ALSO BY KATIE RUGGLE

ROCKY MOUNTAIN SEARCH & RESCUE
On His Watch (free novella)
Hold Your Breath
Fan the Flames
Gone Too Deep
In Safe Hands
After the End (free novella)

ROCKY MOUNTAIN K9 UNIT
Run to Ground
On the Chase
Survive the Night
Through the Fire

ROCKY MOUNTAIN COWBOYS
Rocky Mountain Cowboy Christmas

ROCKY MOUNTAIN BOUNTY HUNTERS
Turn the Tide (free novella)
In Her Sights

RISK
IT ALL

KATIE
RUGGLE

sourcebooks
casablanca

Published by Sourcebooks Casablanca, an imprint of Sourcebooks
P.O. Box 4410, Naperville, Illinois 60567-4410
(630) 961-3900
sourcebooks.com

Printed and bound in the United States of America.
OPM 10 9 8 7 6 5 4 3 2 1

To Jessica Smith, Rachel Gilmer,
Susie Benton, Dawn Adams, and
Mary Altman: you know what you did.

PREVIOUSLY...

CARA PAX AND HER FOUR SISTERS ARE BOUNTY HUNTERS, running a fledgling business out of their beloved family home in Langston, Colorado. All was well until their mother, Jane, stole a priceless necklace and skipped town...*after* using their house as collateral for her bail bond.

Now, shady bondsman Barney Thompson holds the title to their house, and he's willing to use it to coerce Cara and her sisters into chasing dangerous skips for him. To make matters worse, every thief and treasure hunter in the Rockies thinks the necklace is hidden in the sisters' house...including Detective Jason Mill, the potentially crooked Denver cop assigned to the case.

Cara dreams of being a kindergarten teacher, but right now it's all hands on deck. She wants to do her part for the business and to save her family's home, but to really help, she needs to bring in a big, money-earning skip...

Which is why she's breaking into accused killer Henry Kavenski's motel room.

PREAMBULY

CHAPTER 1

CARA TRIED TO ACT CASUAL AS SHE WALKED ALONG THE motel's cracked, weedy sidewalk, but she knew she looked exactly like what she was: a kindergarten teacher—well, almost—who was scared out of her mind. If she told her sisters what she was about to do, they'd yank her home and tie her to a chair to keep her safe. Now that their home and bounty-hunter business were under threat, however, she needed to do more to help.

But of all the cases to take, why did she have to pick a killer?

Stopping at Room 87—the green door with suspicious dark-red splatters that had dried across it—she took a quick glance around before pulling her lock-pick kit out of her pocket. Her fingers trembled, making her fumble the picks.

"Stop it," she muttered. "You're good at this. Quit being a chicken."

This was her chance. She'd watched Kavenski get on the one-ten bus, but she wasn't sure how long he'd be gone. She needed to plant the tracker in his things before he returned...and potentially caught her in the act. The thought of him walking in on her made her shake even harder. Finally, though, the dead bolt released with a *click*, and she exhaled hard, relief and a fresh surge of nerves coursing through her. She'd done it. Now she just had to go inside.

She reached for the door handle, the metal cold and slightly greasy to the touch. It gave under her hand, and the door swung open. Her heart thumping in her ears, she peered into the dim space, the smell of mildew and stale cigarette smoke tickling her nose. Her feet didn't want to move. Once she stepped over the threshold, that was it. When she was inside, she couldn't pretend she'd been just another motel guest, innocently strolling past.

Stop hesitating, she told herself firmly. *Go*. Blowing out a silent breath, she shored up her eroded courage and stepped inside.

A hard hand clamped down over her shoulder and shoved her into the room before she could even suck in a breath to scream.

Her fingers tightened around the lockpick in her right hand and the tension tool in her left. She spun around, the soles of her shoes catching against the worn scruff of the carpet, and held the two tiny steel tools up in front of her as if they were weapons. As Henry Kavenski—who looked even more enormous close up than he did from a half block away—shoved the door closed, she locked her knees to keep them from shaking. Cold sweat prickled along her hairline as her brain frantically scrolled through everything she had done wrong. She wasn't prepared. She should've brought a Taser or even some pepper spray or, better yet, backup. Her sisters were going to be so pissed she'd gotten herself killed in such a stupid way.

From the hard set of Henry Kavenski's mouth, he wasn't feeling particularly merciful.

They stared at each other without speaking, the only sound Cara's heart thundering in her ears and the rapid breaths she couldn't seem to slow. Despite her panic, she still noticed the details that she'd missed during the weeks spent tracking him from a distance. The scruff on his face was just slightly darker than the sun-bleached, tousled hair falling across his brow. His jaw was solid, almost blocky, his nose and mouth drawn with aggressive slashing lines, but the tops of his ears came to the slightest point. That unexpectedly *elven* detail didn't fit with the rest of his solid form and rugged features. Henry Kavenski was more an ogre or giant.

She blinked, pulling her racing thoughts back in line. He still hadn't said a word, and she wasn't sure whether that meant she should be more or less terrified. Their mutual silence did give her a chance to come up with a plan—a fairly dumb plan, but at least it might give her a chance to get out of this alive.

"Who are you?" Her voice shook, but she figured that was only natural.

His scowl deepened. He still didn't make a sound.

Her trembling worsened, fingers tightening around the lock-picking tools. She tried to tuck them behind her in a way that looked natural, but his gaze followed the movement. His eyes met hers again, and she fought to keep from quailing beneath that stone-cold glower. Up until this moment, her foray into fieldwork had seemed like a game. Now that she was caught, just a few feet from a professional killer, it didn't feel like a game anymore. This was just flat-out terrifying, and she scrambled to think of some way she could escape alive.

"What are you doing in"—she mentally grabbed for an imaginary friend's name—"Martin's room?"

His head cocked just slightly in question, although those eerily light eyes didn't soften.

Cara cleared her throat, using the excuse to take a precious few moments to scrabble for composure. It helped slightly, but she knew that all the time in the world wouldn't magically give her nerves of steel. She'd never envied her twin sister's badassery more. "I came here to surprise him. Uh…Martin." Why was her brain working at turtle-slow speed? She knew she'd think of all kinds of credible stories as soon as she left the room—*if* she managed to leave.

The reminder that these could easily be her last minutes alive spurred her to keep going. "I passed my test. My…" She held her hands in front of her, forcing her fingers open to reveal the slim tools. "My locksmith test. Martin gave me some tips when I was practicing for it, and I thought we could go out to celebrate. Mexican. He loves Mexican."

What are you doing, dummy?

She made herself stop adding made-up details about her nonexistent but very helpful friend and finished weakly with "This is his room."

Kavenski still didn't say anything. He didn't even twitch. Instead, he continued to glare at her with those chilly eyes that reminded her of what he was…a killer. A pro. He was most likely contemplating the easiest way to dispose of her body.

Her imagination raced, her heart pounded, and she struggled to swallow around a suddenly dry throat. The air in the musty room thickened as dread filled her.

His considerable bulk blocked the one and only door,

and the window was covered by heavy polyester drapes. Even if she took him off guard with a sudden dash, there wouldn't be enough time for her to open the window—if it *was* openable.

Tension twisted her insides until it was difficult to breathe. She had to say something, or the silence would smother her.

"What are you doing in Martin's room?" she demanded again. Even though she was positive he knew her story was a complete lie, it was all she had.

When he shifted his weight, she flinched, but he just leaned back against the door and pressed the heels of his hands against his eyes. Before Cara could do more than twitch toward the window, he dropped his arms to his sides. She froze, her gaze never leaving his face. The chill in his eyes was still there, but there was a slight droop to his mouth that made him look suddenly human…and extraordinarily tired.

"Are you okay?" The words were out before she realized how ridiculous they were. Still, her mouth kept moving, as if it were separate from her brain. "Have you been sleeping?"

He blinked.

"Not that it's any of my business if you have or not." *Why are you still talking???* her brain screamed at her, but it was no use. This freight train had left the station and was hurtling down the tracks. "Now, if it were Marvin, my friend, then it *would* be my business, but you're not Marvin. You're a stranger. A stranger I don't know. Not that you'd be a stranger if I did know you, so, um, you don't have to answer that, if you don't want to. Don't feel obligated."

"Martin." His voice was unexpected. Deep and smooth and perfect for narrating adventure movies or commercials for gourmet chocolate.

"What?" That unexpectedly delicious timbre threw her off. It didn't match what she'd expected a killer to sound like.

His chest lifted with a silent sigh as he straightened away from the door. "Martin. Not Marvin."

She tensed at his movement, but he just stepped sideways, opening a path to the door. "Right. Martin." She couldn't believe that she'd messed up her fictitious friend's name. It was a stressful situation, yeah, but surely she could keep track of her made-up lock-picking study partners for five minutes.

"You need to stop following me."

Great. Not only had he caught her breaking into his motel room, but he was aware that she'd been tracking him across town. Her sisters were right. She was not cut out for fieldwork. If she managed to survive this encounter, it'd be best if she just stayed home and researched. *That* was what she was good at, not the chasing, tackling, and wrestling parts of bounty hunting.

Cara deflated with a soft sigh, kicking herself for failing so spectacularly. Then she noticed he was eyeing her with the slightest hint of amused resignation, and she realized she hadn't responded to his accusation. *Oops.*

"Following you? What are you talking about?" It was weak, she knew, but everything about this interaction was throwing her off. She didn't know if he was going to kill her slowly and painfully or give her tips on shadowing fellow criminals. It was disconcerting. "I'm here to meet…uh…?"

"Martin," he offered helpfully.

"Right." She eyed the door and then snapped her gaze back to him. It was so tempting, having the path to the exit clear, but she worried that he was just setting a fun little trap for her. Still, she dared take a step forward. When he didn't grab her, she edged forward again. "Since Martin isn't here, I'll just go find him."

Despite those icy eyes and the hard line of his mouth, she was pretty sure he was amused. Strangely, she wasn't as terrified of Kavenski as she'd initially been, and she wondered if she was in shock or, perhaps, under the effect of some fast-acting strain of Stockholm syndrome. Telling herself to wait until she was safely outside the motel room to analyze her jumbled emotional state, she took another cautious step toward the door.

Then he moved, and she froze, her mind clamoring that she should've *known* it was too good to be true. Of course the brutal killer with the ice-cold stare wouldn't just let her walk away after catching her breaking into his room. She'd fallen into his trap, and now she was within grabbing distance, and she was going to die.

When his hand grasped the doorknob instead of reaching for her throat, she stared at him, both relieved and befuddled. With a twist of his wrist, he yanked the door open and looked at her expectantly. A hard breath shuddered into her lungs. Had she not been breathing this whole time? She supposed it was an easy thing to lose track of while waiting to be murdered.

"Oh...um." She took the final step to the now-open door. "Thank you? Sorry for...ah, intruding." Slipping through the opening, she hurried away from the room, jumping as she heard it close behind her with a loud *snap*. Although she managed not to run, she walked fast enough that it hardly mattered. Her heart still wasn't convinced that she was out of danger, and it pounded in time with her footsteps as she tried very hard not to break into a sprint. It was only after she'd reached her car and was cocooned in the familiar safety of the driver's seat that the danger really hit her, and her breathing sped up until she was taking in short, rapid puffs of air.

That was the closest she'd ever come to dying. *I'm such a bounty-hunting failure!* If it had been Molly or Felicity or Charlie trapped in the room with Kavenski, her sisters would've had him tackled and cuffed before he could even glare. It was mortifying that the only reason Cara managed to escape was because a *known killer* had stepped aside and *opened the door*.

As her breathing gradually slowed, she started the car, her fingers trembling just a little now. "It's okay," she told herself out loud. "You just need to walk before you can run. Work your way to the upper levels, rather than jumping right into them." It was clear, now that she'd seen him in all his up-close power and glory, that Henry Kavenski was *not* a skip for a beginner bounty hunter. He'd known that she'd been following him, and he'd obviously set her up, intending to catch her breaking into his room. She needed to find a skip who was a little less deadly and a lot more dumb.

Remembering to bring her Taser would be a good idea, too.

As she pulled away from the curb, Cara felt a strange curl of disappointment in her belly. She should've been relieved by her decision to leave Henry Kavenski to other braver, more experienced bounty hunters, but a part of her didn't want to give him up. After following him around and learning everything she could about him, she'd become, oddly enough, a touch possessive.

She firmly quashed the thought. It was time to focus on a new skip, one whose worst crime was jaywalking or tearing the tags off mattresses.

Pressing down on the accelerator, she left the rundown motel and Henry Kavenski far behind.

Two days later, Cara was regretting her decision to leave Kavenski to the professionals…well, the more *professional* professionals. She clicked through the pile of jobs she'd lined up and made a face. None of them were even close to the bail bond he'd skipped on, and the fifteen percent fee seemed paltry compared to what they'd get for bringing in Kavenski.

"That's the problem, genius," she muttered to herself, tapping the side of her laptop with an anxious fingertip. "You'd have to actually bring him in."

With a Taser or her sisters' help, she probably could manage that, but the real issue was that a part of her honestly didn't *want* to. There weren't a lot of murderers—or criminals of any sort—who would've just let her walk away unharmed. It made her wonder if he really was the vicious killer he was accused of being.

"You're such a sucker." With a sigh, she shut down her computer. "You just think he's pretty."

"Who's pretty?" Her twin, Charlie, charged into the kitchen, heading directly to the fridge. Warrant, their very large and very hairy Great Pyrenees mix, immediately hopped up from his sprawl under the table to follow her, obviously hoping for snacks.

Trying to disguise her guilty jump by standing and slipping her laptop into her backpack, Cara blinked innocently at her sister. "One of the skips." It wasn't a lie.

Charlie frowned at the contents of the fridge before closing the door and grabbing a banana. "Whose turn is it to get groceries? Things are looking a little desperate in there." Leaning her hip against the counter, she raised an eyebrow at Cara. "Speaking of desperate... A skip? Really?"

Despite her discomfort about talking—even indirectly—about the mess she'd made of her encounter with Kavenski, Cara had to laugh. "Come on. You can't tell me that, of all the hundreds of skips we've handled, you've never found any remotely attractive?"

Charlie grinned around her bite of banana, conceding the point without saying a word.

Zipping her backpack, Cara hauled it over her shoulder and glanced at the time on her phone. "Got to get to class. And it's your turn."

"My turn for what?"

"Getting groceries. Don't bring home only junk this time, or Felicity will make you run extra laps." Cara headed for the door as her twin gave a dramatic groan.

"Fine, but I'm still getting Lucky Charms."

"It's your funeral," Cara called, stepping outside and closing the door behind her, rather proud that she'd managed to wiggle out of what could've been an awkward conversation. As she headed toward where her car was parked in the driveway, she felt an uneasy prickle on the back of her neck.

She was being watched.

Trying to look casual, she glanced down the street, but there weren't any parked cars in sight. Her gaze roamed over the neighborhood, but it all looked quiet. Even the ever-present breeze had settled, leaving only the scuff of her shoes against concrete to break the eerie silence.

"Stop it," she ordered herself. "You're getting paranoid." Just to be on the safe side, though, she scanned the trees next to the house, looking for anything suspicious. Since they'd gotten an alarm system installed, the attempted break-ins had dropped significantly, but there was still the occasional treasure hunter trying their luck. *Thanks for that, Mom.*

The forest was still and dark. Despite the lack of any suspicious figures lurking in the shadows, the prickle of unease intensified, and she hurried back to yank open the door.

"Charlie!" she called.

"Yeah?" Charlie stepped into view.

"Make sure to set the alarm when you leave." Still unsettled by the odd stillness of the forest, she frowned. "Or if you stay. And lock the door."

Charlie straightened, meeting Cara's gaze. "Trouble outside?"

"Nothing I can see. Just a feeling."

"Got it." From Charlie's sober tone, Cara knew she wouldn't blow off the warning.

"Thanks."

Dropping her serious expression, Charlie made shooing motions with her hands. "Now get to class before you're late. Your future kindergartners won't teach themselves."

Cara gave her a mock salute before closing the door and hurrying to the car. She hoped that they'd find their mom soon—as well as the valuable necklace Jane had stolen—so their lives could go back to normal. Maybe it was wrong to hope that her only surviving parent would be sent back to jail, but Cara didn't care. Jane had really screwed them over this time. If she hadn't stolen the necklace, used their house for collateral on her bail bond, and then skipped town, Cara would be happily attending classes and doing her usual research. Instead, she was scanning the bushes for danger and breaking into murderers' motel rooms.

Accused murderers, her brain corrected, and she sighed. It was probably a good thing she'd sworn off chasing Henry Kavenski. As far as he was concerned, she seemed to be having a hard time staying objective, maybe because he hadn't actually killed her.

Or because he really *was* incredibly pretty.

CHAPTER 2

CARA'S CHILD DEVELOPMENT THEORIES CLASS WAS A GOOD distraction from the utter chaos of the rest of her life. The two hours flew by, and she was disappointed when it ended and all her worries came crashing back down on her. Not wanting to return to dealing with skips and the possibility of burglars lurking in her backyard, she dragged out the process of packing up her bag.

When she was the last one in the classroom, she knew she couldn't delay any longer. It was time to dive back into the less-fun parts of her life. Heaving her backpack over her shoulder, Cara headed for the corridor. The classroom was on the third floor of Meyers Hall, an ancient brick building that was stiflingly hot in the summer and as cold as a walk-in freezer in the winter. The majority of the students had already made their way outside, and the few remaining were making their way toward the stairs.

Cara followed slowly, still reluctant to get home and have to think about which skip she would choose to take the place of Henry Kavenski. The soles of her tennis shoes squeaked against the highly polished floor, and the sound echoed through the hall, making her realize how quiet it had become. The classrooms had emptied and the rest of the straggling students had disappeared, leaving her alone.

A light scuffing sound behind her made her glance over her shoulder. No one was there.

It's just my imagination, she thought, huffing a quiet laugh at how easily she scared herself. Her amusement evaporated as she continued walking down the hall and the slightly offbeat echo of her footsteps followed her. Despite the uneasiness that prickled the back of her neck, she refused to allow herself to look over her shoulder again. *No one is there. I'm alone. No one is there.* As she repeated the mantra in her mind, she tried to keep from walking faster.

Even as she told herself she was being silly, she couldn't help but tense. Her pace quickened, the sound of her hurried footsteps making her even more anxious. She tried to be amused by how many horror movie clichés her imagination had dreamed up, but it was hard to laugh at her very real apprehension as she rushed toward the stairs. All the crazy, dangerous things that had been happening to her and her sisters lately made her see menace in everything.

"Hey, Cara Pax."

She whirled around, a shriek of surprise trapped in her throat. As soon as she saw who'd spoken, she was glad that the startled sound hadn't made it out. The little weasel had intentionally tried to scare her, and she would've hated to give him the satisfaction of knowing he'd succeeded.

"What are you doing here, Stuart?" she asked, wanting to keep walking toward the stairs but not trusting the creep enough to turn her back. Moving backward away from him felt too much like running, and she wasn't scared of this little punk. Thanks to Jane regularly helping herself to her daughter's tuition money, Cara was several years older than most of her classmates. Stuart Powers couldn't be much over twenty, but he was already mixed up in Langston's shadier side.

He'd been one of the many who'd tried to break into their house. Since Molly and John had caught him in the act, he'd been popping up around campus wherever Cara happened to be. He seemed to have the mistaken impression that she knew where her mom had hidden the stolen necklace—and that she could be intimidated into telling him where he could find it.

"Why are most students in a campus building?" He really did have the most punchable smirk in the history of the world. He stepped closer, and she backed away. Cara was so intent on keeping some distance between them that she didn't even realize he'd cornered her until she felt the press of a recessed classroom door against her back. Shifting closer, he asked, "What do you think I'm doing here?"

Irritation spiked at the question, and she surged forward, knocking him hard enough with her shoulder that he took an automatic step back, giving her an opening. She moved quickly toward the stairs, too annoyed to be worried about what he'd do if her back was turned. "Quit stalking me."

His low laugh followed her, and she straightened her shoulders, fighting the urge to glance back. She wouldn't give him the satisfaction of knowing just how creepy she found him. He was trying to frighten her. What he didn't realize was that she dealt with scarier people every day. She'd faced down *Henry Kavenski*. After that, Stuart seemed like small potatoes.

Still, Stuart's mocking laugh did make her uneasy, as much as she tried to hide it. Campus was her escape from the stress of bounty hunting, and knowing he was lurking around her, following her, ruined that feeling of safety.

Anger filled Cara as she rushed down the stairs, her shoes thumping on each step, creating enough of a clatter that she couldn't hear anything else that Stuart tried to say. When she reached the ground floor, she couldn't keep herself from glancing up to see if he'd followed her. The stairs were poorly lit, the steps quickly disappearing into the gloom, and she felt the prickle of goose bumps ghost down her spine.

That's what he wants, the reasonable part of her brain supplied. *He wants to freak you out*.

Despite knowing that, she still had to hide a shiver as she shoved through the door out into the late-afternoon sunshine. As she strode toward the parking lot, pretending that she wasn't relieved to see the clusters of students scattered around the area, Cara set her jaw. No more chickening out. She was going to bring in a skip and show her sisters that she could be useful in the field. That way, Charlie and Felicity could focus on finding their mom and bringing her back.

Cara was going to do whatever she had to in order to get their lives back to normal. She only had to be a badass for a short time, and then she could go back to worrying about normal things, like class projects and finding a student-teaching position next semester and whose turn it was to clean the bathroom.

Her cell phone dinged, the ringtone telling her it was a work call, and she pulled it out with brisk motions, caught up in a wave of determination. "Pax Bail Recovery."

"Hey there." Barney Thompson's slimy voice made her wrinkle her nose. Between him and Stuart, she was getting a full dose of creeps today. "Which pretty Pax sister am I talking to?"

"This is Cara. How can I help you?" She put on her best professional tone. Before everything happened, she would've blown him off as quickly as possible, but now that he held their mom's bail bond—which meant he'd own their house if Jane didn't show up for her next hearing—Cara had to be polite to him, which just about killed her. That was another thing that needed to go back to normal as quickly as possible. She was going to relish being able to hang up on Barney again.

"I have a job for you."

She had to bite her tongue to hold back a groan. The last skip Barney had wanted them to bring in had almost killed Molly multiple times, and Cara and her sisters had almost been blown up.

At her silence, Barney hurried to add, "He's nothing like the last one. This one'll be easy. A walk in the park, especially for you."

"Why *especially* for me? Cara asked warily.

"Because Abbott loves to get college students to do his dirty work, and aren't you still in your tenth year there or something?"

She hadn't been attending *that* long. Seven years at the most. With effort, Cara swallowed her protest as he continued.

"I'm actually doing you a favor by telling you about him."

"What's he being charged with?" she asked.

"Tax evasion. He owes enough that the judge set his bail high."

That was promisingly nonviolent. "Send over his file, and we'll consider it."

Barney's grunt made it clear he wasn't too happy that she wasn't accepting the job immediately, but he just said "Fine" and hung up.

Cara had barely gotten into her car before her phone alerted her that she had an email. Still suspicious why Barney was so desperate to have them bring in a simple tax-evading skip—rather than siccing his own bounty-hunting dogs on the guy—she opened the file. After scanning the information, she was frowning more deeply. The skip, Geoffrey Abbott, appeared to be an easy job on the surface, but the name teased her brain. It sounded oddly familiar.

Setting down her phone, she started her car, eager to get home and research the guy. Familiar or not, he might be just what she was looking for to replace Henry Kavenski as her first successful capture. Her mood lifting for the first time since Stuart had swooped in to ruin her day, she backed out of her parking space and headed home.

As she drove, she tried to focus on Geoffrey Abbott, but another skip kept wiggling his way back into her thoughts.

"Stupid Henry Kavenski," she muttered, slowing down to turn onto her street. "Get out of my brain."

Despite her determination to drop his case, she knew it wouldn't be easy to let this skip go.

"Why are you doing this again, dum-dum?" Cara muttered to herself as she pretended to examine the for-sale listings plastered over the real estate office's window. In actuality, she was watching a certain skip—one she'd sworn to stop chasing—in her periphery. "You survived likely death once. Stop following the murderer, go home, and start researching the nice, nonviolent tax evader."

Despite the mental lecture, she didn't walk away. Instead, she continued staring at Henry Kavenski's reflected image. Ten minutes ago, he'd parked himself on a bus-stop bench down the street, and he hadn't so much as shifted since.

"We need the money," she argued under her breath. "That's the only reason why I'm giving this another shot. If I can bring in Kavenski *and* Abbott, that'll give us some breathing room while Felicity and Charlie search for Mom."

When she'd walked into the house the day before, ready to start researching a much safer Abbott, she'd found Molly hunched over her laptop, her expression more drawn and deeply worried than it had been since that first hungry year after they'd started the business. Cara had known that they were hurting for money after the whole Jane thing—especially after the burglary—but the tight line between Molly's eyebrows and the anxious downturn of her mouth really brought home how serious things were. Plus, if they ended up losing their house…

Cara hurried to cut off that train of thought, not

wanting to fall down the familiar black hole of stress and worry—especially while she was actively watching a skip. Despite his surprisingly nonviolent reaction to finding her breaking into his motel room, she couldn't afford to get complacent just because Kavenski's shoulders were impossibly broad and his mouth looked both hard and temptingly soft at the same time.

Stop. Even though no one could hear her thoughts, her cheeks still burned with embarrassment. This tiny crush she was developing—on an *accused murderer*—was ridiculous and dangerous, and she had to nip it in the bud immediately.

Mortification won where common sense hadn't, and she started to move away from the real estate office. Her car was parked less than a mile away. She'd leave, drive home, research a more reasonable skip, and forget that she'd ever set eyes on Henry Kavenski.

As she turned, she couldn't resist a final glance at the still figure sitting on the bench. Judging by the lack of other people, the bus wasn't going to arrive for some time, and she felt a shot of curiosity about why he'd planted himself there. In the days she'd followed him, she'd found that he tended to stay out of public places. He'd never parked himself on a busy street for no apparent reason before.

Cara took two steps before succumbing to the need to glance at him again. As she did, she saw his spine straighten in a movement so slight that it was almost imperceptible. If she hadn't been watching him too closely for her own good, she wouldn't have noticed it. Even though she could only see his back and a hint of his profile, there was something about the way he held himself that told her he was alert and prepared for trouble.

Well, I can't leave now, she thought with exasperation— and more excitement than was appropriate. *Things are just getting interesting.*

Pulling out her phone, she leaned against the rough brick wall and pretended to text. Instead, she pulled up her camera app and surreptitiously scanned the area for whatever had made Kavenski tense. There was an older couple setting up a flower stand halfway down the block, a twentysomething guy walking slowly past the bus shelter while staring down at his phone, and a woman pushing a stroller toward the bus stop at a brisk pace.

When the guy looking at his phone passed Kavenski with no apparent interaction, not even a glance, Cara turned her attention to the woman with the stroller. She was wearing oversize sunglasses, and her hair was either very short or tucked up under a trendy knit hat. From her boots to her belted jacket to the thin scarf artfully wound around her neck, the woman was perfectly put together. The baby in the stroller was hidden by the deep sides and the pulled-up sun hood, and everything about them seemed like a picture from a fashion shoot.

When the woman stopped the stroller next to the bus-stop bench and took a seat next to Kavenski, Cara knew something was up. For one, she would eat her phone if that woman would ever set foot on a public bus. Also, Kavenski, for all his hotness, was a big and intimidating guy. No one would casually plop themselves down next to a dangerous-looking stranger, especially with her baby right there.

With both Kavenski and the woman facing forward, it was impossible for Cara to see if they were talking. She was tempted to move closer to the pair to see if she could eavesdrop, but Kavenski had known she'd been following him earlier, and that made her hesitate. It was one thing for her to follow as he skulked around town, but this meeting seemed very shady and purposeful. He'd let her go once, but who knew what he'd do if she had incriminating information on him.

The woman turned her head toward Kavenski for just a few seconds, and Cara hurried to take a few pictures. With the oversize sunglasses, hat, and scarf, it was hard to get an idea of what the woman actually looked like, especially from a distance. The only things Cara was sure of were that she was white, tall, and fashion-conscious.

To Cara's frustration, she saw that the woman's lips were indeed moving. Once again resisting the urge to get close enough to listen to their conversation, Cara watched as the woman reached into the stroller and appeared to adjust the baby's blanket. When she withdrew her hand, however, she was holding something white and rectangular.

Almost bursting with curiosity, even as her heart pounded from fear of discovery, Cara found herself leaning forward, straining to see what the woman had taken from the stroller. In just the split second it took her to pass the item to Kavenski, Cara was pretty sure it was a legal-sized envelope. Before she could see any other details or even take a few steps closer, he slipped the item into his jacket pocket.

The woman stood and pushed the stroller past Kavenski, and Cara realized that she would be passing right by. After a frozen second, she forced her gaze to her phone screen. Her hair fell in heavy curtains on either side of her face, hiding her profile from the woman's view, and Cara was intensely grateful that she hadn't pulled it back that morning.

The seconds seemed to tick by agonizingly slowly as the *burr* of stroller wheels and the sharp click of the woman's bootheels drew closer. Cara didn't breathe as the woman passed just five feet away, and her pounding heart was so loud it made it hard to hear if the footsteps were slowing.

When she couldn't hold her breath any longer, she dared a pseudo-casual glance and saw the back of the woman a half block away. Sucking in a much-needed breath, Cara returned her attention to Kavenski, just in time to see him rocket off the bench right into rush-hour traffic. The movement was so sudden and unexpected that Cara jerked back a step, startled.

"What is he doing?" Without considering the wisdom of what *she* was doing, Cara bolted toward him, her eyes locked on his big, surprisingly nimble form as he played a terrifying game of *Frogger* with oncoming cars. Brakes squealed and drivers laid on their horns as Kavenski shot across the road to the far lane. Turning to face the SUV heading toward him, he raised both hands, palms out, like a traffic cop.

He faced down the oncoming vehicle barreling toward him. The tires squealed as the wheels locked, and Cara instinctively reached toward him as if she could somehow snatch him to safety. His huge frame actually looked small as the five-thousand-pound vehicle bore down on him.

Cara reached the curb, a useless shout of warning building in her chest. Kavenski stared down the SUV, not even flinching as it rocketed closer. Just inches from Kavenski, the vehicle lurched to a halt, rocking back from the force of the stop. Cara's breath escaped her in a rush. She stopped abruptly, realizing that she had been about to run right out into traffic. She'd been so focused on Kavenski's near death that she hadn't even thought about her own safety.

As the driver of the SUV rolled his window down and screamed invectives, Kavenski turned and strode over to a small dog huddled in the center of the lane. Scooping up the tiny furball, Kavenski stepped out of the street, waving casually at the still-yelling driver to continue on his way.

Cara gave a small gasping laugh at Kavenski's nonchalance. He was acting as if risking his life to save a tiny dog was no big deal, while Cara's heart was still trying to pound out of her chest and her hands shook with an overdose of adrenaline. As if he'd heard her slightly panicked laughter, Kavenski met her gaze across the four lanes of traffic. They stared at each other for an eternal moment before the corner of his mouth kicked up in more of a grimace than a smile.

He was the one who broke eye contact, turning with the little dog cuddled gently against his chest. Kavenski didn't seem at all put out by the way the ball of fluff was licking his chin with a tiny pink tongue, but the incongruous picture made Cara laugh again.

Slightly calmer now, she stepped back from the curb, although she kept her gaze on Kavenski, unable to take her eyes off the man. He looked even bigger in contrast to the small dog he held so carefully, but his usual aura of menace had been severely fractured by what Cara had just witnessed. How could she be afraid of a man when he was cuddling a tiny ball of fluff he'd just risked his life to save?

He carried the pup to a convertible that had pulled over to the side of the road with its hazard lights flashing. The driver, a white-haired woman, got out and rushed toward Kavenski, arms outstretched. With the noise of the traffic, Cara couldn't hear what he said to her, but she nodded emphatically several times before he handed the dog to her. Kavenski watched as the woman returned to the driver's seat, clutching the dog against her chest. He didn't move from his spot until the convertible's roof began to extend, enclosing the woman and her dog safely inside the car.

Now that the panic had receded and Cara's brain was working again, she realized that the dog must've jumped out of the convertible into the road. She wondered if Kavenski had insisted that the convertible's roof be closed before he gave the woman back her dog. Cara studied him, rubbing a hand over her lips as her brain struggled to fit the Kavenski she'd researched—who'd supposedly shot and killed two people in cold blood— with the man who'd just risked his life to save a dog, and who was currently watching the owner with the air of a safety-conscious crossing guard.

As the convertible—roof fully closed—drove away, Kavenski's gaze met Cara's once again. Despite the width of the road separating them, she saw his eyes widen slightly, breaking his usual impassive expression. Their gazes clung together until, with a sharp shake of his head, he turned and strode away. Cara stared after him even after he was out of sight. The sound of a box truck rattling by pulled her out of her thoughts, and she started walking to where she'd parked her car.

What had started out as a simple—if dangerous—skip retrieval had gotten a lot more confusing. Remembering his final warning look, she gave an amused huff. If he didn't want her to investigate him, he shouldn't be so fascinating.

———

A few days later, Cara paused, pretending to check her phone as she fought to push away the urge to jump back in her car and drive away as fast as she could. She'd only been to Dutch's Bar once, but that had been in the middle of the day with Molly. At night, it was exponentially creepier. The warehouses surrounding the bar seemed to loom over the space, creating shadows where any number of dangerous people could be lurking. The bar, which had looked nondescript and slightly dingy in the full sunlight, now gave off a menacing air, making Cara sure she wouldn't be welcome or safe there. That didn't matter, though. She was determined to follow through on this new job, and that meant checking out Abbott's possible hangouts…including Dutch's.

She slid her hand over the lump the Taser made in her jacket pocket. The presence of the weapon gave her courage, and she pulled up the photo of Geoffrey Abbott, getting his image freshly lodged in her brain. Slipping her phone back in her other pocket—the Taser-less one—she pulled back her shoulders and strode toward the entrance.

Her confidence wavered as the bouncer eyed her suspiciously, his sharp gaze running over her. The way he frowned as he stared at her midsection made her paranoid that he could see right through her jacket to the Taser in her pocket. She hoped that he wouldn't conduct a pat down, and then wondered if that would be legal for a civilian. Making a mental note to look up the Colorado statute as soon as she had a quiet moment, she focused on the big guy in front of her.

His hand extended, palm out, and Cara offered her driver's license, bracing herself for what she knew was coming. Even though she was legal by almost four full years, she was used to the disbelieving squints. Her small stature and baby face—including dimples—made her appear younger than she was. She'd pulled her dark hair back into a severe bun, to keep it out of grabbing range as well as to make her look more like a serious professional, and she hoped it didn't make her look like a teenager playing dress-up.

The bouncer's gaze flicked back and forth between her and the license several times, and his frown deepened.

Cara sighed as she dug out her wallet. "That really is my authentic, legal license. See? The same birth date as on my student ID."

"Why are you here?" the bouncer asked in a warning rumble.

"Uh…" She didn't expect to be questioned about her motives before she even got inside the place. What kind of dive bar was this? "To have a few drinks, maybe dance a little. Do, you know, bar things."

"Bar things," he repeated expressionlessly, and she nodded too quickly.

"Bar things."

His sigh was deep enough to make his enormous shoulders sag for a moment, and she was pretty sure she was about to be sent away. To her surprise, he handed back her IDs and motioned toward the door. "Don't blow anything up."

"I'll do my best." She would've made a comment about how that was a strange thing to say, except that a skip Molly was chasing had blown a hole in the bathroom wall just a few weeks ago. Besides, she was just glad the bouncer hadn't searched her and found her Taser.

Slipping inside before he could change his mind, Cara looked around, getting her bearings. Filled with people, the bar seemed smaller than she remembered. Loud old-school rock pounded through the space, and the usual beery, sweaty bar smell filled her nose. She'd half expected the music to screech to a stop when she entered, everyone turning to stare, but no one even seemed to notice her.

She took a few deep breaths before moving toward the bar. She'd planned better this time. This was simply a reconnaissance mission. Even if she spotted Abbott, she wouldn't try to make contact. The most she'd do was follow him to his car and get his plate number.

The bartender—a redhead who resembled Jane a little too much for comfort—gave her a suspicious look but handed over the beer Cara ordered without any fuss. Clutching the cold bottle a little too tightly, she wove her way through the throng toward a shadowed booth in the back. From there, she'd be able to watch the crowd while staying somewhat hidden.

Preoccupied with searching for Geoffrey Abbott, she was right in front of the booth before she realized it was occupied.

"Oh! Sorry. I thought this was empty." Even as she apologized and started to turn away, she recognized the man sitting in the corner where the shadows were the deepest, and her head snapped back around. Her first thought was that the gloom was playing tricks on her eyes, because there was *no way* that was Henry Kavenski.

As much as she blinked, though, the face did not change. It was indeed her first attempted skip, possible killer and definite dog rescuer. Cara stood rooted to the spot. She continued to stare, unable to process the fact that, now that she wasn't following him around town, Henry Kavenski just happened to pop up right in front of her. Her stomach was doing an odd fluttering thing that it definitely shouldn't be doing—not now, and never for this guy. He glared back at her, expressionless except for the slight tightening of his lips.

"Hi." Of course she said that. "I didn't expect to see you here." She held back a sigh. Of course she said that too. She was so mortifyingly *not* smooth, especially around Henry Kavenski.

"Didn't I tell you to quit following me?"

Maybe it was because there was more long-suffering exasperation in his tone than actual anger, or maybe it was because she was relieved to see a familiar face in this intimidating bar—even if it was *his* face—but once again, her mouth worked before her brain could stop it. "Yes, but it's really your fault I haven't stopped."

His eyes narrowed, which had the unfortunate effect of making him even hotter than he already was. "My fault." Again, the little threatening rasp he gave the words should've been scary enough to send her scooting out of the bar and back to the safety of home, but she couldn't stop thinking about him diving in front of cars to save a tiny little floof of a dog.

"Yes." Her mouth was operating all on its own. "For being too fascinating."

"It's my fault for being…too fascinating." Resting his elbow on the table, he rubbed the spot right above his temple, making her wonder if he had a headache. She immediately had the urge to feed him a couple of painkillers and massage his neck, but she quashed those tender impulses immediately. Dog rescuer or not, she barely knew this guy—this *skip*. Even despite that, though, she didn't want to walk away from him quite yet.

"Mind if I sit down?" Once again, the words were out before she'd considered whether they were a good idea or not. It was as if her normally repressed impulsive side took over the second she was in Henry Kavenski's company.

He blinked, his face poker-straight and his lips compressed, but he didn't say no, and that was good enough for her. Cara slid into the booth next to him, careful to leave space between them so she didn't intrude on his personal bubble. "What are you doing?" he asked.

"Sitting." A part of her was impressed with her audacity, while the rest was screaming a warning that she was going to get herself killed. After all, maybe it was just dogs he liked, and he had no problem offing people. The couple he'd been accused of murdering—Lance and Bettina Mason—had been a seemingly innocuous pair…at least on paper. There'd been enough evidence to charge Kavenski with homicide, and Cara knew she needed to be cautious. Just because he was the most attractive, and interesting, person she'd ever met didn't mean she should throw all logic out the window. On the contrary, her inappropriate crush should make her even more wary.

"There's an entire empty bench over there." He flicked his hand at the other side of the table.

"I can't see anything from over there." Her tone was apologetic, but she settled more firmly on the battered vinyl seat. This was just the view she needed—if she was willing to ignore the fact that she'd plonked herself down next to an unsettlingly attractive accused killer, which apparently she *was*.

If Henry didn't kill her, her sisters certainly would.

"So find another table." That tone was back—the annoyed yet resigned inflection that was starting to become so familiar. It was oddly reassuring.

"This one is perfect for watching the bar, though." She pretended to take a sip of her beer and scanned the crowd. Unless Abbott was wearing an excellent disguise, she was pretty sure he wasn't in the main room.

A heavy sigh drew her attention back to her booth mate. "Who are you stalking now?" he grumbled.

"Geoffrey Abbott." She watched his face as she said the name. Except for a slight deepening of the crease between his eyebrows, his expression remained impassive. Even if he did know Abbott, she wasn't sure why she'd expected Kavenski to show any reaction. He had his poker face down pat. "He's a tax evader."

The amber liquid in his drink caught the light as he rotated his glass. He hadn't taken a sip since she'd joined him, making her wonder if he was pretending to drink, just like she was. "He's not just a tax evader," he grumbled.

"What do you mean? What else has he done?" Even as she asked, her stomach sank. She'd known this was too easy, especially coming from Barney.

"A lot of bad things. You don't want that mess," he said, rather than clarifying. "Find another target."

"But he was perfectly nonviolent and seemed kind of dumb. That's just what I was looking for." On paper, Geoffrey Abbott was the perfect opposite of Kavenski. Best of all, despite Abbott's objectively handsome face and gym-toned body, Cara hadn't even felt a twinge of attraction to him. She allowed her head to thump against the back of the booth. "I should've known he was too good to be true."

Kavenski stayed silent as she worked through her disappointment. It made sense, now that she thought about it. After all, weren't mobsters traditionally brought down by tax evasion? She stared at the crowd as she mentally ran over his file again. Organized crime ties fit, she had to admit to herself.

"Do you know him?" Even though she was pretty sure she shouldn't continue pursuing Abbott, now that Kavenski had clued her in, she couldn't just turn off her hunt for the truth. There was nothing she loved more than snapping that last piece of the puzzle into place, and she couldn't just leave all the unconnected pieces of Abbott's backstory scattered around willy-nilly.

Kavenski's huge sigh was accompanied by a rolling

of his shoulders, and she tried to swallow her smile. For as dour and supposedly dangerous as he was, he was quite dramatic. Now that she'd been in his company multiple times without him harming her—and with the memory of a recently rescued dog happily licking his chin fresh in her mind—she couldn't dredge up any fear of him. She was pretty sure he noticed her smile, because his eyes narrowed on her mouth. Hurrying to straighten her face into an appropriately serious expression, she stared back at him expectantly.

"I know *of* him," he finally said. "And what I know isn't good. You need to stay away from him."

"See, that's the problem." She played with the bottle in front of her, using her finger to follow a droplet of condensation as it trickled over the label. "I need to bring him in."

"Why?" He shifted slightly, turning his shoulders a little more toward her. It was almost overwhelming to have the entirety of his attention focused on her. He was so...intense. *And hot*, the cheekier part of her brain added. Pushing away that ever-present and extremely inconvenient attraction, she tried to keep her mind on what he was saying. "There are dozens of easier skips out there that you could focus on. Why go after Abbott?"

"I told Barney Thompson I'd do it." Her voice was gloomy. "Usually I'm really good at keeping myself out of trouble. I'm not sure what's wrong with me lately."

"Tell Barney Thompson to go after Abbott himself," Kavenski said with another of his dismissive hand waves. "Who cares if he's not happy? Thompson isn't someone you want to get referrals from anyway."

Resting her elbow on the table, she propped her chin

on her hand as she studied Kavenski. "I wish it were that easy. Thanks to my mom, Barney's holding the title of our house right now."

"Explain."

Despite the depressing subject of their conversation, Cara couldn't help but grin again. He'd sounded so... princely just then, as if he simply needed to know the problem in order to do one of his imperious hand waves and solve all her problems. If only things worked that way. "It's a long story."

"The person I'm meeting isn't here yet, so I have time."

At that, she felt a very stupid, very irrational bolt of jealousy at the thought of him meeting someone. There hadn't been any sign of a girlfriend when she'd been following him around. Was the meeting business or a hookup? *Either way, it's none of your concern*, the practical part of her brain reminded her.

Quickly reining in the ridiculous emotion, she studied his face, wondering if she should share all of her personal drama with a skip she'd been chasing—or maybe still was? With a mental shrug, she decided it wouldn't hurt anything. Most everyone in town already knew all the sordid details.

"My mom stole a very expensive necklace, was arrested, used our family home—that my sisters and I paid for—as collateral on her bail bond, and disappeared." Hearing the words out loud, she felt a fresh surge of anger at Jane. "She hasn't *officially* jumped bail yet, since she hasn't missed her preliminary hearing, but no one's seen her since she got out of jail." Kavenski was extremely easy to talk to, his impassive face showing no judgment.

"Oh, and Mom's friends keep breaking into our house looking for the necklace, and one of them stole money and my sister Molly's car." This made his left eyelid twitch, and she paused, expecting him to say something. When he remained silent, she continued. "I usually just do research, but Felicity and Charlie have spent all their time searching for Mom, and Norah's even more hopeless at fieldwork than I am, so Molly's stuck with doing all the actual skip chasing. She can only do so much, so the business isn't taking in much money, and things are tight."

Remembering how stressed Molly had looked, Cara felt her lips turn down in an anxious frown. She stayed silent until the slightest tilt of his head prompted her to finish her pathetic tale. "On top of that, we could lose our house, and it's the last thing we have of my dad. I wanted to help out, but I seem to be just causing more problems instead of helping."

She'd started out confident, but her voice quavered slightly at the end. It was Kavenski's fault. He just seemed so solid and had a way of listening intently that made it too easy to believe he was a supportive partner, rather than a skip she'd failed to bring in. Speaking of...

"I don't supposed you'd agree to letting me bring you back to jail?" Even as she asked, her stomach twisted at the thought. It might be extremely dumb of her, but she didn't think he was guilty of killing the Masons. Even the huge bounty wouldn't help ease her conscience if she brought in an innocent man.

His mouth quirked in the closest thing to a smile she'd seen on his face, which was not the reaction she'd been expecting. "Can't. Sorry. I have to finish a few things first."

"It's okay." With a sigh, she sat back against the vinyl

seat. She didn't know if it was vomiting her entire story and all her worries at him, or if it was relief from not having to take him back to jail, but she felt lighter than she had in weeks. "I would've felt too guilty anyway. I probably couldn't have gone through with it."

His snort sounded suspiciously close to a laugh. "You're really not good at fieldwork, are you?"

"No." She shrugged. Even though she hated failing at something, she couldn't argue with the truth. "I want to be a kindergarten teacher. I'm working on my education degree—slowly, but I'll finish it eventually. Bounty hunting is not my calling."

Something shifted in his expression as he stared at her, and he rubbed at his temple again.

"Does your head hurt?" She dug in her purse and pulled out a travel-size bottle of ibuprofen. When she offered it to him, his gaze flicked from the painkillers back to her face. She wasn't sure how to read his odd look, so she just waited.

"I'm okay." He wrapped his fingers around hers in order to gently move her hand back toward her purse. Her brain immediately blanked at the contact. All she could think about was how huge and warm and comforting his hand felt. "You need to take care of yourself. If you keep chasing guys like Abbott—and me—you're going to get yourself killed."

For some reason, his concern and careful touch made it hard to hold his gaze without blushing. Looking away, she was starting to respond when her gaze caught on the profile of the very man she'd come to Dutch's to find. Geoffrey Abbott worked his way through the crowd, clearly intent on finding someone. The *someone* turned out to be a woman who looked to be in her early forties, with light-brown hair, a wide, mobile mouth, and strong features that came together into a striking whole. There was something familiar about her, and Cara racked her brain for where she'd seen the woman before.

The two had an intense, low-voiced discussion before Abbott turned away abruptly, his mouth pinched with anger. As intently as he'd made his way into the bar, he now worked his way toward the exit. The woman watched him go. As soon as Cara saw her face in profile, it clicked—that was the woman Kavenski had met.

Cara gently tugged free, set the painkillers next to his untouched drink, and slid out of the booth. Even though Kavenski had warned her about going after Abbott, there wasn't any other solution. Just because an attractive skip held her hand very gently and told her to do something didn't mean she should throw her family's future away. She couldn't let Abbott leave without at least getting a plate number. It'd be simple and danger-free, and might give her the information she needed to decide whether she should drop the case.

"What are you doing?"

Cara gave him a smile. "Nothing dangerous. Thanks for letting me sit with you."

She turned away and slipped through the crowd, keeping her eye on the back of Abbott's head, thankful that he was taller than most of the other bar patrons. By the time she'd worked her way to the door and stepped outside, he was nowhere in sight. She paused, waiting for one of the parked cars to start, hoping that he hadn't parked in the lot across the street or, even worse, walked to Dutch's.

Glancing at the bouncer, she saw that he was watching her grimly. "I didn't blow up anything," she said.

Before he could respond, she saw red brake lights illuminate a car in the far corner of the parking lot. *Jackpot!* It was too far away to see the plate, so Cara hurried across the lot. He was already backing out of his spot, and she moved a little faster, not wanting to attract attention by running but also unwilling to miss her chance.

The back end of his car drew closer as he reversed, and she squinted at the license plate. He started to pull forward toward the lot exit, moving the car away from her, and she trotted forward, hoping to catch the plate number as he paused before turning onto the street.

A loud squeal of tires behind her made her spin around, startled. Bright headlights blinded her as an engine revved. A car was coming at her—fast. *Too fast.* She dodged to the side, but the lights followed, steering toward her as if they were aiming for her. Pivoting in the other direction, she ran toward the row of parked cars, hoping they'd at least take the brunt of the impact, but a glance over her shoulder showed that it was already too late.

The car was going to run her down.

She lunged to the side, knowing it was futile but needing to try to save herself anyway. When the impact came, it was from the wrong direction. She flew to the side as the car swerved past with an angry roar, her body landing with enough jolt to force the air from her lungs. For a long moment, she lay still, trying to figure out why she didn't hurt. Was she in shock? Paralyzed? Dead?

The ground moved beneath her, bringing her out of her daze with a snap. She pushed to her hands and knees, struggling to balance on the lumpy surface, until a grunt made her freeze. She stared at the man beneath her. Tires squealed loudly, making her jolt and turn her head, frantically searching for the vehicle that had tried to run her down. The engine roared as the car peeled away, fishtailing as it turned onto the street. The rumble quickly faded as her attempted murderer raced off, and Cara refocused on the man lying warm and unfairly muscular under her.

"Kavenski?" Sliding off him to land on the asphalt, she blinked several times, trying to make sense of how her night had ended up like this. He turned with her, not releasing her as he ran his hands over her arms, checking for injuries. His gaze was sharp as he looked her over, and his uncharacteristic worry snapped her back to the reality of what had just happened. "Henry Kavenski, did you just save me from death by speeding car?"

He didn't answer, checking her over yet again before climbing to his feet.

Noticing his almost imperceptible wince, Cara felt her stomach twist with worry. He'd taken the full force of their combined fall by putting his body between her and the asphalt.

"Are you okay?" she asked. It took her a moment to notice that he'd extended a hand to help her stand. She accepted it, allowing him to haul her to her feet, but not taking her eyes off him as she scanned him for injuries. He had to have a nasty case of road rash at the very least. "Let me see your back."

When she reached for his shirt, intending to pull it up and examine the damage, he twitched away from her, shifting just out of reach. The move reminded her of just how invasive she was being. Even if her motives were well intentioned, even if she'd spilled her entire life story to him not five minutes ago, they were still mostly strangers, and she didn't blame him for not wanting her to start poking at him.

"Sorry." Dropping her hand, she made a self-deprecating face. "That was rude of me. Do you need me to call an ambulance?"

"No." Every time she heard him speak, she was reminded how gorgeous his voice was. "Didn't I *just* warn you about messing with Abbott?"

Her shoulders drew back at the criticism. "I was just going to get his plate number. Besides, *he* wasn't the one who tried to kill us." She turned to look at the now-empty street bordering the lot. "I don't suppose you got a look at the license?"

He narrowed his eyes at her. "Sorry." The word came out thick with sarcasm. "Didn't get a chance. I was a little busy *saving* your *life*."

"I do appreciate that, thank you." Still, it would've been nice if he'd multitasked just a bit. Even if he'd only gotten a number or two, it would've given them a place to start. Except for the two of them, the parking lot was deserted. Even the bouncer must've gone inside. In all of the excitement, Abbott had slipped away as well, so there was nothing to show for her brush with death except a sore left knee and whatever injuries Kavenski was ignoring.

She sighed and started to limp back toward the bar.

"Where are you going?"

She glanced over her shoulder at him, surprise lifting her eyebrows. "Inside."

"Why?"

"So this night isn't a total loss." As she crossed the lot, she searched for any moving cars. It was going to be a while before she felt completely safe again.

His wordless response sounded frustrated. She could hear him behind her as he followed her to the door, and she pretended to herself that she didn't find having him at her back enormously reassuring. As she reached the entrance, he dodged in front of her so his huge form blocked her from entering. "What exactly are you going to do in there this time?"

She eyed him, more curious than angry. "Why do you care?"

"Because I have better things to do than follow you around saving your life all the time."

An amused snort escaped before she could stop it. "Once. Not that saving my life even one time isn't a big deal, but you made it sound like I make a habit of near-death experiences. And don't pretend you don't do this sort of thing constantly anyway. I saw you throw yourself in front of a moving car to save a tiny Pomeranian just a couple of days ago. Besides, I'll be perfectly safe in there. All I'm going to do is people-watch as I pretend to drink beer."

He didn't budge. "Who are you planning on watching?"

"The woman Abbott talked to."

His eyes actually widened. "Layla? No. That's a bad idea."

She felt a lurch of excitement. She'd figured he'd pretend he didn't know the woman, but now she wondered if he'd actually give up information about her.

"Her name's Layla? What else can you tell me about her? What's her connection with Abbott? What'd she hand to you when you met her and her fake baby the other day?"

His head tipped back against the door with a thump. "Forget I said anything. Just…go home. Pick someone else to follow around. A shoplifter, maybe, or someone with too many parking tickets."

"I'm not following *you* around anymore." For a moment, she wondered why she felt so comfortable poking at Henry Kavenski, an accused murderer—a very *large* accused murderer. Then she remembered that he'd saved two lives—hers and the little dog's—from speeding cars in just the past few days. Maybe she was naive, but she didn't think a cold-blooded killer would have bothered. "I thought you'd be happy about that."

"I am." Despite the words, his voice was a sullen grumble. "Now you need to quit going after Abbott. And Layla. And basically anyone who's ever set foot in Dutch's."

She patted his arm, touched that he was worried about her. "I'll be fine. I've been helping my sisters do this for years. I'm a pro." Honesty forced her to amend her words. "Peripherally, at least. I'm a *peripheral* pro."

Her assurances did not seem to do the trick, judging by Kavenski's groan and the fact that he didn't move out of her way. Instead, he took a step closer, forcing her to crane her neck to meet his eyes. She shifted back, but he followed, and she realized that he was herding her away from the entrance like a sheepdog with a recalcitrant ewe. Rather than being annoyed by this, however, she had to hold back a snort of amusement.

For whatever reason, she was very tolerant of whatever Henry Kavenski did. She wondered if it was because she felt guilty for following him and breaking into his motel room now that she was fairly sure he hadn't killed the Masons. It could also be that he'd endeared himself to her by saving her life. She was almost positive it wasn't *just* that she found him unbearably attractive.

"You can't—" he began.

The door swung open behind him, cutting off whatever he'd been about to say. Kavenski's expression went still and hard as he whipped around to face the entrance, keeping his enormous form between Cara and the door. She shifted to peer around him, curious about who'd just emerged.

The bouncer blocked the entrance just as Kavenski had moments before, his thick arms crossed over his chest. "Leave."

"Both of us?" Cara asked, disappointed. Now that she'd gotten used to the place, she wanted to return to the corner booth. She could be missing important information, thanks to the two large and mulish men standing between her and the door.

"Yes." Even though the bouncer answered her, his gaze never wavered from Kavenski.

"What if I promise not to cause any trouble?" she pushed, her confidence boosted by Kavenski's presence.

"No. Leave."

She studied the firm, almost tense set of his jaw and gave up on the idea of entering the bar again. That didn't mean she couldn't get information, however. "You didn't happen to notice anything about the car that tried to run me down, did you?"

That made his gaze flick toward her for a microsecond before returning to Kavenski. "I didn't see anything."

"Mmm-hmm." She drew out the sound, allowing a touch of the skepticism to seep into her voice. "Took a conveniently timed bathroom break, did you?" A part of her was quite impressed with her sass, even as another, more sensible side reminded her that she wouldn't have dared if she was confronting the annoyed-looking bouncer alone.

He didn't respond, although the angry crease between his eyebrows deepened. Even though she knew perfectly well that he'd seen at least the beginning of her near-death encounter, she was also aware that he wasn't going to admit to anything. With a frustrated huff, she gave Kavenski's back a subtle pat goodbye. Turning around, she headed for her car. She'd just need to try another night. The bouncer was kicking them out tonight, but that didn't mean she was banned forever. Besides, the guy couldn't work every night.

She carefully crossed the lot, still limping slightly, although the initial throbbing ache eased the more she moved. She scanned the area, tensely anticipating any movement, determined to notice any threats before they got close enough to hurt her. Being run over once was plenty, and she'd rather not have a repeat experience. The distant rev of an engine made her jump, making her peer even harder into the harsh shadows surrounding her. Her stomach was knotted and tense by the time she finally reached her car safely.

Unlocking the driver's door, she got inside. As she started to pull the door shut, a monster-sized hand grabbed the edge of the frame, holding it open. Cara jerked away from the opening, her elbow smacking painfully against the center console.

When she finally realized that it was just Kavenski holding open her door, she rubbed her still-tingling elbow and glared. He didn't look as repentant as he should have...not even close.

"Where are you going?" he asked, his voice a warning rumble.

"Home." She knew she shouldn't give information to a skip, but it was hard to be suspicious of a guy who'd just saved her life and then put himself between her and the furious bouncer like a human shield.

"Good." His eyes narrowed, his glare getting icier, but she found that most of her apprehension had evaporated. "You need to keep your distance from Abbott—and Layla."

She made a noncommittal sound before trying to close the door, but he kept his significant bulk in the way.

His expression switched to a glower. "I'm serious. You're going to get yourself killed."

Again, how could she be mad when he was so concerned with her safety? "Thank you—really—but I have a bunch of sisters to look out for me."

Tiredness was creeping up on her, and her knee was starting to throb again. "Besides, I won't be chasing anyone else tonight. I have a paper to finish, and I'd really like to shower after being in there." Her gaze moved toward his grip on her door.

With a grumbly sigh, he released her door and shifted back slightly until he was no longer blocking her.

"Thank you." She smiled at him again. "You might

want to get back to your motel room and get some rest, too." It was silly of her, but she hated to think of him being unprotected and alone.

He blinked, one corner of his full lips twisting down as if he were holding back some expression, but Cara wasn't sure if it was a smile or a scowl. Reminding herself that it was really none of her business—and she would be better off not getting involved—she pulled the door closed and started her car.

Kavenski stepped out of the way. As she left the lot, turning onto the main street, she saw he was standing where she'd left him, wrapped in shadows.

"Be safe, big guy," she said quietly. Pulling her gaze away from his mostly hidden form, she turned her eyes to the road. She needed to go home and let her sisters know what was going on. As much as she was dreading the lectures about to come her way, she needed backup. As Henry Kavenski had said, she couldn't count on him to be there every time her life was threatened, and she seemed to be heading deeper and deeper into danger. It was time to get some help from the real pros.

CHAPTER 3

"HEY." CARA TRIED TO SOUND CASUAL AS SHE WALKED INTO the kitchen. From her spot sitting on the counter, Norah gave an absent wave without looking up from her phone. Molly, who was sitting in Cara's usual spot at the small table that acted as a desk, wasn't as oblivious. Her gaze latched onto Cara, her suspicion clear.

"What's wrong?"

"Why would you think anything's wrong?" Cara knew she was speaking too quickly. Why hadn't she inherited any of Jane's acting ability? "Everything is *wonderful*."

Now even Norah was looking at her curiously. For her to have gotten Norah's attention, she must've been over-the-top unbelievable.

Cara paused, considering how much of her recent escapades she wanted to share with her sisters. "Fine, maybe not *wonderful* exactly." She'd planned to tell them. It was just that this way, it felt as if her sisters were dragging it out of her, rather than Cara making the well-thought-out and rational decision to share information with her family. Pulling out a chair, she plopped down. "Where are Fifi and Charlie? I'd like to get all the yelling out of the way at one time."

"They're in Wyoming, chasing another lead on

Mom." Molly crossed her arms over her chest and leaned back in her chair as if bracing herself for bad news. "You're going to get yelled at twice, so just spill."

"How about John?" Cara knew she was just delaying the inevitable at this point. "Will he be staying here tonight?" It was strange to see Molly without him. Normally, they were joined at the hip.

"No." Molly frowned. "He's gone for a few days, chasing a skip who ran to Texas."

"Ugh. Poor John."

Although Molly made a dismissive gesture, Cara could tell that she wasn't happy being apart from him. "Quit trying to distract me." Molly's laser focus returned, as did her inquisitor stare. "What's going on with you?"

"Felicity thinks you're sneaking around with a guy, but I don't think that's it," Norah said.

Turning her startled gaze to her sister, Cara said, "A guy? What? Why would I be sneaking around with a guy?"

Norah shrugged. "She wasn't sure about that part. Maybe because you thought we wouldn't like him?"

Unable to hold back an amused snort at how her sister was both wrong and also weirdly right at the same time, Cara shook her head. "It wasn't like that. I *was* with a guy—well, *around* a guy—but it wasn't romantic. He's a skip."

"A skip?" her sisters chorused. Even Warrant raised his head off his front paws to stare.

"I was perfectly safe." *Except for a minor brush with death.* "I hardly had any contact with the skip at all." From Molly's expression, Cara's assurances were not helping. "In fact, when I realized that the first skip was going to be harder to bring in than I thought, I switched to an easier target—a harmless one. Total white-collar, nonviolent criminal." Although after Kavenski's warning about Abbott, that last bit didn't feel entirely true.

There was a brief, heavy silence before Molly stood in a jerky movement that made Cara jump. Gripping the top of her head with both hands, Molly started pacing the small kitchen. Feeling like she was a spectator at a tennis match, Cara watched her pass back and forth, not sure if she should say something or stay quiet and let Molly work through it. When her sister was silent for too long, Cara widened her eyes in slightly panicked question at Norah, who gave her the same look back. Molly started muttering under her breath, but that somehow wasn't any more reassuring than her silent stewing.

"Did I break you?" Cara finally asked when she couldn't stand the tension any longer.

Huffing out a breath, Molly stopped pacing. Clutching two handfuls of her hair, she tipped her head back and stared at the ceiling. Cara shifted uneasily. The ceiling-staring and hair-clutching was somehow worse than the silent staring.

"Molly?" she said tentatively. "You okay?"

"I'm fine." Despite her words, Molly was still staring at the ceiling with a ferocious expression. "Who was your first skip?"

Cara really didn't want to say. "That's not important. I was hoping to get your help with the second one. The harmless one." She felt a little guilty for downplaying Abbott's potential danger, especially since she was asking Molly to help her bring him in, so she amended her words. "The *supposedly* harmless one."

That snapped Molly's attention back as she pounced on the correction. "Supposedly? What does that mean? Who is this skip?"

"Geoffrey Abbott." Cara was just glad that her sister wasn't trying to pry Kavenski's name from her anymore. "He was arrested for tax evasion."

"Sound like a mobster cliché," Norah commented, and Cara shot her sister a look. Even though that had been her first impression, too, Molly didn't need any more reasons to worry.

"It does," Molly agreed, returning to her seat and dropping into it. "Why the sudden urge to jump into the field without telling any of us what you're doing?"

"You said it yourself," Cara said, trying to keep any defensiveness out of her words. "It's time for all hands on deck. With Fifi and Charlie chasing down Mom, that just leaves the three of us to take the paying jobs. And if Norah and I both strictly do research, that leaves *you* to do the actual chasing and tackling. There's only so much you can do, especially since John's not around to help."

Molly wasn't making any sign of agreement, but she wasn't contradicting anything, either. Cara knew her sister was just as aware of the reality of their situation as she was, but she pressed on. "Between Mom's theft and Barney holding the title to the house as collateral on her bail, we need all the cash we can get right now."

"I get why you wanted to help," Molly said, still looking thoroughly unhappy with the situation, "but why do it in secret? You could've been hurt, and we wouldn't have even known in time to help."

"I know." Guilt shot through her. This was the only part of the whole situation that Cara knew wasn't justifiable. She just hated being incompetent at anything. Having her sisters critiquing her work at every step would've made everything ten times worse, even if the advice had been well-intentioned. Still, her pride had almost gotten her killed at least once. "It was stupid not to tell you. I realized that last night."

"What happened last night?" Norah leaned forward, her eyes lit with interest.

"Not much." There was no way she was going to share the whole almost-run-over incident. If she knew how close Cara had come to dying, Molly would figure out a way to keep her locked safely in the house for the next fifty years. "I just heard a rumor that Abbott had some unsavory connections, so I wanted to get your help before I brought a bunch of dangerous criminals down on our heads."

Molly still looked furious and hugely worried, but some curiosity crept into her expression as well. "Is the rumor from a trustworthy source?"

Cara's first impulse was to answer in the affirmative, but then she considered the question again. Just because she had the odd and illogical urge to trust Henry Kavenski didn't mean that he was actually trustworthy. "Possibly," she finally answered. "Enough that it's worth looking into, at least. Plus, Abbott went to Dutch's last night specifically to talk to a woman named Layla who caused Ka—ahh…my source enough concern that he shut down any questions about her." It was only when her sisters stared at her again that she realized what she'd let slip. She'd been so concerned about not mentioning Kavenski that she'd blurted out something she'd planned to keep to herself. "Shoot."

"You went to *Dutch's*?" Molly's calm voice was actually more menacing than yelling would've been. "By yourself? Last night? Dutch's?"

The guilty look on Cara's face must've been answer enough, because Molly was clutching her hair and glaring at the ceiling again. "It was fine," Cara tried to assure her. "My source was there, and he's a big guy. I had backup if I needed it."

She immediately regretted her words when Molly slowly turned her head to fix her with a gimlet stare. "Who exactly is this source of yours?"

Cara cleared her throat and then wished she hadn't, since it sounded exceptionally guilty. "Funny story, that."

Molly's eyes narrowed, and there was no hint of a smile as she said, "Do tell, then. I'd love a chuckle right now."

"My source is actually the first skip I went after." Cara tried for a light laugh, but it came out sounding strangled. "I might not have gotten the bounty on him, but at least I got some information out of the deal, right?"

Molly slumped forward until her forehead met the table with a *thunk*. "Tell me," she groaned without lifting her head. "Tell me everything, all at once, so I can just go ahead and have an anxiety-induced aneurysm and die peacefully. I wish Fifi had been right and you were just dating some guy that we would've hated for whatever reason. This is so much worse than I thought."

"It's okay." Cara tried to keep her tone soothing as she reached over and patted the back of Molly's head.

"I'm completely unharmed, and I've learned my lesson. I'll never chase after another skip without backup, even if he is just a tax evader. I promise."

Molly raised her head enough to fix her best and most deadly glare on Cara. "What's the name of this ever-so-helpful skip?"

Fixing her gaze on the ceiling this time so she wouldn't have to see her sisters' reactions, Cara sighed and admitted, "Henry Kavenski."

For several interminable seconds, the only sound in the kitchen was the tap of Norah's fingers on her phone screen. When even that stopped, Cara couldn't take the suspense and snuck a glance at her sister's face. Norah looked just as appalled as Cara suspected she'd be.

Norah turned her head slowly until her horrified gaze landed on Cara. "You went after *this* guy? Have you seen the photos of the crime scene? This was a professional job."

"Why? What'd he do?" Molly jumped up and circled the table so she could peer over Norah's shoulder. Her horrified expression soon matched her sister's. "Cara Evelyn Pax!"

"I know!" Cara dropped her head onto her folded arms so she didn't have to meet the accusation in their eyes. "It wasn't the best plan, but I just gathered research and watched him from a safe distance. I didn't try to bring him in." She was careful not to mention breaking into his motel room and the face-to-face encounter that followed. "I realized that I'd bitten off more than I could chew—plus I'm pretty sure he didn't actually commit those murders—so I switched to the tax evader."

Molly's face was skeptical, and Cara mentally

cursed her inability to lie—or even hide the truth— well. "How'd he become your source if you stayed at this 'safe distance'?"

"When I was at Dutch's, I went to sit at a back-corner booth where I could watch without too many people noticing me, but Kavenski was already sitting there. He let me sit with him and actually gave me some good information."

"The skip you were following just happened to be at Dutch's the one and only time you've ever gone in there, sitting in the very same booth that you wanted?" Molly asked, her disbelief obvious.

"When you put it like that, it does seem unlikely," Cara admitted.

"Do you think he's setting her up?" Norah asked, her still-horrified gaze lifting to focus on Molly.

"No," Cara answered before her sister could. "He wasn't happy that I was there and kept warning me away from Abbott." She started to say that Kavenski had saved her life, but then stopped, not wanting to freak out her sisters any more than she already had. If she told them about her near-death experience, they really would have anxiety-induced aneurysms. "Oh, and he ran out into traffic to save a dog a few days ago. He's really not that bad."

"He saved a dog? Wait... Warning you?" Molly repeated sharply, returning to her seat. She plopped down heavily, as if the weight of the world was sitting on her shoulders. "Did he threaten you?"

"Oh no. Nothing like that." Cara waved a hand, brushing away that idea. "He just told me that Abbott was mixed up in some things besides tax evasion. There was a woman at Dutch's who Abbott talked to—Layla. I didn't get her last name. I did get the impression that she's involved in some shady things." Which also meant that Kavenski wasn't totally in the clear, even if he hadn't committed the Mason murders. After all, his meeting with Layla had been extremely suspicious.

"Well, if she was at Dutch's, that's likely," Molly muttered. Although she still looked unhappy, her initial shock and fury seemed to have passed. "I don't like you going after this Abbott, especially without getting more information on him."

"I did a full background check." Cara was a little offended that her researching abilities were being questioned. Even though she was new to the actual chasing and tackling part of the business, she was confident in her behind-the-scenes skills. "Nothing suspicious popped up. He looked like a straight arrow—except for the tax evasion. Well, and he's one of Barney's skips."

"*Ugh*." To Cara's surprise, Molly simply made a face at the mention of Barney. A month ago, that would've gotten a much more serious reaction, but Cara figured they'd all dealt with so much since Jane disappeared that taking a case from Barney didn't qualify as shocking anymore. Molly absently scratched Warrant behind the ears as her gaze turned thoughtful. "Sometimes a squeaky-clean background is as suspicious as a dirty one."

Cara raised her eyebrows, happy that it seemed the worst was over, but unable to let the seemingly pointed comment go. "There are some of us who just don't like to get into trouble. We do exist."

Molly grinned at her, and Cara knew for sure that

she'd been forgiven. "*You* exist, sure, but I think you're the exception more than the rule…at least until recently."

Before Cara could retort, Norah stood abruptly, drawing both of her sisters' attention. "I'm trying to do a search for open warrants on anyone with the first name of Layla, but I need my laptop for this." She hurried toward the stairs, and Warrant, whose ears had perked up at the sound of his name, followed her.

Molly made *gimme* gestures with her hands. "Let me see the files on the tax evader and Kavenski. Think we can bring both of them in, make this a twofer?"

"No!" Cara clamped her lips together, but the protest had already escaped, and Molly was looking at her much too curiously. There was no chance her sister would let that go. Focusing too intently on digging Abbott's file out of her backpack, Cara tried again, less vehemently this time. "I don't think he's guilty, honestly. He's been really helpful, and I'd like to keep him as a source. Plus, he's a huge guy, so he'd be tough to bring in."

"You doubt my tackling capabilities?" Molly asked, but her voice was teasing. "That's fine. I won't go after him. We'll stick with Abbott. From what you said, he's mixed up with some criminal sorts, so we'll probably trip over another skip or two as we track him down."

"Thanks." It was only when Cara's shoulders relaxed that she realized how tightly she'd been holding them. "Do you want me back in research mode, then?"

Molly studied her, all traces of amusement gone from her expression. "That depends. Do you *want* to work in the field?"

"I thought the idea of me going after skips upset you," Cara said, a little confused by Molly's calm question.

"The idea of you going after them *alone* is what freaked me out. I'm happy to train you to take a more hands-on role in bringing in skips, but you need to have backup and support and a clue about what you're doing out there." Molly's voice was getting more and more high-pitched, as if all her fears of what could've happened to Cara were running through her mind again. Taking an obvious deep breath, Molly steadily met her eyes. "If you want to learn, I'll teach you, but if you want to stick to research, that's just as valuable as having more bodies chasing and tackling."

A surge of relief took Cara by surprise. Until now, she hadn't realized just how much she hated fieldwork. She'd been determined to help, which allowed her to push through her fear, but the moments in Kavenski's motel room had been terrifying, and she didn't even want to think about almost getting run down. She didn't even like scary movies, so real-life fear didn't give her an enjoyable adrenaline rush. It just left her shaking and queasy. Now her sister was offering her a return to her comfortable role as team researcher, and she really wanted to accept it.

But...

"With Fifi and Charlie chasing after Mom, especially since John's gone, you need help," Cara said, trying to tamp down the voice inside her that was screaming to quit arguing and leave the fieldwork to people who actually enjoyed doing it. "You didn't like it when I went out without backup, but what about you? You can't do it alone."

Molly rolled her eyes. "I *have* asked you to be my backup. A lot. Sometimes in really dangerous situations. Have you already forgotten the warehouse with the guns and the bombs and the really super-annoying booby traps? If I need someone to watch my back, I'm not going to hesitate to ask. Even if I don't think I'm doing anything especially risky, you always know where I am, just in case."

As the truth of what her sister said sank in, Cara felt a rush of guilt for running around in secret. If she'd been hurt in Kavenski's motel room or at Dutch's, her sisters would've had no idea where she was or even that they should be worried. "I'm sorry, Molly. I wanted to help, but I went about it in a stupid way."

"You did, and I know you feel terrible, which is why I'm going to bring this whole thing up in order to get my way for *years*." She laughed, and Cara couldn't help but join in. Molly gave her a stern look, but the effect was diminished by her lingering smile. "So what's it going to be? Tackling skips or research?"

"Research." As Cara answered, about a thousand pounds lifted from her shoulders, leaving her feeling lighter than she had for weeks—since her mom had stolen that necklace, actually. "Backup when you need it, of course, but otherwise, I'll stick to research."

"Done!" Molly smacked her palms on the table, and Cara laughed at her sister's enthusiasm, feeling almost giddy with relief. "First thing tomorrow, I'm going to go chat with my favorite cop to see if she knows anything helpful while you and Norah figure out who's doing what researchwise."

Cara nodded, feeling herself settling back into her comfortable role. She was glad she'd done it, though, if only to prove to herself that she really, *really* hated fieldwork.

"Now go get some sleep," Molly commanded, her big-sister bossiness softened by a tiny smirk.

"I've got a paper to finish first." The words ended on a groan as Cara pushed to her feet, her body protesting any movement.

"Are you hurt?" Molly's too-sharp gaze ran over her, even after Cara waved a casual hand to dismiss her sister's concern.

"Just tired." She might've come clean about everything else, but Molly didn't need to know about the incident in the parking lot. Since no one at Dutch's—except Henry Kavenski—had known she was after a skip, there was no reason for someone to purposefully try to take her out. The more she thought about it, the more certain she was that it had been some random drunken bar patron rather than anyone who had a personal grudge against her.

It wasn't like she'd been intentionally targeted. It had just been a case of bad luck and being in the wrong place at the wrong time. The good thing was that Kavenski had been in the right place at the right time, and that he'd taken the very right action when he'd noticed she was in danger. It wasn't something that she'd expected a murderer to do. Every time they'd run into each other, he'd done something to surprise her in the best of ways.

"Cara? You with me?" Molly's voice was loud enough to make Cara realize her sister must've been trying to get her attention for a while.

"Sorry." She gave a sheepish smile. "I'm beat. I might have to skip finishing that paper tonight and just get up early tomorrow." With a grimace, she amended her words. "*Earlier*. Way too early. A ridiculous amount of early."

"At least Fifi's not here to force us to do morning boot camp," Molly offered. "So you'll have that extra time."

"True." That was a slight comfort. "Good night, Moo."

A wadded-up sticky note bounced off Cara's forehead, and she couldn't hold back a grin.

"Good night, Cara." Despite the innocuous words, Molly's tone threatened retribution for the use of her hated nickname.

As Cara walked out of the kitchen and up the stairs, she did her best not to favor her knee, but she had a feeling that Molly saw more than she let on. As she passed the tiny space that Norah claimed as a bedroom, Cara knocked and stuck her head inside.

Norah was tucked into a small corner of the bed, the only spot that Warrant hadn't completely taken over. She looked fully engrossed in whatever was on her computer. The only response she gave Cara's knock was a questioning grunt, eyes never leaving the screen.

"Don't stay up too late," Cara said, knowing full well that her suggestion would be ignored. Once Norah had settled into her researching groove, she didn't give up until she'd found what she was looking for—and usually a whole lot more. Still, Cara had to try. "I'll jump in on research in the morning, so leave something for me to do."

When Norah finally glanced up at that, Cara gave a smile to let her sister know she was kidding—although not about the go-to-bed part. "There is an obnoxiously high number of ways to spell 'Layla,'" Norah said, making Cara laugh.

"I'll help you come up with even more options in the morning."

"Thanks." Norah's tone was dry.

"Always happy to help." Cara tried to imitate Molly's sternest scowl. "Now get some sleep."

"I will." Despite the promise, Norah seemed to be wrapped up again in her search, and Cara withdrew from the room, closing the door behind her.

Yawning so widely that her jaw popped and her eyes watered, she headed for the bathroom. She might long for bed, but there was no way she could rest without taking a shower and washing off the day. Not only did she still smell like the inside of a bar, but she'd gotten up close and personal with the parking lot outside Dutch's. Who knew what kind of disgusting things had been dumped, tossed, or leaked onto that asphalt? The possibilities made her gag a little.

Despite her roll in the goo, however, the day had ended on a positive note. She was back on research duty, she didn't have to hide anything from her sisters anymore, and Henry Kavenski had saved her life. She couldn't hold back the tiniest amazed laugh.

When had her life gotten so exciting—and so stinking weird?

CHAPTER 4

CARA HURRIED DOWN THE STEPS, LETTING HERSELF BE swept up in the crowd as students left their classrooms. The last thing she wanted was to run into creepy Stuart in an empty hallway again. Once she reached the main level and followed the people surging out into the autumn sunlight, she couldn't help but slow her steps and enjoy the warmth beaming down on her. The old building held the chill of early morning, and her classroom had been about the temperature of a walk-in cooler, so it was a treat to feel the sun finally defrost her fingers and the tip of her nose.

As she crossed campus, the crowd dwindled, clearing the pathway enough that Cara could take her focus off the people around her. Tilting her head back, she closed her eyes for a second, the sunlight making the insides of her lids glow red. Even though she'd woken up disgustingly early, she was still in an optimistic mood. She'd finished her paper, emailed it to her professor, and even had time to eat breakfast with Norah and Molly before her first class. They'd divided up the research, and Cara had a lovely, tidy to-do list, which made her content. The beautiful, sunny weather was just the cherry on an already pretty good day.

Then someone grasped her arm, jerking her to a halt,

and she swung around, automatically trying to yank away even before the identity of her grabber registered.

"Don't touch me, Stuart." Her voice was sharp, and she hoped he hadn't heard the slight tremble underlying her words. It was caused by anger, not fear, but from the way Stuart smirked, he not only heard the quaver, but thought it was because he intimidated her. He also didn't release his grip. "Let. Go."

Grabbing his index finger, she yanked it up and back, not releasing him until he yelped and pulled away, leaving pink imprints on her arm where his hand had been. "Ow! Bitch!"

Cara's eyebrows shot up as she moved several feet back, just to make sure she was out of reach. "Me? You're the one who grabbed me."

"I just wanted to talk to you." His voice was a whine as he shook out his hand, and she hoped it seriously stung. Her heart still beat unnaturally fast. So much for it being a good day. Creepy Stuart had ruined any chance of that.

"No." She used her firmest tone. "There will be no talking and no more grabbing and definitely no more stalking. All of that is over." Annoyed that she'd even had to say that much, she turned away and marched toward the parking lot, her sore knee protesting loudly and all her joy in the beautiful day gone.

"Wait." From the slap of jogging feet hitting the ground behind her, he hadn't listened to a word she'd just said. "The least you can do is answer a few questions."

As much as she knew she shouldn't engage, she couldn't just let that pass by unchallenged. Still hurrying toward the safety of her car, she glared at him over her shoulder. "The least I can do is not kick you in the nuts and then call campus security. You need to leave me alone."

He scowled back at her, all his fake surface charm gone. "I'm not doing anything! I know that doesn't matter to you, since you already called the cops on me for trying to be nice."

Don't argue, the rational part of Cara's brain ordered. *Don't even look at him. That's what he wants*. She couldn't stand it, though, and the words just popped out of her mouth. "Trying to be nice? Is that what they call burglary nowadays?"

"I was bringing class notes to you, and you called the cops. Just now, all I wanted was to have a friendly conversation, and you basically broke my finger off."

Only by biting down on the inside of her cheek did Cara manage to not roundhouse kick him in the face. He lied with such confidence, but she knew the truth: Stuart was a sneaky, stalkery, burglarizing creep. She was determined not to play his games any more than she already had. Keeping her lips pressed tightly together, she increased her pace to a speed walk.

"I just have a couple of questions for you. I think I deserve civil answers, at the very least."

Her molars squeaked as she ground them together. Mentally, she ran through every strike, punch, and kick that Felicity had taught her, taking great relish each time her fist or foot connected with Stuart's stupid face in her brain. It allowed her to not take the bait.

She'd never been as grateful as she was the moment she spotted her car in the lot. Stuart was still babbling behind her as she made a beeline for the driver's door, but it was easier to tune him out now that her escape hatch was in sight. At least it was until he grabbed her arm again, whipping her around to face him.

This time, she didn't hesitate. Using the momentum he'd created, she changed her turn into a rotating kick, aiming for his stupid, stupid smirk. Before her foot could connect, he was jerked back out of range, and Cara's leg whiffed by his nose and returned to the ground. From Stuart's startled expression, he wasn't expecting the dramatic backward movement any more than she'd been.

Behind Stuart was a huge boulder of a man who held Stuart's collar in his oversize fist. Cara blinked a few times, overwhelmed by the adrenaline of the moment, before she recognized Henry Kavenski.

"How many stalkers do I *have*?" she wondered out loud.

"I'm not *stalking* you," a red-faced Stuart denied as he struggled helplessly in the larger man's hold. "Wanting to have a conversation is not *stalking*. Seeing you around campus isn't *stalking*. Either you're super paranoid or you want my attention or something, because you're sure creating a lot of unnecessary drama."

For some reason, the overwhelming aggravation she'd felt for Stuart dwindled to almost nothing, his whiny tirade causing only a buzzing fly worth of annoyance now that Kavenski was there. He pulled all of her attention, and she flicked her fingers at Stuart absently as she eyed the bigger man. "Shush."

Stuart's voice became even more strident, but she tuned out the words as she met Kavenski's gaze. "You can put him down now. He's going to go somewhere else."

Kavenski cocked an eyebrow, as if asking her silently whether she was sure that's what she wanted, and Cara gave a firm nod. His huge fist opened, and Stuart—obviously not expecting to be freed so quickly—stumbled before regaining his footing. He opened his mouth as if to resume his complaints, but Cara hurried to speak before he could.

"Shoo. Off you go, and remember to keep your distance if you don't want a kick in the face." She knew she'd be amazed at her casual confidence later, but now she was too interested in why Kavenski was here on a college campus—*her* college campus. She could believe it was just coincidence that they'd both been at Dutch's at the same time, but there was no way he'd just happened to show up here. She narrowed her eyes at him, straightening her spine, determined to take everything he said with a grain—no, a *handful*—of salt. Even though she was a wannabe kindergarten teacher, she'd worked with her sisters' bounty-hunting business for years. She wasn't a naive know-nothing who could be easily manipulated.

At least she hoped she wasn't.

"What are you doing here?" she asked Kavenski, who hadn't taken his eyes off her. It was hard to maintain her skeptical shell when he was gazing at her so...hungrily. As soon as the thought popped up, she squashed it down, feeling her cheeks grow warm. That had to be her imagination. She was just projecting her own emotions onto Kavenski. There was no way he was as attracted to her as she was to him.

She'd just convinced herself when he cleared his throat. "You left this at Dutch's."

Pulling her eyes off his, she glanced down to see the small ibuprofen bottle sitting in the palm of his hand. She automatically reached out to accept the painkillers, and his warm fingers brushed against hers for too short a time as he handed her the bottle. "You tracked me down for that? I meant to give you those. You were the one with the headache."

"I took a couple, but there are still eight left." *Again with the throat clearing.* Between that and his silly pretext for tracking her down, Cara was beginning to truly wonder if her initial impression had been right and this little crush of hers wasn't one-sided. "I figured you might need them. Later. Eventually."

As she opened her mouth to respond, she noticed movement in the corner of her eye. Turning, she saw that Stuart was still there—watching them. Once he noticed he had her attention, he started talking again. Loudly.

"Stuart." His name came out like a gunshot, and he actually went silent, his mouth hanging open as he goggled at her. "Leave. Now."

His shoulders snapped back as he quickly recovered. "You—"

With a sound unsettlingly close to a growl, Kavenski suddenly jerked toward Stuart. The motion was quickly cut off, but it did its job. With a small, startled shriek, Stuart took off at a speed-walk pace that really wanted to be a run. Cutting through the parking lot, he rushed to the pathway that led toward the center of campus, finally leaving Cara blessedly alone…well, alone except for Henry Kavenski.

Refocusing on the thousands of questions bubbling

around in her brain, she asked the first that popped up. "Why are you really here?"

She might have put Stuart from her mind, but Kavenski was still watching him with suspicious eyes. "What's your connection with him?" he finally asked, turning to face her again.

Cara started to automatically answer but snapped her mouth closed just in time. "Nope. I asked first."

"I told you. To return the pills." He studied her for a long moment, his arctic eyes unreadable. "Good thing I did. You have a tendency to find trouble."

"I do not. Well, I didn't used to." She couldn't argue that she'd managed to find her share of dangerous situations over the past couple of weeks. Still, a bail jumper and suspected murderer was calling *her* the trouble magnet? "Until I met you, I was trouble averse."

The tiniest upward quirk of one corner of Kavenski's mouth immediately drew her attention, just because of the rarity of what had—possibly? maybe?—just happened. Did Mr. Hard-Ass actually smile? Was it actually possible without cracking his stone mask of a face? It was almost annoying how much more attractive that hint of a smile made him, especially since he was breathtaking even while cranky. That tiny smile was just overkill.

"Also," she pushed on, needing to keep her mind focused on the conversation, "what do my nonexistent trouble-finding skills have to do with anything? My actual question was 'Why are *you* here?'"

He made an impatient gesture, which she thought was entirely unfair, because he was the one being weird about answering a simple question. "I just told you."

"Okay," Cara said, not letting the way his forearms

flexed as he moved his hands distract her. "Let's try this again. What *exactly* are you doing here in this campus parking lot, just as I happened to arrive?"

That bare hint of a smile was long gone, and a fierce scowl had taken its place. "There's already been one attempt to kill you."

"So?" She shook her head when he stared at her. "I don't mean that my near-death experience wasn't completely scary, because it was, but that doesn't explain why you're lurking behind a Subaru, ready to grab random low-level burglars and dangle them in midair." Her knee gave a dull throb, and she opened her driver's door and tossed her backpack into the passenger seat before plopping down sideways, needing to sit. Once she got comfortably settled, she continued. "Also, isn't it pretty dramatic to say someone was intentionally trying to kill me? I think it's more likely that someone was drunk and dumb, and we were just the unlucky ones in the way at that particular moment."

He opened his mouth and then closed it, glowering at her.

"Well?" she asked when he didn't speak. "What's your answer?"

"To which part?"

"Why are you here?" she asked, finding her patience returning now that she was off her knee and Stuart had disappeared in the distance.

"You're not taking this seriously, and it's going to get you killed."

She couldn't hold back a huff of laughter.

"What?"

Raising one shoulder in a shrug, she looked up at him.

From her position, he looked extra-enormous standing there in front of her, and she marveled at how comfortable she'd become around him. "That's the first time I've been accused of not taking something seriously. Usually, I'm the Negative Nelly of the family, always thinking about possible consequences."

From his renewed scowl, he didn't find this as amusing as she did. "The consequences will be death. Your death." He made a strange face that she couldn't translate—baffled resignation, maybe?—and added in a mutter, "And probably mine."

"It's okay, Henry," she said, his name feeling odd on her tongue. She generally thought of him as Kavenski, but his concern for her safety—as exaggerated as she felt it was—was sweet. Too sweet for an impersonal last name. "I've confessed all to my sisters, and I'm firmly back on Team Research. There will be no more lurking in dark booths at Dutch's for me." That last part almost made her sad. With Henry there in the booth with her, she had felt safe.

His glower finally eased slightly. "Good. Your sisters shouldn't be involved with these people, either."

This time, she laughed outright. "Don't worry. The ones doing the actual chasing and tackling love a heaping helping of danger with their skips. It's the adrenaline rush, something I'm sure you know all about. Me, on the other hand... Well, fear just makes me want to run away." When he looked as though he was about to start lecturing again, she hurried to add, "It's okay. My sisters are smart about it." *Unlike me*. She didn't say that part out loud, since there was a soft, squishy inner part of her that really wanted him to think she was smart and brave.

Well, it was too late for the brave part—and probably for the smart part, too—but she couldn't quite admit out loud how dumb she'd been for chasing after him half-cocked. She was just lucky that he seemed to be fairly decent, as bail jumpers went.

"Why's Powers following you around?" he asked, shifting forward until he could rest a muscular forearm on the top of her door as he bent toward her. His right hand was braced against the car, so it felt as if he surrounded her. Instead of feeling claustrophobic as she would have if anyone else—especially a skip she'd been chasing—had trapped her inside the car with his ginormous body, she felt safe, protected from the outside world. It was probably because he'd saved her life the previous night, but Henry Kavenski didn't set off any of the alarm bells he should've been ringing.

"Powers? Oh, Stuart!" He'd never shared a class with her, so up until a few weeks ago, she'd barely known him. They'd never even exchanged a nod in greeting until he'd broken into her house. Now, she felt as if she couldn't escape him. For a moment, she was sad that her kick had missed his smug little face. "He's after the necklace my mom stole."

Kavenski's expression changed, going from startled back to his usual impassiveness. "You have the necklace?" There was an intensity to the question that he couldn't quite hide, and disappointment flooded her. Immediately, she scolded herself for being silly. Of course he was interested in the necklace. He was a criminal. A double-layered criminal, even, since he'd jumped bail after being arrested for another crime. Even if he *was* innocent of the Masons' murders, he was doing shady things with Layla. The jewelry was worth a fortune and would've been a temptation to even the most sin-free, lawful citizens.

"Of course not. If we did, do you think we'd be hanging on to it, luring every lowlife into our home? Do you *know* how many attempted break-ins we've had since this all happened?"

He peered at her suspiciously, and she looked back, holding his gaze, intensely hoping he believed she was sincere. The thought of Henry Kavenski—*her* skip turned source turned sort-of protector—joining the hordes hunting the necklace filled Cara with bitter disappointment. To her utter relief, he gave her the slightest nod, a bare dip of his chin, but it was enough. He wouldn't be one of the many breaking into her house in search of the necklace.

Pulling her gaze away from Kavenski, she realized that everything around them had gotten very quiet...too quiet. There wasn't even a peep from a bird or squirrel in the surrounding trees. It seemed as if the whole area was holding its breath. Her gaze skipped around the partially filled lot as prickles traced up her spine. Every tinted window and cargo van seemed suspicious, and the vehicles scattered around the lot offered too many possible hiding places. She knew she was just freaking herself out by imagining hostile eyes watching them—as she'd been doing ever since this whole thing with her mother began—but she still wanted to leave. The only problem was that she wanted to keep talking to Henry.

"Want to grab some coffee?" she asked impulsively and immediately felt like the hugest idiot on the planet. He was a skip, for crying out loud, someone who was being chased by law enforcement and bounty hunters and who knows who else. He wasn't just another student who could wander around and go on coffee dates.

That small smile touched his mouth for just a fraction of a second, but the sight of it still warmed Cara's belly, despite her embarrassment. If she hadn't already known he was going to turn her down because it was an utterly terrible idea, the way he straightened and took a step back would've tipped her off. "Probably not a good idea," he said, his voice low and deeper even than normal.

"Right. Okay. Sure." *Cara! Stop. Talking. Now.* She managed to get it together enough to talk like a semi-normal person. "Thanks for the assist with Stuart. I'd probably have gotten into trouble if I'd actually kicked him in the face. Oh, and thank you for returning these." Lifting the pill bottle in her hand, she gave it a shake.

"No problem." He took another step back, and Cara knew that was a hint for her to leave. With a silent sigh, she started pulling her door closed. Before it latched, she heard him say, "Nice form on that roundhouse."

She beamed and gave him a small wave that must've looked incredibly awkward. The truth was that she was too happy about his compliment to really care how dorky she looked. Looking down, she started the car and put it into gear. When she glanced up again, ready to give a final wave, he was gone. Her hand dropped to the steering wheel as she craned her neck to look around, but she couldn't see anyone else in the lot.

Henry Kavenski had completely disappeared.

CHAPTER 5

FRIDAY NIGHT, AS CARA SNUGGLED INTO THE CORNER OF the couch, she was once again grateful she was back on research duty. Nothing beat wearing her flannel hedgehog pajamas and an oversize hoodie to work. Balancing her laptop on her thighs, she twisted around to grab Abbott's file from the end table.

She'd been through the slim file over a dozen times, but she was determined to find a lead. There had to be a detail she'd missed that would be helpful in tracking him. "Geoffrey Princeton Abbott," she muttered to herself. "Wow. Could that name be more pretentious?" She scanned the familiar details. *Forty-four years old, no known children, no known current girlfriend or boyfriend, father dead, mother estranged and living in Portugal.* Tipping her head back, she stared at the ceiling. The file was a dead end. She needed a new source of information.

Kavenski immediately popped into her head, but she promptly shoved that thought away. She needed to let that skip go.

Her phone beeped with a text, and she grabbed it from the back of the couch to see that Molly, who'd been shadowing Abbott all afternoon, had followed her quarry to Dutch's. Molly was parked and watching the bar, waiting for him to leave.

Cara frowned, guilt prickling at her. She hated the thought of Molly being there on her own, with no Henry Kavenski to save her if necessary. She should've told her sister about the possible danger. Even though Cara was ninety-nine percent sure there hadn't been an intentional attempt on her life, she still felt like she'd sent Molly out on her own without giving her the full story.

Resolving to tell her sister about the near hit-and-run once Molly returned, Cara sent a quick text acknowledgment and set her phone on the back of the couch. She flipped through the rest of Abbott's file, frowning. She'd been over and over it, and it still read as more of an inspirational life story than a criminal's background. If anything, it was suspicious because of its total squeaky-clean perfection.

Geoffrey Abbott had grown up in Denver and Aspen and had gone to expensive private schools. After graduating from the University of Colorado in Boulder, he'd snowboarded professionally for a few years before retiring at age twenty-six. He'd bought a high-end hotel in Aspen soon after that, and split his time between a loft in LoDo—Lower Downtown Denver—and his resort. He'd never married, just dated occasionally, and—on paper at least—was the very model of a hard-working businessperson.

The only red flag in the file—besides skipping out on bail—was that the FBI had investigated him, which resulted in the tax-evasion charge. According to Cara's information, there wasn't anything that had triggered the federal investigation, which made her wonder how much dirt she'd missed. She started reading through all of the data again, needing it fresh in her mind before she started digging deeper.

"Huh," she said out loud just as Norah was coming down the stairs. Warrant followed, his tail swishing happily from side to side as he jumped up onto the couch and curled into a large, fluffy ball that covered Cara's toes—and the rest of the couch.

"Did you find something?" Norah's voice was hopeful. Cara knew her sister had been trying to track down any warrants on the infamous Layla, which had to be frustrating.

"Maybe," Cara said absently as she looked up at her sister. "How's progress?"

Norah made a face. "I wasn't getting anywhere, so I've given up on that avenue of investigation until we can get a last name—and spelling—for Layla. Any chance your new source knows more about her?"

"I'm sure he does, but I don't know how to get ahold of him until he pops out of a bush in front of me. He's changed motels again, and I never got his phone number." *I wish*, a small part of her brain whispered, but the rest of her quickly shushed that wistful voice. When Norah's face fell with obvious disappointment, Cara hurried to add, "I promise I'll ask if I stumble over him in the shrubbery."

"Thanks." Norah perched on the sofa arm and peered at the contents of the file over Cara's shoulder. "What were you huh-ing about a minute ago?"

"This." Cara tapped the line of text she'd just been looking at. "St. Thomas More Academy in Colorado Springs. Abbott spent part of his junior and all of his senior year there. Isn't that basically the rich-kid alternative to juvie?" As she asked the question, she handed the file to Norah so she could open her laptop.

"I believe so. Wasn't that the place where one of the students died of heat exhaustion?" Norah asked, leaning closer to see the laptop screen. The school's website wasn't much help, except to confirm that it was a military-style private school with a strong emphasis on discipline. Cara returned to her general search and found a number of news articles detailing the incident that Norah had mentioned.

"That's the place," Cara said as she continued scanning the Colorado Springs *Gazette* article. A fifteen-year-old boy died during a group ten-mile run. There was a police investigation, but no one had been found to be at fault. Switching over to the file again, Cara noted the name of his previous school. "He was in Aspen at the Anchor Academy until February of his junior year. Guess I'm going to be checking the police blotter for crimes committed by minors right around that time."

"Good plan." Norah made a face as she pushed herself back to her feet. "I wish I could help."

That made Cara focus on her sister with her full attention. "You look nice. Are you going out?" She felt bad that the question came out sounding so incredulous, but Norah never wanted to go out or do anything social.

"Yes." Norah scrunched up her face again. "Dwayne's completed his parole, so he was able to leave California. He wants to meet for dinner."

"Oh! I didn't know POS was in town. Will he be stopping by here to pick you up?" Cara often forgot that Norah's dad was still alive, since he was usually serving time or on parole. She would never say it out loud, but Cara didn't think it was fair that Dwayne was still alive and kicking, while her and Charlie's dad, Victor Chavis, had died when the twins were only two. Cara couldn't really remember her biological dad, except for brief, blurry flashes that she worried might just be imagination, but according to everyone who had known him, Victor had basically been an angel living on earth. Dwayne, on the other hand, proudly went by the well-earned nickname POS.

"No, I'm meeting him at that family buffet place in Langston," Norah answered, and Cara tried to shove away any lingering pangs of grief and anger at the unfairness of life. "Mom still has that protection order out on him, so he can't come to the house." Norah's voice was pragmatic.

"Poor Norah." Cara couldn't keep the sympathetic amusement out of her voice, especially after her sister made an exaggerated *yuck* face. "You have to hang out with POS at a restaurant with a sneeze guard?"

"It's okay." Norah pulled a long sweater on over her tunic and leggings. "He'll get arrested again soon enough, so I only need to suffer through this every three to five years."

That made Cara laugh out loud. "That's a very healthy attitude."

Norah shrugged as she headed for the door. "It's been like this my whole life, so I've had twenty-three years to get used to it."

"Well, tell POS I said hi."

"I will. Text me if you find out anything interesting." Norah had opened the door, but she wasn't leaving. From the longing in her expression, Cara knew that she was dying to dig in and do some research, rather than eating wilted iceberg lettuce and lukewarm canned corn at the buffet. Knowing POS as they did, Norah would end up paying.

"You know it. Do you have some money?"

Norah nodded as she patted her pocket. "Mind if I take your car?"

"Of course not." Cara held up one hedgehog-covered leg. "As you can see, I'm not planning on going anywhere tonight, except maybe to the kitchen to get me and Warrant a snack." At his name—or possibly at the word *snack*—Warrant thumped his tail a few times. "Have as much fun as you can. Hopefully, your visit will be quick and painless, like pulling out a splinter."

From Norah's expression, she wasn't holding out much hope of that. "Thanks," she said a little hollowly. She finally left, calling out just before she pulled the door shut, "Turn the alarm on."

"Right." The rule was that the alarm was always on at night, if the house was empty, or if only one person was home. Putting her laptop and the file on the coffee table, Cara pulled her toes out from underneath Warrant and moved over to the alarm controls. Setting one to Occupied, she moved to lock the two dead bolts securing the front door.

Once she was fully alarmed and locked inside, she looked over at the dog, who'd stretched out to cover the entire couch. "Since I'm up, I might as well get some research snacks, right?"

Warrant's tail thumped against the cushion again, making Cara more certain that he'd learned the word *snacks*. It made sense. Snacks were his very favorite thing in the world.

She made some microwave popcorn and filled her water bottle before returning to claim her spot. It took some battling with Warrant, but she finally wedged her way back into her corner on the couch. Grabbing a handful of popcorn, she flipped up her laptop screen. "All right, Warrant. Let's see what Geoffrey-with-a-G did to get shipped off to military school."

Pulling up the Aspen Times police blotter, she quickly found that the paper's archives didn't go back far enough for her needs.

"Guess we're doing this the hard way." Cara typed in the year Abbott had transferred, along with Anchor Academy and Aspen. When hundreds of thousands of search results came back, she tried adding various other words, including arrested, theft, and—feeling especially morbid—murdered. Nothing incriminating popped up. She scrolled through the disappointing results with one hand while popping a few popcorn kernels into her mouth with the other. Deleting murdered, she tried adding died to the other keywords in the search bar and hit Enter.

"That's it," she murmured, clicking on the second result listed. It was an old newspaper article about the memorial service for an Anchor Academy student, Doug Lear. In late January, just a few weeks before Abbott had transferred schools, Lear had died of alcohol poisoning. Two students, one male and one female, had been questioned by the police about their involvement, but only the male student had been charged with hazing and expelled.

The doorbell rang, and Cara groaned. "Please go away," she said under her breath, dropping a forgotten handful of popcorn kernels back in the bowl. In response, the doorbell rang again. Warrant lifted his head and gave her a pained look. "Normal dogs would bark a warning at visitors—especially unwanted ones." When Warrant just stared at her with liquid eyes and his ears pressed back, she sighed.

The bell rang for the third time, and he slunk off the couch and up the stairs. She assumed he was going to jam himself under Molly's bed, the place he usually hid during thunderstorms and July Fourth fireworks. The doorbell pealed again, making her swear. She huffed, carefully placing her popcorn, computer, and water bottle down.

She didn't want to answer, didn't want to deal with anyone rude enough to show up at someone's house at seven thirty in the evening without being asked—not to mention someone who repeatedly rang the doorbell, hurting poor Warrant's ears, rather than taking the hint and leaving. Only the thought that it might be someone needing help was enough to leverage Cara off the couch. She stomped to the door and peered through the peephole. The person she saw on the porch just enraged her more.

"Go away, Stuart!" she called through the door, leaving the alarm and dead bolts engaged. There was no way in heck she was going to open the door for Stuart Powers.

"I have to talk to you!" Stuart shouted back, louder than he needed to be heard through the door.

Cara winced. All the neighbors had to be listening

to this. The Pax sisters were already the pariahs of the neighborhood, so this would be one of many, many transgressions for the neighborhood association to gossip over. "Go away, Stuart! I'm not going to talk to you!"

"I'm not leaving until we talk!" He rang the doorbell several times in a row, and Cara shot a worried look toward the ceiling, hoping that Warrant wasn't freaking out too much.

"I'm calling the cops, then!" She made a face as she shouted the threat. She really didn't want to have to call the police. Although most local law-enforcement officers would handle the situation well, there were a few—especially a certain detective—who would take pleasure in making everything a thousand times worse. The way her luck was going, she was almost certain to have Detective Mill show up at her door. Ever since Molly and John had gotten his crooked partner arrested, Mill had been keeping an uncomfortably close eye on all the Paxes. He'd jump at the opportunity to take this call.

Stuart laughed loudly as if he could read her thoughts. "Do it! They'd love to get another chance to look around Jane Pax's house!"

Swallowing a groan, Cara squeezed her eyes closed and tried to think. Molly would rush home if she knew what was happening, but Cara didn't want her sister to have to deal with Stuart, either. Charlie and Felicity— both of whom would've had a ball tossing Stuart into the street—were chasing after Jane. John Carmondy would've been her next choice, but he was out of town, too.

"Ugh," she muttered as softly as possible. "Now would be a good time to jump out of the bushes,

Kavenski!" Since the doorbell continued to chime, she assumed he hadn't heard her almost-silent call for help. She decided to just wait Stuart out, pressing her hands over her ears when the constant dinging of the doorbell grew insanity-inducing. Her head was starting to throb, and she knew that poor Warrant had to be in the middle of a doggie meltdown.

Finally, she couldn't stand it any longer. "I'll take my chances with the cops." Pivoting toward her phone, she started to take one step and then froze. A guy dressed all in black—from his knit face mask to his military-style boots—stood just a few feet away. He jerked to a stop, obviously not expecting her movement, and they stared at each other. Her first oddly calm thought was that their new alarm system had betrayed her, and she flicked the quickest of glances toward the alarm controls. The screen was blank and lifeless. The intruder must've disabled the security system.

Quit obsessing about the alarm and move! her brain screamed, breaking her paralysis, and her legs obeyed. She dove sideways, toward her phone, and yelled to the idiot who was still poking rhythmically at the doorbell. "Stuart! Call the cops! Someone's in my house!"

The chiming paused but then picked up tempo, and she knew that either Stuart was the most evil little woodchuck in Colorado, or he was in on this—whatever *this* was.

She'd almost made it to the coffee table, her hand extended toward her phone, when a burly arm wrapped around her middle, jerking her back before her fingers could close around the device. Her heart pounded so loudly in her ears that she could barely hear the doorbell.

Cara started screaming, the tiny, practical part of her brain that wasn't blind with panic hoping for once that her nosy and judgmental neighbors *were* listening. Anything to bring the cops to the house to help.

Cara was yanked back, her spine pressed tightly against the intruder's chest, surprise stealing her breath for a moment. Her elbow automatically swung back, and her assailant's breath was driven out in an audible *whoosh*. Desperately trying to remember her training, Cara stomped on the foot behind her, cursing her stocking feet as her heel came down on the hard surface of a steel-toed boot. The arm around her middle tightened again, and Cara twisted, trying to turn enough to aim a heel strike at the intruder's nose, but he anticipated her next move and dodged the blow. The side of her hand glanced off his knit-covered cheek, the miss sending her off-balance.

Her body rocked to the side, but she didn't wait to regain her footing before kicking out again, hoping to hit his knees. Her sole slammed against his shin, but it wasn't hard enough to make him release his grip. Balling her hand into a fist, she let it fly in a backswing toward the side of his face. Before it could connect, he lurched forward, taking both of them to the floor.

This is bad! She grimaced with effort as she fought to get out from underneath him, but wrestling had always been her weakest point in the basic self-defense training Felicity had given them. Now, with panic swamping her brain and keeping her from remembering the techniques she'd been taught, Cara was reduced to ineffective squirming and glancing backward blows that only managed to tire her out.

She sucked in a breath, prepared to start screaming again, when something pricked the side of her neck. Her head swung back, and the back of her skull connected with his face. She felt a fierce sense of satisfaction as she heard a male voice start nasally swearing. She desperately hoped she'd broken his nose.

When he reared back after she head-butted him, she struggled frantically, using her breath to fight rather than scream, but her arms grew heavy and the living room was already getting wobbly around the edges.

Darkness crept in from the sides of her vision, and she prayed that she wasn't dying. She tried screaming again, but her lungs were having trouble getting enough air through her vocal cords, and her yell turned into a pathetic whimper.

Her phone chimed from the coffee table, and she renewed her struggles, hating that she was so close to a rescue and yet it was impossible. There was no way to get to her phone, and she wasn't even able to scream. Not even the nosiest neighbor would hear her cries for help over the constant dinging of the doorbell.

As the darkness edged in, she gradually stopped fighting, her limbs turning leaden and uncooperative.

All she could manage was a final mutter. "I'm... going to...*kill* you, Stuart." Then everything went dark.

CHAPTER 6

CARA'S HEAD WAS POUNDING, AND ALL SHE WANTED TO do was fall back into the oblivion of sleep, but she was too cold for that. Besides, the bed was hard, and someone was talking loudly. She made a face without opening her eyes, wishing whoever it was would be quiet, since the noise was making her head hurt even more. There were times when it was hard to live in a house with all her sisters. Peace and quiet were rare. She shifted, trying to roll to a more comfortable position on her side, but her arms weren't cooperating.

The strangeness finally registered, and her brain snapped to full awareness as her eyes flew open. She was on the floor on her front, her head turned toward a wall, and her arms were pulled behind her. Panic rose in her, making it hard to think, and she blinked hard at the rough board in front of her. The pounding in her skull increased, the pain tearing viciously through her head. Scattered images flashed through her brain—struggling with a masked man, the constant ringing of the doorbell, the painful prick in her neck—overlying the terrifying unfamiliarity of her surroundings. Her heart beat so quickly it was almost a drone, and a scream built in her lungs. Gasping in a rough breath, she forced herself to count the knots in the rough planks that made up the wall. It took thirty-eight before she calmed enough for her brain to work again.

The room was dim, but a small amount of light creeping in around some kind of window covering made her fairly certain it was daytime. Now that she had shaky control over her panic, she lifted her shoulders, arching her back to give her enough space to turn her head to face the other direction.

The room was tiny and bare. Except for her, some cobwebs, and a solid layer of dust, the space was empty. The rough boards that made up the walls and floor made her think she was in a cabin—not a fancy, ski-resort-type vacation cabin, but the type that someone threw together so that they'd have some protection, no matter how rough, against the winter snow and winds. A shack.

She spent a dizzy moment debating whether she'd rather be tied up in a cabin or a shack before the panic started creeping back in, and she jerked her thoughts back on track.

Focus.

The person in the other room had gone quiet, and the complete silence was unnerving. The events of the evening before—had it just been last night?—ran through her memory, and she instinctively yanked at her hands until her wrists burned from the friction.

Calm, calm, calm.

Her breaths were quick and tight, and she forced herself to slow them, dragging in long, ragged inhales until her heart stopped pounding so hard. The pain and pressure in her head eased along with her panic, which helped her start thinking rationally again.

Okay. Hands are tied. Feet?

She attempted to move her legs, but they were strapped together at the ankles. The restriction threatened to bring another wave of panic, so she focused on making a mental to-do list. First, she needed to get off the floor, at least to a sitting position if she couldn't stand. Trying to stay as quiet as possible—since she didn't want whoever was in the other room to know she was conscious—she rolled to the right, just enough to draw her legs up underneath her.

It was a relief to see that she still wore her hedgehog pajamas and her hoodie, but the drag of fabric against the rough floor sounded loud to her ears. Pausing, she listened so hard that her head started pounding again. When no one came bursting into the room, she let out the breath she was holding in a long rush and lifted her upper body until she was on her knees.

A wave of dizziness hit her, and she swayed, blinking rapidly against the spinning room. When it finally passed, she wondered if she'd hit her head or if her symptoms were a result of whatever her kidnapper had injected her with. The thought of him drugging her filled her with fresh rage, and she clenched her teeth together hard enough to make her molars squeak.

A hard shiver shook her, distracting her from her anger, reminding Cara of how cold she was. Her fingers were numb, either from the tight bonds or from the chilliness of the room, making it impossible to feel what they'd tied her with. Twisting, she examined her ankles and saw that they'd been secured together with two zip ties. She made a face, wishing it had been duct tape or knotted cord—something she could've picked at.

From her position on her knees, she looked around to

see if she'd missed anything she could use as a weapon or to free herself, but the room was just as empty as she'd thought. There was a window, though, covered with a cheap plastic shade. She tried to shuffle toward it on her knees, but the ties around her ankles were too tight to allow for movement. She debated standing, but worried that she'd topple over, creating a crash that could bring her abductors in.

She paused, realizing that they hadn't gagged her. Did that mean they didn't think she'd wake to yell, or was there no one around to hear? The walls weren't soundproof in any way. She could hear the twittering of some kind of bird and the occasional sweep of the wind. Her stomach tightened, and she swallowed with a suddenly closed throat. The idea of being in a murder cabin was infinitely scarier when it was in the middle of nowhere.

They don't care if I scream, because no one will hear.

The drag and thump of a chair being pulled over old floorboards reminded her of the other occupant of the cabin, and she corrected herself. *No one who hears will care.*

Panic was bubbling up again, and she forced it down. *Stop it. Not productive.* What *would* be productive was getting to the window. She might not be able to escape with her feet and hands tied, but she could at least get an idea of where she was.

Having a goal helped keep her calm, so she added to her to-do list: *Second, get over to the window.*

Getting to her feet was out, she'd decided, and moving on her knees wasn't working, so what were her other options? She rolled onto her hip and pulled her legs in front of her. Shuffling around so her back faced the window, she bent her knees and pushed herself back, scooching her butt along the floor. It was slow going, the rough floorboards catching on her pajama pants and threatening to pull them down. She wished desperately for polished wood that she would've slid smoothly over, but then caught herself before a semi-hysterical laugh escaped. If she was making wishes, she should do a better job—like wishing for a pocketknife and a cell phone or not being kidnapped in the first place.

She made slow, painful progress across the small room, using her bound hands as leverage to raise her hips slightly off the floor. Falling into the rhythm of the push-lift-back motion, she didn't realize she was so close to the wall until her shoulders hit against it with a *thump*. She felt the board behind her bow slightly under the impact, then heard a sharp crack as a piece of the rotted-looking window trim popped free of its moorings. She watched in helpless horror as the broken strip of wood toppled toward the floor. Without hands to catch it, she tried to twist underneath to muffle the sound, but the board bounced off her shoulder and landed with a painfully loud clatter several feet away.

She tensed as she heard the sound of a chair scraping against the floor before heavy footsteps approached the door. All of Cara's thoughts dissolved into white noise as she pressed her back against the wall, trying to disappear into the rough planks.

The door swung open, revealing the black-clad, ski-masked intruder who'd broken into her house, drugged her, and taken her to this scary cabin in the middle of nowhere. Fury sparked inside her, but her fear stayed

dominant. She was tied up and weaponless, and she had
no idea what this guy wanted from her. He had the upper
hand by a mile, while both of hers were bound helplessly behind her back. Half-started plans swirled in her
head, but she wasn't able to hold onto a thought before
another one shoved into its place.

Without a word, he moved toward her, and she
braced, ready to fight however she could manage.

"What do you want?" she demanded—or tried to. Her
voice came out in more of a pathetic croak.

Instead of answering, he pulled something out of his
pocket. "You weren't supposed to be awake yet." His
voice sounded wrong. It wasn't the menacing growl of a
kidnapper. It was a normal, pleasant tenor that could've
belonged to one of her instructors at school or a news-
caster giving a weather report. It threw her off, making
her still for valuable seconds.

He bent down and reached for her, and she snapped
out of her moment of surprise. Bending her legs, she
kicked out, aiming for his knees. He dodged so only
one of her feet glanced off his lower thigh, but it landed
hard enough to make him grunt. She threw herself sideways away from him, rolling even as she knew it was
hopeless. She was bound and still woozy from being
drugged, while he was almost twice her size and almost
assuredly armed. Still, she turned onto her back to try
to kick him again, not willing to give up while she still
had a chance to fight him off. He lunged, knocking her
onto her side as the weight of his body kept her legs
pinned. Flipping her onto her front, he held her down
with terrifying ease. She felt the sharp prick of a needle
entering her neck for the second time in who knew how

many hours, and she swallowed a scream. Turning her head, she tried to bite the hand holding the syringe, but he pulled away just in time before casually backhanding her across the face.

Her head bumped against the floor as her cheek throbbed from the blow. She fought to keep struggling and stay conscious, but the darkness crept back in until everything went black.

It felt like just an instant later when she was blinking open blurry eyes, but her kidnapper wasn't in the room anymore, and there was pale, pinkish light squeezing in around the window shade. She was still close to the window, slumped on the floor on her side. As she struggled into a sitting position, her head spun, and nausea rose. Squeezing her eyes closed, she focused on keeping the little that was in her stomach down where it belonged. After a few moments, things settled, and she reopened her eyes.

The reality of her situation hit her at the sight of the empty room, and she had to choke down bile again. Swallowing hard and tightening her jaw muscles, she forced herself to think productive thoughts. Except for the residual drugs in her system making her groggy and nauseated, she was unhurt. Her captor—the one she'd seen, at least—was masked, which meant that he wanted to hide his identity from her. He wouldn't have bothered if he was planning on killing her.

Now that her stomach had settled, she scooted closer to the window and awkwardly rolled to her knees, trying to keep as quiet as possible. She couldn't hear any

sounds coming from beyond the wooden door, but that
didn't mean she was alone in the cabin. The last thing
she wanted was for someone to hear and come knock
her out again.

No, her brain corrected. *The last thing you want is for
someone to hear and come shoot you in the face.*

With that cheery thought, Cara refocused on the
window. The sill came to her chin, so she was just tall
enough to see out once she used the side of her face to
push the shade over. It rustled as she moved it, unsettled
dust floating in the air, tickling her nose, and making
her wish she had at least one hand free to rub her face.
She shook her head slightly at the ridiculous thought. Of
her current most urgent needs, scratching an itch was a
pretty low priority.

The view outside the window focused her stray
thoughts. *No wonder they didn't gag me.* There was
nothing out there except miles of sparse, sunburnt grass
stretching farther than she could see. If it weren't for the
mountain peaks in the distance, she would've thought
the cabin was on a prairie, rather than the high plains in
the middle of the mountains. Although she'd only driven
through Field County a couple of times, the rocky, flat
openness seemed familiar, and she was almost certain
that's where she was.

Her brain worked as she smashed her cheek against
the window, trying to see as much as possible from her
awkward vantage point. No matter how hard she looked,
though, there were just open high plains. She couldn't
see a driveway or even a two-track trail leading up to the
site. It was as if aliens had dropped the cabin from the
sky—with her in it.

Fear started nibbling around the edges of her mind, so she quickly smashed down her irrational thoughts. *The driveway is on the other side of the cabin*, she told herself firmly. *I just can't see it. In fact, there's probably a road and other houses and an entire shopping mall on that side. I just have the room with a wilderness view.* Even though she didn't really believe her assurances, the possibility that she wasn't in the middle of nowhere was enough for her to get a grip on her panic.

Knowing her sisters, Molly and Norah had most likely figured out who'd taken her and where they were keeping her in the first couple of hours. In fact, Molly probably had a plan in place—and eighteen backup plans—and she and Norah could very well be about to mount a *Save Cara* mission at this very moment.

That thought both reassured Cara and terrified her. As much as she wanted to be rescued, she didn't want her sisters to be in any danger.

So start rescuing yourself, dummy. Resolve filled her, erasing the last of the hopelessness the sight of her barren surroundings had caused. She'd get herself out of here and save her sisters. It was time for her to be the hero.

She pulled back slightly to examine the window and swallowed a curse. Shiny silver screw heads dotted both sides of the wood bracketing the glass, angled in a way that meant those screws had been driven right into the surrounding frame. Even if she managed to reach the lock at the top of the window, there was no way it would be opening unless she broke the glass, making a loud crash in the process. She set that idea aside for plan C or D.

Easing her head away from the window, she allowed

the shade to fall back into place. It made a light smacking sound as it tapped against the frame, and Cara froze, straining her ears for any indication that someone in the other room had heard. There was only silence except for the wind whistling outside.

She moved carefully so that she was on her knees facing the door. By arching her back, she could just reach one of the bands holding her ankles together, and she wished desperately she had a knife or box cutter. Without some type of sharp-edged tool, she could only brush the hard plastic tie with her fingertips, and that did nothing to help.

Swallowing a sound of frustration, she sat on her heels and curled her shoulders forward, easing the ache in her spine. Her mind hopped from one escape plan to another, each more implausible than the last. She was bound and stuck in a room. It would take several minutes of trying for her to open the door even if it was unlocked—which she doubted.

Okay. What's the first step?

The answer was clear enough: *Get out of the zip ties.*

She mentally flipped through possible ways to accomplish that. She wouldn't be able to break them, there didn't seem to be anything in the room that could be used as a cutting tool, and they were tight enough to block most of her circulation, so she doubted she could work them off over her hands or feet.

She abandoned a half-thought-out notion to convince her captors to untie her. If—when—they returned to her bare room, it was doubtful they'd be here to free her. It was much more likely that bad things would happen. The longer she could escape notice, the better.

A creak of wood came from the other room, making her tense and stare at the door. Her thoughts raced, along with her heart. Had she made a noise? Did they know she was awake? Would the masked man come in and drug her again—or worse? Her breathing sped up until her vision grew wavy around the edges, and she forced herself to calm. *Focus on the next step*, she repeated over and over in her mind until she'd managed to lock down her panic enough to function again.

Giving up on the idea of getting out of her zip ties for now, she focused on the next part of her plan. *Get out of the cabin*. Her backup plan, in case she was really and truly stuck in this wooden shack, was to find some way to communicate with her sisters—phone, radio, fireworks, or whatever she could manage.

Even though she wasn't positive that being outside the cabin in the middle of the wilderness would be the safest thing, it felt good to have a solid goal. Besides, the most urgent danger was a masked man who kept shooting knockout drugs into her system. If she could escape her captors, she could deal with whatever the empty high plains could throw at her…probably.

Pushing away thoughts of bears and mountain lions, Cara shifted onto her hip and then into a seated position. One of the wooden floorboards creaked beneath her, and she froze in place, holding her breath. Her blood rushed through her ears too loudly to hear anyone coming, so she carefully maneuvered her body so that her back was to the door. Despite it making her feel incredibly vulnerable not to be able to see someone coming into the room, she knew it was the fastest way she could travel while bound the way she was. Drawing up her knees, she pressed her feet against the floor and scooted herself backward, ignoring the way the rough floorboards grabbed at her pajama pants. The rustle of her clothing and the occasional creak from the floor made her tense, but there was no way to prevent every sound unless she stayed perfectly still, and that would get her nowhere—literally.

She was horribly tempted to glance over her shoulder at the door, to try to catch a glimpse in case someone entered, but she forced herself to keep her gaze focused on the shade-covered window. It was getting brighter outside, and the sunlight peeking around the shade was shifting from pale pink to golden. She wondered how long she'd slept—if it had been almost twelve hours or actually longer than that. It was a creepy feeling that she'd been out so long, especially since she knew her kidnapper—or kidnappers—had been with her at least for part of the time. They could have done anything to her while she was drugged.

She shoved that thought away. Instead, she tried to focus on making each motion as quiet as possible as she made her way across the floor like a backward inchworm. It seemed to take endless time to cross the tiny room, but when she finally allowed herself a quick glance over her shoulder, she found that she was just a few feet from the door.

Scooting closer, she looked up at the small cast-iron knob. Not only did she have to figure out a way to open the door—provided it wasn't locked—but then she'd have to venture out into the rest of the cabin, possibly confronting one or more of her captors. Her brain instantly created an image of a whole army of ski-mask-wearing, gun-toting bad guys, all waiting for her to try to get away. Suddenly, breaking the window and escaping that way seemed a lot more appealing.

Knock it off, she told herself firmly, banishing all thoughts of her probable bloody death. Resolutely, she pressed her shoulders against the wall, leaving space at her lower back so her hands didn't get squashed. Bending her knees, she tucked her bound feet close and pushed up, using the wall for leverage. Her hoodie rubbed against the wood, making a *shushing* sound. Wincing, she tried to raise herself as slowly as possible, but the creak of the wood and rustle of fabric still sounded terrifyingly loud in her ears.

Her quadriceps burned as she inched higher, balancing on feet that were too close together. It reminded her of chair pose in yoga, and she almost let a frantic gasp of laughter escape before she bit back the sound. *Who would've thought that yoga had practical, lifesaving applications?*

Inch by inch, her shoulders crept up the wall as her thighs trembled from the effort of the painfully slow movement. In an effort to find her balance, she rocked a little on the soles of her feet, the small swaying motion adding to the difficulty of the maneuver.

If I get out of here alive, she silently promised herself, *I will first kiss Felicity's feet in thanks for pushing us every morning, even when we whined about it. Then, I will ask her to make us work even harder from now on.*

The slight shake in her legs increased until her whole body trembled, and she told herself it was just muscle strain, not complete terror. With a final push, she

straightened to standing, letting out her breath silently in
a relieved *whoosh*. There wasn't time to waste, though,
so she didn't allow herself to rest. Shuffling sideways,
she turned so the doorknob was at her back and in reach
of her bound hands.

The plastic zip tie cut into her wrists as she closed her
fingers around the cold metal knob. It turned silently in
her grip, and her stomach jumped with hope and apprehension. It couldn't be so easy, could it? What kind of
kidnappers didn't even lock the door?

Trying her best to not think of what might be on the
other side waiting for her, Cara pushed at the door, but
it didn't budge. *It must have a dead bolt on the other
side*. Of course it wasn't actually unlocked. Her disappointment was cut with a thread of relief. As terrifying
as it was to be locked in a strange room, at least she was
alone and unhurt. A huge part of her didn't want to go
out into the rest of the cabin and face unknown dangers.

Before she released the knob, she pushed at it again,
just in case the door was simply stuck, rather than
locked. As she pressed, she glanced to the side. When
she saw the black iron hinges, she blinked as realization
struck. Immediately, she felt like a huge idiot.

The door opens in, dummy.

She mentally smacked herself for being stupid as
she drew a deep, bracing breath and shuffled forward.
Without the door or wall to help support her, it was hard
to balance, and she wobbled with each tiny, mincing step.
As tightly as her ankles were bound, she could barely
push the toes of one foot ahead of the other, and it took
much too long for her to inch along the rough floorboards.

The latch gave a *snick* as it released, and the door

opened. As soon as it was clear of the jamb, she released
the knob slowly, her fingers aching from the awkward
angle. She started shuffling in a half circle, turning to
face the door, all too aware that any sound would carry
farther now.

As she inched closer to the door, her anxious impa-
tience got the best of her. She shoved her foot forward
too quickly, knocking herself off-balance. Her upper
body swayed unsteadily, threatening to tip her over.
Sucking in a panicked breath, she jerked on the zip tie
around her wrists, automatically attempting to get her
hands in front of her to catch her. The motion pitched her
forward even more, bringing her face just inches from
the door. She knew that if she fell against the door, it
would slam closed, letting everyone in and around the
cabin know that she was awake and attempting to escape.

Desperately, she clamped down her abs and steadied
her swaying upper body, dragging her torso back in line
with her bound feet. For a moment, she stood still except
for the fine tremor making her muscles vibrate, her brain
replaying the close call over and over.

*I promise to ask Fifi to make us do more core work,
too.*

The thought of home and her sisters and her normal
routine helped calm her enough to plan her next move.
She needed to free her legs at the very least. From
her view out the window, they were very likely in the
middle of nowhere, and she couldn't shuffle her way
over miles of rough terrain. She needed to find a knife
or some type of sharp edge she could use to cut the zip
ties. The kitchen would be best, since that was normally
where knives lived.

With renewed determination, she used her chin to nudge the door open a little more, just enough so that she could see out. As she peered through the crack, her stomach knotted, but she relaxed slightly when the army of imagined bad guys wasn't there. All she could see was a rough wooden wall and the arm of a ratty-looking sofa. Her immediate relief disappeared, since she knew that the kidnapper—or kidnappers—could very well be in the part of the room she couldn't see. Were they watching the door? Creeping closer toward her? The suspense was too much to handle, and she used her chin to open the door even more, the need to know overcoming her caution.

Using the frame to balance, she pushed far enough into the opening to see the entire room. Her heartbeat thudded in her ears as she looked wildly around, her muscles tensed and ready to fight, even as she knew that, bound as she was, there'd be little she could do to protect herself. At best, any struggle would end with her once again drugged and unconscious. At worst...

Now wasn't time to think of the *worst*.

Tamping down the desire to hide, she forced herself to look around the room. The space was empty. All the air rushed out of her as relief made her head spin. She glanced over everything again, more calmly this time, making sure that she hadn't overlooked anyone. The area was mostly living space, with a small kitchen lining one wall. The worn couch was the only furniture except for an equally battered wooden table with a couple of camp chairs pulled up to it. From her angle, Cara couldn't see much except the glare of the morning sun out of the single window. There were two doors besides the one to her room. One was slightly ajar, revealing a bathroom, and the other appeared to be a front door. Her heartbeat sped up again at the sight, making the possibility of escape seem so real.

She shouldered open her door the rest of the way and started her agonizingly slow shuffle. Even though it would've been faster to sit and scoot backwards, she couldn't bring herself to get down on the floor again. Despite her slow and wobbly progress, she felt infinitely less vulnerable on her feet.

She'd feel even better with a knife. Cara headed for the kitchen, even though the sparse furnishings made her worry that the drawers and cupboards would be empty. No matter. All she needed was one sharp edge.

A movement in the corner of her eye caught her attention, and she whipped her head around just as a large form passed by the window. She froze and then tried to rush her steps, terrified that whoever was outside would be coming through the front door any second, catching her out of her room but still bound and helpless. But as soon as she hurried, as soon as she let the spike of fear overwhelm her, her body overbalanced, and she tumbled toward the floor.

Landing on her side with a heavy thud, Cara held her breath, not even noticing the dull throb of pain in her shoulder and hip. She stared at the front door, unable to move as she waited for it to open and let in her kidnapper. Even if he hadn't heard her hard landing, there was no way he wouldn't see her immediately now, sprawled across the floor as she was.

Another movement at the window broke her fixed, terrified gaze, and she looked over to see a man cross it again, moving away from the door this time. He'd shoved his ski mask up to his forehead and was holding a cell phone to his ear. As he passed, she stayed completely still, not daring to breathe until she couldn't see him any longer.

Once he was out of sight, she sucked in a breath and swiveled around until she was sitting with her back to the kitchen. She pulled her legs in and scooted backward as quickly as she could. The kidnapper could be leaving, or he could've just forgotten something. If that was true, then he'd be coming through the door within seconds. She needed to have her arms and legs free before that happened.

She could hear him speaking, but his words were muffled. Her hands bumped against the refrigerator, and she hurried to turn to face the bottom row of cupboards. She went for a stack of drawers first, biting down on the top drawer pull and yanking it open, revealing a few loose forks and spoons scattered with some drinking straws. The man's voice was getting louder again, becoming clear enough that she could make out an occasional word.

"We're…around…want…Kavenski."

She paused for a half of a second at the name, her brain racing to make sense of it. *Henry* was involved? She'd assumed that this was part of Jane's mess, that she was being held ransom for the priceless necklace her mother had stolen, but that wouldn't involve Henry Kavenski…unless he was in on it, too.

Her mind revolted at the idea, even as her practical side reminded her that he was supposedly a killer. Why would he hesitate at kidnapping?

Because it's me*!* the soft, squishy, naively romantic part of her wailed. *He wouldn't hurt me!*

Shaking off the distraction, she refocused on her task. It didn't matter at the moment who'd engineered her kidnapping. What was important was getting her hands and feet free so she wasn't completely helpless. Quietly closing the top drawer with her forehead, she used her teeth to open the second one.

There!

With a fierce sense of triumph, she stared down at her find. Tangled in a mess of wooden spoons and a can opener and a pair of tongs was a bread knife. Before she could fish it out, the kidnapper crossed the window again, and Cara went still. The man was a stranger and extraordinarily ordinary looking. His features were average, his appearance so nondescript that Cara knew she'd have trouble describing him accurately if she managed to get away. Still, she fought her panic in order to take in the details, knowing he was an important part of solving her kidnapping.

He'd pushed up his face mask into a rumpled mass on his forehead, and several strands of light-brown hair stuck out from underneath. His nose didn't look bruised or swollen, so she knew that there were at least two kidnappers. She'd head-butted the man who'd grabbed her from her house *hard*. She was positive she hadn't seen him before while shadowing Kavenski or during her trip to Dutch's, and she was fairly sure she'd never seen his picture in the course of her research. His jacket was rugged but expensive and looked new. She took a mental picture, cataloging every detail of his face for when she escaped—because she was going to get out of this cabin. Meanwhile, the kidnapper was scowling, the phone jammed so tightly against his ear that his fingers were white.

Please don't look in here. Please don't look in here.

Repeating her mantra over and over, Cara didn't move as he stomped past the window. Even after he was out of sight, she still couldn't breathe, her gaze fixed on the front door. The knife was right there, almost within her grasp, but it wouldn't do her any good if he was about to come charging into the cabin. She wished desperately that she were more like one of her sisters. Molly or Fifi would've already freed themselves, and they'd have been planning a way to ambush their kidnapper right now. Charlie wouldn't have let herself get kidnapped in the first place. Her twin always seemed to be ten steps ahead of her skips.

Not helpful. The practical voice in her head was right. She needed to focus and use that common sense she prided herself on. If he did storm into the cabin, she needed to have the knife out. Even if she couldn't use it on him, she could hide it somewhere on her. That way, she'd at least have it when she woke up from her next drugged sleep. Tearing her gaze off the door, she studied the knife, wondering if she could pick it up by tucking her chin against her chest. Quickly dismissing that idea, she ducked her head into the drawer. Holding it with her teeth would give her a better grip. Feeling like she was in the scariest version ever of bobbing for apples, she mouthed the handle, nosing the other utensils out of the way until she could get a good grip with her teeth. Clamping down on the unforgivingly hard plastic, she winced at the immediate ache in her jaw. Only when she had hold of it did she think of how she must look with a knife gripped in her bared teeth.

You go, you swashbuckling pirate! Biting down harder to force back a hysterical giggle, she lifted her head, wincing at every clank and rattle of the other implements as she pulled the knife free. She paused, listening, but the man's voice continued without a suspicious pause.

"Don't think…won't…" His words grew almost clear before growing muffled again as he strode past the window, heading away from the door again.

Cara's shoulders dropped in relief. He was pacing. That was why he kept crossing the window. Depending on how long his phone conversation continued, she might have time to free herself. She paused, knife in her teeth as she leaned against the drawer to close it. Now that she had a sharp surface, she wasn't exactly sure how to use it to cut through her bonds.

She dropped the knife, wincing as it clattered against the floorboards and spun to rest a few feet away. With a nervous glance toward the currently empty window, she shuffled closer on her knees. The man outside had gone quiet, and Cara was tempted to go still, not wanting to make any sound that might draw him inside. But if his phone conversation was over, she knew it wouldn't matter how silent she was. He'd still come in and see her, and she needed to be free before that happened.

Still on her knees, she moved so the knife was behind her, right next to her toes. Arching her back, she reached for the handle blindly. Even when she craned her head to look over her shoulder, she couldn't see what she was doing. Her spine protested, and her shoulders ached with strain as she felt for the knife. When her fingers brushed the cool metal, she nearly started to cry with relief.

Fumbling, she finally managed to close her fingers around the handle, clutching tighter than necessary because she feared dropping it and having to go through another painful struggle to get it into her grip again. The man outside was speaking again, his words becoming more distinct as he drew closer to the window, but Cara couldn't take in any of what he was saying. Her heart was beating too loudly to make out anything else.

Leaning back again, she used her thumb to lightly feel the edge to make sure the serrated side faced up. The obvious dullness of the blade made her anxious that, after all of this, it wouldn't cut her bonds, but she pushed away the worry. Tightening her fingers even more, she eased the blade between her ankles and the plastic strap. She jerked the knife up and toward her, feeling the plastic dig into the front of her shins. Trying to keep her breathing even and not dissolve into terrified, fast pants, she jerked the knife up again.

With a *pop*, the plastic gave, opening with a sudden release of tension that made her tip forward. She caught herself before she fell on her face and repositioned the knife under the next zip tie securing her lower legs together. Her heart was pounding from excitement as well as fear, escape so close she could almost taste it.

The second tie snapped after four sawing jerks of the knife, and the third plastic strap only took two. Blood rushed to her toes, making her realize how numb they'd been before, and she squeezed her eyes closed at the swarm of painful pricks invading her feet. After the initial shock of feeling, she forced her eyes to reopen, trying to think of the best way to cut the tie binding her wrists together. She wedged the knife, blade facing up, between her newly freed feet and tried to rub the zip tie against it, but she wasn't able to hold it still. Her gaze jumped around the small kitchen as she searched for a place to wedge the handle. Her eyes settled on the drawers.

Grabbing the knife from its unsteady spot between her feet, she struggled up, still off-balance with her hands bound behind her back. Turning away from the top drawer, she pulled it open just enough to slide the handle in, the blade sticking up out of the drawer.

With her hip, she closed the drawer and leaned against it, using her body weight to hold the knife steady as she moved her hands up and down the blade, sawing at the zip tie. The knife shifted slightly, making it hard to find purchase, and panic left her clumsy, only capable of broad, rough movements. The ridiculousness of what she was trying to accomplish hit her. She was using a cartoon-like solution to her very real, very deadly problem. *This will never work.* Gritting her teeth, she forced away her doubts and pressed the zip tie more firmly against the blade. *It will work.* She had to believe it, or she might as well sit on the floor and cry. The blade slid uselessly along the edge of the tie until the serrated edge finally caught against the plastic.

A sob of desperate relief burned for release, but she managed to hold it back. Tightening her muscles, she prepared to rip the tie over the surface of the knife, but a soft *click* made her freeze. Her gaze shot to the front door. Terror gripped her for a fraction of a second, and all she could do was stare at the rotating doorknob.

In her fight to get her hands free, she'd momentarily forgotten to track the whereabouts of the man on the porch. Breaking out of her paralysis, she released the pressure on the drawer and yanked the knife out with her still-bound fingers. She held the blade, rather than the handle, but at least she had a possible weapon in her grip.

The door swung open, revealing the man, his ski mask pulled down into place, covering his identity again. He froze for a brief second, his eyes widening with surprise, before he reached into his coat pocket.

He's going to kill you! Cara's brain warned, and she strained to pull her hands apart, ignoring the sharp pain as the ties cut into her wrists, needing them free so she could protect herself. If he caught her again, all her efforts would be useless. He'd take away her knife and tie her up again, probably locking her inside the room this time. Or worse. This—with her feet free and a knife in hand—was her chance, as pathetic as it may be.

The man strode toward her, pulling his hand out of his pocket. Instead of a syringe, he was holding a matte black pistol.

Her gaze locked on the gun. All the air left her lungs in a *whoosh*, and she gave her wrists a final, panicked yank. The partially cut zip tie snapped, and her hands separated with such force that she almost let go of the knife. She managed to hold on, despite the dull blade digging into her fingers, and she fumbled to grasp the handle instead before thrusting it out in front of her.

The man stopped a few feet out of slashing range, his gun pointed at her. She couldn't look at the deadly weapon, so she focused on his face—at least the small circles around his eyes and mouth that she could see. He'd obviously recovered from his initial surprise, and his startled look had changed to one of amusement. In her peripheral vision, she saw his gun hand drop slightly, enough to give her a spark of hope that death might not be as imminent as she'd feared. Sucking in a breath, she clutched her knife tightly, worried that the painful pins and needles in her hands would make her drop it.

Unexpectedly, he laughed, the sound a scornful huff. "Don't you know you're not supposed to bring a knife to a gunfight?"

She stayed silent, his attempt at a joke just making her more uneasy.

"Too bad Kavenski doesn't care what happens to you."

Even though she'd already known that Henry was somehow involved, the sound of his name from her kidnapper's mouth made her tense.

"Thought he was more into you than that, did you?" he asked, but Cara barely heard him. He was raising the gun again to point directly at her chest. "Guess we made the same mistake. Abbott's going to be disappointed. Sorry about this."

Her muscles tightened as she prepared to dive out of the way, even as she knew it was hopeless. She couldn't dodge a bullet. At this range, there was no way he could miss.

As his finger curled around the trigger, Cara knew that black barrel would be the last thing she'd see.

CHAPTER 7

HENRY KAVENSKI LOOMED BEHIND THE KIDNAPPER, snaking a huge arm around the other man's neck and hauling him back away from Cara. The gun went off as the man's arms flailed in surprise, and Cara jerked in anticipation. She had no way of knowing if the bullet had missed her, or if she'd been hit and adrenaline kept her from feeling the pain, but she couldn't just stand by and watch. Holding her knife outstretched in front of her, she lunged toward the grappling men. As she paused, not wanting to accidentally stab her rescuer rather than the kidnapper, Kavenski twisted the gun out of the man's grip. The kidnapper elbowed him hard in the gut, but Henry just gave a grunt before swinging the gun toward the other man's temple. The butt connected with a thud, sending the kidnapper to the floor. Tense and ready, Cara stared at the downed man, expecting him to jump back into the fight, but he lay limp and still.

Kavenski stood over the unmoving stranger, but his intent gaze was focused on Cara. As their eyes met, she felt a crashing wave of relief broken by a tiny bit of residual fear. After all, there was a chance she was wrong about him, and he wasn't any less deadly than the man currently sprawled across the floor.

At least he's not pointing a gun at me, she reasoned,

and the last bit of wariness crumbled away into nothing. Kavenski had never tried to hurt her and had saved her life twice now. She shifted her weight as she continued to stare at him, still not quite believing that he was here and she wasn't dead. Her legs still felt unsteady, but it was a huge relief to have her limbs unbound again. She held Kavenski's gaze in silence, keeping her eyes off the limp figure on the floor, not wanting to think about if he was unconscious or…worse.

"Is that a bread knife?" Kavenski's question made her jump, his words abnormally loud after the long, tense silence.

She glanced down at the knife in her hands, still outstretched in front of her. He was right. Her weapon was a bread knife. Although the serrated edge had been sharp enough to cut her zip ties, the tip wasn't even pointed. It curved into a harmless half circle that would be dangerous only to defenseless loaves of bread. "Yes." The word came out as a sad little croak, so she cleared her throat and tried again. "It was the only thing available." She gestured toward the drawer she'd found it in. "The kitchen isn't very well stocked."

His eyes closed for several seconds, his face unreadable, and Cara wished she could hear his thoughts. On paper, he didn't seem like a guy she should trust, but this was the second—possibly third—time he'd saved her life. It was no wonder she wanted to throw herself into his burly arms and take comfort against his rock-hard chest.

She gave her head a small shake, needing to knock her brain back to normal.

"Let's go," he said before she could straighten out the tangle of her thoughts. "More will be coming."

"More?" The word came out as a groan, even as she crossed the cabin toward Kavenski. "How many kidnappers *are* there?"

"Too many," he answered grimly, waving her toward the door. "Abbott can afford an army."

She made a wide circle around the unconscious man, horror-movie images flashing through her mind. A part of her was certain that just when she relaxed, he'd reach out and grab her ankle. The thought made her shiver. It was as if Kavenski'd had the same thought, since he yanked the other man's hands behind his back and secured them with a zip tie he'd pulled out of his pocket.

As she watched him secure the man's legs next, she couldn't help but ask, "What's with everyone having such a ready supply of zip ties?"

He glanced up, the corner of his mouth tucking in. That expression was becoming familiar, but she still wasn't sure if it hid irritation or amusement. "Don't you?"

"Maybe I should." She'd definitely decided to carry a pocketknife and an extra cell phone and to possibly invest in a medical alert bracelet like Norah wore... and maybe start hauling around a gun and some hand grenades.

Giving the last zip tie around the man's ankles a final tug, Kavenski frisked him, removing a cell phone and a folded knife from the unconscious stranger's pockets. He straightened and gestured toward the door, his gaze running up and down her body in a way that was both clinical and intensely intimate. "You injured?"

"No." She glanced down at herself. So much adrenaline was running through her that she wasn't positive she'd feel it if one of her legs fell off. As she did, her head gave a particularly vicious throb, reminding her of her headache. "Just a little groggy. They shot me up with some kind of sedative twice—at least twice." She shivered as she corrected herself. The thought of being injected with something while she was unconscious was somehow even worse than being aware of when the needle went in.

Stepping forward, he cupped her jaw and gently turned her face up until her startled gaze met his. His other hand covered her eyes for several seconds, blocking the light long enough for Cara to start feeling awkward. He dropped that hand but kept the one cradling her face as he studied her eyes. She stared back, knowing he was checking to see if her pupils were reacting, but still feeling her stomach twist with familiar attraction and something dangerously close to affection. His eyes softened, his gaze warming as he went from studying her pupils to actually looking at *her*. His fingers stroked over her cheek, just the smallest movement, but filled with such unexpected tenderness that her legs went shaky again—but not from fear or adrenaline this time.

When he finally released her, she couldn't hold in a disappointed sigh. Even though she knew it was not an optimal time for them to be gazing into each other's eyes, she still missed the feel of his hand against her face.

"I'm okay, then?" she managed to ask, pretending the quaver in her voice was caused by the close call with death and not his touch.

He gave a slight lift of his chin, which she took as an affirmative. Her skin still felt chilled with the absence of his warm hand, but she pushed away the sensation. Now wasn't the time to get all stupid over a guy—especially this guy.

"You'll live," he said, reaching into his pocket and withdrawing a small bottle of ibuprofen. Popping off the lid, he shook two tablets onto his palm and held them out to her.

She accepted them with a wry smile. "You got your own?"

He rewarded her with one of his barely-there smiles. Despite the situation, the sight of it warmed her insides. Reminding herself that now was not the time to get mushy over Kavenski, she focused on the tablets in her hand. Her mouth was cottony enough that she knew she wouldn't be able to take them dry, so she hurried back to the kitchen sink. There was a clank and groan after she turned on the faucet, but the water that flowed out looked clear. Putting the pills in her mouth, she cupped her hands and drank, only realizing how thirsty she was when the water hit her dry throat.

"Let's go. I've got water in the car," Kavenski urged, and she forced herself to turn off the tap and follow him through the front door. She couldn't help glancing back at the bound kidnapper, unable to trust that he wouldn't break his zip ties and surge up to attack them like some sort of supervillain.

With her attention on the immobile body, Cara crashed right into Kavenski's back. Grabbing handfuls of his coat, she regained her balance, peering around his broad form to see why he'd stopped in the middle of the porch. Her hopes when she'd looked out the back window were immediately crushed. There wasn't any sign of civilization in this direction, either. The

scrubby grassland stretched in all directions, only stopping at the distant mountain peaks. A half-collapsed
barn fifty feet away was the only structure besides the
cabin. Cara followed Kavenski's narrowed gaze and saw
a cloud of something hovering right above the ground
in the distance.

"Is that smoke?" she asked in a low voice. The tension on his face made her nervous.

"Dust."

It took a moment for his one-word answer to register.
"Oh! A car?"

"Three."

"Oh." She swallowed. "Coming this way?" He didn't
answer, but then he didn't need to. She could tell that the
dust cloud kicked up by the vehicles was getting closer.
Dragging her gaze away from the incoming cars, she
scanned the more immediate vicinity. "Where's your
car?"

"There." He jerked his head toward the collapsing
barn before taking the porch steps in one long-legged
step. Pulling out the phone he'd just taken off the kidnapper, he chucked it far away from the cabin without
breaking stride. "Hurry."

Cara trotted after him as he picked up the pace to a
jog. Her gaze kept drifting over to lock on the approaching vehicles, and her stocking toes kept catching on tufts
of rough grass while small rocks bit into the soles of her
feet. She forced her attention back to her footing and
just missed stepping on a small, round cactus the size
of a tennis ball.

Even though she avoided getting a foot full of spines,
she gave a small yelp as she dodged.

"What's wrong?" Twisting to look over his shoulder, Kavenski focused on her feet and seemed to take in the situation in less than a second. He turned, scooped her up so she was folded over his shoulder, and then started running for the old barn again. The shock of suddenly being flipped upside down took her breath away. It took three strides before she processed what had happened, that he'd tossed her over his shoulder like a bag of potatoes.

The hard wedge of muscle smacked into her solar plexus. Even factoring in the possibility of more cacti, Cara was pretty sure that being carried this way was more uncomfortable than continuing to run in her socks would've been. Mentally, she chided herself for being whiny. *Just appreciate the ride. Besides, he runs faster than you could without shoes.*

The worst part was that she couldn't see anything. Pushing away from his back a little, she twisted her neck and managed to spot the dust cloud. It had transformed into three SUVs that were approaching too quickly for comfort, and Cara suddenly didn't mind the jolting. From her angle, she couldn't see any part of the barn, so she had no idea if they were even close.

Kavenski abruptly stopped and hauled her off his shoulder, setting her on her feet with more speed than finesse. She automatically took a step back to catch her balance, but it wasn't needed. His firm grip on her hips didn't ease until she was steady. As soon as she wasn't wobbling, he turned to shove open a small door in the side of the barn—or what used to be a door, at least. The boards were worn, and several had worked free of their nails, leaning drunkenly to the side. The wood cracked as Kavenski forced it in enough to allow him to step inside.

"We're going inside?" When Kavenski had indicated that his car was by the barn, she hadn't expected it to actually be *inside*. The place looked like a stiff breeze could send the whole thing crashing down around them. "Is that safe?"

He gave her a look, and she made a face as she stepped through the narrow opening after him. The usual barn smells of hay and manure were faint, overtaken by the odor of dust and disuse. Patches of the roof were gone, allowing in a considerable amount of light, and the aging wooden siding had shrunk, creating wide cracks in the walls. The car parked inside looked out of place, too new and clean and modern to belong in this ancient building.

"Yes, I know that it's silly to worry about being crushed to death by a collapsing barn when there's a whole convoy of bad guys coming, but it's still a valid concern."

He dipped his chin slightly, as if giving her the point, before turning his back toward her. "Climb up."

It only took a second for his command to click in her brain. He wanted her to climb *him*. Swallowing an inappropriately timed giggle born of terror, she obediently put her hands on his thick shoulders and hopped onto his back. He caught her thighs as she wrapped her legs and arms around him, careful to keep her grip around his neck loose so she didn't choke him.

He made his way quickly to the car, carefully picking through the junk that littered the floor. When she heard the soles of his boots crunching against who-knew-what, she gripped him a little tighter, grateful he hadn't made her walk through the mess in her socks.

"Did they see us run in here?" she asked, her voice low, trying to hear over her thundering heart. She kept expecting to run out of fear, to go numb from her constant state of terror, but it hadn't happened yet.

His shoulders lifted, pressing against her arms. "Not sure, but I'm assuming the worst."

"What are they doing here?" She was still whispering as he set her down by the passenger seat. "It was only two guys up until now—at least when I was awake." The correction reminded her of all the terrible things that could've happened when she was unconscious, but she forced away the mental images. It wasn't the time to dwell on that, not when she needed to keep her brain functioning. She couldn't dissolve into a terrified puddle until they were safe.

"I wasn't where I was supposed to be," he said, incredibly unhelpfully. "Get in."

She pulled open the passenger side door and climbed inside. Twisting around, she watched as he started opening the oversize sliding door. After sliding only three feet, the door stopped, the warped wood not wanting to move. Cara opened the car door, intending to get out and help push. Before she could leave the car, a sharp crack rang out. A chunk of wood right next to Kavenski's head disappeared, leaving another hole for sunshine to creep through. Cara flinched, her head jerking back against the seat. Someone had just *shot* at them.

Sprinting back to the vehicle, Kavenski dove into the driver's seat, starting the car and slamming it into reverse before Cara could blink. She yanked her door closed, still stunned at the close call. If Kavenski had just been inches to the left, his head would've been blown off. Her heart wrenched at the thought.

"Seat belt," he snapped, and she grabbed the strap automatically, yanking it across her body and clicking the buckle into place. She started to ask what the plan was. Before she could say anything, a small cylindrical object flew over the car, landing on the hood with a light *thunk* before rolling toward the front. Even though she'd never seen one before, she immediately knew what it was.

A hand grenade.

"Hang on," Kavenski said grimly, and Cara grabbed for the dash, even as her practical brain told her that clinging to a bit of plastic wasn't going to help her—not if they were blown up by a freaking *hand grenade*. Cara felt a surreal sense of unreality as her gaze locked on the innocuous-looking object—one that could blow them to bits in less than a second.

The car tore backward, leaving the grenade to fall to the ground, and crashed through the mostly closed doors behind them. Cara yelped, squeezing her eyes closed and then immediately snapping them open again, not wanting to see but still needing to. The impact brought the rest of the wall down, ancient boards splintering, destroyed chunks raining down on the car like a merciless wooden hailstorm.

The tires bumped over the remains of the door as the car flew backward, giving Cara a clear view of the barn's collapse. The entire front of the building sagged, seeming to droop in slow motion before crumbling into a jagged pile of broken lumber.

"Head down!" Kavenski bellowed, reaching out to shove her face down toward her knees. Cara curled up as well as she could with her seat belt on, just as she heard a sharp *crack* and hiss. Needing to know what had just happened, she glanced up and saw the hole in the windshield, cobwebbed cracks radiating out from that center nucleus.

The car skidded as it rotated, and Cara swallowed a shriek, her terrified gaze shooting toward Kavenski. His stony expression was weirdly soothing, and she took a tiny bit of hope in the determined set of his mouth. This was not a man who was going to let himself be blown up, and she was lucky enough to be in the passenger seat of his car.

He shifted gears, and the car tore forward, jerking at the abrupt change of direction. "Head down," he ordered again, and she ducked back into her curled position, her forehead just above her knees.

Then the whole world exploded.

The back window shattered as a world-shaking *boom* seemed to fill her head, so loud and all-encompassing that she felt the shock through her whole body. They flew forward as if a giant had shot them out of a slingshot, flinging them impossibly fast across the rough terrain. Cara clutched the seat by her knees, her teeth clenched so tightly that pain radiated up to her temples. For the first time, she wasn't at all tempted to look up. She could *feel* what was happening, and it wasn't anything good.

Wind rushed through the car, howling, the sound competing with the roar of the rapidly growing fire behind them. The whole world was lit up in an inferno of red and orange. Although Cara knew they were alive, it still felt like they'd been caught in the center of the explosion, and how could anyone have lived through that? It was hard to believe that they'd made it through intact, and she stared down at her body, needing to see physical evidence of her survival.

She blinked at her knees, taking stock of each body part. Her sore face and lingering headache—as well as a few stinging or sore parts—proved that she hadn't died. She took a deep breath, the first real one since the grenade had hit their car, and let it out slowly, allowing herself a second to relax with relief. With what felt like a huge effort, she unlocked her neck muscles enough to turn her head and check on Kavenski.

To her shock, he looked…the same, grim and ferociously determined to get them to safety. Except for a scratch beading blood on his cheek, he didn't appear any different than he had before their world exploded. She felt a surge of gratitude that he'd come for her, that he'd risked his life over and over to save her own.

His jaw muscles were still locked tight, but he was in one glorious piece. She couldn't stop herself from reaching her trembling hand toward him, needing tactile evidence that her mind wasn't making this up, that he—and she—had both survived. Her trembling fingers touched his forearm, and the feel of his clenched muscles made the entire thing seem real. All her breath left her in a rush that made her head spin.

At her touch, his gaze darted toward her quickly before returning to whatever was in front of them. "You okay?" His voice was gruff, but the obvious concern made her smile.

"I think?" She sounded just as she figured anyone would after so many near-death experiences in less than fourteen or so hours. "Unless I'm dead, and you're just my ride to the afterlife."

His rough chuckle sounded as if it had been torn out of him. "Doubt we'd be going to the same place, sweetheart."

As crazy and terrifying as their current situation was, Cara still laughed. The sharp pop of another crack appearing in the windshield cut her off. Twisting around in her seat, she saw that the rear windshield had shattered and collapsed on itself, only the film lining the glass keeping the pieces from separating. Wind tore through the opening along with a thick cloud of dust, and she coughed as she tried to peer through the dirt fog the wheels were kicking up. Vaguely, she could make out the shapes of at least two vehicles much too close behind them.

"They're behind us," she said, raising her voice to be heard above the wind. "About sixty feet back." Turning back around, she examined the front windshield, happy to see that most of the damage was on the passenger side. Although there were some cracks on the driver's side, it wasn't enough to limit Kavenski's field of vision.

He gave a grunt in acknowledgment, but his attention remained focused ahead of them. Although the ground had appeared flat when she was looking from the cabin, it wasn't anything like a road—not even a dirt one. The car dipped and lurched, knocking Cara's teeth together when it flew over a particularly deep hole. She clung to the door handle, trying to keep from turning around to stare at their pursuers. There was a *thump* right as a hole appeared in the dashboard just a few inches to her left.

"Get down," Kavenski ordered, and she curled over once again as the reality of what had just happened struck her. A bullet had buried itself in the dash right next to her.

"They're really determined not to let us get away, aren't they?" she asked, her words muffled by her position. She was glad for that, since it hid the shake in her voice.

"Yeah, they are. Get on the floor."

She released the seat belt before wedging herself into a ball in the foot well, trying to make her body as small a target as possible. It was hard to keep her head down, though. The thought of Kavenski being unprotected and vulnerable was unbearable, and his concern for *her* safety made it worse.

"Want me to drive?" she called out. She'd be terrified, but at least she wasn't the size of a linebacker. Even not curled into a ball, she'd make a smaller target, one that would—hopefully—be harder for the men behind them to hit.

"No." The car jerked to the right suddenly, and Cara swallowed a startled yelp. Before she could recover her breath, they changed directions again, swerving to the left this time. She braced herself the best she could as the quick turns continued.

"Are you sure you don't need me to drive?" she yelled, smacking her head on the underside of the dash as they hit a bump big enough to launch the car into the air. When the wheels touched down, Cara thumped her head again.

"No. Quit micromanaging." Except for an almost undetectable tightness in his voice, he sounded much too calm for the situation. His even tone, just loud enough for her to hear over the wind and engine noise, made everything—the chasing and shooting and the bullet hole in the dash—seem surreal. She peeked up, raising her head just enough to get a glimpse of him, needing to see that he was fine and bullet-hole free. Without turning his head, he ordered, "Stay down."

She subsided, figuring that it would be good for at least one of them to remain uninjured. Mentally, she rehearsed what she'd do if he was shot. Would it be easier to shove him to the side and take over at the wheel, or just sit on his lap?

The car continued to swerve, so Cara kept herself braced. The deliberate turns reassured her that he was still in one piece, although she stayed tense, expecting at any second for a bullet to hit him.

Her stomach swooped as the car dipped down and then up again before making a hard left. She held her breath as the rear tires skidded sideways. She expected them to spin out, giving their pursuers time to catch up—or at least to get close enough to shoot more accurately. Kavenski somehow managed to wrestle the vehicle back into a straight line. As they accelerated, Cara heard the distinctive ping of gravel hitting the car's underbelly, and her head popped up.

"We're on a road?" For some reason, her heart leapt in hope. A road meant civilization, which meant more people and law enforcement and not being outnumbered by the bad guys who were trying to kill them.

"Yes. Stay down." His huge hand covered the back of

her head, encouraging her to tuck back into her small ball. The gesture should've seemed oppressive, but it felt oddly reassuring. He gave her back a light pat as he withdrew, and that was more comforting than it should've been.

Now that they were on the gravel road, they traveled even faster in more of a straight line, following occasional curves in the road, but without any of the swerving from earlier.

"You okay? You're not hit, are you?" she asked, needing to raise her voice even louder than before. Their increased speed meant that the air rushing through the car was even more thunderous.

"I'm good." This answer was as matter-of-fact as his others, but there was a warm edge to it that made her want to examine his face. She resisted the urge and kept her head tucked down.

"Good." Her words sounded rough, even to her own ears. "Are they still right behind us?"

"Not *right* behind."

Somehow, that wasn't reassuring. "Do you have a destination in mind, or are we just getting away?"

"There's a town about fifteen miles from here. I'll drop you there."

Her head shot up so she could glare at him. "You're going to dump me in some random mountain town while you face Abbott and his guys alone?"

"Down." Cara tucked back into a protected ball as he continued, completely ignoring her indignant question. Obviously, he was determined to play the martyred hero while she hid like a coward. "There's a police station there. You'll be safe. You can make a report and then call your sisters."

"My sisters!" Her stomach lurched at the reminder.

They could be following her trail into danger right this moment. "Do you have a cell phone on you?"

"A little busy right now." The car's tires slid across loose gravel as he rounded a curve. "Let me get us clear, and then you can use it."

"Of course. Sorry." Despite their own life-threatening situation, she was almost more frantic with worry about her sisters. She'd been so preoccupied with escaping that she hadn't even thought about them putting themselves into danger. She knew her sisters. They'd risk their lives in a second trying to save her. "What if they track me to the cabin?"

"How would they manage that?" he asked.

"You did, and they're wily about finding people. It's their job." The more they talked about it, the more certain she was that her sisters were just a few steps behind her—and about to jump right into the hornets' nest she'd left behind.

"Even if they do find the cabin, they should be safe enough. Most of Abbott's men are still chasing us."

"Oh." All the wind had been taken out of her sails. "Well, that's…good, I suppose?" Her own words made her laugh. "Guess we found the silver lining."

"Guess so." Although Cara couldn't see his face, she was pretty sure he was smiling.

CHAPTER 8

THE CAR LURCHED OVER A BUMP AND MADE A SHARP RIGHT turn. The squeal of protesting tires could be heard over the wind, but then Kavenski wrestled the car back into a straight line and everything smoothed out. The rattle of gravel hitting the undercarriage disappeared as the road became blessedly even. It was strange to be grateful for asphalt, but Cara definitely was thankful for paved roads at the moment. The car picked up speed, and the wind caught at her hair. She shivered, huddling into a smaller ball to try to retain heat.

"You can sit up now," Kavenski said. "Put your seat belt on."

As Cara uncoiled from her spot in the foot well, she gave a pained grimace.

"What's wrong?" he asked, his gaze intense as it flicked from the road to her and back again. "Are you injured?"

"Nothing major." Despite her words, she couldn't hold back a grunt as she sat in the seat and straightened her legs, making him glance sharply at her again. "My muscles are just protesting being kidnapped and tied up and drugged twice, that's all."

The corner of his mouth twitched. "That's all."

"Yep. Phone?"

He pulled it out of his pocket and handed it to her.

As Cara looked down at the screen, hope made her heart beat faster for just a second until she saw the *No Service* icon. She held it up and moved it to all the different spots that she could reach while buckled in, but no bars popped up. With a disappointed sigh, she lowered the phone to her lap.

"No reception," she said. He didn't look surprised.

With the useless phone in her lap, she twisted to look through the ruined rear window. The road curved behind them, partially blocking her view, but she couldn't see any other cars. Turning back around, she looked through her side window, since the windshield was almost opaque from the extensive cobwebbing. They were climbing a slope that curved around a bluff, dotted with evergreens and aspen trees that were bright yellow with their autumn leaves. It would've been beautiful if the circumstances were different. If, say, she'd been taking a scenic drive in the mountains with her strong yet often silent boyfriend—who *wasn't* a potential felon—rather than escaping for her life.

The thought reminded her of what she'd been too frantic to consider up until that point, and she turned away from the view to face him. "Why are you here?" Before he could answer, she added, "Not that I'm ungrateful for the assist, but what's your involvement in this?"

His tight-lipped glance told her nothing. Her stomach squeezed as suspicion wormed its way back into her brain. It just made sense that he was after the necklace. *Everyone* who was even slightly shady had been breaking into their house and stalking them and lurking in the trees around their property. Why wouldn't Henry Kavenski, a bail jumper mixed up with several shady criminals, want a piece of that multimillion-dollar prize?

"What's wrong?"

She stared at his profile, as if his true motives were printed on the hard plane of his cheek. Unfortunately, it wasn't as simple as that. She either had to trust him or not, let that worm of suspicion grow or squash it completely. The car slowed as it eased around a hairpin turn before speeding up again. Cara squeezed her eyes closed for a long moment, trying to get her muddled thoughts in order.

"Seriously, what's happening in your brain? Are you still worried about your sisters?"

This was the first time he'd ever tried to get her to spill her thoughts, rather than the other way around, she realized. She seized on the excuse he'd given her so that she didn't blurt out her suspicions. "Of course I am. Do you think the guys that were chasing us have gone back to the cabin?"

He darted a quick glance at the rearview mirror. "Doubt we'd be that lucky."

Cara turned around again, but all she could see were the rocky outcroppings that bordered the road. Between those and the trees, it was impossible to see more than fifty feet behind the car. The idea that their pursuers were just around the last bend was unnerving, especially when she wasn't sure whether she could trust the man right here with her.

"I don't know if I'd rather they be following us or at the cabin in case Molly and Norah show up."

"What about the other two?" he asked, steering the car around another hairpin turn.

Her brain was trying to go in so many directions at once that his question didn't make sense. "Other two SUVs? I thought just the one stayed behind."

"No. Sisters. Don't you have four?" Kavenski didn't look at her as he answered, focusing hard through his cracked side of the windshield. When Cara glanced out her window, she saw why he was so carefully watching the road. After the last sharp turn, the road straightened, running along the edge of a cliff. Only a measly, spindly guardrail separated their lane from the drop-off below. From Cara's perspective, it looked like they were just inches from the edge, as if just a slight swerve could send them plunging down the sheer rock face to crash into the river that snaked so far below.

Dragging her gaze from the precipitous drop, she focused on Kavenski's profile. Even though she knew he might be a villain, at least he was a *pretty* villain. Looking at him was as good a distraction as any. "How did you know how many sisters I have?"

Somehow, he managed to roll his eyes at her without taking his gaze off the road. "*Everyone* knows about the Pax sisters. I did even before you started following me around."

"Ugh." She made a face, pressing her cheek against the headrest so that she didn't give in to the train-wreck temptation of looking at the vast emptiness beyond the guardrail. "There's another thing I can thank Jane for—notoriety among Langston's criminal element. Thanks, Mom!"

Kavenski followed the curve in the road, and Cara

was forced to squeeze her eyes closed when it felt like they tilted toward the cliff edge. "No need to thank her. You were well known before she stole that jewelry and took off."

His mention of the necklace hung in the air between them. Straightening her shoulders, Cara looked at him again, needing to see his expression when she asked her question. "Are you after the necklace, too? Do you have some criminal connection with my mom?"

Although his poker face didn't reveal much, the slight widening of his eyes appeared to be from true surprise. "What would I do with a hot, recognizable piece like that?"

For a confused second, Cara thought he was referring to Jane, and a weird jolt that felt unnervingly like jealousy zipped through her. Then her practical brain clicked back in, and she understood that he was talking about a piece of *jewelry*, not a piece of... "Fence it, of course," she hurried to answer before her thoughts could meander off too far in that inadvisable direction. "Don't you have underworld connections?"

"Underworld connections?" Despite the tense cliff-edge driving, the corner of his mouth twitched up in an actual smile. In a flash, though, all hint of amusement was locked down, covered by his usual impassive mask. "Is that something that people actually say out loud?"

A huff of laughter escaped her. When she'd started following him, she'd never expected him to be *funny*. Everything about this man kept surprising her. "I don't know. I'm usually in front of a screen, researching. I'm not out on the streets actually dealing with the *underworld*."

Although his smile was still of the blink-and-miss-it variety, it clung a little longer than the last one. "First, quit calling it the underworld. Second, I have no interest in your mom's necklace."

His words felt true, but she had to be sure. The blunt method of questioning seemed to be working pretty well, and it was distracting her from the treacherous road they were traversing, so she blurted out her next thought. "If you're not after the necklace, then why did you show up at the cabin? Why risk your life to save me if you're not getting anything out of it? And how did you even know where I was being held—or that I'd been kidnapped in the first place?"

This time, his mouth twitched down, holding the unhappy grimace for a beat longer than his sudden smiles. "Geoffrey Abbott called me."

She blinked at his grim profile. After a few seconds of silence, she prompted, "Why did Geoffrey Abbott, the tax evader, kidnap me? And why did he tell you about it?"

He heaved a huge sigh, as if the explanation was both too tiring and painful to stand, and Cara almost apologized for forcing him to explain. Just in time, she caught herself before the words escaped. The very least he could do was tell her what was going on. After all, she was the one who'd been kidnapped.

"There's a reason I warned you to stay away from him. I was supposed to meet him at one of his buildings in Langston. If I showed, he said he'd let you go."

"But you didn't go there." Cara's brain was working through the pieces as she realized she'd been putting together the wrong puzzle. From what he'd said so far, it didn't seem like the necklace had anything to do with the kidnapping. "You came to the cabin. How'd you know I was being held there?"

"I didn't." One of his massive shoulders lifted in a partial shrug. "It was just my best guess."

"Good thing for me that you were right," she muttered under her breath. Although she wanted to know more about how exactly he'd figured out where she was being kept, there were more important questions to ask. "What did Abbott want from you?"

"Information." For such an innocuous word, it sounded unnervingly ominous gritted through tight lips.

After a quick glance at his profile showed that she likely wouldn't have much luck getting him to expand on that single-word answer, Cara moved on to a different subject. "If the necklace has nothing to do with this, why'd they grab me? You and I are...barely acquaintances." That was the truth, even though it often felt as though she'd known him forever.

"They were given bad intel." His features hardened as he glared ferociously through the cracked windshield, making Cara glad she wasn't the cause of his anger.

As she considered his answer, she glanced out her window again and immediately wished she hadn't when the open expanse made her dizzy. The sunny morning was beautiful, giving the cliff faces a golden sheen and lighting up the bright-yellow aspen leaves. The river snaked beneath them—*way* beneath them—a dark-blue stripe against the lighter rock. The car followed another sharp curve at Kavenski-level speed, and Cara's right hand instinctively grabbed the door handle. It was silly, she knew that, and a handhold wouldn't help her if the entire car plummeted off the side of the mountain, but it still felt a little reassuring to have a grip on something.

Forcing her attention off the view from her window and back onto Kavenski, she focused on the puzzle at hand. It was hard to understand why anyone would think the two of them were even casual friends, much less that she was important enough to be used as leverage against him. Perhaps Abbott had seen them sitting at the booth together that night, or witnessed him saving her from being run down just after. But even that didn't seem like enough to make anyone think she was *important* to Kavenski, unless…

She groaned out loud when the answer hit her, so bright and obvious and ridiculous that it made her want to punch someone. "Stuart Powers. That little…" No epithet seemed horrible enough for the sneaky little worm who'd gotten her into this mess in more ways than one. Barney had warned her that Abbott liked to use college students as his minions, and it was no surprise that Stuart had been willing to sell his soul for a little bit of money. A glance at Kavenski told her that he'd arrived at the same conclusion. "He saw us together on campus and told Abbott that we were a thing." It seemed monumentally unfair that she had to deal with all the bad parts of being in a relationship with an unnaturally attractive felon but didn't get to experience any of the good bits.

Kavenski gave a slight tilt of his chin that she interpreted as a nod.

"So Stuart's involved in this?" Since she already knew the answer, she kept talking. "The little weasel gets around. Is *Abbott* after the necklace, then?"

"Not specifically." Rounding another curve too

quickly for Cara's comfort, Kavenski sped up even more as a straight section of road opened up before them. "If it fell in his lap, I don't think he'd mind, but he's more preoccupied with taking out his main rival right now."

She checked the phone screen, but the *No Service* message stayed stubbornly in place. "What does Abbott—" She broke off as Kavenski tensed and the car jumped forward, pressing her back against her seat. Seeing his tight-jawed stare move to the rearview mirror for a fraction of a second, she whipped around in her seat. A black SUV had appeared behind them. It was still a quarter mile away, but it was gaining quickly.

A hopeful part of her wondered if it might be someone else behind them—a family out for a scenic drive, possibly. After all, there had to be loads of black SUVs in Colorado. Then a second, matching SUV came around the final turn into view, and that tiny hope was squashed.

"I'm pretty sure that's Abbott's people," she said, barely able to hear herself over the wind screaming through their car and her heart pounding in her ears.

Although Kavenski didn't respond, the tension in his grip on the steering wheel and his intent focus told her that he agreed. She didn't know where to look, since every view was scarier than the last, so she focused on the phone in her lap, trying to will it to find reception. Even a single bar would help, but it remained disconnected to any hint of a signal.

Needing to do something besides sit there like a lump as they hurtled along on the cliff edge and the SUVs drew closer and closer to their rear bumper, Cara tapped out a text to Molly. Her fingers shook, making her clumsy, and it took three tries before she was able to enter her sister's phone number correctly. *Alive for now. Traveling through Field Cty. No signal. Will update when I know location. Love you!*

Even though the text sat uselessly on Kavenski's phone now, it would hopefully keep attempting to send and would go through as soon as there was a signal—if they managed to get out of this mountainous, reception-less wasteland. It wouldn't give Molly much information, but it would at least let her know that Cara was alive and hopefully keep her sisters away from the guarded cabin.

"Hang on," Kavenski gritted out. Shoving the phone into her hoodie pocket, Cara grabbed the door handle with one hand and braced her other against the dash.

How did my quiet, normal life turn into the scariest scene in an action movie? Glancing at Kavenski's determined profile, she was glad that if she had to be in a high-speed chase on terrifying mountain roads, at least she was with him. "You know, hanging on isn't going to help when the car goes over the cliff."

He laughed—actually laughed—and she stared at him.

"Having a getaway driver who literally laughs in the face of death is not reassuring!" Her voice rose to a shriek at the end as he whipped around a turn. The tires squealed in complaint, and she couldn't blame them. He'd just managed to straighten the car when the next turn loomed, and he swung the wheel to the right, the muscles in his forearms bulging as if he were keeping them on the road through sheer might.

Cara clenched her jaw, holding in a scream and a

torrential mix of cursing and praying and unsolicited driving advice that wanted to pour out of her at the highest decibel possible. She knew it wouldn't be useful and would only distract Kavenski when he was doing his best to keep them both alive. The scenery whipped past her window in a nausea-inducing blur, and she tightened her grip on the handle until her fingers went numb.

They swung into another turn, tires skipping sideways over the pavement, making Cara squeeze her eyes closed and swallow another scream. It was worse not knowing what was coming, though, so her eyes popped open again. Not daring to loosen her grip on the dash and door handle, she looked in the side-view mirror rather than turn around. Immediately, she wished she hadn't given in to the impulse.

One SUV was right behind them, so close that she couldn't see its left headlight. "How'd they catch up to us?" she yelled over the shrieking wind. Even that cacophony wasn't enough to cover the rumbling of the SUV's engine. Her skin crawled at their closeness, knowing that they could easily shoot her from this distance.

"Only the best and fastest for Geoffrey Princeton Abbott." Kavenski sounded almost eerily calm, but Cara could see the strain in the tension of his body and the hard-held lines of his face.

"I'd like to point out that it's really unfair I've been kidnapped and am being chased down by a guy I barely know, all because they think we're dating, which we're n—*ot*!" The last word turned into a startled yelp as they rounded a curve and the back of a station wagon appeared right in front of them. They flew up behind the other vehicle, rocketing toward the back of the slow-moving station wagon, and Cara clutched her handholds even harder. "Car! Car!"

Kavenski whipped the wheel to the left, and they swung into the other lane. Cara barely had a chance to suck in a gasp of relief before they'd shot past the car and darted back into their lane.

The SUVs followed closely, barely losing any ground as they passed the station wagon and closed in on Kavenski's car again. Cara could only hope that the driver of the slower vehicle called the cops to complain about their unsafe driving.

They flew along the curved road cutting through the top of the pass, and a national forest information sign whipped past before Cara could read it. The back of their car slid toward the center line, the tires struggling to hang on to the asphalt in the sharp curve. Kavenski gripped the wheel with grim determination, the lines of his face sharp and hard with tension. Suddenly, there was a crashing sound, and the car lurched forward. Cara was thrown back against her seat from the force of the hit, her head jerking painfully.

"Did they just ram us?" she asked in shock.

"Yes." Kavenski's voice was grim as he pushed the car even faster. It shuddered with effort as they approached another sharp turn, but it wasn't enough. They pitched forward as the SUV bumped their back end again.

Cara bit her cheek to keep her scream inside and braced herself for the next hit. The car slid sideways as Kavenski jerked the wheel sharply, forcing them into the next hairpin turn. As the engine shrieked, the smell of burning rubber filled Cara's nose. The wall of rock outside her window got bigger and bigger, and she shoved herself sideways toward Kavenski, sure that they were about to smash into the cliff.

The back end of the car spun out, smacking into the rock in a glancing blow that jolted Cara hard enough to knock her head against the side window. The pain didn't register, as fear took precedence in her brain.

The car's wheels grabbed the asphalt and propelled them forward. Cara sent up a prayer of thanks that their vehicle, although battered and crumpled in spots, was still functional. They flew up the incline and around another curve, and Cara locked her gaze on the side-view mirror, watching for the pursuing SUV.

"What's the plan?" she asked, needing to know. Right now, she felt like they were just flying by the seat of their pants, and that didn't work for her. Unless it was an impulse stop by an ice cream shop, she wasn't a fan of spontaneity…especially when it became a matter of life and death.

Kavenski flicked her a lightning-quick glance before focusing on his driving again. "I told you. Get to the next town. Drop you off at the PD there."

"How far is that, do you know?" She hated the idea of darting to safety while he drove off with SUVs full of professional killers still following him, but she knew she wouldn't win that argument. In fact, he probably wouldn't even participate in that argument. Her brain spun with possible alternative plans. She couldn't stop shivering, although she wasn't sure whether it was from the cold or from stress and fear. The wind whistling through the car had grown icier, and patches of snow were caught on protrusions in the rock wall bordering one side of the road. They'd started pretty high up, judging from the thin, dry air at the cabin, and they were climbing even higher.

"Five or six miles." The engine gave an unhealthy-sounding shriek as they rounded the next turn.

Cara felt her lips pull down into a grimace. Five miles seemed like a long way when being pursued by kidnappers with higher-powered vehicles. Her gaze moved to the side-view mirror again, and her heart gave a sharp snap in her chest. The SUV following them around the turn was barreling toward their back bumper. "Incoming!"

Before the SUV could connect, Kavenski jerked the wheel to the left. They flew over the center line into the oncoming-traffic lane. The SUV darted up next to them, and Cara found herself staring at the driver just a few feet away from her window. The ski mask covering the driver's face made the whole situation so much worse. She stared, mute with fear, as he lowered his window and lifted a handgun...pointing it directly at her.

CHAPTER 9

KAVENSKI SAID SOMETHING TOO LOW FOR CARA TO HEAR over the rush of the wind and the thrum of her frantically beating heart. The car shot forward just as the gun went off. With a sharp crack, the back-seat window shattered, the safety glass crumbling around a gaping hole.

"Cara!" Kavenski yelled, reaching toward her as if he was going to retroactively ward off a bullet with his bare hand.

"I'm okay!" She was screaming the words, unable to believe that she hadn't been hit. "It missed me! I'm not hit!"

Cara couldn't stop twisting her head around and staring at the shattered window, knowing how close that bullet had come. The broken glass made her feel even more vulnerable as the SUV started catching up to them again.

Forcing herself to face front, she realized that Kavenski was still trying to check her over for injuries while he drove. "Just drive!" she ordered, gesturing toward the windshield. "I'm fine."

Even though his expression was grimmer than she'd ever seen it, he turned his full attention back to the road. Bracing for the next turn, Cara felt her arms shake as she clung to the door with one hand and the dash with the other. A part of her randomly wondered if there was such a thing as overdosing on adrenaline. If so, she had to be approaching her limit—*if* she hadn't already shot by it.

Their car flew around the sharp curve, centrifugal force pulling her toward Kavenski. Her arm ached with the effort of holding on to the door handle, the cliff edge too close for comfort. From the way that he kept glancing at the narrow shoulder, Kavenski didn't seem too happy about their position, either.

As they rounded the final part of the turn, the car skipped sideways, the tires squealing as they sought to find traction. Cara's fingers tightened as she cringed back against her door, certain that they were going to fly off the road and tumble to their deaths. Metal screeched against metal as the side of the car scraped against the guardrail, and Cara hoped desperately that her text to Molly had gone through. If she was going to die on this mountain, she at the very least wanted all her sisters to know that she loved them before she was literally flung off a cliff.

The car bounced off the guardrail toward the center of the road, straightening and shooting forward. Cara blinked several times before the truth sank in. "We're not dead?"

"Not yet," Kavenski answered through a set jaw, his fingers pale as he gripped the wheel.

Sinking as far down in her seat as her seat belt would allow, Cara stared through the damaged windshield, willing the town to pop up in front of them. Instead, a dark shape appeared, and her spine snapped straight. The shattered glass, held together only by the inner film, mottled the scene in front of her, making it impossible to make out any details…except that it was getting bigger—fast. "What's that?" she asked, her voice trembling.

"Truck." The way Kavenski snapped out the word made it sound like a warning, but there was nothing she could do except sit there and watch the distorted blob get larger and larger. She sent a frantic glance to her right, checking if, by some miracle, the lane next to them had opened up, only to see the masked driver pushing the SUV faster and faster until the two vehicles were almost parallel. Despite the driver's face being covered, she could still see the gleeful look, the cold amusement that she and Kavenski and some innocent truck driver were all about to die. There was nowhere for their car to go.

Kavenski suddenly braked, making Cara lurch forward before the seat belt and her grip on the dash stopped her. The first SUV shot past them, but the second managed to stop, filling the right lane as effectively as the other one had. The truck in front of them blared its horn, long blasts that turned wavery in Cara's ears as time seemed to slow. The semi was getting so close that it filled the windshield, blocking out everything else. She could only stare and listen to the thrum and hiss of air brakes as she waited to be obliterated.

As she braced her feet against the floor, both hands in front of her on the dash—despite knowing that none of that would do any good when they were hit head-on by a freaking semi truck—the car jerked to the left. The unexpected movement startled Cara out of her fatalistic paralysis, and she turned her head to look at Kavenski.

The car shot toward the edge of the road, flying over the miniscule shoulder and over the edge of the drop-off, just as the semi hurtled by behind them.

They weren't going to be obliterated by the truck after all. No, they were going to be smashed to bits at the bottom of the cliff.

Cara's frightened scream somehow turned into an inhale instead, ripping against her throat and getting trapped inside her lungs. The tires bounced off the rocks, picking up speed with each jounce. When her terrified mental scream eased enough for her to think, she realized that they weren't in the free fall she'd expected. Instead, they were on a steep rocky slope, one that she would hesitate to hike down, much less drive.

"Did you just hurl us off a freaking cliff?" she demanded once she'd recovered enough to speak. Her voice still held a terrified squeak, but she felt that higher pitch was fully justified. "I thought the whole goal was to *not* fling ourselves into the void!"

The car hit a sapling, shooting them to the right. "Better this than…" He paused as the car hit a particularly big rock and they went airborne for a horrifyingly long moment. The car landed again, bouncing hard enough to make Cara's teeth clack together, and then continued hurtling down the mountainside. Kavenski picked up where he'd left off, as if there hadn't even been a pause. "…being hit by that semi."

Cara watched, terrified, as rocks and evergreen branches flew by her window fast enough to blur. At the moment, this didn't seem like a much better alternative than instant death. At least that would be over fast. Watching their downward slide was too terrifying, so she turned and latched her gaze on Kavenski. In just the short time she'd known him, she'd started to rely on his unflappable expression to calm her down. Whether they'd be crushed to death at the bottom of the cliff or not, her screaming and flailing wasn't going to help. Staring at him, she could almost believe that he was still driving on a gravel road—well, a really bumpy, terrifyingly treacherous gravel road.

There were subtle signs of tension in him, now that she was looking so closely. He had a death grip on the wheel, and his jaw was clenched so tightly that there were white streaks underneath his tan complexion. But even as they basically tumbled uncontrollably down a mountain, he was still in control, fighting to keep the car going in the general direction he wanted it to go.

Dust, thick and choking, billowed up from behind the car and drifted into the broken rear window. Releasing the dash with one hand, she covered her mouth and nose with her arm, trying to breathe through the fabric of her hoodie to filter the air slightly. The right side of the car lifted, bucking underneath her as it hit ground again. A loud *bang* echoed across the cliffside, and the jolting became a hundred times worse.

"Blown tire?" she asked, her voice still embarrassingly high-pitched. Just when she'd started to think that things might miraculously work out, something like this happened.

"Yeah." His voice matched his grim, determined expression as he jerked the wheel sharply. The car obeyed somewhat, but the flat tire didn't allow him to maneuver well enough to miss a large pine tree altogether. The car flew closer, the right rear corner smacking against the tree. It bounced off, sending them sliding in a diagonal trajectory that Cara was pretty sure wasn't even close to where Kavenski had originally planned to take them.

The car lurched and jerked, ricocheting off larger rocks and gnarled trees as if they were in a giant pinball game. Kavenski twisted the wheel to muscle the car back into a nose-first position, but it was too late. Momentum had taken over, sending them on an uncontrollable dive down the slope.

Cara grabbed on to the door handle with one hand and reached out with the other, needing the comfort of human contact during what could be the last moments of her life. Releasing the wheel, Kavenski grabbed her hand, tightly enfolding it in his huge mitt.

The car rotated until it was completely sideways, skidding down the mountain driver's side first. Smaller pieces of earth and rock bounced along with them, a tiny landslide knocked loose by their careening vehicle. A larger boulder protruded out of the side of the hill, and Cara stared at it through the driver's window. As they got closer, she held her breath, hoping that they would slide right by, but they weren't that lucky. With a loud crunching sound, the front of the car slammed into the huge rock.

The force of the hit spun the vehicle again, turning it so that the trunk was heading downhill first. Cara swallowed a scream and clung to Kavenski's hand. Somehow, it was even more terrifying to fly *backwards* down a mountain. She didn't have to worry about that long, however. As it smacked into trees and rocks, the car flipped around in nausea-inducing changes of

direction until a sharp ridge of rock brought it to a sliding stop.

She didn't even have enough time to take a relieved
breath before the car was moving again, this time flipping onto its side. The metal groaned, and small rocks
and bits of safety glass rained over them through the
smashed windows. Unable to hold back her shriek of
terror, she released Kavenski to grab her door handle
with both hands, clinging for dear life as the car slid for
what felt like forever before toppling over again, this
time landing upside down. The air left her lungs in a
rush, not giving her enough oxygen to scream. Instead
she clung to her handholds, mentally shrieking as the car
was tossed around like a toy.

All the blood rushed to Cara's head as she reached
up—no, down—to brace her hands on the ceiling. Her
body was squashed and confused, gravity pulling her
down while her seat belt held her strapped to her seat.

The car continued to slide, picking up speed, bouncing over rocks and dirt like a three-thousand-pound
saucer sled. The upside-down view through the broken
windows was blurred and surreal, and Cara couldn't
catch her breath as they flew down the slope. Sharp bits
of wood and stone pinged against her skin, and thick
dust made it even harder to breathe. It felt like they'd
been hurtling down the mountain forever. Cara squeezed
her eyes closed, mentally chanting *At least we're still
alive. At least we're still alive.*

The car jolted with a protesting creak of metal and
plastic, slipping twice more before coming to a shuddering stop. Cara froze, her eyes still locked shut, unable to
believe that they'd truly come to a halt. She held very

still, waiting for the car to start moving again, to plunge them off a final cliff. As they'd crashed down, flipping from side to top, she hadn't really believed they'd survive. Now that the car wasn't moving, she didn't dare believe the nightmare was over.

It was unbearably quiet—even the engine must have been killed at some point—with only the light patter of pebbles that had followed them down the slope landing on the body of the car and the slight whine of the wind disturbing the utter peace. A tiny bubble of hope rose in her, expanding until her entire chest was filled with elation.

They'd done it. They'd survived.

A rough voice cut through the silence. "Cara? You with me?"

It felt strange to speak, as if the trip down the mountain had taken fifty years and she'd forgotten in the meantime how to form words. When she first tried, a cough escaped instead, forcing the coating of dust and dirt from her throat. Her second attempt was more successful. "I think I still have all my pieces." It was hard to tell, though. She tried to do a mental inventory, but her upside-down position was messing with her senses. "I need to get down."

"Hang on."

She laughed weakly at that and then wondered how she was able to find amusement in the current situation. "No choice but to hang on, really." Her voice cracked on the last word, and she coughed again.

A click from the driver's side was quickly followed by a heavy thud, and Cara forced her eyes open. The light was strange in the remains of the car, too bright in places and completely dark in others. She focused on Kavenski, who was untangling himself out of the heap he'd landed in after letting himself out of his seatbelt.

Seeing him freed made her feelings of claustrophobia worse, and she fumbled with her own seat-belt latch, forgetting his request to hang on. The car shifted slightly, tortured metal groaning, and she gripped her seat belt with both hands and froze, her fear of being trapped overwhelmed by a more immediate fear of imminent death. A strangled whimper escaped her throat as she turned to look through what remained of her window.

There was only empty space.

A single tree trunk kept them from falling into the chasm. It wasn't like the fairly steep but survivable slope that they'd just traversed. This drop would be straight down to the river below. There was no way they could live through that.

The car creaked again, and Cara very carefully turned her head toward Kavenski to see him inching toward her across the car ceiling that had been turned into an unsteady floor. Her terror must've been obvious, because he started talking in a tone more soothing than she'd thought him capable of.

"It's going to be okay, Cara." In a crouch, he shifted another inch closer, and the car rocked ever so slightly, as if they were in a sailboat on a still lake...right at the top of a waterfall. She gripped her seat belt tighter and concentrated on not losing her mind with fear. "Just stay calm. I'm almost there. We'll get you free and then both get out of here."

She wanted to tell him to knock it off, that his gentle tone was too weird to handle, and that it was freaking her out, but she didn't know if she was capable of saying anything at the moment. Instead, she concentrated on his face, on the eternally calm expression that was marred by dirt and a few streaks of blood.

"Good job," he said, as if she'd done anything except hang there frozen and stare at his face. "I'm just about there." He was close enough to touch her shoulder, and he pressed her up slightly, taking a little pressure off the areas where the seat belt kept her secured. Shifting over again, he reached for the latch, the maneuver forcing them to press so tightly together that her cheek was flat against his thigh.

The car creaked as something snapped, making the passenger side dip. Cara's stomach swooped at the movement, and she released her grip on the seat belt to clutch at the man in front of her. He'd gone still, which scared her almost more than the rocking car.

"Okay." His voice was rougher than it had been a few seconds earlier. She actually preferred that to his unnaturally gentle tone. "Going slowly isn't working. We're going to get out. Get ready to move fast in three…two…one."

As soon as he got to *one*, she heard the click of the seat belt and then the pressure across her chest and waist released. Before she could drop onto her head, however, he was yanking her back into the space above the driver's seat, both of them tangled in a mess of limbs. There was a thump and then the sound of breaking glass, and the car rocked more violently than it had since they'd stopped sliding.

Cara's breath caught, turning from what would've been a frightened noise to a choked cough. She stared at the squashed and twisted doors, and she knew that they'd be impossible to open.

"It's okay." He sounded a little winded as he shoved her headfirst through the opening where the driver's side window had been. As soon as she realized what he was doing, she tried to help, grabbing at the rocky ground outside to haul herself out of the car. The trip down the mountain had flattened the car, leaving the window openings narrow and misshapen, but she was able to fit through with some wiggling. As soon as her feet cleared the window, she turned around and saw that Kavenski had his arms out and was working to get his broad shoulders through. Grabbing handfuls of the back of his coat, she pulled on him, her stomach twisting as the breadth of his chest filled the entire opening.

She set her jaw. They'd made it this far—through bullets and a cliff dive and a *grenade*, for Pete's sake. She wasn't about to lose him because he was too much of a muscled tank to fit though the smashed window. Getting a better grip at the base of his biceps, she used all the strength she had to haul him out.

His body moved, but it was in inches. The car shifted again, and the crack of wood breaking echoed across the slope, amplifying the sound so it was even more terrifying. Cara redoubled her efforts.

"We've got this," she told him in a hoarse voice. "I'm not letting you go."

Kavenski didn't pause in his efforts to escape the car, but he did give her a narrow-eyed glance.

"What?" she puffed, her muscles straining. She hadn't expected torrents of gratitude, but his look had been more exasperated than grateful.

"Inspirational...speaking," he gritted out as he dragged himself forward, his muscles vibrating with the strain, "isn't...your thing."

She opened her mouth to retort, their back-and-forth strangely reassuring in a crazy way, but then the sound of splintering wood filled the air again. This time, the car lurched sideways, away from them, yanking Kavenski along with it.

Taken by surprise, Cara stumbled forward, pulled by her grip on him, but then she planted her stocking feet and resisted being towed along. Kavenski caught at the rocky ground, searching for handholds, and his fingers locked into a narrow crevice. She tightened her hold and threw herself backward, putting all her weight into being an anchor while she wished she were bigger and stronger, feeling like a hummingbird trying to save an eagle.

With a horrible grinding, tearing sound, the car toppled forward. Cara held on and watched, terrified that Kavenski was going to be dragged along with it. His hips and then legs slid free as the hunk of twisted metal and shattered plastic tumbled over the edge of the cliff. Cara toppled backward, and Kavenski followed her down, landing on her with enough force to drive the remaining air from her lungs. She didn't care about breathing at that moment, though. She just appreciated the feel of his huge, intact, *alive* body flattening her against the rocky ground.

The crash of the car landing far below them was as loud as the grenade had been, but somehow worse as the sound bounced around the peaks. Cara flinched at every echo. It had been too close a call. They'd been so close to being inside the vehicle when it fell, so the sound of its destruction hit Cara hard.

Kavenski's weight lifted as he pushed himself up. Hovering above her, he inspected her with an intense gaze. "You okay?"

"I think so." Now that he wasn't on top of her, she could actually breathe again, but a part of her missed the secure feeling of being pinned by his bulk. "Give me a minute. I have to wait for the adrenaline to subside before I know if, you know, one of my legs fell off or something."

His huff of air could've been just an acknowledging grunt, but Cara liked to think that it was a laugh. He rolled to the side so he was lying on his back next to her, and it felt oddly intimate, as though they were in a bed together—if the bed was a sheet of rock.

As her heartbeat started to steady, her aches and pains let themselves be known. Her entire body felt as if she'd been tossed into a cement mixer, but she couldn't feel any pain that stood out more than any other.

"Everything still attached?" Kavenski sat up and then rose to a crouch, as if he could tell she was mentally cataloging her injuries and ready to report.

"Yeah. Sore, but nothing needs immediate attention." She started to sit as well, but it was harder than she'd expected, her muscles protesting any movement. Flopping back down, she allowed herself one miserable groan before making her next attempt.

Kavenski offered a hand up, his mouth twitching in that way that was equivalent to a grin from anyone else. She gave him the flattest stare she could manage while scrambling to her feet with his help, hiding her pleasure at getting him to smile.

His humor disappeared quickly once she was standing. "We need to get moving."

Everything rushed back. "Right. They'll be looking for us." She peered up the slope, but she couldn't see the road. That was good, though. If they couldn't see their pursuers, hopefully she and Kavenski couldn't be seen, either.

"Most likely."

"Won't they think we've gone down with the ship?" She waved in the general direction of the cliff without looking at it. Their close call was too fresh in her mind.

"At first. They'll eventually check out the wreckage and know that we weren't in it. Abbott tends to be... thorough." Kavenski was back to his expressionless, almost harsh way of speaking, and Cara was strangely glad. That soothing voice had been disturbingly unlike him, and she mentally filed away the fact that if he pulled out his gentlest tone, they were probably very close to death.

Focusing on the subject at hand, Cara looked around. The part of the slope they were on wasn't too steep for them to traverse on foot, but it would be difficult in just her socks. She dropped her gaze to her feet.

Kavenski pulled off his coat, silently eyeing the rips now decorating the sides where they'd caught on the edges of the car window. The sight reminded her that he'd gone through an even more traumatic event than she had. "Are you hurt?" she asked, feeling guilty she hadn't immediately checked. The man was so stoic that he could be missing a body part, and he'd probably just rub some dirt on it and walk it off.

In response, he flipped his hand in a dismissive

gesture, which Cara took to mean that, like her, there was nothing life-threatening wrong, although she guessed he had to be even sorer than she was. As she studied him, looking for signs of more minor injuries, he pulled a folded knife out of one of his pockets and flipped it open.

Her attention caught, she watched as he used the knife to hack off both sleeves of his coat. Although she couldn't imagine why he was mutilating his outerwear, she kept her mouth shut, figuring she'd eventually figure it out if she kept observing. Once the sleeves were removed, he put on the remains of his coat, which now looked like a hacked-up vest, and put away the knife.

When he pulled out a few zip ties, Cara couldn't help but flinch. He met her gaze. "Don't worry. They're not for tying you up this time."

This time? Somehow, his words weren't as reassuring as he'd probably meant them to be. Warily, she watched as he banded the cuff of the separated coat sleeve and pulled the tie tight. He did the same to the other sleeve and then held them out to her.

She accepted the sleeves but held them in front of her, eyeing them uncertainly. "What am I supposed to do with them?"

"Put them on." When she didn't immediately follow his command, he gestured impatiently toward her feet.

Looking back and forth between the sleeves and her socks, it finally clicked what he was aiming for. "Oh! They're boots…well, sort of." Still not sure how exactly they were going to work, she lifted her foot and pulled one of the sleeves on so the zip-tied end was by her toes. When Kavenski didn't tell her she was doing it wrong, she put the other one on as well. Immediately, she felt warmer, the insulated fabric making her skin tingle a little painfully as her feet thawed.

Crouching next to her, he pulled the top of the sleeve up past her knee and then secured it with a zip tie. "Too tight?" he asked.

Having his hands on her legs, even for such a practical purpose, made her heat up in a way that had nothing to do with sleeve-boots. Every touch from him instilled such a sense of comfort that she wondered how she'd ever thought him capable of cold-blooded murder. "No." Her voice came out low and husky enough to make her cheeks heat up.

Either he didn't notice her face turning red or he was content to ignore it as he added a second zip tie right below her knee, checking wordlessly with her once he'd tightened it. By the time he'd secured the second sleeve, she was feeling very warm, and her heart was beating in double time.

She shook off her reaction as he moved away, telling herself firmly that it was neither the right time nor the right place nor the right man to get silly about. To distract herself, she took a few practice steps. Although her improvised boots didn't have a hard sole to protect her from sharp rocks, they provided a layer of warmth and cushion her socks didn't offer. Also, they were much more waterproof than fuzzy fleece.

"These are great. Thank you."

Kavenski just dipped his chin slightly in acknowledgment before turning his gaze to the area around them. Cara felt a sudden surge of gratitude.

"Thank you for coming to get me," she continued,

feeling a little awkward when his silent attention returned to her. "From the kidnappers. I don't really mean anything to you, so you could've just run, and then they would've killed me, so I appreciate the rescue."

He studied her for long enough that she was having a hard time not shifting uncomfortably under that steady stare. "It wasn't an option."

"What wasn't?"

"Running. Let's go." He started off, and she followed, wanting to question him more but too busy keeping up while getting used to the strange feeling of her sleeve-boots. The footing was uncertain, with loose pieces of shale to slip on and protruding rocks to trip over, so she kept her focus on their path, darting occasional glances at Kavenski's back to make sure she wasn't falling too far behind.

He must've been pacing himself to her speed, because he was always right in front of her when she looked up, and she knew he could move faster than her with his longer legs and regular boots. She wondered if he knew where he was going or if he was making an educated guess. Knowing Kavenski, he had a full topographical map of the mountains in that robot brain of his.

She snorted a laugh, and he glanced over his shoulder at her, his eyebrows drawn together in either question or condemnation. "Sorry. Just amusing myself back here."

After he turned back around, she gave a small hop to get over a medium-size rock in her way. As she landed, her sweatshirt swung, and something hard in the front pocket bumped against her hip.

"Oh!" she said as realization hit her. Reaching into the pocket, she pulled out Kavenski's phone. He'd turned around at her first exclamation, and she held the cell out to show him. "I forgot I had it on me. I can't believe it didn't fall out in all the commotion." *Commotion* didn't seem like the right word for their terrifying, life-threatening experience, but it made her feel strangely better to reduce the event to something no more scary than a hectic day at home. Pressing the button to turn on the phone, she held her breath, watching the screen intently as she waited for it to light up. There were several cracks zigzagging across the front, but she was still hopeful. After all, her twin was always cracking the screens of her phones, and they continued to work...well, until Charlie dropped them in the toilet or ran over them with a car or something.

When the screen stayed dark, Cara's shoulders drooped with disappointment.

"Nothing." She offered the dead phone to Kavenski, who glanced at it before slipping it into one of his coat—well, vest—pockets. She appreciated that he hadn't tried to turn it on himself, but just trusted that she hadn't been able to make it work. When he turned and started walking again, she fell in behind him with a silent sigh. A working phone wouldn't have done much good for them out here anyway. Even if they managed to miraculously get a signal, it wasn't as though they could call for a Lyft.

The slope they were walking on grew steeper, and Cara was forced to concentrate all of her attention on keeping her footing. The material of her makeshift boots wasn't too slick, and the lack of soles allowed her to grip with her feet to help keep her on the path, but she would've given quite a lot for a pair of hiking boots, especially when the sharper small stones dug into her feet.

Kavenski kept looking back more and more to check on her, and she wondered if that was because of the treacherous footing or because she was muttering invectives under her breath as she did her best to keep up without sliding down the slope.

A cluster of loose shale sent one of her feet slipping down the incline, almost making her lose her balance. Kavenski whipped around as the small rocks rained down the stone slope, but she caught herself before she tipped over.

"I'm okay," she said, making sure her next steps were secure as she caught up to him. She didn't want to fall, but she *especially* didn't want to topple over while Kavenski was watching. For some unexplainable reason, she wanted him to think she was competent and brave, rather than a damsel in distress. He'd done the bulk of the rescuing so far, but she wanted to do her part to ensure their escape.

Despite her assurance, he was still eyeing her as if she was about to fall off the cliff at any moment. When she came to a stop next to him, he finally looked away. Cara glanced up, too, realizing that she'd been so focused on not dying in the car and then having to pay close attention to where she was putting her feet that she hadn't really looked at what was around them.

Her breath caught as she took in the view. It felt like being in a sporting goods commercial. The exposed rock that they were crossing looked over an entire panorama of mountain peaks, sloping down to a thick skirt of evergreens and blaze-yellow aspen trees before finally reaching the winding river at the base of the valley. The air was thin and chilled, but it felt clean, and the sun shone merrily down on the gorgeous view. Cara squinted at the clear blue sky, feeling a bit aggrieved. It was much too nice a day, considering all of their near-death experiences.

"What's wrong?" Kavenski asked. His focus had returned to her while she'd been taking in the view.

"Nothing important," she said, feeling a bit sheepish. "It's beautiful out here, but I wish it were a planned hiking trip, and not me in pajamas with sleeves on my feet."

His grunt sounded like he agreed with that sentiment. "It's just going to get steeper if we continue across here. We're going to head for those trees, instead." He pointed to where the scattered evergreens first cropped up, appearing to be rooted in sheer rock. Cara could appreciate that tenacious clinging to life after the day they'd had. The slope seemed too steep to walk straight down, though.

As if he could read her thoughts, he added, "We'll switchback down."

It was still intimidating, but Cara gestured for him to lead the way. He seemed comfortable in the mountains, while she'd only taken a hike or two on groomed trails. Most of her wilderness time had been spent in the fairly flat national forest bordering their backyard, so she was willing to cede control to the more experienced of their twosome. She followed his path exactly as he wove back and forth, creating a zigzagging line that would eventually lead them down the slope.

Focusing on her footing again, she lost track of how

many steps they'd taken and how many turns they'd made. When every glance at the trees just showed a frustrating lack of progress, she kept her gaze trained on the rock in front of her feet, with only occasional checks to make sure that Kavenski was still right in front of her.

He was another distraction. Her gaze would catch on his tall, well-built figure and get stuck there, mesmerized by the play of muscles under his cargo pants. It wouldn't be until her foot landed on a particularly sharp pebble or she stubbed her toe on an outcropping that she would realize that she was staring again. She'd never been so fascinated by a man before, and it was disconcerting, especially since she should've been completely focused on their terrifying situation. After priding herself on relying on logic and reason, even in relationships, it was uncomfortable to realize that she was just as susceptible to losing her mind over a tight pair of buns as the next person.

Not the time or the place for crushing on someone, Cara told herself. *And definitely not* this *someone*.

She'd been concentrating so hard on not looking at the trees—or Kavenski's muscled bits—that the brush of pine needles against her shoulder took her by surprise. They'd made it to the trees without falling to their deaths, so Cara took that as yet another win.

"Where do we go from here?" she asked, looking around. The trees blocked some visibility, but she felt so much more secure with something to grab onto in case she slipped or, worst-case scenario, something to block her from falling off a cliff.

Kavenski pointed, which didn't really tell her anything. Falling in behind him again, she trudged along, keeping an eye on her footing. It was still very rocky, although more dirt and pine needles covered the stone. She dodged around patches of snow, not wanting to test how waterproof her improvised boots were.

Even though she looked around as much as she could when she wasn't staring at the ground in front of her, she had no idea where they were headed. It all looked the same to her, and the lack of any signs of civilization—no roads, buildings, or even power lines—made her uneasy.

"So..." she started when she couldn't stand not knowing any longer. "Do you actually know where we're going, or are you just improvising? Because I feel like we're at the beginning of one of those survival movies where we think we're following the path, but we get lost and have to spend the winter fighting mountain lions for scraps."

She was pretty sure she heard a snort, although it was hard to tell since Kavenski didn't turn around. "We're headed east."

After waiting a few steps for clarification but only getting silence, she gave him a verbal nudge. "East is good. Langston is east...I assume. Do you have a specific destination in mind?"

He gave her an offended look over his shoulder, but she just gave an exaggerated shrug.

"Can you blame me for asking?" She waved in the direction of her feet. "I'm wearing sleeves on my feet, after all." She was also getting thirsty, tired, hungry, ached all over, and she had to pee, but she didn't want to whine too much.

"The town of Red Hawk," he said, facing forward again. "Specifically, the Red Hawk police station."

Oh, right. That had been their original plan before Kavenski had driven them off a cliff. "That's right! It's only, what? Five miles away?"

"Five miles on the road."

"Oh." She looked around with fresh dread at the wilderness stretching around them. This time she was glad that the trees limited her visibility. She'd rather not see exactly how far the nothingness went. "I don't suppose we're taking the shortcut."

His laugh didn't sound very amused. "Nope."

With a sigh, she settled in for a very long, very rocky walk.

CHAPTER 10

IT WAS IMPOSSIBLE TO KNOW HOW MUCH TIME HAD PASSED. The sun seemed to have shifted in the sky, but Cara had never had to pay attention to the sun's location to figure out the time. That's what cell phones were for. She promised herself that she'd start wearing a watch as soon as they managed to get home safely. She also threw in a promise to take a wilderness safety course.

"How long have we been walking?" Her voice sounded loud. Before she'd spoken, it had been silent except for the crunch of their footsteps and the sweep of the wind.

Squinting up at the sky, Kavenski said, "About an hour."

Of course he knows how to tell time from the sun. She silently sighed, feeling like deadweight again. *This isn't your fault*, she reminded herself. *Not that it's Kavenski's fault either, but it* definitely *isn't your fault*. Still, she didn't want to break out with the whining. "Mind if I stop to pee?"

In answer, he came to an abrupt stop. "Don't go too far."

"I won't." She definitely wouldn't be wandering away from her wilderness guide. Finding a spot behind a particularly bushy pine tree, she took care of business.

It was awkward enough that she added another item onto the Things to Hate about Abbott list, which was already really long. She picked up a handful of melting snow and rubbed it between her palms, hoping to feel like she'd washed up, but she just ended up with wet, numb hands. Making a face, she wiped the melted snow off on her pants and rejoined Kavenski.

"You don't happen to have any power bars in those handy pockets of yours, do you?"

Even as he checked, he shook his head. When he pulled out a small item, she got excited, even when she saw it was a roll of breath mints. She held out her hand eagerly, expecting him to give her one, but he passed her the entire thing.

"Don't you want any?" she asked.

"I ate this morning. You didn't." He started walking again, and she followed.

"Thank you." She ate the mints one at a time, enjoying the small sugar rush. Her mouth didn't feel so dry anymore, and her bladder was empty. Except for being completely exhausted and sore everywhere, she didn't have much to complain about. The ground had leveled out quite a bit as well, which made it easier to walk. Although she still had to keep an eye on the ground in front of her, each step didn't threaten to send her sliding off a cliff.

Finishing the mints, she tucked the wrapper in her hoodie pocket. When her hands were buried in the fleecy warmth, she realized how cold they'd gotten. The sky was overcast, and the aggravatingly cheerful but warm sun had disappeared. She studied the gray clouds carefully. They reminded her of the storms that rolled in almost every early evening during late summers in Langston.

"Do you think it's going to rain?" she asked Kavenski, shivering as the breeze picked up.

"No." Before relief could spread through her, he spoke again. "It might snow."

"Snow?" The word was more of a yelp. She wasn't ready for snow, and she wouldn't be for a solid month. It was barely fall weather in Langston. She looked down at her hoodie and then at her sleeve-boots. "I don't even have a hat." When she heard her words, she wanted to laugh. A lack of a hat should probably be the least of her worries. "Do you think we'll get to Red Hawk before it storms?"

"Doubt it." He was starting to get that tight-jawed, clenched look he'd had when they were having grenades tossed at them, which made her more anxious about the upcoming weather. "We need to cross the river."

"The river," she repeated, trying to wrap her head around everything that a water crossing would entail. "The one that's way down there?" Even though he couldn't see her, she pointed in the general direction of where she'd last seen the river. It had looked tiny and far away, and the wrecked car had fallen for what had felt like a long time before it hit bottom. That was going to be a long descent in sleeve-boots—and an even longer climb back up. Another problem hit her. "Are we going to have to swim across?"

"It's low enough now that we'll be able to find a spot to wade across."

Cara was quiet for a minute or two, absorbing all the ramifications. The dark clouds seemed to be racing in to cover the sky, only allowing the sun to peek out for a few seconds before the world darkened again. "Okay. First things first. It's getting colder really fast, and I might have just spotted a snowflake. Should we find a sheltered spot to wait out the snow?" She couldn't help but picture them trudging right off a cliff during a whiteout.

He gave her an approving look over his shoulder before pointing at something Cara couldn't see. "There's a structure of some kind in that direction. We'll head toward it."

Even squinting, she couldn't spot what he was referring to. "Do you have ultimate-supreme vision? Because all I'm seeing are trees and rocks."

"Ultimate-supreme vision?" When she just shrugged, he pointed again. "Look there when the sun's out."

She trotted a few steps until she was walking next to him rather than behind him, so he didn't block the view. Now that she was waiting for a peek of sunlight, it felt like forever before there was a gap in the clouds. It only lasted for a moment or two before the sun disappeared again, but when the landscape was lit up with sunlight, she thought she saw something in the direction that Kavenski had pointed.

"What was that flash?" she asked, peering through the trees as she tried to catch the burst of light again. "Is someone signaling over there?"

"The sun's reflecting off something shiny—probably a window."

"Oh, that's clever!" Without thinking about it, she reached over and gave his shoulder a pat. "Good eye. I was thinking we'd have to huddle under a bush to wait out the snow, but a house would be so much better. Maybe whoever lives there has a phone we can use. I just hope it's not a Unabomber type who tries to kill us for trespassing. I've had enough of that for today—for a lifetime, really."

The corner of his mouth twitched up, and she felt a surge of accomplishment for getting a rare Kavenski smile—well, his sort-of smile, at least. She'd need to work up to getting him to actually show teeth in a full-out grin.

"We'll hope for no Unabomber, then," he said as evenly as if they were talking about the weather. Now she couldn't hold back her own smile.

"I'm glad you came to rescue me," she said impulsively, and then felt her face heat as she realized how strange that sounded. "Not just because I would probably be dead a few times by now if you hadn't been here."

His sideways look told her clearly that she was just digging herself deeper into an awkward hole.

Giving up on trying to make sense, she just blurted out her thoughts. "You're making everything easier in this whole messed-up situation, and I'm glad I'm not trying to do this by myself." After a pause, she couldn't help but add, "Although I probably wouldn't have driven us off a cliff, but that ended better than I expected, so I won't hold it against you."

The sound he made was a pearl-clutching huff of offense that made her snicker. "You would've rather been hit by that truck?" he asked.

"No, but I don't think my solution would've involved cliff diving in a car."

"It was the best spot. If we hadn't blown a tire, it would've been a smooth ride down to the bottom."

Cara bulged her eyes out at him. "Did you forget about the flipping-upside-down thing?"

Waving a hand, he made a sound of dismissal. "We were fine."

"We almost went off the edge of a cliff—a *real* cliff."

"But we didn't."

"It was close." She shivered as she thought about just how close it had been.

"We didn't die, and that's all that matters."

She was quiet for a few beats and then said, "I think that's a good motto for this whole kidnapping adventure."

"Adventure?" he repeated.

"Escapade?"

"Fiasco."

"Yeah. That's the right word for it." She resisted the urge to companionably take his hand. They were escaping attempted murderers and kidnappers, not going for a stroll in the woods, she reminded herself. Still, what she'd said was true. If she had to be lost in the mountains with sleeve-boots and an approaching blizzard, there was no one she'd rather have with her than Kavenski. "Can I ask you something?"

The only change in his expression was the slight quirking of an eyebrow. "Can I stop you?"

"Sure." Honesty prompted her to continue. "But I'll probably just ask later, since this is really bugging me. You can choose not to answer, though." A part of her did want to know, but on the other hand, she wasn't sure if she wanted to hear the truth. After all they'd been through in just the past few hours, she felt as if she was starting to get to know him, and everything she was learning contradicted the facts in his file. "You didn't really kill those people, did you?"

"Which people?"

She blinked. "It's a little unnerving that you would need me to clarify which murder I'm referring to."

His mouth slanted into the most fully formed smile that she'd seen on him.

Forcing herself to ignore how gorgeous that made him, she managed to frown. "It's even more unsettling when you look all happy about these multiple killings."

"Not the killings, you're just…" He slashed down a hand, as if physically cutting off his thought.

Now she was intrigued. "I'm what?"

He stayed silent for so long that she was pretty sure he wasn't going to answer, but she waited him out, her gaze fixed on the side of his face—well, as much as she could without tripping over something and falling flat on her *own* face.

"You have an…interesting way of putting things," he finally said, surprising her with both his willingness to answer and the answer itself. "It's cute."

Now she was the one who couldn't hide her grin. "You think I'm cute?"

Stoic McStoneface actually rolled his eyes. It was just a quick upward flick before he returned to his usual neutral expression, but she caught it. "Of course." His voice was even gruffer than normal. "It's not an opinion; it's a fact. You are *objectively* cute."

"Mmm." She reluctantly let it go, but she couldn't stop smiling. Henry Kavenski, who was objectively

a super hottie, thought she was cute. The temptation
to take his hand was even greater now, and she only
resisted because she realized that he'd never answered
her question. Now she was even more reluctant to
find out that he was a stone-cold killer—because if he
was, her excitement that he found her objectively cute
became objectively creepy. "Did you kill Bettina and
Lance Mason?"

"No." From the look on his face, he hadn't been
planning to tell her the truth. He paused as he stepped
onto a raised section of rock and then offered her a
hand up. "I'm not telling you anything else about it,
so don't ask. The more you know, the bigger the target
on your back."

That actually made her laugh, although the sound
didn't hold much mirth. Grasping his proffered hand,
she hauled herself up next to him, mentally cursing her
lack of real boots when the bottoms of her battered feet
throbbed painfully with the movement. Reluctantly, she
released his hand as they continued forward again.

"I don't know very much right now, but I'd say my
back target is pretty darn huge. *Ow!*" Something sharp
had poked the ball of her foot. Grabbing Kavenski's
arm for support, she lifted her foot, turning her knee
outward so she could see her sole. She plucked a long
pine needle out of her sleeve-boot and then gingerly set
her foot down again. "For such a tiny thing, that hurt
a lot. My queendom for a pair of hiking boots," she
muttered. When nothing else poked into her skin, she
allowed her foot to take her full weight and released her
grip on Kavenski.

He was frowning at her feet as they started walking

again. "When we get to shelter, we'll trade. You can have my boots," he said.

"Thank you, but no. I'll be fine." She ignored the complaints of her sore and abraded soles. Every other part of her was cold from the wind that had started whipping around them, but the bottoms of her feet throbbed with heat, and her left big toe still ached from being stubbed on a rock several minutes earlier.

Kavenski gave her a look that she was pretty sure was supposed to make her quake in her sleeve-boots and agree to whatever he was suggesting, but Cara was past the point of being scared of him. He'd put her safety before his too many times for her to believe he'd ever hurt her. Not to mention, she was starting to get hungry again, and she was sore and thirsty and tired enough to be contrary just for the sake of being contrary. Besides, she had a good reason for not following his suggestion.

"Your boots would be enormous on me. Even if I managed to lace them tight enough that they didn't fall off, I'd trip over every rock and probably get blisters since they'd be loose and rubbing against my ankles and heels. Thank you, but no thank you—and *where is that damn house already?*"

This time, his glance was less chiding and more startled.

"Sorry," she said, even though she felt more surly than apologetic. "I'm just...done with this day." It probably wasn't even midmorning, and already it was the worst day of her life.

"Shouldn't be too much farther." Before she could complain that he was being unhelpfully vague, he continued, "Do you want me to carry you?"

"No. That'd be weird." Realizing that she'd been less than polite when he was being so nice, she added a belated "Thank you, though."

She tried to peer through the trees, but the heavy clouds had completely covered the sky, not allowing any glimpses of the sun. The dim light created impenetrable shadows between the trees, making it difficult to see more than twenty feet in front of her. The dark spaces reminded her that anything could be hiding in these trees.

Though she wasn't as worried about wild animals as she was the human kind.

"Do you think they'll come after us on foot?" she asked, automatically keeping her voice low in case there were any unwelcome listeners. "Or will they wait for us to almost make it to Red Hawk before they burst out of the shadows and shoot us dead?"

"That's a little pessimistic."

She lifted her shoulders in a shrug and then winced. Every part of her was sore. "You say pessimistic, I say realistic. We're running out of lucky chances."

"Sure you don't want me to carry you?" he asked, obviously having noticed her slight grimace of pain.

"I'm sure. Let's save that for when we're under fire and I'm unconscious and bleeding out."

The sound he made was strange, kind of like a laugh disguised as a cough. "Good to know."

"What's good to know?"

"That you get morbid when you're hungry."

"And thirsty." She'd reached the point where she didn't care if she was whining. Her upper lip just couldn't stay stiff any longer. "And tired and sore and really annoyed about being kidnapped and shot at."

"Don't forget about the grenade being tossed at you."

Cara scowled at the mention. "Oh, don't worry. I haven't. That's definitely on the list." After a pause, she added, "You never answered. Were you trying to distract from the fact that Abbott and his guys are after us?" The groaning of the wind was loud enough that someone could be driving a tank toward them right now and she wouldn't hear it until it was on top of them. *Not that it'd be easy getting a tank up here*, her brain interjected, making Cara shake her head, trying to wrangle her straying thoughts even as she started to imagine approaching helicopters and heavy weaponry. *Stop*, she ordered the more lurid parts of her imagination. *Not helping*.

"Doubt they'll come after us on foot," he said, but there was a very slight emphasis on the last two words that made her uneasy.

"So they *are* coming in tanks and helicopters." She marched forward more quickly, grimly determined to reach the structure before the invading army attacked. Maybe the Unabomber-type homeowner would have some useful weapons they could use to defend themselves.

"Wait...what? Tanks?" From the bemusement in his voice, she'd actually managed to knock him off-balance, but she was so preoccupied with mentally preparing for war with Abbott that she couldn't appreciate it properly.

Ignoring the way her feet ached with each step and how her skin felt like it was stretched too tightly from the dry, cold air, she hurried through the thickening trees. Kavenski easily caught up with her, and they walked in silence. The snow was starting to fall in small, spindly flakes that stung her skin where they landed, lending extra urgency to her steps. She was amazed by how dark it had gotten, seeming more like dusk than midmorning, when just a short time earlier the sun had been merrily shining from a bright, clear sky.

All too quickly, the few flakes turned into a flurry. The wind drove them into Cara's eyes and bit at her exposed skin. The light dusting of snow seemed to grease the rocky ground, making each step more treacherous than the one before—but she had no choice. She had to keep going. Her heart beat faster than their quick pace warranted. The building cold and howling wind made it all too easy to understand how people could freeze to death in a mountain blizzard.

Just as she was starting to doubt that the reflection they'd seen earlier was anything human-made, Kavenski caught her arm, pulling her to a halt. She followed his gaze and spotted the stacked row of peeled logs that couldn't have been natural. They'd found the structure they were looking for.

Without a word, Kavenski took the lead, and Cara let him. If he wanted to be on the front lines when they met a bear or one of Abbott's guys, he was welcome to it. She was just as happy tucked safely behind his brawny form. Besides, he broke the wind, and his back gave her something to focus on besides the worsening storm.

They approached as quietly as possible, given the obstacles. Kavenski stepped over a large fallen tree, and Cara wished for his long legs as she scrambled over it much less gracefully. As she landed on the other side, she slipped on some loose, pebbly dirt covered in snow but caught her balance before she fell. Turning,

Kavenski gave her an *Are you okay?* glance, and she nodded, annoyed with her clumsiness.

As they crept closer, more of the log wall came into view. It was more cabin-sized than a full-on house, although it was larger than the shack where she'd started the day. Cara eyed the unlit windows uneasily. The Unabomber's twin could easily be watching them, waiting for them to get close enough to push the button, setting off the bomb he'd planted in preparation for when the FBI raided his mountain hideaway. The wind settled briefly, creating an eerie quiet that was broken by a *snap*. Swallowing a startled yelp, Cara grabbed the back of Kavenski's coat-turned-vest as she braced for the coming explosion.

Nothing happened. The expected hail of bullets never came. Kavenski gave her a questioning look as the wind picked back up, tossing tiny, icy pellets of snow at their faces. Her gaze dropped to the small branch that had broken under her sleeve-boot. Giving Kavenski a sheepish look, she released the handful of his coat, smoothing down the fabric as if to erase her entire embarrassing reaction.

Despite the false alarm, she quickly grew unnerved again as she returned her attention to the dark windows. Now her fears didn't center on loud dangers such as tanks and helicopters. The quiet, scary things—such as Abbott's people crouched silently in the cabin, waiting to ambush them, or odd, weapon-obsessed mountain folk who'd shoot any trespassers on sight—seemed so much worse than any rumbling machinery.

Kavenski made a sharp gesture, one that she was fairly certain meant *stay put*. Reluctantly, she halted and watched him continue to pick his way through the rocks and scrubby trees. Instead of heading for the front porch, he slipped behind the back of the cabin, quickly fading to a shadow in the false twilight of the gathering snow and then disappearing completely.

CHAPTER 11

LEANING AGAINST AN ASPEN TRUNK, CARA KEPT HER EYES locked on the spot where she'd last seen Kavenski. After her steady feeling of being watched, she was surprised to be so bothered by her solitude now. The wind continued to howl, and the snow picked up even more, creating a sheet of white that blurred the structure in front of her. Despite the cabin and the trees—*and the possible tanks and helicopters*, her lurid imagination insisted on adding—that bit of the mountain felt completely desolate, making it hard to believe that civilization still existed, much less that there was a town with a police station a few miles away.

Shaking herself out of her postapocalyptic imaginings, she peered through the wind-tossed snow, waiting for Kavenski to reappear on the other side of the cabin. Seconds ticked by, turning into minutes, and Cara grew increasingly cold and worried. She shifted her weight, wishing once again that she was in the habit of wearing a watch. Time seemed to stretch uncomfortably long, and wild thoughts ran through her head.

What if something had happened to Kavenski? Could he have been grabbed or hurt or found by Abbott's guys? Or maybe the threat wasn't human-made at all. Maybe there was a mountain lion making a snack out of his insides *right now*. Despite knowing that her fears were unlikely, Cara still pushed away from the tree she'd been leaning against and took a step toward the cabin.

"It's clear." Kavenski materialized in front of her, making her jump a foot in the air. He paused, eyeing her. "What's wrong?"

She waved a cold hand, her worries seeming silly now that an unharmed, un-snacked-on Kavenski was standing next to her. "Nothing. Just felt like you were gone a long time."

"Had to break in." He started toward the front of the cabin, and she followed him, feeling both relieved to have him next to her and a trifle aggrieved at herself for needing him there to figuratively hold her hand. He led the way up the few roughhewn front porch steps and to the heavy wooden door.

As he turned the knob and pushed the door open, Cara glanced around for any evidence of how Kavenski had gotten into the locked cabin. "Did you have to break a window?" she asked when she couldn't find any sign of damage.

"No." He stepped inside and moved so she could enter the dim space. "I picked the lock." As she passed by him, he gave her a slanted look. "Something you seem to know a little about."

Feeling along the wall, her hand encountered the reassuringly familiar shape of a light switch. Holding her breath hopefully, she flipped it up and was happily shocked when the room filled with light. "That's why you took so long," she said absently as she took in the interior of the cabin. Compared to the kidnappers' shack, this one was surprisingly cozy. The living room, kitchen, and dining area made up the open lower level as in the other place, but this was larger and furnished with a comfortable-looking couch and coordinated chairs, as well as a small dining table. The rugs and wall hangings made it feel warm, even though the potbellied wood-stove in the corner wasn't in use.

Closing and locking the door behind them, Kavenski gave one of his stuffy-sounding huffs. Cara bit back a smile. The sound was so grandmotherly, completely incongruous with his hulking form and usual scowl. "I was faster than you were that day."

She wandered farther in, checking things out more thoroughly as he moved from window to window, clos-ing all the blinds. When she realized what he was doing, she moved back toward the light switches. "Should we keep the lights off so Abbott's people don't spot the cabin?" she asked.

"No." He climbed the spiral stairs to the loft. "Even if they're out in this storm, it's highly unlikely that they'll track us here, and the blizzard's only getting worse. I'm just taking precautions." As he disappeared into the loft, she resumed her exploration of the cabin, reassured.

Everything she saw made her relieved that they'd stumbled upon this particular place. It looked like a seldom-used vacation cabin, a much safer shelter than the messy, explosives-rigged, Unabomber-occupied shack her imagination had conjured up. When Kavenski came back down the stairs, she picked up their earlier conversation. "That was an unfair lock-picking compari-son, by the way. My hands were shaking. I even beat my sister Charlie's best time, and she's fast. I bet I could make your skills look like a first-grader's."

His eyes narrowed as he crossed his arms over his chest. "My skills would blow yours out of the water."

"That's it. We're having a pick-off as soon as we get back to Langston." Cara realized that she'd been so distracted by the cabin and their light banter that she'd been talking as if they'd continue to be friends after they made it off the mountain. The reality was that he wouldn't be able to settle into a relaxing life after this. Even if he hadn't killed those people—and she believed him when he said he didn't—he'd still been arrested for murder and skipped bail. Until that was dealt with, he'd always be on the run.

"You're on." Kavenski sounded like he'd forgotten his complicated situation, too. Before Cara could say anything about it, she spotted a door next to the spiral stairs leading up to the loft. Excitement filled her as she hurried over to it, her sleeve-boots sliding a little on the polished wooden floor.

"Is this a bathroom?" Yanking open the door, she felt for the light switch and flicked it on. A huge smile spread across her face at the sight, and she hopped a little. She would never have thought that a simple bathroom would make her so happy. "It's heaven with a toilet," she said, stepping inside. Her happiness waned a little when she saw that there wasn't any water in the bowl. Fate couldn't be cruel enough to offer a bathroom with no running water, could it?

Moving back into the main room, she found Kavenski stacking some small logs into the woodstove.

"There's no water," she said mournfully, shuffling over to where he was crouched. "Could I use your knife?"

His eyebrows shot up as he glanced at her. "For what?"

"To take my fake boots off." She took the folded knife he'd dug out of his pocket and held out toward her. "What did you think I wanted to do with it?"

"Wasn't sure how you were going to fix the lack of water with my knife." He turned back to his perfectly arranged pyramid of wood and lit the fire starter tucked at the base.

Plopping down on the end of the couch closest to the woodstove, Cara cut the zip ties securing the sleeves to her lower legs. She marveled at the ease of cutting through the strips of plastic when it had been such a struggle to free herself just hours before. Her chilled fingers tingled as they came back to life, but her feet were hot from all the walking she'd done. A pulse thumped intermittently in her soles, and she grimaced at the soreness.

"Is there a way to turn the water on?" she asked, sliding the sleeves off her feet.

"Should be." Kavenski straightened to his full height, looming over her. "I'll go look."

He crossed the room and disappeared through a door next to the stairs as Cara watched the tiny fire grow, licking at the larger logs and leaving trails of soot on the bark. The flames were mesmerizing, and she stared at them for several minutes. Sitting down made her realize how bone-deep her exhaustion went.

The sound from the other room made her start, pulling her out of her stupor. She glanced toward the door Kavenski had gone through, hoping he'd succeeded in turning something on, something that would lead to being able to flush the toilet and take a shower.

It took some effort to push herself to her feet, but she finally managed. Since Kavenski had started a fire and was likely well on his way to getting the plumbing to work, she thought she should contribute something toward their survival. She'd never been a fan of camping. Charlie had dragged her out to the woods to sleep in a tent many times while they were growing up. Even as a kid, Cara never saw the fun in sleeping on the hard, cold ground, not showering, and peeing out in the open when there were beds and bathrooms readily available.

Now, she felt her lack of outdoorsy skills. If Kavenski hadn't been there, she would probably already be dead of exposure…or from falling off a cliff.

Shaking off the sudden rush of inferiority, she tried to focus on what she could do. Her gaze moved around the cabin and settled on the row of kitchen cabinets.

Food, she thought. *We need food*. As if in agreement, her stomach rumbled and squeezed in on itself, letting her know exactly how hungry she was. Crossing her fingers that the cabin contained something edible, she walked to the kitchen on tender stocking feet. Away from the immediate vicinity of the woodstove, the floor was cold, but it actually felt good on her soles.

Even though she was pretty sure it would be empty, she checked the fridge first. The darkened interior held a lone box of baking soda. The freezer was equally unlit and empty except for a pair of ice-cube trays. The first cupboard she opened revealed stacked plates, and the second held glasses and mugs. On the third, she hit pay dirt.

"Score," she said under her breath, scanning the labels

of the stacked cans of food. Pulling out some soup, she looked over her shoulder as Kavenski returned to the main room. "Did you get the water turned back on?"

The corner of his mouth twitched in a way she was starting to recognize as warm amusement. "Yeah. Well pump's on."

"I love indoor plumbing." Cara bounced a little on the balls of her feet, but their soreness made her stop. "And I found food, so we're golden."

She started rummaging through drawers, searching for a can opener and trying very hard not to think about her desperate hunt for a knife at the other cabin. Despite her attempt to convince herself that it wasn't at all the same, she was hugely relieved when her fingers closed on the metal handles of an opener.

As she straightened, she felt heat behind her, as though her back was to a furnace, and she went still. Reaching around her, Kavenski turned on the sink faucet. Even the miraculous trickle of water that turned into a steady flow wasn't enough to distract her from his proximity. Despite the warmth he was radiating, a shiver trembled up her spine. With his chest right behind her and his arm stretched along her right side, she felt surrounded...but not in a claustrophobic way. His big form seemed to be curled around hers, as if he were keeping her safe, blocking any threats with his own body. Maybe it was because she'd been kidnapped, drugged, and almost died several times over the last eighteen hours, but she was craving the feeling of protection he was unintentionally providing.

Breathe, dummy, Cara scolded herself, but having him so close seemed to have short-circuited her brain.

It's not like he's doing this on purpose, after all. He can't help it that the kitchen is small and he's so incredibly big.

As if to prove the practical side of her brain right, he seemed oblivious to both their intimate position and her extreme reaction to his closeness. Giving a grunt of satisfaction, he turned off the water and moved away. She couldn't stop herself from watching as he walked to the bathroom. Only when he went inside and out of her line of sight did she exhale all the air in her lungs in a heavy rush.

Suddenly, waiting out the storm in a small cabin with Kavenski seemed like a really dumb idea.

"The other option is freezing to death on your lonesome outside," she muttered, turning back to the soup. "That would be less awkward, but more…well, deadly. Quit being an idiot." It was easy to be practical without him right behind her.

I wonder where we'll sleep tonight?

Her gaze was drawn upward, and she studied the beams that held up the loft floor as if she could see the furnishings with X-ray vision. Her heart skipped a beat. "You're being stupid again." Dragging her attention back to preparing the basic meal in front of her, she started searching for a pan. "If there's only one bed, you can sleep on the couch, doofus."

"You say something?" Kavenski asked as he emerged from the bathroom.

"What? No. Just talking to myself about…nothing." She found a small saucepan and clutched the handle as tightly as she could. Her cheeks had to be red. She could feel them burning almost as hotly as the bottoms of her feet. When his eyebrow quirked and his lips parted as if he was going to say something more, she hurried to change the subject. "Think it's safe to turn on the propane stove?"

He frowned at the appliance as if he had X-ray vision as well and could examine the inner workings just by looking at the exterior. "Better not. Just use the top of the woodstove."

Still a little flustered by her earlier thoughts, Cara concentrated on opening the cans to have an excuse not to look at him directly. "I didn't see power lines the entire time we were walking. How is there power?"

"Solar panels and a small wind turbine. Hear it?"

She listened. At first, she could only hear the howling wind, but then there was a lull. "That kind of buzzing, humming sound?"

He dipped his chin in a nod as he prowled around the space, checking in drawers and the lone closet. She glanced at him occasionally now that his focus wasn't on her, finding herself too fascinated by him for her peace of mind. "They're powering a battery bank in there." He waved toward the utility room.

"We're lucky the cabin we found is owned by people who like their luxuries, and not the family who loves to rough it." She paused for a moment, then asked, "Do you have any money?"

That pulled his attention away from the books lining a small shelf. "Why? Were you planning on robbing me?"

Making a face at him, she dumped a couple of cans of chicken and vegetable soup into the pan. "Yeah. I'm going to rob you and then ask for your help getting me out of these mountains. You have my nefarious plan all figured out." When he didn't say anything in response, she continued. "Since we're using these people's cabin and eating their soup and about to use their bathroom and their bed—beds—um..." She stumbled when she realized her insecurities were showing, but then she plowed on. "Anyway, I thought we should leave them some money. Obviously, I don't have any cash on me, so that leaves you."

"Yeah." The short answer to her long explanation made her roll her eyes at the soup pan.

"Yes in that you agree in theory, or yes in that you have money you're willing to give to the nice people who own this cabin?" She lifted the pan slightly before setting it on the circular cast-iron plate on top of the woodstove. "And this soup we're about to eat."

"We'll leave some cash." He started up the spiral stairs to the loft, and Cara followed, curious about the upper level. The bed question nibbled at her mind as well. She'd feel more settled after she knew if she was going to be bunking on the couch.

As she rounded the last curve of the staircase and got her first glimpse of the loft, she felt her stomach flip. There was one bed, and it wasn't even a big one—a double at most. Letting out a small huff of disappointment, she resigned herself to a night on the couch. Immediately, she mentally scolded herself for acting like a princess when things could be so much worse.

Crossing to the French doors at the far end of the loft, she peered out into the dimness. The balcony wasn't very wide, but the blowing snow was so thick that it was hard to see the railing. She shivered a little. It was too easy to imagine all sorts of dangers lurking in the murkiness of the storm.

"Cold?"

Kavenski's question made her turn to see him in front of an open closet, watching her. "Not really," she answered, a little surprised it was true. Even this far from the fire, the cabin was quickly warming up. "I'm just creeping myself out."

"Doubt Abbott's guys are out in this," he said in a matter-of-fact tone that was strangely comforting. It was as if the universe wouldn't dare to go against his word when Kavenski said something with such confidence. "They aren't any kind of wilderness experts."

His assurance brought up a hundred more questions about how he knew what Abbott's people were like, and how Kavenski was involved in all this. She knew that conversation would take a while, and there was soup heating on the stove, so she let it go…for the moment, at least. Her gaze shifted to the bed again, all fluffy and cozy-looking, draped in thick quilts and stacked with an abundance of pillows. "We're definitely stuck here for the night?"

He moved to stand next to her to look out the French doors. "Doesn't look like it's stopping anytime soon, and it'll get dark in a few hours. Safest to stay put where there's heat and food." He turned his head to look at her. "You don't want to stay?"

"It's fine. I mean, I'd rather stay where it's warm than venture out there again." She gestured toward the glass in front of them. "I just have a weird Goldilocks feeling, like the owners of this cabin are going to pop in at any second and find us sleeping in their bed." *There's that bed reference again. Just let it go, Cara. He won't*

notice if you don't make a big, awkward deal about it.
Of course she couldn't just let it go. "Or on their couch,
or wherever."

His inscrutable expression gave nothing away as his
gaze landed on the bed. "Doubt anyone will be hiking
in this. If they're coming here, it'll be tomorrow at the
earliest."

Seizing on the change of subject that didn't have anything to do with beds or sleeping together, she asked,
"That's the only way to get here? Hiking? How'd they
even build this place?"

He gave a small shrug before heading back to the
closet he'd been checking out earlier. "Some people will
pay a lot for privacy."

"Huh." Cara thought about it for a long moment. "I
think I'd prefer to have a nice paved road and driveway
that an ambulance could drive up, just in case."

His half smile touched his lips, but he didn't agree or
disagree, just waved toward the contents of the opened
closet. "Clothes in here if you want to change. There are
some boots and a winter coat in the closet downstairs
that look like they'd fit you."

She blinked silently at him for a moment. It warmed
her insides that he'd cared enough about her comfort to
bother, even if it was just so she could walk faster when
they hiked the rest of the way to Red Hawk the next day.
"Thanks," she finally said, realizing when his expression turned quizzical that she'd been quiet too long.

"You'll probably find other things in there." He
nodded toward a dresser but didn't exactly look at it, an
unusual awkwardness in his stance that tipped her off to
why he was acting so strangely.

Her nose wrinkled. "I'm not stealing someone's used underwear," she said resolutely. "That's a line I'm not crossing."

He muttered something that Cara interpreted as "Suit yourself, but please stop talking about underwear." Striding toward the spiral stairs, he said more audibly, "Soup's likely hot."

She hesitated by the closet, tempted by the idea of warm, dry, clean clothes that weren't the pajamas she'd been wearing since being kidnapped the night before. Maybe she could squeeze a shower in before eating?

"Come eat. Water heater needs to fill first," Kavenski called from the bottom of the stairs as though he could read her mind. Her stomach grumbled agreement, so she reluctantly left the strangers' clothes and jogged down the stairs.

This is great, her internal voice said sarcastically. *Now the owners will find you in their house, in their bed, and in their clothes*.

"Hush," she muttered, and hurried to rescue the soup before it boiled over. "It's not like we could ask them first." Still, guilt nibbled at her. Staying at the cabin with Kavenski felt almost too comfortable. It made her feel like they weren't in the middle of a desperate situation. She needed to remember that indoor plumbing or not, they weren't safe yet.

As she descended the stairs, the wind roared down the woodstove flue, creating an eerie whistle. Cara shivered and glanced at the covered window. Despite the cozy cabin and Kavenski's reassuring presence, deadly danger still lurked outside.

CHAPTER 12

THE SOUP TASTED HEAVENLY, BUT THE HOT SHOWER HAD been even better. Cara's borrowed clothes—yoga pants and a long-sleeved T-shirt—were slightly long and a tad snug around her chest and bum, but it still felt wonderful to change. Even though it had been less than twenty-four hours since stupid Stuart had shown up on her front porch, it felt like months had passed since she'd felt safe. She could almost smell terror on her clothes, as if her fear had worked itself into the very fibers of the fabric.

The cabin owners either had to be forgetful packers or have lots of friends visiting, because there were plenty of sample-size toiletries and toothbrushes in their unopened packaging. Cara had even discovered a comb and a package of disposable razors. Afraid that the blow-dryer would push the limits of the solar batteries, she towel-dried her hair and then combed it out, leaving the strands lying damply over her shoulders.

She walked out of the bathroom, the dry heat of the woodstove feeling harsh after the warm steam from her shower. Her skin felt instantly tight, so she got a glass of water from the kitchen and chugged it. Her head already hurt from hitting it against the car window. She didn't need a dehydration headache making things worse.

"What are you doing?" she asked curiously as she joined Kavenski by the fire. He was sitting on the edge of the couch, hunched over as if he was examining something on the coffee table. For just a moment, she contemplated sitting on the couch with him, but then her practical side won out, and she headed for the chair instead. As she curled up with her bare feet tucked underneath her, she eyed what looked like two handheld radios sitting on the table in front of him. Her heart gave a swift beat of excitement. "Radios?"

He sat back, his legs sprawled wide. "Walkie-talkies," he corrected. "No batteries."

"None?" She wasn't sure what the difference was between walkie-talkies and radios, except that the first was sold as a toy and the other was used by first responders. *Range, maybe?* It didn't really matter if there was no way to power them.

"None. I checked the whole cabin except the bathroom." He glanced over at her.

Interpreting his silent question, she shook her head. "Nothing battery-operated that I found." Stupidly enough, her cheeks warmed at the words, and she was annoyed at her reaction. *Battery-operated* just sounded so suggestive. Not wanting him to guess why she was flustered, she hurried to keep talking. "There's a blow-dryer, but I didn't find anything else that needed powering up. All the toothbrushes are the manual kind. What about flashlights or smoke detectors?"

"Wrong sizes." His wide shoulders twitched in a shrug. "Doubt they'd have the range to communicate with anyone useful anyway."

Even so, it was frustrating to have a communication

device that they couldn't use. "What about a satellite phone?" After he shook his head, she suggested without much hope, "Internet?"

"No."

Making a sound of disappointment, she settled a little deeper in her chair. "I suppose I should be happy that there are walls and food and a fire. Oh, and a bed." *For Pete's sake, why do I keep bringing up that bed?*

He didn't react except for a grunt she took as agreement.

"What time is it?" She looked around for a clock but didn't see one, not even on the stove. She felt a ping of longing for her home, with its multiple clocks and phones and internet—not to mention the sisters, Warrant, and her own bed.

"Around seven."

Now that she had eaten and showered, she expected to be exhausted, but instead she was wired. The expansive windows made her feel like a tropical fish in an illuminated tank. Despite Kavenski's assurances that Abbott's guys weren't outdoor people, she still felt exposed. Unable to sit still without the distraction of conversation, she popped up and walked over to the bookshelf.

"Ugh," she muttered after skimming over the titles on the spines.

Kavenski gave a huff that sounded suspiciously close to laughter, and Cara remembered that he'd checked out the books earlier.

"Do you think they actually read these, or are they just for show?" She pulled one out and flipped it open. The book was pristine, its sober navy-and-burgundy cloth cover spotless enough to have fit in any bookstore. The spine even gave a soft creak, as if it had never been opened before.

"Show," Kavenski answered with absolutely no hesitation.

"Yeah." Closing the volume, she slid it back between its equally untouched-looking brethren. "I can't imagine anyone reading these for *fun*."

Disappointed at the reading selection, she roamed the cabin, peeking in cabinets and the closet, feeling a renewed pang of guilt for nosing around when the owners were kind enough to let them use the cabin—albeit unknowingly.

She was distracted from her remorse when she opened a cupboard next to the fridge to find several board games. "Score!" she cried, although her voice was somewhat muffled as she reached in to pull out the stack. They were obviously older, and the boxes were creased with use, but they'd be better entertainment than those books.

"Batteries?" Kavenski guessed.

Somewhat deflated, she glanced down at the Monopoly box. "Well, no. Games. I suppose that batteries would've been more useful. At least these will help distract us from our situation." As Cara spoke, the thought of her sisters popped into her head again. They had to be beyond frantic by now. She didn't know if it would be better if Molly had gotten the text before the phone was destroyed or not. All she could hope was that her sisters didn't cross paths with Abbott or any of his people in their search for her.

Blinking suddenly hot eyes, she focused on the pile

of games she was holding. Setting them on the counter, she flipped through them, sorting them into two stacks: fun and not fun. Returning the not-fun ones—including Monopoly, one she'd hated since she was a child, thanks to Charlie's habit of reducing her to homelessness and bankruptcy—back to the cabinet where she'd found them, she grabbed the three that had made her *yes* pile.

"Okay," she said, bringing the games over to the coffee table. "We've got Connect 4, Battleship, Life, and Clue." Taking a seat across the low table from Kavenski, she glanced up at him expectantly.

Instead of picking a game, he stared at her.

"Well?" she prompted when he held his silence. "Which one? Don't get too invested yet, though, since we have to check if all the pieces are still there. Can't sink a battleship if it's already lost."

His stare didn't waver, but she waited him out this time. "You want to play a game," he finally said. "With me."

"Yes." She drew out the word, not understanding why he seemed so incredulous. "It's just the two of us here, so no one will ever know that tough and scary Henry Kavenski played a kids' game. Please? Your cabinmate is bored and needs a distraction." When he didn't look convinced, she started to get a touch aggravated. "A cabinmate, I might add, who was kidnapped last night and almost died several times because some wannabe crime boss needs information from *you*."

Even though he held his stony expression, Cara thought she detected a hint of softening and pushed her case.

"Let's play Clue," she said, moving the other games to the side. "It seems like something you'd be good at."

"Why do you say that?" His words had enough snap to make her meet his narrowed gaze.

"Why play Clue?" she asked, confused. For someone who didn't want to choose a game, he sure seemed to have strong opinions about this particular one. "We don't have to if you'd rather pick one of the others."

"No, why would you think…" He paused, looking at her more intently than her simple question called for, and she stared back as she tried to puzzle him out. "Never mind," he finally said, his focused intensity fading a bit. "If we're going to do this, let's play."

"We are going to do this." She gave him her best commanding schoolteacher glare, which she might have stolen from Molly. "We are going to play a game, and we are going to have fun—or at least be distracted somewhat from the life-threatening circumstances we are currently in. Got it?"

His mouth twitched, and the crease on his forehead finally smoothed. "Got it. Not Clue, though. Doesn't work with two people."

"Oh." A little disappointed, she exchanged the game box with another one. "Battleship, then?" His chin dipped in acceptance.

As she pulled out the pieces, she eyed Kavenski's position on the couch and frowned.

"On the floor, buddy," she ordered, shifting back so she could pull the table away from the couch to give him more room. The warmth radiating from the woodstove felt good on her back.

"Why?" Although it came out as a grumble, he did lower himself from the couch to the rug.

"Because you could see right over the top to where I'm strategically locating my fleet." Even sitting on the floor, he seemed enormously tall, and she gave him a suspicious glance. With a long-suffering sigh, he shifted his upper body down so that the middle of his back was leaning against the front of the couch.

"Better?" He sounded so martyred that she was almost distracted from the way he'd stretched his sprawled legs under the table. They weren't close to touching her crisscrossed knees, but just being inside the V of his legs felt weirdly intimate.

She made a sound that she hoped conveyed a grudging affirmative, although she worried that she might have sounded a bit like a dying duck instead. *Focus on the game*, she told herself, giving her ships her attention. They were both quiet as they arranged the plastic pieces, the click of the pegs connecting to the board the only sound except for the crackle of the fire and the muted howl of the wind outside. She started getting excited about the game. Unlike Monopoly, she'd almost always beat her sisters in Battleship. She attributed her winning streak to planning her ship search, rather than just randomly calling out letters and numbers. Wind whistled down the flue again, but it didn't seem so creepy this time. If she didn't think about all the events of the day, she could almost pretend that she and Kavenski were vacationing in a remote cabin by choice.

The thought of the two of them taking a voluntary trip together made her stomach swoop and clench in both good and bad ways, and she peeked at him over the tops of their game boards. Since it seemed as if she couldn't get away with anything without maximum embarrassment, he immediately looked up and met her eyes.

"What?" he asked.

Willing her cheeks not to redden, she tried to play it cool, lifting her eyebrows in imitation of his expression. "Ready?"

"Yep. Shoot." His mouth twitched at the double meaning, making her smile.

"Okay." She rubbed her hands together with honest glee. Even when she wasn't trapped in a cabin trying to distract herself, she loved games. One of the reasons she'd decided to major in elementary education was because a big part of her job would be playing with kids. She couldn't wait until she had her own class of kindergartners, but for now she'd just have to play with Kavenski. "D-six."

"Miss. A-one."

"Hit." She scowled at him. "On the first try?"

"I'm good at shooting games."

"This isn't really considered a shooting game." Although she considered herself to be a good sport, she couldn't help but pout a little as she inserted the red peg into one of the holes in her destroyer.

"Well, then I'm good at shooting games and Battleship."

"Humph." Her eyes narrowed as she thought. Now she really wanted to win. "J-ten."

"Miss. A-two."

"Hit." She grumbled under her breath as she inserted the peg in the second, and last, hole. "Sunk."

Even though his expression stayed as stony as usual,

smugness positively radiated off him as he put a red peg in the top of the game board.

"You're trying to punish me for making you play a game, aren't you?"

A small smile appeared for a microsecond—just a tiny flicker before his typical scowl returned—but it was enough to warm her insides and erase all her annoyance at losing her destroyer so quickly. When it only took four more turns for him to find her submarine, however, all that irritation returned in a hurry.

"How have I still not found any of yours?" she grumped. "C-eight."

His eyebrows bunched together. "Hit."

Her hand, which had already been reaching for yet another white peg indicating a miss, paused. "Are you serious?"

His crabby look was answer enough, and she gave a victorious whoop as she grabbed a red peg. It didn't even sting as badly when his next guess hit the middle of her sub.

"C-nine," she guessed, unable to hold back a grin. She wasn't winning, or even close, but it was fun to finally find one of his ships.

"Miss."

That took the wind out of her sails a little, but she was still hopeful, even when his next turn sank her submarine.

It took only two more turns for him to stumble onto her battleship, but she almost didn't care, since her next guess had to be a hit. "B-eight."

"Miss."

"Wait...what?" She stared at the top of her board.

With the latest miss, the single red peg was completely surrounded by white ones. "That's impossible."

"No, it's not. You missed."

"I can't have missed. There aren't any ships with only one hole." When he lifted one shoulder in a shrug, she narrowed her eyes at him. "You're cheating!"

"Am not." He widened his eyes in what she thought was supposed to be an innocent look, but it just emphasized the devilish glint as he ever so casually reached for his board. She popped up as quickly as she could, needing to see his ship arrangement before he could fix things.

All of his ships were clustered in a corner, nowhere near where she'd managed to get a hit. "Did you *move* them?" she demanded.

"Well, sure."

She blinked, not having expected him to just admit it outright. "You're not allowed to just move them."

"Why not? Real ships can move."

"But—"

"If a ship's taking fire, you're just expecting it to sit in the same place, waiting to be sunk?" He tsked. "Not in my navy."

A laugh sputtered out of her. "In this game, the rules say you can't move them after you start, not unless you're a Cheaty McCheaterface." She reached over and grabbed one of his ships, intending to put it back where it'd been when she'd hit it, but he caught her hand and tried to retrieve it.

"I'm not losing any ships on my watch," he said, using both hands to try to pull the plastic piece from her grasp. She quickly figured out that he was trying very hard not to hurt her, and she was willing to use that to her full advantage. Her position bent over the coffee table took away her leverage, so she stepped onto the wooden surface.

She could tell that he was surprised by her move, and she used that to twist out of his grip. As soon as she was free, she jumped off the table and ran, unable to hold back a gleeful shout of triumph. Who knew that years of wrestling things away from her sisters would build necessary life skills?

She didn't even manage to get a stride in before a thick forearm caught her around the middle. With a laughing shriek, she was pulled off her feet and back against Kavenski's chest. Holding her with one arm, he tried to pry the ship out of her hands, but his gentleness was still his greatest weakness.

Squirming and breathless with laughter, she managed to cling to the game piece, but she wasn't able to free herself from his hold. As she tried to wiggle out from under his left arm, she managed to get him off-balance, and he took a step back. Suddenly, they were both falling, tumbling down to land on the couch.

Kavenski's back hit the cushions as she landed on top of him, the hard surface of his chest and abs knocking the breath out of her. Slightly stunned, she stared down into his equally startled face before she regained her bearings. Once she realized what had happened, she started giggling.

He attempted to frown, but it wasn't even a good effort. There was too much laughter in his eyes for him to look menacing. "Return my ship."

"Or what?" The words came out so breathless and husky that Cara almost didn't recognize her own voice.

"War." His arms had been banded around her, keeping her from rolling off the couch when they'd fallen, but now they moved. She only had time for a short, silly moment of regret that he wasn't holding her any longer before his hands were moving over her, searching for the sensitive places most vulnerable to tickling fingers.

"Nooo!" she cried out, her laughter picking up again as she clamped her arms against her body, flattening herself against him and tucking her head beneath his chin, trying to minimize exposure. Still, he was relentless until she gave up. "Okay, okay! I'll give you your ship back."

Only when his hands moved to flatten against her lower back did she dare raise her head. Looking at his amused face, she wondered how she could've ever thought of him as closed-off. Now that she'd gotten to know him better, she could see all sorts of things chasing across his expression.

"Here." She carefully placed the battleship on his forehead. "But know that you are a cheater, cheater, pumpkin-eater, and I'm never playing board games with you again."

He glanced up, as if trying to spot the ship, and she laughed. "Never? What if we're snowed in here for weeks?"

She felt her eyes widen as trepidation filled her. "You think we're going to be stuck here that long?"

"Probably not."

When she saw the slight upward curl of his lips, she thumped her fist lightly against his chest. "Rude. You scared me." She tried to infuse her huff with more annoyance than she actually felt in order to hide that she was really enjoying lying on him like this. "And no. Even if we were snowed in here for *months*, I wouldn't play with you."

That wicked curve of his mouth was back. He gave a small shake of his head so that the game piece toppled off onto the sofa. "You wouldn't play board games."

"Right." Her voice was both sultry and absent as she studied his mouth. Normally, his lips were set in a hard line, but now that they were relaxed and actually smiling a little, he was a hundred times sexier. That was a problem, since she was already having a hard time keeping her head on straight when it came to him. She shouldn't be playing with him, or wrestling with him, or—and this was the most important—lying stretched on top of him, her body touching his from chest to toes. "No board games."

"So other games are still a possibility?"

Her lips parted as she tried to think of a rejoinder, knowing she needed to shut him down hard, but her body's insistent need was distracting her, making it hard to think logically when she just wanted to go along with this flirty conversation and feed the hunger she could see in his eyes. It was the same hunger that pulled at her belly, urging her to do something extraordinarily stupid, like lean down and kiss him.

His eyes heated even more, as if he could read her thoughts and approved heartily. One of his hands skimmed up her back and under her hair, his fingers burrowing through the strands until his palm cupped the back of her skull. It took hardly any pressure for him to urge her head down until their mouths were just a breath apart.

For a long moment, they froze in that position. Cara could feel the heat from his breath and skin brushing her lips, and she was so tempted, more than she'd ever been before. She wasn't sure if he moved or she did to close that last fraction of an inch, but either way, their lips were touching, and she wanted it more than anything.

At first, the kiss was exploratory, their lips brushing and grazing as if trying to figure each other out. Then it was as if a switch had been flipped, and Kavenski's bossy side showed itself again. His mouth took over the kiss—or tried, at least, but Cara held her own. Ever since she'd first seen his mug shot she'd been wanting to do this, and now that she had her chance she was going to explore the way she so desperately wanted.

Their mouths dueled playfully, each trying to take over. It reminded Cara of how gentle he'd been while trying to get the game piece back, except that this was more intense and a lot more enjoyable. She nipped at his lower lip, drawing a groan from him that ended in a growl. Pressing his lips more firmly to hers, he wrapped an arm around her back and shifted both of them in a dizzying whirl.

By the time Cara realized that she was no longer on top, he was kissing her again, and she found it hard to care that she no longer held the position of power. Besides, he was still playing the back-and-forth game with her, giving and taking as they explored each other. It was impossible to focus on anything except the kiss, the feel of his lips and tongue and teeth as they moved against hers, and the secure press of his chest over her, bearing her down into the sofa cushions.

Everything about the horrible, ugly past day fell away, leaving only Henry Kavenski and his talented, beautiful mouth.

CHAPTER 13

HENRY'S WEIGHT PRESSED HER INTO THE COUCH JUST enough for Cara to feel secure without being suffocated. That was Henry in a nutshell—safe but exciting. She smiled against his lips at the thought before getting lost in the feel of him again. With his mouth on hers, she could forget about everything outside their cozy cabin. It felt like the two of them were the only people in the world at the moment.

A muted roar followed by a sharp cracking sound yanked Cara out of her kiss-induced tunnel vision. Henry turned to look at the woodstove, where the fire blazed ferociously for a few seconds—fueled by the gust of wind down the stovepipe—before settling back down to a flickering smolder.

There's a metaphor in there somewhere, Cara thought, torn between irritation that the noise had interrupted the most intense kiss she'd ever experienced and relief. Things were already so messy. They didn't need to throw another container of gasoline on the raging dumpster fire that was their current situation, no matter how amazing that fire had felt.

Henry turned his attention back to her, and their mouths were suddenly too temptingly close together. Catching her rogue gaze focusing on his lips, she yanked her focus back to his eyes, which were another issue. The blue that was normally glacially cold burned like the hottest flame, and she felt warmth rushing to her face—and other parts of her body that were already overheated.

She wasn't sure where to look, so she settled on right above his eyes. There couldn't possibly be anything sexy about eyebrows. "Umm…" Her brain hunted for something—anything—to say, but all she could concentrate on was how incredible his lips had felt against hers. His forehead creased, and his eyebrows pulled together, his silence continuing until she couldn't help but meet his eyes again, needing to know what he was thinking. As soon as she did, she wished she'd just kept kissing him, because the hot hunger in his gaze was quickly being replaced by resignation. He closed his eyes and sighed.

"Yeah, you're right." He moved away from her, and she pushed up to sitting, drawing her legs in closer to her chest. Instead of sitting next to her on the couch, he moved to the armchair. Even though the practical part of her knew that this was best, she still hated how cold she felt without his huge body pressing her so securely into the cushions.

Cara blinked as his words finally registered. "I didn't say anything."

"You're thinking that we shouldn't have done that."

Her first instinct was to argue, but that logical part of her brain had been telling her how stupid getting physically involved with Kavenski would be. Even though the rest of her was screaming at the reasonable part to be quiet and let her enjoy their explosive chemistry, she couldn't deny that going any farther—or even just continuing the kiss—would be monumentally dumb. Her tumbling thoughts and conflicting emotions kept her quiet.

Henry dipped his chin as if agreeing with something she didn't say. "Like I said, you're right. You're already much too involved in my mess." He stood abruptly. "We should get some sleep. Expect an early start tomorrow."

"Okay." The mention of sleep set off a whole new avalanche of heated mental images, but she tried to hide the direction of her thoughts. "I'll stay down here. You can have the bed upstairs."

He frowned at her. "It's going to be hot this close to the stove."

"I'll be fine." Despite her words, she could already feel the radiating heat baking her skin. *It's just residual kissing heat*, she assured herself. *As soon as he leaves the room, I'll cool down again.*

"Don't be stupid," he said. She glared at him, but he just scowled right back and continued, "You're going to cook down here."

She opened her mouth and closed it again as too many responses ran through her head, her thoughts jumbling before they could make it out of her mouth. If she kept protesting, she'd sound like she was being stubborn for no reason or, even worse, make it obvious how much she wanted him. Finally, she just threw up her hands. "Fine."

His glare still in place, he hesitated for a moment, as if he hadn't expected her to give in so easily. She hid a tiny smile, glad she was able to throw him off-balance, even if just for a moment. Quickly, he seemed to shake it off and headed over to add more logs to the fire.

"Want some water?" she asked, heading to the kitchen and opening cupboards until she found a couple of water bottles.

"Sure. Thank you." Again, there was a tension-filled pause, making her wonder if he was feeling as tempted as she was. A glance at his closed-off expression made her quickly dismiss the crazy thought. Henry Kavenski never lost his cool, rational head—at least not while she'd been around.

At the sink, she filled and capped the water bottles, and she decided to make it her personal mission to get Henry to lose a little bit of his self-possession. Now that his facade had cracked, showing her the blazing emotions behind his mask, she wouldn't be satisfied until she broke through completely. A wicked grin spread across her face. Of course, surviving the hike to Red Hawk tomorrow would be the priority, but if she could get an expression or two out of the man on the way, that would be a bonus.

"What?" he asked suspiciously as he accepted the filled water bottle she offered. Her smile must've lingered.

"Nothing." She tried to put all the innocence she could in that one word before heading up the stairs, feeling his eyes on her back the whole way.

Once she saw the bed again, her skin prickled with renewed heat. It just looked so *small*, especially because Henry was so *big*.

"Act like an adult," she muttered under her breath. "He's obviously not bothered by the possibility of temptation, so you need to just suck it up and keep your hands to yourself. Of all the bad things that happened and the even worse things that *could've* happened today, having to share a bed with a hot guy in a luxurious cabin with a bathroom and a decent supply of board games does not even belong in the negatives column."

"Are you talking to me?"

Henry's voice was so close that she jumped a foot and a half before whirling around to see him at the top of the stairs.

"No." Her mouth wanted to open again to spew out guilty-sounding nonsensical babble to relieve the growing pressure the situation was building inside her. Having him standing there, looking so kissable, was not helping matters. Somehow, she managed to snap her jaw closed after the one word, but that left a sizzling, almost unbearably charged silence in its wake.

His eyebrows rose a fraction in a way that looked almost amused. Reaching back, he grabbed a handful of his shirt and pulled it over his head. Before Cara could close her eyes, she had the image of Henry's broad, hair-dusted chest imprinted onto her brain.

"A little warning next time you decide to get naked would be nice." Her voice sounded choked to her own ears as she whirled around to face the bed. Her body heated from the inside out.

The sound he made could've been a scoff or a laugh or even a suggestive growl, but Cara dragged her brain away from the strip show happening behind her and tried to think about other things. She had to, or she would self-combust immediately.

"What side of the bed do you want?" As soon as the words were out, she wanted to slap a palm over her face. Why was she making this so weird? The only reason they were in this situation was because they were trying to survive, but her brain kept insisting on turning everything into a scene from a romantic comedy.

When he didn't answer, she risked a glance at him, making sure to keep her eyes above chin level. To her relief—and disappointment—he'd pulled on a T-shirt and a pair of sweatpants. Both fit much too tightly, and the pants barely covered his shins, so she assumed that the original owner must be a quite a bit smaller than Henry.

He looked back and forth between the spiral stairs and the French doors leading out to the balcony. "I'll take the side closer to the stairs," he finally said, although he didn't sound happy. "Too many possible points of entry into this place."

"You weren't complaining when you broke in earlier," she said, placing her water bottle on the nightstand next to her side of the bed.

His scowl deepened. "Not helping."

"Sorry." Despite her apology, Cara had to duck her head to hide her smile. Her amusement disappeared when she glanced toward the balcony doors, however. Henry had turned the lights off downstairs, so the cabin was only lit by the fire in the woodstove. The exposed French doors somehow made things spookier. Her imagination conjured up all sorts of nightmares waiting just beyond that dark glass. Now that he'd mentioned it, she could easily picture someone scaling the balcony and breaking into the bedroom while they slept. She shivered, unable to look away.

"Get in bed." Henry's voice broke the frightening spell, and she turned her head from the French doors and the unknown that lay beyond them. He must've misread her hesitation as a reprimand for his bossiness, because his tone mellowed when he continued, "You're cold."

Rather than explain why she was freaked out, she took the excuse he offered and folded back the covers to reveal a bare mattress beneath. "You didn't happen to see any sheets when you were nosing around, did you?"

Wordlessly, he turned and opened the closet, pulling a set of folded flannel sheets from the top shelf. As he brought them over, Cara pulled the covers off all the way. For some reason, she half expected him to dump the sheets on her and watch while she made the bed, but he did his part with the hospital-cornered efficiency that screamed boot camp—or nurses' training.

As she held a pillow under her chin so she could slide a case over it, she studied him curiously. She'd investigated his background, but she'd been focusing more on the crimes he was accused of and possible places he might be hiding out. This small detail made her realize how little she actually knew about the facts of his life.

"Were you in the military?" she asked, making him pause with another pillowcase in his hand.

"Not really."

Frowning, she said, "That's not a good answer, as answers go."

For that, she got an amused upward lip twitch in response, but no clarification.

"Were you trained as a nurse?" She was determined to get some answers out of the man. For as close as she felt to him, she knew very little about the details of his life.

He blinked. "As a medic, yeah. How'd you guess?"

"The hospital corners on your sheets." She could tell he hadn't expected that answer, and she gave herself a point for surprising him. "Plus, there's that way you look at me when you think I might be injured. It's clinical, but also…not." Her skin warmed as she thought about the way his eyes blazed with concern for her whenever she was shot at or almost blown up or driven off a cliff.

He made a *hmm* sound, even as his gaze locked on her. The heat in his expression made her squeeze the pillow she still held to her chest.

"Yeah." Her voice was husky. "That's the look, except with a double helping of lust."

A laugh burst out of him, and she gave herself a solid ten points and a high five for that.

Ducking her head to hide her pleased smile, she dropped the pillow onto the mattress and flipped the thick quilts over the newly made bed. As she climbed in, giving a little shiver at the cool flannel against her bare feet, Henry crossed the room and checked the lock on the French doors. When he turned back around, she could see he was scowling again.

"What's wrong?" She drew the quilts up to her chin, feeling like a kid hiding under the covers from the things that went bump in the night—although Abbott's boogeymen were all too real.

"That lock's too…" His voice trailed off as he met her eyes, finishing with a brusque wave of his hand as if he was dismissing his concerns.

"What?" His uncharacteristic hesitance made her even more worried than she'd been before he'd answered—or *hadn't* answered. "What's wrong with the lock?"

"Nothing's wrong with it." When she raised her

eyebrows skeptically, he relented. "It's just not the kind I would've chosen if this were my place."

She couldn't hold back a snort.

"What?" He echoed her earlier question.

"As if you'd have French doors on your house." He gave her a look but didn't argue, and she grinned in triumph. "Your dream home is probably an underground bunker with enough supplies to last through a nuclear winter."

He looked slightly put-out, but she noticed he still didn't deny it.

"You wouldn't even want a window, much less a French door with a piddly lock."

"I'm fine with windows." He sounded a bit grumpy that she'd read him so well. "As long as they have bullet-resistant glass and solid locks."

"And bars?"

Shooting a final glare at the French doors under discussion, he circled to the other side of the bed. "No. Not crazy about bars."

His grim expression reminded her that he'd been behind bars, at least for the short time before he'd bonded out. Her urge to tease him more about his love of home security faded, and she burrowed deeper under the covers before changing the subject. "Did you check all the doors and windows downstairs to make sure they're locked?"

His *What do you think?* look was answer enough. Before he got into bed, he paused for a fraction of a second, making Cara wonder if he felt any of the heavy sexual tension that she did. Then he was climbing in, as expressionless as always, and suddenly his muscular body was very, very close. She went still, not wanting to accidentally touch him but, at the same time, really wanting to intentionally touch him.

Quit being ridiculous, she scolded herself before turning onto her side so she was facing away from him. The problem with that, she soon discovered, was that she was now looking right at the French doors of doom. Not only was the darkness outside eerie and filled with possible dangers, but the flickering firelight created spooky, shifting shadows around the loft.

She closed her eyes, which helped shut down her imagination as far as murderous intruders went, but it made her so much more aware of the other person sharing the bed with her. Even though she was on the very edge of the bed, he was close enough that she could feel his heat on her back, radiating more warmth than the woodstove downstairs. He didn't move, didn't shift or squirm or even breathe audibly, and she found herself straining to hear him.

Even as aware of him as she was, she jolted, her eyes popping open, when a huge hand settled lightly on her upper arm.

"We're safe here tonight," he rumbled quietly. "No one's out looking in this snow. Even if they were, they couldn't find us. Go to sleep, and stop worrying."

Her exhaled puff of air came out too fast. "I can't just stop worrying because you order me to."

His only answer was a pat on her arm before his hand withdrew. She immediately missed it, the way his broad palm covered most of the space between her shoulder and elbow. Even with her long sleeves, she could still feel the comforting heat of his hand. He was still and quiet again, and she was back to staring tensely at the shadows, which wasn't helping her attempt to sleep. Giving up, she rolled to her back and then to her other side, making sure to stay in her little section of the too-narrow mattress.

"How long do you think we'll be hiking tomorrow?" she asked, more to break the charged silence than anything else.

"Hard to tell." He was staring at the lofted ceiling. Even in that position, flat on his back, he still looked huge to her. "Depends on how much snow we get, what the terrain's like, what obstacles we encounter."

"Obstacles like big rocks or obstacles like bears?"

In the dim, red-tinted firelight, she could see the corner of his mouth twitch. "Hopefully neither."

"Hmm." The way the past twenty-four hours had gone, she wasn't going to rely on hope or luck. "I think I'll expect the worst. That way, I'll be happily surprised when we're not dismembered and eaten."

"Probably a good idea."

Cara realized that despite the gory subject of their conversation, talking to Henry had relaxed her. Now that she was facing him, she couldn't see any of the shadowed corners of the room, which helped settle her imagination as well. Having the bulky shape of his body under the covers was comforting, and she closed her eyes again—this time because she was truly tired, and not just to hide from scary things. To her surprise, she was actually relieved to be sleeping right next to Henry. Now that they were all tucked in, it didn't seem like the unbearable temptation that she'd expected.

CHAPTER 14

SHE'D WORRIED ABOUT BEING ABLE TO FALL ASLEEP WITH
Henry, but it turned out that wasn't a problem. Waking
up…now *that* was a problem.

It was her own fault. For some reason, her unconscious self thought it would be a fantastic idea to wrap
herself around him like a four-armed octopus clinging
to a treasured toy. More of her was stretched on top of
Henry than was on the bed. Her head was using his chest
as a pillow, and she'd even grabbed a handful of his
T-shirt and was clutching it in her fist. She kept her eyes
closed for a moment, not wanting to move. She hadn't
felt so comfortable and safe in…well, *ever*.

When she finally allowed her eyes to open, she
blinked as she adjusted to the thin early-morning light.
Most of what she saw in front of her was his borrowed
shirt, stretched too tightly over his endless expanse
of chest. Luckily, she didn't see any sign that she'd
drooled. Worried that he'd wake up and see how she
was clinging to him, she decided to just peel herself
away from him as quickly as possible, like pulling off a
body-size Band-Aid.

The problem was that she didn't really want to move.
Her spot on top of Henry and under the covers was
lovely and warm, and the air stinging the tops of her

ears had a cruelly cold edge to it. She knew the floor would be icy against her bare feet, too. It didn't help to know that this would most likely be the last time she was warm and comfortable that day, since it'd be filled with hiking and fording rivers and dodging bullets and probably more hand grenades when Abbott caught up to them.

Her body tensed, so she pushed thoughts of Abbott away. If these were the last comfortable moments for her, then she was going to enjoy every one. She relaxed against Kavenski for a few indulgent minutes. Without lifting her head, she couldn't see whether he was awake or not.

He was still on his back, unmoving except for the rise and fall of his chest under her cheek. One of his arms was draped over her waist. Although he wasn't holding on to her, she doubted she'd be able to slip off him without waking him—not with his ninja reflexes. That was another good reason for her to stay exactly where she was.

Not knowing whether he was awake or not was making her aware of every tiny motion she made. Even breathing took on an intensity with her chest pressed against him. Overly conscious of all the places where they touched, she found herself holding her body completely still.

Quit being ridiculous, she scolded herself. Bracing her hands, Cara pushed off his chest enough that she could look at his face.

He was wide awake, watching her.

Of *course* he was. Although she knew he couldn't stay awake all the time, she couldn't imagine him ever sleeping. Being unconscious would make him too vulnerable.

Their eyes locked, and her *good morning* evaporated along with every thought in her head. All she could focus on was the obvious desire that filled his normally stony expression. All that intensity, all that desperate hunger was for *her*—boring, cautious, lackluster bounty hunter and wannabe kindergarten teacher Cara.

He wanted her.

Without even realizing what she was doing, she lowered her head toward his, drawn in like iron to a magnet. She stopped when their lips were only a breath apart, never breaking their connected gaze.

What are you doing? a tiny, practical part of her screamed—the part that usually ran her life in an ordered and measured way. For once, she ignored it. She knew that this was dumb. It was foolhardy to involve herself any more with Henry Kavenski, who'd already swept her up into his personal tornado of trouble. Because of him, she'd been kidnapped, almost shot, almost blown to bits, driven off a cliff, and dragged through a blizzard wearing sleeves on her feet. A smart person would try to get far away from Henry as fast as she could. A smart person wouldn't be a fraction of an inch away from kissing him. A smart person wouldn't like him so darn much.

"Guess I'm not that smart," she whispered, making Henry's mouth quirk slightly.

"I disagree. You're too smart to get involved with me," he said, as if every one of her thoughts had flashed across her forehead like a digital sign.

"Guess I'm an idiot, then." Without allowing herself

to think of all the reasons she shouldn't be doing this, she closed the tiny gap between their mouths and pressed her lips to his.

As if he'd been waiting for her to take that final step that tipped them over the edge, he burrowed his fingers through her sleep-mussed hair and pressed down on the back of her head, sealing their mouths more closely together. Their kiss went from a gentle press of lips to a wild ravaging of mouths in less than a second, as if that initial contact was the spark igniting the banked heat that had been smoldering between them since their kiss the previous night.

Exhilaration rushed through her, lighting her up from the inside, and she knew this had been inevitable since the moment she first opened his file. It made no sense to get involved with this bail jumper who'd brought truckloads of trouble down on her, but it was too late for second thoughts. She'd driven right off that cliff with him. She was involved.

Without breaking the kiss, he rolled them both over so she was beneath him, being pressed into the mattress by his heavy form. It was her turn to wrap her arms around him, one hand cupping the back of his skull while the other clutched at the muscles of his unyielding shoulders. It wasn't until he released her mouth to explore the line of her jaw that Cara was able to suck in a harsh breath, but breathing wasn't that important a concern right now, not when Henry was teasing a sensitive spot right below her ear with just the slightest nip of his teeth.

Her fingers dug into his back, and she made a frustrated sound when the fabric of his shirt prevented her from touching his skin. She yanked at the T-shirt, trying to tug it up and off his body, but their closeness prevented her from removing it. He pushed himself up enough for her to drag it over his head, and then he finished pulling it off his arms before tossing it away.

The faint dawn light illuminated the hard surface of his bare, lightly furred chest, and she pushed at his shoulder until he was on his back and she was once again on top. Straddling his waist, she sat up so she could fully explore the skin that had just been revealed. As frantic and intense as their kiss had been, she felt as if she'd been waiting a long time to be able to touch him freely, and she wasn't about to rush the experience.

From his agonized groan when she traced the muscled lines of his chest, Henry was very willing to rush things.

"Patience is a virtue," she teased, flicking one of his nipples with the edge of her short fingernail.

His abs jumped, and his moan turned to a growl. "I've been patient." Grabbing the bottom of her shirt, he yanked it up, and she willingly raised her arms so he could pull it off. "I've wanted to do this since I first spotted you tailing me. I've been *plenty* patient."

With that, their positions were reversed again, and his stubbly cheek brushed the underside of her chin as he nibbled down the side of her neck. The influx of sensations made goose bumps rise under his touch, and she shivered as he worked his way to the top of her chest. She ran her fingers through his hair, clutching the strands convulsively when he finally drew her nipple into his hot mouth.

Releasing it, he blew out a breath that made her gasp as the hot air hit her breast. "You're even more beautiful than I imagined you'd be." He made his way down to her belly, and she couldn't believe that she'd just chided him about a lack of patience when she was about to scream if he kept up his torturously slow pace. Her stomach muscles twitched and flinched under the dual sensations of his smooth tongue and lips and the rasp of his stubbly jaw against her skin.

"You imagined me?" she managed to say, not caring that it didn't make much sense. She was so lost to everything she was feeling that she was impressed she was able to get a few coherent words out.

He pressed his rough cheek to her lower belly and groaned, the sound vibrating through her. "All the time. Thoughts of you kept me awake at night."

"Like a nightmare?" Her laugh turned into a hiccupping gasp as he yanked her borrowed pants down her hips.

"You *do* haunt me," he admitted, although his low chuckle took any sting out of his words. Then he was sliding down her pants, pulling them off her ankles and tossing them in the same direction that their shirts had gone. His mouth followed a path up her calf to her inner thighs and then higher, and she lost any hold she'd had on the thread of their conversation.

His mouth and fingers brought her to the edge, erasing everything from her mind except the feel of him. She called his name as she reached for him, wanting him over her, inside her, as close as they could possibly be, but he resisted her insistent tugs on his hair. Instead, he continued touching and kissing her, seeming to know exactly how much pressure in just the right spot would drive her absolutely wild. Her back arched as the sensations drew her muscles tighter and tighter until her pleasure peaked. As her climax rushed through her, intensifying with every puff of his breath on her damp skin, she clung to him, needing to anchor herself. He allowed her grip as he rested his scratchy cheek on her belly.

As the pleasure ebbed, leaving behind a warm, pleasant lassitude, she ran her fingers through his hair and let her breathing return to normal. She felt him sigh, the rush of his breath hot against her skin, before he eased away from her and sat up.

"What about you?" she asked, pushing up onto her elbows so she could see him.

"No condoms," he said with a rueful grimace, and she blinked, startled by the fact that she'd completely forgotten about the need for protection.

"Right," she said, feeling a little flustered by how open his expression was, such a change from her normally reserved rescuer. "Too bad the cabin owners didn't provide them along with the toothbrushes and board games."

The corner of his mouth twitched upward as his eyes glinted with humor, and Cara felt a rush of affection. The Henry who'd just given her the most amazing orgasm of her life was the same guy who hadn't flinched as he drove them off the cliff. There were so many facets to the man in front of her, and she wanted to know them all.

Just staring at him was rekindling the heat inside her. "It's safe—pregnancy-wise, I mean. And otherwise, at least in my case." She waved a hand at her body, even as she mentally sighed at her not-very-smooth delivery. "If you're okay…?"

"I'm clear." As if her words had flipped a switch, his need for her was burning in his eyes. "You're sure? Even though I've brought you nothing but trouble?"

"There's nothing I want more," she said completely honestly. Then a grin tugged at her mouth. "And you haven't just brought me trouble. You also brought me an orgasm. Any chance of repeating that?"

With a laughing growl that only Henry could pull off, he dove for her, flattening her to the bed in a way that reminded her of their play-wrestling the night before. Instead of tickling her, though, he kissed her everywhere, making her sigh and moan instead of laugh. The tension built inside her again, heat and pleasure rising until she was frantic for him.

She urged his face back to hers, needing him too badly for his light caresses. When she kissed him, his intensity matched hers. All teasing disappeared, leaving only raw hunger. She clutched his shoulders, digging her fingertips into the unyielding muscles of his upper back, trying to pull him impossibly close. Any space between them was too much.

When he slid into her, it was perfect, as if they were made to fit together. Her legs wrapped around his hips, pulling him even more tightly against her, and he groaned his pleasure against her mouth. All her worries fell away, and she didn't think about all that was wrong with being with Henry. Her entire being was focused on what was truly, incredibly *right*.

The feel of him, inside her body and out, was simultaneously stimulating and comforting, and she felt at that moment that she could spend the rest of her life connected to him. She'd never felt like this with anyone else, not even a hint of the almost desperate connection that attraction and danger and proximity had caused.

He rocked into her again, and she arched, pleasure tightening her muscles and heating her skin. Her hands swept down his back, needing to feel as much of him as she could reach before he drove into her again. She clutched his shoulders, loving how broad and heavy and *safe* he felt, as if he were a wall protecting her from the rest of the world.

His hips picked up speed, and she lost herself to the incredible sensations building and growing until it felt like her skin couldn't contain that much pleasure. As she tipped over into another orgasm, she gasped his name, and his movements grew wilder, as if his ever-so-tight control had finally snapped.

Even as she rode her climax, she opened her eyes to watch him come, not wanting to miss the moment when his impassive mask melted away completely, leaving only pleasure so intense it was almost painful to see.

They rested together, chests heaving against each other as they caught their breath. Even as limp and wrung out as she was, Cara couldn't stop touching him, running her fingertips over his corded wrist. As her breathing eased and her skin started to cool, Henry gathered her against him in a hug so encompassing and careful that her heart filled with affection and something even stronger. Unable to resist, she pressed her lips to his, trying to convey without words how tender and strong her feelings for him were. He kissed her back with gentle ferocity, their eyes meeting when they finally shifted away.

"I hate to say it…" His voice was rough.

"We need to go." She finished what she knew he was going to say. "I know. Our timing sucks."

A smile flickered over his face and then disappeared. Although his impassive mask descended, this time it was different. She could still see the lingering warmth in his gaze as she reluctantly climbed out of bed. The floor was freezing on her bare feet, shocking her back to reality as she hurried over to the dresser. The previous evening, she'd thought that wearing someone else's used socks was weird—even if they had been washed. This morning, she didn't care about that. All she wanted was a barrier between the icy floor and her toes. Teetering on one foot and then the other, she yanked on a pair of thick woolen socks.

"Wear layers today." Henry's voice was closer than she'd expected, making her jump and almost lose her balance. Placing her now-stockinged foot back on the floor, she nodded, but he was facing away from her, stretching. His corded arms reached up toward the ceiling as the muscles in his back stood out in defined relief. Cara suddenly found her mouth was dry, but she was unable to pull her gaze off him. He glanced over his shoulder, probably because he was still waiting for a verbal reply.

"Right," she hurried to say, dragging her gaze back to the open drawer. She couldn't keep watching him without wanting an immediate repeat of what they'd just done, but Abbott wouldn't wait for them to leave their cabin love-nest. She needed to get her head back in the game and be sensible. "Layers."

When she looked at him again, he was already halfway down the spiral stairs, with just his head and shoulders showing. "What time do you think it is?"

She hated the feeling of not knowing, of not being able to just glance at her phone and see the numbers. Once they managed to get back to Langston, she vowed to never take her phone for granted again—and to never put it down. If she had to hang it around her neck on a chain, that's what she'd do. If she'd picked up her phone before answering the door the night she was kidnapped, everything would've turned out differently.

"About six." He continued down the stairs, and Cara watched him, infatuated by the graceful way he moved and the heat and tenderness in his eyes when they landed on her. She waited for the top of his head to disappear before she shook herself out of her Henry haze and threw on a T-shirt. She slipped down the stairs after him and headed to the bathroom to clean up. Once she finished and opened the door, she immediately searched him out where he stood in the kitchen, his gaze locked on her. Even though she knew she was being ridiculous, she couldn't tear her eyes away until she climbed the stairs again and he disappeared from view.

Without the distraction of watching Henry, the cold air of the loft was much more noticeable, so she started adding layers. When she had on so many clothes that she felt like a well-stuffed sausage, she stripped the sheets off the bed and carried them downstairs. Henry was in front of the woodstove, messing with something in a pan.

"That smells good," she said as she headed to the bathroom, determined to act normal. The only response she got was a distracted grunt, which oddly made her smile. It was just so *Henry*. At the thought, she mentally caught herself. *Don't think that you know him*, her practical side warned. *Twenty-four hours on the run and one night in bed together are not a relationship.* Even as stupid as she knew she was being, she couldn't help but feel connected to him.

Dropping the sheets on the floor, she was hit by a pang of guilt at the sight of their dirty laundry, and she wished there was a washer in the cabin. The thought made her give an amused snort. "Bathroom's not enough for you now?" she asked herself under her breath. "Getting a little greedy, aren't you?"

"What?" Henry asked, glancing over his shoulder before quickly returning his attention to the pan.

"Nothing. Just telling my inner princess to chill." He gave her another look, but she just smiled and shrugged. "I wish we didn't have to leave the very nice cabin owners a pile of dirty laundry."

His own shrug wasn't at all concerned. "The cash'll make it all better." Wrapping a dish towel around the handle of the pan, he carried it to the kitchen counter where two plates were waiting. He dumped a huge pancake onto one of the plates. "Here. Eat."

She watched him return to the woodstove with the pan and a bowl of batter before turning to the beautifully browned pancake that covered the plate. "Did you actually cook on that thing? I'm impressed. I mean, heating soup is one thing, but how'd you even regulate the temperature to not char the outside and leave the inside raw?" There was a bottle of syrup—the fake, sugary kind that had a reassuring amount of preservatives in it—on the counter, and she spread it liberally over the pancake. Using a fork, she cut out a bite-size piece, realizing that she might have spoken too soon about the insides not being raw, but it was cooked and fluffy and perfect all the way through.

"Dumb luck," he said, making her laugh. She pressed her fist to her mouth to keep from sending chewed bits of pancake flying across the counter.

"Well, your luck is on point today," she said once she'd swallowed. "Which is a good thing, considering our situation." The reminder made her stomach lurch, but she ignored her worries and shoved another bite of pancake in her mouth. She'd need all the fuel she could get before they headed out.

He made a sound she took as agreement as he worked a spatula underneath the half-cooked pancake currently in the pan and flipped it with a competence she found strangely attractive. Shoving another bite in her mouth, she poured them each a glass of water as she glanced around the kitchen.

"I don't suppose you found any coffee?" she asked hopefully. When he shook his head, she sighed and took a long drink of water. "Oh well. That's just my needy princess side again."

Since he was turning toward her, pan in hand, she saw the quick flash of his smile. He dumped the newly cooked pancake onto his plate and left the pan on one of the kitchen stove burners to cool. They finished their meal in silence, although it was surprisingly comfortable. After the kiss and the bed-sharing and the unconscious cuddling and then the very conscious and intense sex, she'd expected more awkwardness, but it was as if they'd settled into their own weird routine, in which they cooked and ate and ran from kidnappers and sometimes kissed and did...other things.

The memory of that moment—well, several long moments—in bed with his head between her legs made her cheeks heat, and she ducked her face to hide it, concentrating on her last bite of pancake.

"Something wrong?" he asked, because of course he noticed the exact thing that she wished he wouldn't see.

"No." She grimaced when the word came out too quickly to be believable. "Except for, you know, everything outside this cabin." Waving her empty fork in a circle above her head, she indicated the mountains around them. As beautiful as the wilderness was, she couldn't forget that they were being pursued by potentially murderous thugs.

As if he'd needed the reminder as well, his mouth hardened, and he reached toward her empty plate.

"Nope." She snatched up her plate before he could take it and then reached for his, catching it at the same time he did. They both held on in a polite sort of tug-of-war. "You cooked, so I clean up." When he didn't yield, she gave a little tug and added, "Besides, you'll know better than I do what would be useful to bring with us."

At that, he released the plate, and she took the dishes to the sink. As she washed, he prowled the cabin, creating a pile of supplies on the table. Steam rose from the hot water filling the sink as Cara scrubbed a plate and watched him dig through the closet by the front door. She couldn't seem to get enough of watching him, and she was pretty sure the feeling was mutual, judging by the way his gaze kept returning to her. The scene felt strangely cozy, and she hurried to say something to break the too-comfortable silence before she was overwhelmed with warm and ill-timed thoughts.

"I don't suppose there's a backpack somewhere in here?" She refocused on the sink so she could rinse the plate without dropping it. "That'd be useful to carry all of the supplies."

"Not really." There was an odd note in his voice that made her turn to look at him. Henry held up a dark-green pack by one strap.

"What is that?" Cara felt her eyebrows draw together as she turned her head to the side to get a better look. When she realized what he was holding, she started to laugh. "A fanny pack?"

Making a wordless sound that managed to convey all of his disgust, he returned it to the closet.

"Oh no," she said, still trying to control her amusement. "You need to wear that. I need to be the only person in the universe who has seen wild and dangerous Henry Kavenski wearing a fanny pack." Just saying the words made her crack up again.

"No. My pockets will hold more than that thing." The gleam in his eyes made Cara stop laughing. She didn't trust that wicked look of his. "You should wear it."

"Nope." She held up her wet, soapy hands as if to ward off the pack. "You know I'm already going to be the anchor around your albatross's neck. You don't want to be weighing me down any more."

He blinked, still looking more amused than she felt comfortable with. "Anchor around my albatross? I don't think that's the saying."

Waving a hand in dismissal, she turned back to the sink and drained the water. "The albatross thing never made any sense to me. They're birds. They can fly. Why would they hold you back? An anchor, now, that makes sense. That would definitely slow a bird down."

She heard his snort behind her but focused on wiping the cast-iron pan. When that was done, she cleaned the rest of the kitchen and then moved to scrubbing the bathroom. By the time she came out, Henry had extinguished the fire in the woodstove and was sweeping the floors. The pile of supplies was gone except for their two water bottles, but the fanny pack was nowhere in sight, so Cara assumed that he'd managed to get everything to fit in his pockets after all.

"Put those on," he said, pointing toward a pile of clothes next to the closet.

"I don't know if I'll be able to move if I add even one more layer." Despite her words, she stepped into the bright-pink insulated coveralls. They were slightly long and baggy on her, but, like all of the other clothes she'd borrowed—well, taken—they'd work until she had access to her own closet again. The boots were especially welcome after her trek in Henry's coat sleeves the day before.

"Will these fit in your pockets?" he asked, holding out the water bottles. She tried, skeptical that they'd be deep enough. To her surprise, the bottles slid right in, with only the caps poking out of her side pockets. She pulled on a hat and gloves that he'd set out for her, and then waited for him to do a final sweep of the cabin. In all her heavy layers, she was warm enough that sweat made her scalp prickle. When he placed some bills on the counter, she pulled off her gloves and hurried over to write a quick note on a paper towel with a pen she'd found in a catch-all drawer. She hesitated, trying to think of what information to reveal and what to keep hidden. Finally, she decided to just keep it short and sweet.

Thank you, cabin owners! Your place saved our lives during a snowstorm.

Best wishes from two lost hikers

As she set the note by the cash, she noticed that the bills were all large and there were several of them. It would more than cover the clothes, food, and other items they'd taken, with enough left over to have the place professionally cleaned. She slid a sideways look at Henry as he pulled on a pair of borrowed gloves, torn between approving his generosity and suspicion about why he was carrying so much cash and how he'd gotten it.

"Is that money from the envelope of cash Layla gave you at the bus stop?"

His head whipped around as he fixed her with a sharp stare. "How'd you know she gave me cash?"

Cara couldn't keep her smugness from showing. "I didn't...until now."

The corner of his mouth twitched, but she didn't know if it was from irritation or amusement. "No, that money isn't from Layla." He waved her toward the door, his expression set in a way that made it clear she wasn't going to get any more information out of him. Making a mental vow to press him for more details later, she hurried out of the cabin.

As she stepped outside, Cara turned and gave the interior a final glance. As much as the first cabin had been a place of budding nightmares, this one had been a welcoming safe haven, the place where she and Henry had kissed for the first time. It had given them an escape from the storm, and she knew she'd always remember it fondly, as she would a treasured vacation spot. Knowing what dangers lurked outside its walls, she was sorry to leave the cozy little place. She'd definitely miss the bathroom.

Henry shifted his weight, and she took the hint, closing the locked cabin door behind them just as the sharp crack of a gunshot echoed through the trees.

CHAPTER 15

CARA DUCKED AUTOMATICALLY AS SHARDS OF WOOD AND bark exploded from the aspen tree a few feet from her. Henry grabbed her arm and yanked her toward him. Wrapping an arm around her shoulders, he hustled her along the path toward the trees. Hunched over, Cara ran, trying to keep up with Henry's longer legs.

Another shot rang out as they reached the tree line. Pulling her behind him, he took cover behind a pine and crouched. She followed him down, huddling as close to the ground as she could, hoping to present the smallest target possible. A loud blast made her jerk back. Only then did she realize that Henry had a pistol in his hand and was returning fire.

Clamping her hands over her ears, she moved as close to his back as possible. As much as she didn't want to be in the line of fire, she hated that he was using his body to protect her. The thought of him getting shot made her jerk in horrified reaction. He must have felt it, since he reached behind him to pat the side of her leg in reassurance.

Resisting the urge to grab that hand and squeeze it tightly, she stayed still, not wanting to distract him or throw off his aim. There was a pause in the shooting, and the silence that fell over them was so deep it made Cara uneasy.

Henry picked up something off the ground and held it back behind him, offering it to her. Confused, she accepted the rock with shaking fingers, not sure what he wanted until he made a throwing motion. Comprehension dawned, and she rose slightly to steady her base of support. Using every ounce of skill she'd honed during four years of high-school softball, she chucked the rock as far as she could throw it.

It clunked faintly against a tree trunk before dropping to the ground in a rustle of dead leaves. Immediately, a hail of bullets peppered the area where the rock had landed, and Henry held a fist behind him without taking his attention off where the gunfire had originated. Despite the terrifying situation, she couldn't hold back a tiny, proud grin as she soundlessly bumped his fist with hers.

She found the next rock by her feet, slightly smaller than the first one, but heavy enough to travel some distance. Cocking back her arm, she hurled it in the same direction, trying to send it even farther away from them than the last one had gone. It made it only a few feet past the first stone before it landed in a clump of brush, but it spooked two sage grouse. The birds exploded from the undergrowth in a flurry of wings, moving so suddenly that Cara flinched back.

Turning, Henry grabbed her hand and took off through the trees. She followed, moving as quietly as possible, dropping behind him whenever the path narrowed, but never releasing her grip. Behind them, the gunfire grew gradually quieter and more distant, and Cara hoped that the sage grouse hadn't been hit.

The snow was thin on the ground in the more heavily

wooded area, and Cara was grateful that they weren't leaving clear prints for Abbott to follow. She was also very thankful that she had decent boots to run in rather than the jacket sleeves from the day before. The trees thinned too soon, and the snow lay thicker on the ground. Dropping her hand, Henry led the way toward the edge of the trail, where the wind had blown the rocky surface clear. Trying very hard not to peek over the edge to the steep incline below, Cara kept her gaze locked on the back of Henry's jacket, pretending as if nothing could happen to her when he was there.

As if to mock that illusion, a bullet pinged off the rocky ledge by her feet, right as the distant bang echoed in her ears. With a yelp, she jumped over the next section of path, startled by the closeness of the unexpected shot.

"You hit?" Henry whirled around, looking intensely worried.

"No, just spooked," she answered, her breath coming in short huffs from the adrenaline and exertion.

His expression barely lightened as he urged her to move in front of him. Even though she hated that he'd put himself in danger for her again, she didn't take time to argue. Instead, she tore as fast as she could down the path. Another shot echoed across the silent slope, and Henry grunted.

Terrified, Cara twisted around. "Were *you* hit?"

"Grazed," he said, but she wasn't reassured. With how tough Henry could act, *grazed* could mean that the bullet barely brushed against his heart.

Before she could press the matter, he'd grabbed her and urged her into a crevice in the rock before planting himself in front of her. It wasn't large enough to be a cave, more like a depression in the rock face, but it hid them both from whoever was shooting at them— although it was a tight squeeze. Cara's face was pressed against his back, and she was right up against the wall of the crevice. In that position, she couldn't see anything, but she trusted that Henry would get them out of this situation alive. After all, they had a pretty good record of surviving whatever Abbott had thrown at them so far.

Despite this, her heart still thundered as they waited, pressed as closely together as possible. Everything was quiet except the rasp of her breathing, and she tried to take shallower, silent breaths. There was the slightest scuff of a boot against rock outside their improvised shelter, and Henry lunged forward so quickly that she almost fell forward at the loss of his support.

Pivoting to face the way they'd come, he raised his gun and fired three times in quick succession. Cara's body jerked with each loud bang, but the silence that came after was even more nerve-racking. She didn't dare move or say anything. All she managed to do was keep her eyes locked on Henry's grim profile until he turned back to her.

"Let's go," he said in a low voice, reaching for her hand. She grasped it, falling in behind him, unable to stop herself from peering over her shoulder. "Don't look."

His words came too late. Cara had already seen the two fallen figures just ten feet from their hiding spot. One of their faces was turned toward her, and she recognized the features of the second kidnapper, the one who'd almost shot her at the cabin.

"Is one of them Abbott?" she asked.

"No." Henry tugged her forward, forcing her out of her paralysis, and she tore her eyes away from the fallen men as she stumbled after him. Her feet started working automatically, even as her brain tried to process what had happened. Gradually, the numbness faded, and she kept her mind on moving as quickly as possible along the path behind Henry. She knew she'd need to deal with her reaction later; now was not the time. They were still in survival mode.

From behind, Cara could see the torn spot at the top of his left sleeve where the bullet had creased his skin. A little blood stained the fabric around the hole, but it wasn't much. He'd been telling the truth when he'd said that the bullet had only grazed him. Relief coursed through her, warming the spots that were still numb from the violence and horror. Henry was okay, and that was the most important thing right now.

"I think we've lost them."

Even as quiet as it was, Henry's voice made her jump. Giving a nervous glance over her shoulder, she asked, "Are you sure?"

He tipped his head as if considering the question—or listening for approaching footsteps. "Fairly sure. We should keep moving, though."

They continued walking for what felt like an eternity, but couldn't have been more than an hour. The early-morning sun still frosted the new snow with pinkish-gold light, giving everything a glow that seemed too perfect to be real. The wind had died down to nothing, and the air felt powdery and almost warm on Cara's cheeks.

"I feel like I might have too many layers on," she

said, keeping her voice low as she followed Henry down the trail. She felt a pang of guilt for making such a selfish complaint when two men were dead behind them, but then she reminded herself how many times those guys had tried to kill her. They wouldn't have mourned her or Henry for a second.

"See how you feel now that we've stopped running," he said, giving her an assessing look over his shoulder. "If you're still warm, you can take off a layer."

"Okay." They'd moved to a trail a safer distance from the edge, and her feet sank into the six inches of powder with each step. It was so light and fluffy that walking through it wasn't much harder than if there hadn't been any snow at all. For the second time that morning, she offered mental thanks to the boot gods as she tried to imagine how miserable she would've been if she'd tried to wear Henry's coat sleeves on her feet again. It had been bad enough on dry, mostly snow-free ground when they weren't running for their lives.

As they left the open area and began winding through another patch of trees, the snow on the ground thinned, since most of it had been caught by the branches. Keeping an eye out for any movement—from either humans or wild carnivorous animals—she jumped at every scratch of pine needles against their jackets and the *shush* of snow falling from the trees.

"Are you sure you know which way to go?" she asked, more to fill the eerie silence than because she doubted him.

"Yes."

That didn't help. He needed to contribute to the conversation, or she'd be stuck giving a monologue just to keep herself from freaking out whenever a squirrel made the tiniest noise. "How do you know?"

"Because we need to go east."

It took her a few seconds to get it. Once she did, she felt a little silly. "Right. Toward the sun."

Rather than mocking her, he just gave a grunt of agreement, which she appreciated. What she didn't like so much was that they'd fallen back into silence, and the tiny sounds were starting to make her tense up again. *Maybe it's good to be able to hear everything*, she thought, scanning the area around them. *We want some warning before someone starts shooting at us again or a mountain lion starts gnawing on our heads*. Somehow, that thought wasn't as reassuring as it should've been.

After they walked quietly for a while, the trees started to thin, and the ground grew snowier under their boots. Cara was forced to concentrate on where she placed her feet, so she could only give an occasional quick upward glance to make sure that Henry was still right in front of her and hadn't been carried off by an eagle or something while she'd been staring at the ground.

As the tree cover tapered off completely, the trail they were on grew narrower and more sloped until it blended into the rock face altogether. The snow hadn't been able to pile onto the angled surface, so the stone was mostly bare, but that didn't help much. The soles of her boots slid across the smooth, hard surface, sending a surge of panic through her. She caught her balance and managed to stop her slow, sideways skid, but she didn't want to take another step forward.

The ground under her feet sloped dramatically, making her stomach lurch. It reminded her of standing at the top of the hill when she'd gone snowboarding for the first time, and she was sure that it was too steep to survive the plunge. This time, though, the exposed rock wasn't a groomed ski trail. If she fell, she would most likely die.

"Hey." The unusually gentle note in Henry's voice brought her attention away from the slope that could easily kill her with one misstep. While she'd been preoccupied with staring downhill, he'd moved closer and was standing right next to her. Her gaze locked on his face, which was a thousand times more reassuring than looking at the rocky slope. "You can do this. We just need to make it over there, and it levels off somewhat."

When she just stared at him with wide eyes, unable to take that next step that could send her sliding down the mountain, he reached over and took her hand. "Wait," she protested, her voice sounding higher than normal. "Now I'll just pull you down with me. We both don't have to die." She tried to make it sound as though she were joking, but she couldn't hide her all-too-serious worry that her clumsiness would kill them both.

He raised his eyebrows in mock-offense. "You think you'd be able to pull me down? Please." Still holding her hand, he turned and started to make his way across the sloping ground. Pretty sure that he'd just drag her across with him if she didn't move of her own volition, Cara took one shaky step and then another. The tread on her boots gripped the surface of the rocky ground, and she relaxed a tiny bit as she followed Henry, her fingers clinging tightly to his. It was easier, she quickly found, to keep her eyes on his back, rather than looking down.

The lack of trees made the area look dizzyingly huge and empty.

It was hard to believe that her feet could grip on such a vertical slope, and every muscle in her body was tight with the fear that just one bad step could sent her plummeting down. The steepness of the ground made her light-headed when she glanced down the hill. It appeared almost vertical, and every bit of physics knowledge in her screamed that there was no possible way for them to stand on such a slope. She swayed a little, her head spinning with fear and vertigo. Henry's hand tightened on hers.

She took it step by single step, trying not to think about how far she still had to go. With each successful movement, she felt her confidence grow. Henry had been right. She could do this.

Just then, her boot slid on some loose bits of shale. Her leg pulled to the side, making her body lurch, and she knew she was going down. This was it. The slope looked steep and endless to her panicking mind, and she was furious with herself at the same time. After everything— bullets and car chases and hand grenades—a little bit of loose rock would be the end of her. Her throat clenched on a held-in scream as she braced for the moment she started falling. Her feet slid faster, sweeping out from under her as her free arm pinwheeled, trying to grab something, anything that could keep her from plummeting to the rocks below. Her shoulder wrenched as her body dangled over open space, nothing beneath her feet but emptiness.

She swung in midair, dangling from Henry's hand.

Before it even registered that she wasn't going to

die, he hauled her upright. She managed to get her feet underneath her, although her legs shook violently, barely supporting her weight.

"Okay?" he asked as she panted for breath.

Ignoring the way her legs trembled from residual fear and adrenaline, she gave a nod, not wanting to speak and hear how shaky her voice was. She was also sucking in too much air in long, heaving inhales to be able to get an intelligible word out. As she calmed, her breath came more easily, although her legs still felt wobbly.

"Ready?" He didn't even sound breathless, and he was the one who'd been holding her entire body weight.

Again, she nodded, her steps tentative as she followed him across the slope, clinging even more tightly to his hand than before. She carefully placed each foot, testing every step before daring to put her entire weight down. Only when she had her breath back and thought she'd sound somewhat normal did she say something. "You're really strong."

He shot a slightly bemused look over his shoulder. "Thanks?"

"You're welcome." That didn't seem right, though. "I mean, I should be thanking you for keeping me from falling down the mountain." She pictured herself tumbling end over end, cartoon-style, picking up snow as she went until she was stuck in the center of a huge snowball that smashed into the rocks below.

His only response to that was a barely audible grunt, which made her smile. He was really bad at accepting any kind of gratitude, which she found oddly endearing. It made her want to heap gratuitous praise on him just so she could watch his discomfited reaction. Glancing at their locked hands, she resisted the urge, grateful enough for his reassurance and help that she didn't really want to tease him.

Her foot slipped again, just a few inches, but it was enough to remind her of their precarious position. Forgetting about poking at Henry, she focused on where she was placing her feet, not looking up until she walked right into his back and realized that he'd stopped.

"What's wrong?" she asked, looking around now that their feet were planted and she didn't have to worry about taking a dangerous step. They'd reached another thin patch of trees, where the ground—as Henry had promised—wasn't sloped as severely as the section they'd just crossed. The sun was brighter, and the patches of snow covering the tree branches were dripping onto the rocky ground below, making it sound as if it was sprinkling.

"Nothing's wrong," he said, although the way his eyebrows drew in toward each other contradicted his words. "Just trying to decide on the best way."

Peering around him, Cara saw what he meant. If they continued straight, they'd run into a patch of loose, broken pieces of shale. After nearly being taken down by a few poorly placed pebbles, she could only imagine how treacherous crossing that would be. The other route took them up above the trees, and she made a face.

"We're going to have to go up more before we can go down, aren't we?"

His look was a little bit amused but even more sympathetic, which surprised her. "Yeah. You okay?"

"Sure," she answered honestly. Having Henry— especially this helpful, even *kind* version of Henry—there made everything feel achievable. There was something about his calm confidence that kept her from panicking, and holding on to his hand felt like a literal lifeline. As they started up the rocky surface that could generously be considered a trail, she could almost pretend that they were on a fun hike in the mountains. Her only complaints were her aches and pains from the day before and the sweat that was prickling underneath her multiple layers of clothes. With the bright sunshine beaming down and their brisk pace, she was starting to get overheated.

Reluctantly, she dropped Henry's hand so she could unzip her coveralls to her waist. He immediately stopped and turned toward her when she released him. As he watched, she pulled her arms out of the coverall sleeves and then pulled off her fleece top. Leaving the top part of the coveralls to hang down around her hips, she tied the fleece around her waist.

"Okay," she said. "I'm set." She waited for him to start walking again, but he extended his hand toward her instead. After a surprised pause, she took it, lacing her fingers with his. Only then did he start walking again. On this flat section of rock, she wasn't in much danger of falling unless she really tried, so she didn't need him to catch her. Still, she was pleased he'd offered. She liked having that reassuring physical connection.

Although climbing up was easier than going down, especially when the trail wasn't sloped, it still took most of her concentration to stay on her feet and keep up with Henry. Every step higher was frustrating in that she knew they'd have to go that same distance down again to get to the river. She tried not to think about that, focusing on one step at a time.

Once they'd crossed above the area with all of the broken shale, they started making their way down, criss-crossing back and forth across the face of the slope.

"If we could go straight down, we'd get there in one-tenth the time," Cara commented as they made yet another hairpin turn.

Henry gave her a wry look over his shoulder. "Yeah, but the idea is to get there in one unbroken piece."

"Good point." She climbed over a sharp, protruding rock edge. Before she could say anything else, a distant hum caught her attention. Tipping her head, she tried to identify the sound. "Do I hear traffic? Are we close to the road?" She wasn't sure if that was a good thing or a bad thing. If they could hitch a ride with a kindly Good Samaritan, that would be wonderful, but with their luck, they were more likely to stumble over some of Abbott's people out searching for them.

Henry cocked his head as if he was listening. "That's the river."

Cara's heart gave a little leap of excitement. "We're getting close?"

Lifting one of his shoulders in a half shrug, he said, "Close enough to hear it."

She narrowed her eyes at the back of his unhelpful head, but her spirits were still buoyed by the sound of rushing water. It helped that more vegetation was cropping up on and around their trail as well. Twisted, stunted pine trees with roots that seemed to be embedded directly into the stony mountain provided occasional handholds, and the melting snow mixed with the sparse dirt to provide a stickier walking surface than the slick bare rock.

The trees and shrubs grew thicker, forcing them to stop holding hands so that they could use both to push aside branches and scramble around protruding roots. The ground grew steeper and rougher, with frequent short drop-offs that made the trail look like uneven stairs designed for a giant. The closer they got to the river, the more the air cooled. Despite the fresh bite of cold, Cara appreciated the dampness after a day of extreme dryness.

Henry jumped down a three-foot drop before turning to help her. His hands gripped her hips as she hopped off the edge, and she marveled that she trusted him so completely, knowing he wouldn't drop her. He lowered her down while giving no sign that she weighed more than a few pounds. Their eyes met for a charged moment, just long enough for her to catch the hungry flash in his before he released her and turned back around.

The slick ground didn't give her an opportunity to dwell on Henry's mixed signals, since it required all of her concentration to stay upright. The mud had thickened, as the temperature was just warm enough to melt the snow and keep the ground from freezing. The muck clung to the bottoms of her boots, weighing down her feet, and was both sticky and slippery enough to be treacherous. She almost missed the smooth bare rock from the start of their hike.

The sound of the river grew to a roar as the ground leveled out to a rock-strewn shore. The spray from the water hitting the protruding rocks misted over Cara's cheeks, adding another level of cold. Her heart sank as she eyed the rushing current.

"Do we absolutely have to cross this?" She didn't

want to complain, but the question slipped out anyway as her nerves picked up. To distract herself, she pulled out a water bottle and took a drink before holding it out toward Henry. His attention was focused on the river, so she had to tap his shoulder with the bottle before he reached for it.

His brows drew together in an unhappy frown, which she took as a *yes*. "Abbott's still after us. We have to keep moving. Let's head over there," he said, pointing to the right.

Cara followed willingly as they carefully picked their way through rocks and vegetation along the bank. The reminder about Abbott spooked her, and her entire body tensed with the need to run to safety. When Henry stopped, however, she eyed the new stretch of river doubtfully.

"Are you sure this is the best spot?" she asked. "It looks even wider here."

"Wider, but slower and shallower."

"Too bad there isn't a convenient bridge." Leaning forward, she peered at the river as it twisted away from them, but she couldn't see any way to cross it without getting her feet wet. There weren't even any handy fallen logs or stepping-stones to use.

"There never is." Henry sounded grim, and Cara raised her eyebrows at him.

"Aren't *you* optimistic."

He gave her a sour look. "Why should I be? Nothing's gone right since…I was arrested." There was the tiniest pause that made her think he was going to say something else, and that made her infinitely curious. He turned back to the river before she could probe for answers. When he started stripping off his coat, she was immediately distracted. "Take off all your layers except for one, and leave your boots on," he ordered.

"Won't our boots stay wet?" she asked, even as she started pulling off her clothes.

"Better than ripping up your bare feet trying to cross." He stepped out of his boots to pull his pants over his feet before placing his feet right back into the boots again. Cara copied him, stripping off everything except her boots, a thin pair of leggings, and a long-sleeve T-shirt. She shivered in the chilly air as he bundled all their clothes together, wrapping his coat around them to create an improvised pack. Hoisting it up, he strode straight into the river.

"Okay, so we're just…doing this," Cara muttered as she followed. Even though there was no reason to delay—and she wanted to get as far from Abbott as fast as possible—she still would've liked a few moments to work up her nerve rather than just jumping right in.

The first few steps were the worst, as icy water rushed in to fill her boots. At least the water wasn't running very fast here. Instead, it eddied gently around her ankles, so clear she could see every detail of the riverbed.

"Step where I do."

Henry's order focused her attention back on him, and Cara did her best to place her waterlogged boot in the exact spot that his foot had just left. The water grew deeper, now sloshing around their shins, and it was harder to see where his feet landed. The movement of the current made it seem as if they were moving sideways, and it made her a little dizzy and disoriented.

"Don't look down. Keep your eyes on my back."

She immediately lifted her chin and did what he said. Although it was impossible to see where he placed his feet when her gaze was up that high, she instantly felt steadier.

They were almost at the halfway point, and the water ran around his knees and her thighs. It pushed hard enough that Cara felt unsteady, and she was forced to slow her steps so she didn't lose her balance. Henry's longer stride carried him more quickly through the water, and the gap between them widened.

Not liking that he was too far away to grab onto if she needed to, she tried to speed up and lengthen each step, but the water fought against every stride, wanting to push her downstream instead. He glanced over his shoulder and frowned before stopping to wait for her to catch up.

"Keep moving," she yelled over the roar of the river. "I'm fine." As much as she wanted her security blanket of a man close, she knew there was no practical reason for him to stay in the river longer just to make her feel better.

He ignored her, still watching her progress as the water flowed around his tree-trunk thighs. She struggled to move faster to reach him, but a large shape upriver caught her attention. Turning her head, she caught a glimpse of the dark wood of the massive broken tree branch caught in the frothing current.

"Henry!" she shouted, pointing at the hazard, but he barely had time to turn his head before the branch struck him, knocking him sideways into the water.

CHAPTER 16

HER HEART STALLED OUT IN HER CHEST AS CARA WATCHED Henry go down, so stunned to see him fall that her own body swayed for a fraction of a second before she caught herself. He hit the water as she lunged toward him, but she was too far away, and her hands caught on nothing but air. In the next moment, her brain kicked in, and she didn't have to rely on useless instinct.

Her leg muscles burned, the thigh-high water turning her attempted run into a nightmarishly slow slog. To her relief, he had a grip on a larger rock protruding from the surface, and he was struggling to regain his feet.

He'll be fine, she assured herself as she fought the current to get close enough to help him stand. *Wet, but fine*.

Just as she stretched out a hand, a heavy surge of water hit him, knocking him back. To Cara, it seemed as if he fell in slow motion, his head bouncing off the rock that he'd been clinging to. He went limp and dropped into the fast-running water.

Without pausing to think, she jumped after him, desperately reaching out, trying to grab an arm or a foot or even a handful of clothes—anything she could use to keep him from being carried away from her. She landed chest-first in the quickly flowing water, the icy temperature stalling her lungs and her brain. Her arms moved too slowly, and Henry's limp form was carried out of her reach as the current sucked her down below the surface. She struggled to get her feet under her, but the raging water twisted her body until she was battered and unsure which way was up.

Stunned by the intense cold, she was helpless as the river carried her downstream. The only thought that kept her from panicking completely was that she was being swept in the same direction as Henry. There was still a chance she could save him.

Her arm brushed a hard surface, and she pushed off it. Her lungs strained with the need for oxygen, and she shoved herself toward what she hoped desperately was the surface. When her head broke through the water, the air cold on her wet cheeks, she sucked in a rasping breath that sounded like a sob. The river rocketed her downstream as she strained to keep her face out of the frothing water. Her shoulder hit a rock dividing the current, sending her spinning off to the side. She knew she had to get out of the water if she was to be of any use to Henry. Every bit of her skin was numb from just her short immersion, and she couldn't feel her fingers.

The cold erased her ability to think, and panic threatened to take over as the river churned around her. Icy water slapped her in the face, stealing her breath. *Henry. Save Henry.* She clung to the thought, repeating it over and over until the panic retreated just enough for her to get her bearings. A glimpse of the far bank gave her a target, and she forced her numb arms to swim. Propelling herself toward a protruding rock, she wedged herself against it as she gasped for breath.

The current hammered against her as Cara fought to get her feet underneath her. She stood, surprised to find that the water only came to her waist. When she'd been mostly submerged, the river had felt endlessly deep. She slogged through the water to the bank, stumbling over slippery rocks and the uneven riverbed, the current maliciously trying to shove her back down, but somehow she managed to keep from falling in again.

When she finally reached the bank, her body begged her to collapse, but she knew she was Henry's last chance at survival. She ran downstream alongside the river as she scanned the water, hunting for a glimpse of him. *Why did he have to wear black?* she wondered desperately, trying to see beneath the white foam churned up by the speeding water hitting rocks and other submerged obstacles. In her panic, she resolved to make him wear blaze-orange clothing from this point on…if he wasn't already gone.

Stop! she ordered as she ran faster, the heaviness of her soaked boots feeling like an anchor. She was tempted to take them off, sure that she could get to Henry faster without them, but she didn't want to stop even for the few seconds needed to remove them. Instead, she set her jaw and pushed her legs to go faster despite the waterlogged weights attached to her feet.

A not-quite-right flash of color caught her attention, and she realized that she'd almost run right past Henry. The water tumbled over him, the white froth and reflected sunlight disguising his submerged form. Splashing into the river, she ran toward him, her breathing rough and uneven from her frantic sprint. It was deeper here than the point where they'd tried to cross, the water reaching her waist, then higher. The current shoved at her legs, trying to make her tumble over, and she automatically braced herself as she reached into the freezing water and grabbed onto Henry.

A huge wave of relief crashed over her at the feel of him in her grip. She finally had a hold on him, and her fingers tightened. She was determined not to let the river snatch him away from her again. Her joy at reaching him was quickly flattened by the realization that she couldn't move him, and paralyzing fear filled her again.

He wasn't getting any oxygen, but Cara couldn't think about him drowning or she wouldn't be able to function. Instead, she shoved down her rising panic and forced herself to look at things in a logical, step-by-step manner.

"Okay," she said out loud, the high pitch of her voice nearly sending her into a helpless flurry of terror again. "Okay, okay, okay. Why won't you move?"

Feeling along the length of his body, not letting herself think about how still and cold and lifeless he seemed, she realized that his hip had gotten wedged under the protruding lip of a boulder. The current had pushed a thick waterlogged branch up against his other side, trapping the lower half of his body against the rock.

With numb, shaking hands, she shoved the branch, fighting the weight of the pressing water until the wood was caught by the current and carried past the other side of the rock. Once that was gone and Henry was no longer caught against the side of the boulder, his body began shifting away from her.

"No, you don't." She caught his leg, clutching too hard since she couldn't feel her fingers, and there was no way she was letting him go again. Hand over hand, she worked her way up his body until she could grab underneath both of his arms. Water pounded against them, the force of it even stronger now that it was pulling at both her legs and Henry's huge, inert form.

She hauled him backward, the water providing buoyancy now that he was no longer caught. Knowing he had to get oxygen, praying he wasn't already too far gone to save, she moved so quickly that she overbalanced and fell back in the water with a splash. The water surrounded her body, the painful cold of it numbing all the skin it touched almost instantly. The current threatened to drag her farther downriver, but she fought against its strong pull.

Keeping her grip on Henry made regaining her feet awkward, but she wasn't about to let him be carried away from her again. She finally managed to stand, her muscles aching from the effort of holding him, and she backed toward the bank. This time, she went slow enough to control her movements, even though her brain was screaming at her to run, to get him out of the water as quickly as she could.

"Slow is fast," she muttered under her breath, hardly able to spare the oxygen needed to make words. "Fast is slow, and slow is fast."

Step by backward step, she dragged Henry to the edge, water coursing off both of them as the river grew shallower until the pebbles covering the bank crunched and shifted under her boots. She dragged him as far out of the water as she could manage, but he became heavier and heavier with no water to help support him. His feet were just an inch from the swirling water when she conceded defeat and eased his upper body to the ground.

His stillness was terrifyingly obvious now that he was out of the river and the current wasn't moving his limbs. Frantically searching the corners of her mind for a long-ago lesson on how to help a drowning victim, Cara tried to turn him onto his side. When he didn't budge, she sat on the ground next to him, placed the soles of her soaking-wet boots against his side, and pushed with her legs until she was able to leverage him up and over.

Water streamed from his nose and mouth, and his skin was a bluish-pale that made even his tan skin look wrong. *He looks dead.* The thought was there before Cara could push it away, but she clenched her teeth and refused to believe it. It was so wrong that Henry—always so strong and protective—was lying on the bank, completely helpless. He was her wall, protecting her from all possible dangers, but now he couldn't even breathe for himself. Her jaw set.

After all the times he'd rescued her, now it was her turn to save him.

After all they'd gone through, all the brushes with death they'd survived, she wasn't about to let him accept defeat because of a poorly placed rock and some cold water. With a final shove, she turned him over onto his back and then scrambled to kneel next to him. She tried to check for a pulse, but her fingers were so numb that she couldn't even feel his skin, so she rested her head on his chest to listen.

He was too still and quiet, making her heartbeat so loud that she couldn't hear anything outside her own body. Sitting up again, she tilted his head back, pinched his nose shut, and mentally thanked Molly for making them take a first-responder course when they'd started their business.

She blew a breath into his lungs, let it escape, and then did it again, her brain throwing unwanted comparisons to how it felt when he kissed her versus the cold, unresponsive mouth under hers now. It was almost a relief to move to chest compressions, the regular rhythm of the heel of her hand against his sternum allowing her to blank her brain of anything but counting.

Shifting back to his head, she gave him two more breaths, and then moved back to chest compressions. Back and forth, mouth to chest to mouth again, her motions became both a blurred rush and an excruciatingly slow crawl. It was between the seventh and eighth chest compression when she heard a choking noise and froze, her locked hands hovering above his previously motionless chest—a chest that was now heaving with the effort to cough.

Grabbing his arm, she helped him roll to his side, amazed and tentatively ecstatic when he did most of the work himself. As he hacked and choked and expelled what looked like the whole river's worth of water from his lungs, she couldn't stop rubbing his arm and back and side—everywhere that muscles tensed and moved when they'd been so limp and lifeless just a few moments ago.

Best of all, he opened his eyes, and his dazed expression quickly firmed into his normal Henry-ness. That was when Cara burst into relieved tears.

"What?" The question was little more than a croak, but he was awake and alive and actually talking, and that made her cry even harder. He struggled to push himself up, and still sobbing, she helped steady him. Once he was upright, she didn't let go, clinging to his arm with one hand and his wet shirt with the other. He wrapped an arm around her, holding her in that careful and secure way that was becoming so wonderfully familiar. "What's wrong?" he asked, and the demanding tone was so exactly him that it was glorious.

"Nothing," she finally managed to get out semi-coherently. "Nothing now. Everything was wrong when I thought you were dead."

"Dead?" He coughed again, and she clung tighter, irrationally worried that this was just a breathing, talking fluke and he'd fall over at any second, actually dead this time. Despite her worries, he stayed sitting up, his gaze only getting sharper and more focused. "What happened?"

"You fell." Her voice quavered as she mentally relived the moment when he went down. "Hit your head on a rock." She reached toward the spot and hovered her fingers over it without touching the lump, for fear of hurting him. "I chased you until you got stuck on a rock, and then I hauled you out and did CPR." Her gaze fell to his chest. "I didn't break any of your ribs, did I? The instructor said that's common."

His mouth actually quirked, and she wanted to yell at him that this wasn't a time for smiling or laughing or any type of amusement, because he'd come much too close to dying for anything to be funny for a very long time. "My ribs are fine," he said. "My head, though…" He reached up and, unlike her, actually probed the spot where the rock had connected with his skull. His expression went blank in a way that she took as a wince of pain.

"Concussion?" she asked, still so off-balance by his *almost dying* that checking his other injuries was strange, making her feel as if they were concentrating on the wrong thing.

"Doubt it." He went to stand, and she hurried to scramble to her feet so she could help balance him. Once upright, she reached for him and swayed, not sure if she was clinging to him to help her balance or his. Either way, it was good to feel the living tension in his muscles and the warmth of him after he'd been so cold and still.

She frowned, sliding a hand under his single wet layer to feel the skin over his abs. The physical exertion of performing CPR had warmed her, thawing her fingers and toes, but his skin felt cooler than usual, even clammy.

"Not that I'm complaining," he said, the words sounding soft around the edges, "but is now the time to feel me up?" He wasn't quite slurring, but she still looked at him sharply.

"You're too cold," she said, looking around them for the first time. "Should we start a fire?" There were plenty of downed branches and other fuel around, but they were all wet, thanks to the melting snow. Also, unless Henry knew how to light a fire by rubbing two sticks together—which wouldn't really surprise her, knowing Henry—they didn't have any way to start it.

"Where are our other clothes?" he asked, taking in the area as well.

"You dumped them all in the river when you went down like a felled redwood." There was a tiny edge to her voice that she knew was because she was worried, but she still felt bad about scolding him for something that wasn't his fault. "Sorry. You couldn't help it. The branch hit you hard."

"The branch. Right." Comprehension lit his eyes, and she knew he was remembering what had happened. "C'mon. We need to walk." As he turned, his legs wobbled and he started to go down. She tried to catch him, but his weight carried her to the ground with him. He managed to turn and take most of the impact of the fall, while she tumbled down on top of him.

The sign of weakness panicked her, and she hurried to roll off him. She knew he had to be in terrible condition to fall from just taking a step, and her stomach twisted into knots as she crouched next to his head.

"Sorry." He grimaced, already trying to push up to a sitting position.

"Just take a minute," she said, pressing his shoulder with her palm. She wasn't strong enough to keep him down if he really tried to get up, but he must've agreed that it was a good idea for him to rest for a moment, since he stopped attempting to rise. The fact that he was willing to lie there scared Cara almost as much as when he'd fallen.

She rubbed his arm, almost recoiling when she felt how cold he was. Suddenly concerned that hypothermia was making him compliant, she stretched out over him, plastering her front to his. His mouth quirked, that wry expression so Henry-like that she almost sobbed again with relief.

"What are you doing?" he asked, his words shuddering slightly as his muscles shook, his body doing its best to warm him.

"Getting you warm." She felt her own shivers ripple

through her as her clammy clothes stuck to her chilled skin, and she made a face. "Well, warmer, at least."

"We can't stay." His teeth clicked together audibly. "Abbott…"

"I know." Tucking her face into his too-cool neck, she chafed her hands up and down his arms, trying to generate some heat. She wished she were bigger—or at least had a dry blanket for him. Even if they'd had time, there was no way she could start a fire, not without dry matches. Why hadn't she done Girl Scouts as a kid?

Henry wrapped both his arms around her, holding her tight to his shivering body. "You're so nice," he said.

Her head popped up, worry stabbing at her insides. "You're not going into shock, are you?"

"What?" His eyes looked clear, and the pupils were symmetrical, giving her hope that he was thinking clearly. "No, I'm okay—just cold."

Despite his words, she continued studying his face closely.

His brows drew together, even as his mouth twitched with amusement. "I can't give you a compliment without you thinking I'm delirious?"

"Well…"

His huff was shaky but clearly a laugh, and relief trickled through Cara at the sound.

"You don't normally say things like that," she said, attempting to rub some warmth back into his sides. The places where their bodies touched were starting to heat, with just the extremities still numb with cold. "You tend to show your love in actions, rather than with words."

When he stilled, she realized what she'd implied. *Love.*

"Not that you…umm… Are you feeling warmer?"

"Yeah." His gaze stayed locked with hers, unreadable emotion there, before dropping to her mouth. "A lot warmer."

The flash of heat that shot through her made her forget ever being cold. She ducked her head, not even realizing that she'd moved until she felt his breath on her lips. *Not the time or place, Cara!* Knowing that her inner killjoy was right, she pulled back and tried to focus on practical things, but it was hard. Henry Kavenski had just professed that he didn't *not* love her. "Did you want to try to stand?"

As if he could read her mind, his mouth crooked up, but the look in his eyes was filled with affection and something else that she didn't want to think about too hard, not when she was trying to be practical. "Sure." Instead of getting to his feet, though, he pulled her tighter against him for a long moment before finally releasing her.

Reluctantly, Cara peeled herself off him, immediately missing their full-body contact. Her skin cooled as she stood, and she hopped a little, trying to warm up again. Henry pushed himself up to a sitting position and then paused for a moment, just long enough for her to start worrying that she was going to have to haul him over her shoulder and carry him to Red Hawk.

She reached down to offer help, but he pushed himself up on his own, getting steady on his feet before taking her outstretched hand. The press of his palm against hers made her brave, and she stood on tiptoes to say quietly in his ear, "I don't *not* love you, too."

He gifted her with a full, gorgeous smile, using his

grip on her hand to pull her in flush to him. "We'll make it," he promised, cupping her jaw so she met his resolute gaze. "You'll be safe."

"I know." She didn't even hesitate. With Henry, she always felt secure.

His eyes blazed with heat and something else, something like longing, and then his lips were on hers. She returned his kiss just as fiercely, determined to keep him safe as well. Breaking the kiss, he met her eyes for another intense moment before reluctantly releasing her and turning around. When he swayed, she reached out to steady him, but he managed to catch his balance. He started walking upriver, and she bit her lip with concern. Despite his best efforts, he was obviously not his usual steady self.

"Are you sure we shouldn't get you warmer first?" she asked, hurrying to catch up.

"Physical activity will work," he said. If she didn't hear the slightest burr in his voice, she would've felt a lot better, but she had a feeling that Henry wouldn't show any weakness…until he collapsed again. "Besides, the sun's out."

Hiding her anxious concern, Cara followed him along the bank. They were so close to safety. All she had to do was climb a cliff, possibly carrying an almost-drowned Henry. *No problem.* Despite the overwhelming task ahead of them, she was determined. He'd kept them safe up until this point. Now it was her turn.

CHAPTER 17

A SHORT TIME LATER, HENRY CAME TO AN ABRUPT HALT.

"What is it?" Cara asked.

He pointed to the beginning of a faint path that led up the slope before moving toward it. "Here's our trail."

As she followed, she tried very hard to be grateful for an actual path rather than their trailblazing method of getting down to the river. Her adrenaline rush was fading, however, and exhaustion was starting to set in. Her legs felt like they weighed eighty pounds each, and her soaked boots weren't helping. Every uphill step was an effort.

Henry is alive, she told herself, trying to think of all the positives to take her mind off how much she just wanted to collapse and sleep for a week. *The sun is shining. The wind isn't blowing…too hard. No one is shooting at us…at this second. Henry is alive.* She realized that she'd counted that one twice, but it—he—was worth a double count.

The thought of him brought her gaze to his back just in time to see him sway, only catching himself from falling over by grabbing the twisted branch of a stunted pine tree and using it to hold himself upright.

"Whoa," she said, hurrying to get close enough to support him in case he started going down again. "You okay?" It was a stupid question. She knew that as soon as it left her mouth. If he'd been even close to okay, he would never have wavered.

"Yeah." His paleness under his tan and unfocused eyes told a different story. "I just need to...sit for a second." His knees softened, his body sagging as if he was about to plop down right on the trail.

"No, no, no," she said, her tone halfway between panic and sternness as she looped her arms around him in a hug that was meant to keep him standing. "No sitting. We're walking. That'll get you warm and to a hospital, both at the same time." She hoped that Red Hawk had a hospital—or a doctor, at least.

He leaned in to her for too long a moment, and she had to lock her knees to not collapse under his weight, but then he straightened with a grunt of effort. She eyed his face, which didn't look any better than it had a minute ago, but at least he was standing independently.

Although he didn't say anything, he gave a grim dip of his chin and started trudging up the path again. His pace was slower than normal, and every so often a step would waver, threatening to dump him onto the muddy path. Forgetting her own dragging exhaustion, she focused on Henry's back, trying to push him up the slope with just the strength of their combined will.

He paused, swaying slightly, and Cara knew she had to get him moving again. "Let's go, big guy," she said in the most upbeat tone she could manage. Resting her hands on his back, she pressed him forward ever so slightly, afraid that too hard a push would knock him over onto his face, and then she'd never get him moving again. "I didn't get soaked dragging you out of that water so that you could fall over and die on this trail." He gave her a glance over his shoulder, and she was enormously happy to see a spark of sardonic amusement. That was the Henry she knew, the one who'd manage to get up this mountain.

He started walking again, slow and close to stumbling at first, but then he seemed to catch his stride. Without seeing his face, she wasn't sure how close he was to total collapse, but at least he was moving forward and wasn't swaying at the moment. The path gradually turned from what appeared to be a narrow deer trail into a wide, well-worn hiking route, and Cara was so grateful for its relatively even surface that she wanted to cry. Instead of having to navigate their way up the mountain, they could just grimly follow the trail, trusting that it would lead them to civilization.

Once they were far enough from the river that the trees thinned again, the wind picked up, cutting through her thin single layer. *It'll dry our clothes*, she thought, reaching for positives even as she clenched her teeth together to keep them from chattering. Henry was visibly shivering, making dread cling to her insides.

When she wasn't staring at him, she was checking for Abbott over her shoulder. As she glanced behind them for the thousandth time, a movement down by the river caught her eye. She immediately focused on the spot below them, but she couldn't see whatever it was that had grabbed her attention. *Maybe it's a deer, or a bear, or men with guns...* Swallowing hard, she turned her attention back to a wavering Henry.

"Faster," she ordered, desperate to warm him up and put more distance between them and whatever was by the river. He gave her an incredulous look, but his not-quite-focused eyes made her even more determined. "Let's go. Move it. You said you went to something like boot camp, so show me how it's done. We're running this trail now." Her body screamed a protest as she picked up a jog, but she ignored it, everything in her concentrating on the man in front of her.

His steps picked up a little speed, but he was still just walking, and the toes of his boots dragged across the rocky surface of the path. She darted another quick glance into the canyon. Even though she couldn't see anything, her heart beat faster as nervous tension slid up her spine.

"Fine," she said, putting all the attitude she could dredge up into her words. That was all that was left except for panic and terror. "I'm passing you, then. Try to keep up, slowpoke." She darted around him, taking the lead and hating that she couldn't keep her eyes on him in case he started to go down. When she heard the shuffle of his boots behind her picking up speed to a stumbling jog, the flood of relief was so strong it made her dizzy.

She allowed herself a glance over her shoulder to see that Henry was just a few strides behind her, and his gaze looked a little more focused...as he stared directly at her ass. She cleared her throat loudly, and his eyes locked with hers as his steps became more even and measured.

"Nice view," he said, and she couldn't even be embarrassed, because she was just so thrilled that he was looking almost like himself—well, a completely worn-out version of his normal self.

"Thank you," she said primly, delighted to see the corner of his mouth twitch up in a Henry-type grin.

The rest of the hike was brutal. They alternated between jogging and walking when the slope got too steep or the footing was tricky. Henry kept his focused expression, but the pallor underneath his tan grew worse, and his features drew tight with strain. Cara was so focused on keeping an eye on him and also making sure she didn't fall over herself that she almost ran into the trailhead post.

"Careful," he warned, his voice gruffer than normal.

She dodged just in time to not hit the sign head-on, and then stopped and stared for a full five seconds at the etched letters that proclaimed Red Hawk was point-two miles straight ahead. "Did we…" She didn't even want to dare to hope, in case it was an illusion and they had ten miles of upward slogging to go. "Did we actually make it?"

"Looks like," he said in words that were barely more than a grunt. She stared at the sign once again, still marveling that their hike from hell was almost over.

Henry grunted again, although this time it sounded more like air had been knocked from his lungs. Whirling around, Cara jerked back, bumping into the trailhead sign she'd just been so gleeful to see.

Geoffrey Abbott stood between them and the safety of Red Hawk, holding a pistol aimed right at them.

Cara took a sideways step, trying to get between the two men, but Henry must've had the same idea, since their sides bumped together. If she hadn't been hyper-focused on the gun in Abbott's hand, she would've glared at Henry. Why did he always get to protect her?

Why couldn't he let *her* save *him* from danger every once in a while?

"Kavenski," Abbott said, a certain smugness in his tone that exponentially increased Cara's desire to punch him in the face. "You know, all of this could've been avoided if you'd just given me what I wanted the first time I asked."

When Henry didn't respond, Cara asked, "What did you want?" She needed to keep him talking until her racing brain could come up with a plan that didn't end with her or Henry getting shot.

Abbott's gaze flickered toward her. "Just for him to tell the truth. That's all."

"What truth?" She hated that her voice shook when she wanted to sound as impassive as Henry.

"Your boyfriend didn't tell you?" Abbott sounded positively gleeful. "He's taking the fall for someone— someone I'd love to see finally go down."

"Why?" Now Cara wasn't just drawing out the conversation to distract Abbott. She was honestly interested in why Henry wasn't fighting the false charges with every resource he had.

"That I don't know. Kavenski? Care to share?"

"I have the evidence you need," Henry said, his voice deadly calm. "I'll take you to it. Hurt Cara, and I'll kill you."

His flat tone made her shiver with its utter certainty. Even if she hadn't seen him take down two of Abbott's men on the trail, she wouldn't have doubted his willingness to kill for her safety. In a morbid, violent way, she almost found it sweet. As Abbott's attention turned to Henry, Cara let her eyes dart around, trying to find someone or something that she could use to get them out of this situation. A tiny movement in the brush a few feet away from Abbott's feet caught her attention, and a rough plan began to form.

Tipping his head to the side, Abbott looked as if he was considering Henry's offer, but then he offered a cold smile. "No. It's not worth it. You're too slippery for me, Kavenski. I'm cutting my losses."

The gun barrel shifted to point directly at Henry's chest. Cara's mind raced. She was out of time.

"Don't!" She shifted, subtly bumping against Henry's side. He stiffened at her shout, but then shifted over slightly as if he could read her mind. "After all that work you went through, kidnapping me and chasing us through the mountains and everything, you're just going to give up on getting the evidence?" They shuffled over another tiny step, and Cara felt a spark of hope when Abbott moved to the side, keeping himself directly across from them.

"Like I said"—Abbott took aim again—"not worth it."

Out of time, Cara bumped Henry over another step. They were in position now. The rest of her pathetic plan was up to nature.

Abbott took a deliberate step forward, his gun hand not wavering, and Cara tensed. As Abbott's very expensive leather shoe stepped down in a patch of brush, a sage grouse burst from her hiding place just inches from his foot, flying up in a mad flutter of wings. Even though Cara had planned for that to happen, she still jerked at the movement, her tensed muscles reacting to the sudden burst of noise and motion.

Taken by complete surprise, Abbott staggered backward, his arms—and the gun—flinging up to protect his face. Recovering from her start, Cara lunged forward, ready to tackle him in her best bounty-hunter fashion. She was just a fraction of a second too late. Henry got to him first.

Moving so quickly it was hard to believe he'd almost drowned just a short time earlier, Henry hurled himself at Abbott. Grabbing the gun barrel with one hand, Henry clamped his other over the top of Abbott's fist. Jamming the pistol up, he twisted it out of the other man's grip, making him shriek with a crunch of broken fingers. Muscles tight with the need to move, Cara held back, not wanting to jump in and make Henry lose his advantage. As she watched, in awe of his efficiently brutal movements, he tossed the gun to the side.

Distantly, Cara heard it clatter down the incline they'd just ascended, but she couldn't look away from the fight happening in front of her. Pulling back his fist, Henry swung, but he staggered when Abbott dodged. As Cara sucked in a harsh breath, she felt her stomach seize with terror when Henry gave his head a shake, his eyes unfocused. He'd used up everything he had, the last tiny bit of focus and energy he'd held in reserve. Henry swayed, looking like an enormous tree about to crash to the ground.

A gleeful grin crossed Abbott's face as he yanked a switchblade from his pocket with his unbroken hand. He crouched, ready to spring at a disoriented Henry. Cara felt her molars grind together. There was no way she was letting this mob-boss wannabe hurt her Henry.

Charging forward, she drew on every self-defense

training session that Fifi had drilled into her brain. Her muscles remembered every endless repetition, falling into the correct form as she threw a straight punch right into his midsection. When he bent over, his arms clutching his middle, she snapped a front kick right at his face. Even as she moved instinctually, finding an opening and seizing it, she marveled that she was fighting—and winning. She heard cartilage crunch, and his eyes rolled back, right before he toppled over onto the ground, unconscious. For the hundredth time that day, she was grateful she was wearing boots.

When she looked away from the limp Abbott, she saw Henry blinking at her, a slow smile spreading over his face. "You're nice *and* you're amazing."

"Thank you." Warmth spread through her chest, erasing the chill of watching Henry almost get shot and then stabbed. "You're pretty amazing yourself."

They exchanged a smile before Cara turned back to Abbott's unconscious form. "I don't suppose you have any more zip ties on you?"

"No pockets." He patted his legs as if in proof, and she noticed he swayed a little. He obviously couldn't haul Abbott over his shoulder at the moment.

"Hmm… I don't want to leave him here. After all that, what if he wakes up and gets away?" She eyed Henry, considering their options. "If we each grab an arm, think we can drag him to the police station?"

That earned her another smile. "I like how you think."

"Ditto."

"Where's the hospital—if there is one. Do you know?" Cara asked a short time later as they emerged into a small gravel parking area marked with a trail map, a limp Abbott dragging behind them.

"No hospital," Henry said, his voice slightly slurred. He was staying on his feet and hauling his share of Abbott's weight, so Cara was hopeful he'd make it the rest of the way. "We'll go to the station, dump this guy, and have the paramedics meet us there."

"Good idea." She just hoped that none of the Red Hawk officers knew what bail jumper Henry Kavenski looked like. They reached the road, and she looked in both directions. There were some cabin-type homes, but nothing that looked like a police station. "Which way?"

He waved to the left with his free hand, the gesture lacking his usual forcefulness, and she could hear that his steps were dragging again. Swallowing her worry, she trudged to the left, using both hands to hold on to Abbott's arm. It had been tempting to drag him by the feet instead, letting his head bounce off the pavement, but she'd been merciful. She did hope he woke up with some aches and pains, though.

The houses were getting closer together, and a few shops came into view. All the buildings, even the businesses, seemed to be going with the mountain motif. Everything was logs and carved bears and chalet-style roofs. To her relief, the town was quiet, with no people in sight. It would've been hard to explain why they were dragging Abbott's limp form across town.

Once she spotted the building, she knew that it had to be the police station, even before Henry waved her in that direction. Only the cops could build such a utilitarian structure in this cutesy little town. She sped up, dragging Abbott behind her, thoughts of concussion and nearly drowning and hypothermia and all sorts of other things that could be wrong with Henry spinning through her mind.

He kept up—barely. His boots shuffled against the pavement, the sound of his stumbling footsteps so painful to hear from a guy who usually moved so soundlessly. Even as bad off as he was, however, he still held up his half of Abbott's weight, *and* he even opened the door for them as they entered. That reassured her he was alert and aware enough to be polite.

She dropped Abbott's arm as they passed a short row of chairs, assuming Henry would leap at the chance to finally sit down after she'd forced him to march—and run—up the side of a mountain. Without slowing, she went straight for the desk sergeant's window. The cop, a woman not much older than Cara, looked back and forth between her and Abbott's sprawled form with startled eyes.

"Can you please arrest the unconscious guy and call for medical help?" Turning to look at Henry, she jumped when she found him standing right behind her. "What are you doing? Go sit before you fall over." Turning back to the cop, she added, "He fell in the river and hit his head."

The officer reached for a radio, but before she could call for either backup or medical assistance, Henry spoke.

"I'm Henry Kavenski. I skipped out on bail, and she"—he tipped his head toward Cara without meeting her eyes—"is with Pax Bail Recovery. She found me and is bringing me in."

"Henry," Cara protested, completely shocked by his unexpected—and unwelcome—confession. Before she could protest or deny or do whatever she needed in order to keep him from going back to jail, he gave her one of his tiny smiles…and then collapsed onto the tile floor.

CHAPTER 18

THE NEXT COUPLE OF HOURS WERE A CHAOTIC BLUR.

After paramedics arrived and whisked Henry and Abbott away in a couple of ambulances—both with their own police escort—Cara was ushered to the tiniest interview room in the history of police stations. There, she told the entire story to two officers, answered their questions, *re*told the story, and then repeated the entire process when the Colorado FBI agents arrived.

When she was finally alone in the tiny room, she rested her head on her folded arms, overwhelmed with exhaustion and worry for Henry. Although they'd assured her that both men were still alive, she wouldn't—*couldn't*—believe it until she saw and hugged him herself.

A tap at the door brought her head up with a swallowed groan. Although the cops had been fairly gentle with her once they realized she was mostly the victim—and the bounty hunter who'd brought in two wanted criminals—she didn't think she had it in her to tell the story one more time. She needed food and sleep and a hug from Henry—not necessarily in that order.

The door swung open, and the first officer she'd met stuck her head in. "Your sisters and brother are here." When the cop pushed the door open wider and stepped out of the way, Cara felt a surge of hope.

"I'm free to go?"

"With Abbott in custody, you should be safe at home. We've filled in the Langston police chief on the situation, so they'll be keeping a close eye on you. If we or the FBI have more questions, we have your phone number."

Cara stood, holding back another groan and forcing a polite smile. The Red Hawk cops didn't know that siccing the Langston PD on her family wasn't a good thing. She hurried out the door, deciding to file that in the deal-with-later pile. For now, she was happy to escape the miniscule interview room and see for herself that her sisters—and brother?—were unharmed.

As soon as she stepped into the waiting room, she was mobbed. Molly, Charlie, Norah, and Felicity all tried to hug her at the same time, squeezing the air out of her until she couldn't even answer their barrage of questions.

"Are you okay?"

"What happened?"

"Are you hurt?"

"Who took you?"

"Was it that skip?"

Even Molly's boyfriend, John Carmondy, was there, wrapping his arms around the entire group like a huge, muscled shield.

With a shaky laugh of sheer relief that all her sisters were unharmed, Cara gently extricated herself from their family huddle. "I promise to tell you everything, but can we go home first? And maybe hit up a drive-through for food?"

"Of course." Molly swooped in and gave her one

hard final hug. "Anything for you, Cara. It's the rule—
get kidnapped, and we're nice to you for at least a day."

"Well, a few hours, maybe." Charlie's teasing tone
was belied by the tight grip she had on Cara's hand. Her
fearless sister was actually trembling. "Don't get carried
away here."

Their laughter was mostly from relief, but it felt
good. Cara had survived. Now she just had to make sure
that Henry did, too.

"He did *what*?" Molly was the one who asked the
question, but all of Cara's sisters—along with her one
honorary brother, John—were staring at her with wide
eyes. She'd managed to put off the interrogation from
the time they'd all descended on the Red Hawk police
station until they got home, but now the entire family
was gathered around their small kitchen table demanding answers.

"He just…blurted it out." Cara's hands flung from
her mouth outward in a wide word-vomit gesture. She
still couldn't believe it. After all of his evasions and
dodges, Henry had just turned himself in to a cop at a
tiny police station who didn't even know who he was.
He could've gotten patched up at the hospital, given a
fake name, and then disappeared again. Instead, he'd
given up his freedom and any chance to exonerate
himself, just so she could get the bond-recovery fee. It
was…incomprehensible.

"What'd he say afterward?" Charlie asked. "Did he
give any explanation?"

"He fell over and had to be taken to a Denver hospital in an ambulance. He's under guard there, and I can't get in to see him." Cara felt a renewed surge of frustrated helplessness. She knew he was still alive, but she couldn't get any more information about his condition. "I don't get why he did it. How're we supposed to track down the real killer now?"

"Um…you do realize that *he* is the real killer, right?" Felicity asked tentatively.

Cara was shaking her head even before her sister finished her question. "He's not, though." When her sisters exchanged concerned looks, she gave a huff and leaned forward, fighting through her exhaustion. She'd dozed the hour it took to drive back to Langston, but she felt like she could sleep for days, maybe weeks. First, though, she had to fix this. Then she could rest. "I know most skips say that, but I believe him when he told me he didn't kill those people. Why would he have stuck around Langston if he'd done it? If he was guilty, he would've disappeared right after he skipped—kind of like Mom did."

"Lots of skips stick around," Molly countered. "They don't have money to leave, and they have friends and family members who hide them."

"Henry has money." Cara remembered the large pile of bills he'd so casually dropped on the counter of the cabin. "He wasn't staying with friends, either. He was in a ratty motel. Besides, would a killer have risked his own life to save a near-stranger from kidnappers? Would he have turned himself in because he knew I needed the money? You saw those crime-scene photos. A bad person slaughtered those people, and everything

Henry's done has convinced me that he's a good guy. Also, Abbott said that Henry was taking the fall for someone. I just don't know *who*."

There was another exchange of looks, and Cara braced herself for the next round of her sisters trying to convince her that Henry was a killer. There was no changing her mind, though. Even though she and Henry had been running from Abbott's people for less than thirty-six hours, she felt like she truly knew who Henry Kavenski was—and that he was a good, moral man.

"Okay." Molly looked at Cara expectantly. "What's the plan?"

Cara blinked, taken off guard by the simple question. "The plan?"

Before Molly could answer, John gave a wide grin. "Does this mean we get to be PIs? Because that was my next career choice if bounty hunting had been a bust."

"Wait." Cara was still trying to process that her sisters weren't trying to convince her of Henry's guilt anymore. "You're going to help me solve this and clear Henry?"

Molly gave a clap and stood. "Okay, Norah and Cara, you're on research. Fifi and Charlie, find out everything you can on this Abbott guy. Carmondy, you're with me. We'll track down Stuart and squeeze the little weasel until he pops."

John gave a whoop. Pushing off the counter he'd been leaning against, he wrapped Molly in a backward hug. "This is why I love you, Pax. We have the same idea of what makes a date fun."

Cara considered protesting her research role, but since her first and last attempt at a simple skip retrieval had morphed into life-threatening kidnapping and attempted murder, she decided that she should stick to what she was good at. It was hard to watch her sisters make plans to actively search for the person—or people—who could exonerate Henry, though. He was hers to save.

Felicity interrupted her somewhat greedy thoughts with a hug from behind. "I'm glad you're okay," she said. "Plus bringing in not one but two skips… impressive."

Patting Felicity's encircling arms, Cara leaned her head back against her sister. "I'm pretty impressed with myself too. Seriously though, thank you for pushing us so hard during our workouts. I channeled you when I had to force Henry to run up a mountain after he'd just drowned, *and* I got to kick a mob boss in the face."

Fifi looked a little startled before a Cheshire cat grin spread over her face. "Did you hear that?" she asked, loudly enough to get all the sisters' attention. "Cara wants me to push you even harder in the mornings." The communal groan that this elicited just made Felicity's smile wider. "Tomorrow we're starting a half hour earlier. Prepare for pain." With a final squeeze that contradicted her bloodthirsty words, Felicity released Cara and headed for the door.

Charlie took her place, although she gave Cara a fist thump to the shoulder rather than a hug. Charlie wasn't big on gestures of affection, which made her hug and hand-holding at the Red Hawk police station rare and precious. "Nice job, Twin. I think that's the highest bounty any of us has ever brought in."

"Thanks." Cara tipped her head back to smile at Charlie. "Although it was kind of unintentional, so I don't know if that counts."

"If the money's there, it counts." With a final whack on Cara's shoulder, Charlie followed Felicity out the door.

"Let's go find us a weasel to pop, PI sidekick," John said as he ushered Molly after them.

Although Molly allowed herself to be towed, her eyes narrowed. "Who're you calling 'sidekick,' sidekick?"

John gave one of his deep bellowing laughs as they disappeared out the door, and Cara couldn't help but smile at the sound. Even though she'd been gone for just a couple of days, it'd felt like an eternity, and she'd had moments when she hadn't thought she'd see her family again. She'd missed them all, even John.

Once Molly had closed the door behind them, Cara looked at Norah as the house went quiet.

"Ready?" Norah asked.

"Let's research." They both stood at the same time, as if it'd been choreographed, which made Cara laugh. When Norah gave her an inquiring look, Cara just waved her sister toward the stairs. "Don't mind me. I'm just happy to be home."

Norah's expression changed as she reached out to grab Cara's hand. After giving it a tight squeeze, she let go and hurried out of the kitchen. When Norah said quietly, "I'm glad you are, too," Cara grinned at the softly spoken words.

Norah glanced back, giving her a pained expression when she spotted Cara's smile. Like Charlie, Norah wasn't one for big displays of emotion.

"I've also missed being on the research team," Cara said, taking pity on her sister and changing the subject to something less emotionally soppy. "Adrenaline rushes are exhausting and traumatizing. Give me a nice, safe computer screen and a snack any day."

Without looking back, Norah just held her fist behind her. Cara bumped it in researcher solidarity.

It's good to be home. Now she just had to bring Henry home, too.

━━━━━━━━━

Cara's eyes felt gummy when she looked up from her laptop screen and blinked at the black bedroom window. "When did it get dark outside?" she asked, but Norah just hummed a non-response, staring at her own screen.

"We should probably get some food." Cara set her laptop aside and stretched, feeling the lingering aches in her muscles from the past few traumatic days. She was still exhausted, and her vision had gone fuzzy around the edges, but she couldn't sleep while Henry was locked up for something he didn't do. "Norah? Food?"

"In a bit," her sister said absently from her perch on Cara's bed as she leaned even closer to the screen.

"Why?" Cara felt her stomach jump with a flash of hope. "Did you find something?"

"There's a woman who keeps popping up. She's listed as a past associate of Geoffrey Abbott, *and* she was interviewed by the police when Kavenski killed—um...I mean, someone killed that couple and framed Kavenski. She was the one who discovered the bodies, said she was a close friend of the murdered couple." Norah turned her laptop so Cara could see the screen. "Her name is Layla Baron."

"Layla? *The* Layla?" Peering at the photo, which

appeared to be a publicity shot at some sort of formal event, Cara felt an itchy sense of recognition. "That's her. That's the woman who met with Henry, the one I saw the night that..." She let her voice trail off right before saying *the night I was almost hit by a car*, since she didn't want to freak out her sister. "Ah, I saw her at Dutch's," she rephrased lamely, glad that she was talking to absentminded Norah rather than one of her less distracted sisters who would've pounced on her verbal misstep. She'd also seen the same woman giving money surreptitiously to Henry, and her heart started to beat faster. Could Layla Baron be their link to the real killer?

"I'm surprised she's hanging out at Dutch's." Norah rotated the screen back so she could frown at the woman's picture before her fingers tapped at the keyboard again. "She looks a little too high-class for that place."

"Geoffrey Abbott was supposedly high-class, too."

"Funny you mention that." Norah's fingers paused. "Layla Baron went to Anchor Academy in Aspen with Abbott—well, until he was expelled. She graduated from Anchor the following year."

"That's an interesting coincidence." Grabbing her phone, Cara tapped out a text to Molly. When there wasn't an immediate response, she tried Charlie, and then Felicity. As she waited for her sisters to answer, she paced the short distance between the two beds.

The seconds seemed endless, and Cara knew she wouldn't be able to stand sitting at home doing nothing to help Henry while waiting for a return text. She stopped in front of Norah and smiled.

Norah shrank back. "What?"

"How about we go out to eat? Maybe some chicken wings?" Grabbing Norah's hand, she hauled her sister off the bed.

"Dutch's?" It came out as a mournful but resigned sigh.

Cara smiled. "Dutch's."

Reaching back, Norah closed her laptop and left it on the bed. She followed—well, was towed by—Cara out of the bedroom. "I thought you were done with fieldwork."

"This is still research, just more...*active* research than usual." Cara knew her sister was smart to protest, though. "We'll just go, have some bar food, see if we see any familiar faces, let our more adventurous sisters know if we do, and then come right home."

Norah groaned, although she didn't pull away from her sister's tugging hand. "Fine, but I want it on the record that I think this is a stupid idea."

"Noted." Even though she knew Norah was probably right, Cara couldn't help but feel a zing of excitement that she was actively helping to search for the person who had framed Henry for murder. Maybe her sisters weren't so crazy. There was something to be said for fieldwork and adrenaline rushes after all.

"Okay." Norah slid to the edge of the booth seat, looking like a spooked bird about to take flight. "We've eaten wings and looked around, but Layla Baron isn't here. We should go home now."

Although Cara sighed, she couldn't say her sister was

wrong. Even the crowd at Dutch's seemed mellower than the other time she'd been there. It was a disappointing stakeout all around.

"Fine. Let's go. Wait." Her eyes narrowed as she recognized a weaselly face across the bar. "Excuse me for just a second. I have a throat to punch."

Norah just blinked at her, wide-eyed, apparently too startled by Cara's uncharacteristically violent urge to be anxious about being left alone.

Cara wove her way through the crowd, her gaze locked on her target. When she was just five feet away, he spotted her approaching. Face paling, he tried to dart toward the exit.

"No, you don't." Lunging forward, she caught him by the arm. Twisting it behind his back, she pinned his front to the end of the bar. The red-haired bartender glanced over at them and then away, looking bored, and none of the patrons seemed too concerned about a wannabe kindergarten teacher trapping a guy against the bar. Dutch's did have its perks.

"Let me go, Cara!" Stuart wriggled in her grip so she shoved his arm a little higher, making him yelp. Her first instinct was to feel guilty for intentionally hurting someone, but then she remembered his part in everything.

"Not until you answer some questions. You helped Abbott kidnap me!" Granted, it was more of an exclamation than a question, but she was still pissed about Stuart's role.

"No, I didn't! I—" He cut off sharply when she yanked his arm again. "I didn't know he was going to kidnap you! All he wanted was for me to try to get you to open the door. Ow! Stop! Fine! He wanted to know who you were, just basic stuff. Nothing he couldn't get out of the campus directory."

"The campus directory? My friends are listed under my name?" Her voice was heavy with sarcasm as she pressed Stuart harder against the bar. In a way, she was glad that she'd found him before Molly and John could. Making the weasel squeak was cathartic.

"No, but…I mean, it's really on you for being friends with Kavenski. Everyone knows he's Baron's toy poodle."

The name startled her into letting up the pressure, and Stuart yanked away. "Layla Baron?" she clarified.

"Yeah." He stepped back out of reach, his face twisted in disgust. "Kavenski even went to jail for her. Loser."

Cara reached for his arm again, new questions bubbling in her mind, but Stuart dodged her hand and almost ran for the door. After watching him go, her brain working at a hundred miles an hour, Cara made her way absently back to the booth, processing the new information. She was snapped out of her thoughts when she saw her sister's anxious expression. "Sorry, Norah, but now I really want to talk to Layla Baron. According to Stuart, she's who Henry took the fall for. Will you hate me if we stay just a little longer?"

Norah looked doubtful. "You know the odds of her actually showing up here while we're waiting for her are pretty low, don't you?"

"Yes, but at least I feel like I'm doing *something* to help Henry." She gave her sister her best entreating expression, and Norah sighed audibly.

"Fine." Norah gave her a stern look. "We'll give it another half hour. That's it."

Cara nodded, happy to have gotten that concession.

"So what did Stuart say?" Norah asked, and Cara filled her in on their brief conversation as her gaze roamed the bar patrons. A half hour passed, and Cara wheedled another fifteen minutes out of Norah. Once that deadline had passed too, Cara heaved a huge sigh.

"You're right. She's not coming here tonight. Sorry for making you stay here so long," Cara said, disappointment hanging heavy in her belly. "We can go now."

Looking relieved, Norah stood. "Do you think I'll be knifed if I use the bathroom here?"

"Maybe?" Cara made a so-so gesture with her hand. "I'd say the odds are around seventy-thirty that you'll survive." She smiled to show that she was joking... sort of.

"I'll risk it. I really have to pee." With a determined expression, Norah headed for the narrow back hallway that contained the bathrooms.

Cara pulled out some cash for a tip and then turned, her eyes scanning the crowd for a final time. After almost three hours of disappointment, she wasn't really expecting to see anyone else she recognized, so her gaze skipped over the woman talking to a guy in a battered trucker hat before zooming back to her striking, memorable face.

It was her. Layla Baron was actually there.

Now that she'd found the woman, Cara wasn't sure exactly what to do. Pulling out her phone, she sent a group text to her sisters and then started the audio recording app before dropping her phone back into her jacket pocket. Taking a deep breath, she walked toward Layla.

You wanted to have an active role. You chose to come here. This is what you wanted.

When Layla spotted her approaching and narrowed her eyes, Cara had a hard time remembering why she wanted to talk to the intimidating woman. All of her questions scattered as she got closer and stopped a few feet away.

"Can I help you?" Even though she was standing in the middle of a scary dive bar, Layla's tone was all frost and wealth.

"I hope so." Cara forced out a tentative smile. "I wanted to talk to you about Henry Kavenski."

There was the slightest widening of Layla's eyes before she returned to her fake smile. "Of course, but it's too loud in here. Let's go outside."

"I'd rather stay in here." Even though the clientele was a bit sketchy, there was still safety in numbers and Cara didn't want to lose that. Besides, Norah wouldn't know where she'd gone, and she wasn't about to ditch her timid sister at Dutch's, of all places. "This won't take long."

Layla's gaze shifted to a spot behind Cara for just a second before she gave another of her artificial smiles. "Of course. Let's move over by the door, though, where it's quieter."

Cara gestured for Layla to go first, feeling more secure following the woman than having her at her back. They'd only gone a few steps when a loud crash behind her made Cara whirl around. The man in a trucker hat that Layla had been talking to earlier had another guy pinned against the bar. One or both of the two must've had friends with them, because there was a muted roar as ten more people jumped into the fight. Suddenly, it was chaos.

"This way." Fingers closed around her upper arm and a blunt cylinder pressed into Cara's side, right above her hip, as Layla's cool voice spoke directly into her ear. "Come along now, unless you want your internal organs to be the new wallpaper in this dump."

Cara froze, unable to do anything but stare at the black gun muzzle pressed against her. Layla gave her a sharp nudge from behind to get her moving. Cara's feet stumbled into motion, moving toward the door as she resisted the urge to look around for Norah. She didn't want her sister anywhere near Layla or her gun.

The bouncer shoved past them, heading for the fight, and they moved out the door unseen. It was eerily quiet outside without the shouting and pounding fists and blasting music. With the gun and a tight grip on her arm, Layla hauled Cara toward the side of the building.

She felt numb, and she wondered if she'd been terrified so often over the past few days that she'd started to become immune to fear. Then Layla jammed the gun into her side, and Cara realized that she could indeed feel afraid. After all the close calls she'd just been through, she couldn't believe that she was going to die in such a stupid way. She'd walked right up to a woman she'd suspected of being a murderer. It was her own stupid fault she was in this pickle.

"You're quite persistent, aren't you?" Layla said in such a posh, chilly tone that Cara almost laughed at the strangeness of it all.

"I was trying to mind my own business," Cara said, her voice quavering despite her best effort to imitate

Layla's cool confidence. Then again, the other woman was the one with the gun, and it was easy to be self-assured when she held all the lethal cards. "Did you have me kidnapped?"

"Of course not." Layla hauled her closer to the back of the bar, and Cara tried to put on the brakes. Nothing good could come of anything in a grubby alley behind Dutch's. "That was all that moron Abbott's idea."

Although she knew it wasn't a good sign that Layla was telling her things, Cara still wanted to know. "So he could get information out of Henry? Information about you?" She took Layla's silence as an affirmative answer. "Like that you killed your friends?"

"They weren't my friends." Layla almost hissed the words, and she jammed the gun so tightly against Cara's side that she had to grit her teeth to keep from crying out. "They were my accountants—at least until they tried to blackmail me. Idiots."

"Why would they blackmail you?" Cara's teeth had started to chatter, and she clamped them so tightly together that it hurt her jaw.

"They were greedy and nearsighted, and Abbott pushed them into it." Layla sounded so casually normal that the press of the gun felt surreal. They rounded the corner, fully in the alley now despite Cara's attempt at delaying them. "He's had an issue with me ever since he was expelled for that silly thing in high school and I was cleared. It's not my fault that he was weak enough to fold during his police interview."

Swallowing her protest that a boy dying was not a silly thing, Cara asked, "Did you try to run me over with a car?" If she was about to be killed in a gross alley that smelled of pee and garbage, she at least wanted her curiosity satisfied.

"No. *I* didn't, and he was supposed to be aiming at Kavenski."

Before Cara could respond, Layla slammed her face-first against the rough surface of the wall and shifted the gun so that the muzzle now rested against her temple.

"Everyone's going to hear that go off if you shoot me." There was nothing Cara could do to control the shake in her voice. This was it. If she was going to save herself, she had to do something *now*.

"That's what suppressors are for, you stupid girl."

Cara felt it, the intention, the tensing of Layla's muscles that screamed that she was really about to go through with this, that she was going to shoot Cara in the head and leave her there in the alley behind Dutch's like so much garbage.

No. Cara's thoughts grew calm, and her shaking stopped. *That's not going to happen.*

She dropped her head forward, just slightly, as if she were giving up. Then she slammed it backward, her skull connecting with something on Layla's face that crunched under the force. The pressure against her temple dropped away, and Cara twisted in the woman's hold, fiercely determined not to die.

"You *bitch*!" Layla gasped, her voice sounding nasal and choked.

A yell from behind them echoed distantly in Cara's ears, but she was too busy fighting the grip on her arm. She fumbled for the gun, hoping frantically that she would knock it away from Layla. The gun went off, a sharp bark, surprisingly loud for what Cara had thought a silenced weapon should sound like, and she felt a sharp slice of pain along the top of her shoulder.

"FBI! Drop your weapon!" There were shouts coming from all directions, but the words didn't make any sense to Cara's brain. She grappled for the gun, grabbing Layla's wrist with both hands and ignoring the pain as the other woman clawed at her arms.

Layla's narrowed eyes went wide for a fraction of a second, and Cara saw a completely terrified Norah holding a jagged piece of concrete that she'd just crashed into Layla's head. In that split second of distraction, Cara lost her grip on Layla's wrist. Looking furious, Layla aimed the gun at her again.

"Hit her again!" Cara shouted, breaking Norah out of her paralysis. She raised her chunk of concrete, but Cara knew her sister would be too late. Layla needed less than a second to pull the trigger and bury a bullet right into Cara's chest.

Before the gun went off, an enormous shape hit Layla from the side, tackling her to the ground. As she went down, Layla's head bounced against the pavement, and she went limp. Cara could only stare at the two figures on the ground, unable to comprehend that she was alive and Layla was unconscious and *Henry* had just saved her life…again.

Norah let the chunk of concrete tumble to the ground, and the heavy *clunk* it made when it hit seemed to release Cara's paralysis. Suddenly, they were swarmed by people in protective vests with FBI emblazoned on them.

"Cara!" The big guy in an FBI jacket who'd just tackled Layla pushed himself to his feet, leaving the unconscious woman to the other agents. He swept Cara up in an enormous hug, moving her away from Layla's fallen form, and she hung limply in his grip, her brain trying to process what was happening.

"Henry?" she finally managed to say, her voice breathless from how tightly he was squeezing her. "Aren't you in jail? Why are you dressed up like an FBI agent?"

He finally set her down, although he kept a firm grip on her upper arms. Either he was shaking, or she was shaking, or they both were shaking, because she could feel her body vibrating almost violently. He moved his hands to cup her face, and she determined that they were both trembling right before he kissed her, hard.

She wouldn't have imagined that anything could distract her from the fact that she'd almost been shot in a dirty alley, but Henry was doing a pretty good job of making her forget everything except the feel of his mouth on hers.

When they finally separated, she couldn't look away from him. They stared at each other for what felt like a long time before she finally cleared her throat. "FBI?"

"Yeah."

"Undercover?"

"I was, yeah. We knew Layla had killed Bettina and Lance Mason, but we don't have enough to convict her. I was working for her, pretending to take the fall for cash, so I could get the evidence we needed. Bringing in her former associate and current rival—Abbott—was a bonus." A flash of guilt passed over his expression. "I'm sorry I dragged you into my mess." He cradled her face so gently, as if she was something precious.

"That's okay." Her voice sounded a little faint, but she was just glad that she was upright and able to talk at this point. "I was the one who jumped into your mess—at first, anyway. The kidnapping, though, that was pretty much your fault."

"Yeah, it was." His hands kept moving, stroking her hair and then down her arms, and she realized that he was checking her for injuries in his tender way. She wrapped her arms around his waist, needing to feel him, to have concrete evidence that he was alive and well and out of jail. Despite his protective vest separating them, the feel of him was hugely reassuring while at the same time threatened to reduce her to relieved tears. She forced them back, needing answers.

"Why didn't you tell me you were with the FBI?" she demanded, wanting to smack him for deceiving her but not willing to let him go quite yet. "I was worried about you going back to jail."

"I was trying to keep you out of it." His broad palms skimmed down her back, so familiar and reassuring that she couldn't hold on to her indignation. "By the time I realized that I'd fallen for you, we were spending most of our time together running from killers and trying to stay alive. It never seemed like the right time."

"Hmm…" She knew she would grill him more about his lack of communication later, but for now she was too happy that he was here and safe to be appropriately stern. "So now that this is over, are we?"

"Over?" He went still, peering intently down at her face as if he was trying to read her expression. "No. I don't ever want us to be over."

She couldn't stop a huge grin from spreading over her face. "Good."

"I have to go home to Bozeman, Montana, for a few days to wrap things up, but I'll be back as soon as I can."

"You'd better."

Someone hovered next to them, and Cara tore her gaze from Henry's face to find an anxious-looking Norah.

"Sorry about the failed rescue," Norah said, her gaze dropping to her feet.

Cara grabbed her in a hard hug. "It was a good effort," she said. "If Henry hadn't tackled her, your second hit would've knocked her out. It's not your fault that Layla has an impossibly hard head." Norah hugged her back but didn't say anything. Cara wasn't sure how to console her sister. After all, they both knew that if it hadn't been for Henry, Norah's second hit would've come too late. Cara would've been shot.

Norah tightened her arms even more, and Cara grunted. "I was really scared you were about to die," Norah said shakily.

"Me too."

It wasn't until Cara pulled away that she realized they were both crying. "The other sisters better answer my texts *lickety-split* from now on." She wiped her eyes roughly with the backs of her hands and leaned into Henry's hand on her back.

Instead of laughing, Norah was staring at her shoulder. "You're bleeding. Were you hit?"

She felt Henry stiffen as they both looked at her shoulder. He pulled her shirt away from the stinging injury so they could see it.

"Just a scratch," she said, relieved that there wasn't a bullet lodged inside her that she hadn't noticed because of shock or adrenaline or whatever. "It's already stopped bleeding."

"We're still getting that looked at. The paramedics are staging at the front of the building," Henry said, taking her other hand and leading her that way. Cara went willingly, happy to get away from the gross alley and the waking Layla, even if she was currently disarmed and surrounded by FBI agents. Norah trailed close behind, still looking spooked. Cara couldn't blame her.

Despite her sister's presence, Cara couldn't help but squeeze Henry's hand and lean closer against his arm. It was such a relief that he was out of jail and everyone knew that he wasn't a murderer.

Her phone beeped in her pocket, and she pulled it out with her free hand, hiding her wince as the movement pulled at the scrape on her shoulder. As she unlocked her screen and saw the text from Molly pop up over the other open app, she smiled.

"I recorded Layla's confession," she said, stopping the audio recording. "Will this work as your evidence?"

Henry actually looked startled before his expression eased into a smile—a real one, not one of his tiny lip twitches. "You're pretty amazing."

"I know, right?"

Norah snorted a watery laugh. That set Cara off, although Henry just looked at her as if she was crazy for laughing—but he also looked like he loved that crazy part of her, too.

CHAPTER 19

As soon as Cara sat on the porch swing, Warrant climbed up next to her and tried to wiggle onto her lap.

"What's with you?" she asked, scratching behind his ears when he finally settled with half of his body stretched over her thighs. "Were you worried about me, too?"

She'd been dealing with concerned sisters—and her honorary brother—all week since the whole Layla incident. She couldn't really blame them, since she'd been kidnapped and then re-kidnapped and then was almost killed, but she was feeling a bit claustrophobic. Today was the first day that she'd been allowed to be alone, except for the furry white beast sprawled on her lap. She ignored the tiny voice in her brain reminding her that she didn't really want to be *alone*. Even though Henry had only been gone a week, she missed him fiercely.

With her toe, she moved the swing just slightly, since Warrant didn't care for the rocking sensation, and enjoyed the peace. Even when their irate neighbor Mr. Petra glared at her from his screened-in porch next door, she just smiled and waved. His grumpiness was normal, and normal was so reassuring.

A car cruised down the street, catching her attention. She watched it closely, not recognizing it. Instantly, she was on high alert, her mind throwing out possibilities. Was it treasure hunters? One of Jane's sleazier friends? Had Detective Mill changed vehicles to stalk them more easily? The sun reflected off the windows, preventing Cara from seeing inside the vehicle.

When the car came to a stop at the curb, she tensed, her fingers slipping into her jacket pocket and wrapping around her phone. The driver's side door opened, and a large, familiar form got out. She relaxed, releasing her grip on her cell as he made his way up the front walk. Everything inside her warmed with pleasure at the sight of him.

"You're here," she said, unable to stop a huge smile from spreading across her face. "In a suit, too." He looked really good in that suit—even better than he had in his clingy wet long underwear or his FBI gear.

"I'm here." He paused at the base of the porch steps, actually looking uncertain. Warrant raised his head to look at Henry, then thumped his tail against the swing and dropped his muzzle onto her lap again. Henry cleared his throat, and Cara stared at him, completely thrown by his obvious awkwardness. "I've been assigned to the FBI office in Denver."

This made her smile even more broadly. Although he wouldn't be in Langston with her, Denver was close enough to make her happy.

After climbing the porch steps, he leaned against the railing in front of her. If she swung hard enough, her knees would touch his, and her whole body lit up at the thought of that tiny touch. A week had been too long. Her body was starved for him. "I've found an apartment in Langston," he said.

Her heart gave a happy little jump. "Why not in Denver?"

If she wasn't quite certain that he was physically incapable of blushing, she would've thought that a bit of red was creeping up from his collar. Despite his uncharacteristic shyness, he met her eyes boldly. "Because you're here."

Now she was blushing, too. Her heart pounded faster than it had when she'd been kidnapped.

"When I was undercover, I couldn't do this, not without putting you in danger."

"Do what?" She swallowed, pretty sure she knew but needing to hear it from his own mouth. He'd been such an enigma, and she didn't want to have to guess what he was feeling or thinking anymore. She just wanted him to say it out loud.

"Ask you out."

There it was, as bald and obvious as she'd wanted, but now she realized that she had to reciprocate. "Okay. Right now? Because I want to change first to something with less dog hair on it."

He grinned, and it was beautiful. "Tonight?"

"Sure." She couldn't stop herself from smiling back.

"Tomorrow, too."

That made her laugh. "All right."

"And the day after that."

"Are you booking me up?"

"Yes." His smile faded into an intense look that warmed her from the inside out. "I want all your days."

She rocked the swing so that her knees brushed against his. "I think that can be arranged."

"Good." Leaning forward, he placed his hands

on either side of her legs, stopping the motion. She watched, still amazed that he was there, right in front of her, within grabbing distance. He moved closer until their lips were almost touching. Before he could kiss her, she stopped him with a hand against his chest.

"Hold on." She leaned back and gave him her best stern-teacher frown. "I didn't hear a word from you for a *week*, and now you're here, looking all sexy in your suit, trying to kiss me?"

She tried very hard not to find the way he ducked his head adorable. After spending so much time with tough-guy Henry, however, she couldn't stop her heart from melting at his show of uncertainty. A bashful Henry was basically irresistible. Somehow, she managed to keep from folding.

"It took me longer than expected to get my life in order," he said, settling back on the railing but holding her gaze. She marveled at how *open* his expression was, his impassive mask nowhere to be seen. The small glimpses she'd seen of this man while he was undercover were just a preview of who Henry Kavenski really was. "All the time we've spent together, I haven't had anything to offer you. Just about everything about me was a lie—even my name."

That startled her. She hadn't considered that even his name wasn't real. "What's your name?"

"Benedict Henry Weaver." His words came out in a rush, as if saying it was a relief. "Nice to meet you." His smile—his real, true, not-undercover smile—creased his cheeks, and it was impossible for Cara to hold her stern frown in the face of the radiance of it.

"Nice to meet you, too, Benedict Henry Weaver."

He winced. "Henry. Please."

Swallowing a laugh, she nodded. "Good thing I don't call you Kavenski anymore."

"Yeah." His smile slipped away as his expression turned earnest. "He's gone, and now I'm just Henry Weaver, local FBI agent who's not at all undercover, and who's crazy in love with Cara Evelyn Pax."

The words jolted her. This was the last thing she'd expected after his week of silence. "You *love* me?"

"So much. I don't even care that it happened so fast. I love your kindness and the way your logical mind works and that stern-teacher voice you use sometimes and how you got so offended that I cheated at Battleship. I love how brave you are, and how you're so loyal to your sisters." He leaned in again. "So can I kiss you now?"

"As long as you promise never to leave again." The memory of the last hellish days without Henry replayed in her head, allowing her to scowl at him in spite of the ecstatic butterflies dancing in her belly. "It's been a rough week."

"I'm sorry." He grimaced as he palmed her cheek gently. "I wanted to be someone you'd consider being with."

She smacked his shoulder lightly. "Dummy. Even when you were accused killer and bail jumper Henry Kavenski, I was seriously considering being with you. I love you."

"I know." That wry quirk of his lips was achingly familiar, and it did crazy things to Cara's heart.

"You do, do you?" Although she tried to play it cool, her voice came out husky.

"Sure. You told me you don't *not* love me. It's the logical conclusion."

She laughed before leaning forward and grabbing a handful of his very nice suit jacket. Tugging him close, she met his hot gaze. "Kiss me, Benedict Henry Weaver."

"Happily."

EPILOGUE

NORAH PAX STARED AT THE DOOR. IT WAS FAIRLY NON-descript, as doors went, but what was on the other side frankly terrified her. She paced the alley, five strides north and then five strides south, back and forth ten times until she was in front of the entrance again. She was relieved that there wasn't any window for someone to see her strange behavior.

Just as she had that thought, the door to the neighboring business—a café—opened, and a man with a full garbage bag stepped into the alley. Giving her a curious but friendly look, he started to raise his free hand. The thought of having to make conversation with this stranger terrified her even more than what was behind the door. Ducking her head and pretending she didn't see the guy, she yanked open the door in front of her and stepped inside.

It was…quieter than she'd expected. No rock music blared, and no muscle-bound men tossed their weights noisily back on racks. There were only mats and a ring and equipment neatly stacked against the far wall. It even smelled nice, not like the mix of body odor and vinyl that most gyms had.

Only one person was there—a very large, muscular person—and he was staring right at her, scowling.

"What do you want?" he barked.

She didn't mind the directness. It was comforting, really, that he didn't hide his purpose in politeness. "I need to learn to fight."

"Why?"

"So I won't be useless next time someone tries to blow up or shoot my sisters."

His glower didn't lighten as he studied her with eyes as dark as night. "Come in, then," he finally snapped, and Norah started to smile.

This might just work out after all.

INTO THE FRAY

CHAPTER 1

NORAH WANTED TO CLOSE HER EYES, BUT THEY REFUSED TO cooperate. Instead, she stared fixedly at the fist swinging toward her face, even when the knuckles got so close that she went cross-eyed.

The fist stopped abruptly, close enough that Norah's eyelashes brushed against the battered knuckles. The gym was completely silent until her belated indrawn breath broke the quiet. For the thousandth time, she mentally gave thanks that no one else was there. It limited the potential embarrassment, at least. Physical pain, Norah could handle. Mockery, not so much.

"If you're not going to block, you should at least move your face." His voice had a raspy edge to it that distracted her for a moment, just long enough for her eyelashes to flick against his knuckles three more times.

When the meaning of his words finally registered, she pulled her head back and her focus away from that huge, scarred fist. She hadn't expected the almost-hit to come so fast. It hadn't given her time to think through each step of blocking his punch, so she hadn't done anything—not even duck. That had always been her issue when Felicity, one of her sisters, tried to teach her self-defense. If she wasn't able to run through her mental what-to-do checklist, her brain froze until it was too late. That was probably part of the reason she'd almost watched her sisters die multiple times over the past few weeks.

He dropped his arm to his side and regarded her with his head cocked slightly to the right. Although he was frowning, that had been his default expression since she'd walked into his gym yesterday, so she didn't take it personally. "It's better to move *before* the punch lands."

When he paused, she figured he was waiting for her to say something. There really was no necessary response, however, since everything he'd just said made sense. Still, in the interest of moving on to the next step, she gave a nod and said, "Okay."

His scowl deepened. "Don't just agree. *Do* it next time."

She studied him as she mentally debated how to respond. It was an interesting face to look at, with his almost-black irises and prominent cheekbones and the scars mottling the left side of his neck and jawline, but she couldn't really enjoy it because the majority of her focus was on what to say next. *Okay* hadn't gone over well, so that was out, but that was usually her go-to phrase when she wanted someone to stop staring at her and continue. She tried, "I will."

To her satisfaction, that seemed to do the trick. Although his expression was still snarly, he took a step back and settled into the defensive position he'd just shown her—base solid and hands ready to protect his face. Despite his burly form, he looked light on his feet, and she knew from their very short acquaintance that he could move surprisingly fast. One of his slashing black brows lifted in a soundless command. Twitching her tank top into place, she moved to mimic his stance.

They were only ten minutes into their first session, but the position already felt natural. It just made physiological sense, and there was nothing that Norah appreciated more than when things were logical. If only punches didn't come so quickly, she was pretty sure she'd actually be able to remember how to counter them.

"Let's try this in slow-motion," he said, as if he'd read her mind. He started extending his arm, the muscles stretching out from their bunched positions. Even when he wasn't flexing, though, his arms were huge. As his fist gradually drew closer to her face, she ran through the steps in her head.

Shoulders up, tuck my chin, thrust palm, connect with the side of his wrist, shove his arm away, move my face in case I miss, and return hand to guard position.

"Good." The compliment was a mere grunt, but it still warmed her insides. "Again."

Over and over, slightly faster each time, he threw punches at her face. Gradually, her movements became automatic, and she didn't have to think about each step. Her body just started doing what needed to be done.

"Okay," he said, shifting his balance back. Norah felt a line of sweat tickle her spine, and she wished she could take off another layer. If she took anything else off, however, she'd be down to her underwear, and Dash was much too attractive for her to be that close to naked in front of him. "Let's work on breaking some holds." His voice was even as he continued, either ignoring the fact that she'd turned bright red or not noticing that she suddenly resembled a stop sign. As warm as the gym was, he probably just thought she was overheating because of the physical effort, rather than embarrassment.

He was waiting again, so she gave him a slight lift of her chin in response. That seemed to be what he'd been waiting for, because he shifted closer and waited for her to imitate his ready stance.

"If I grab you, what's your first impulse?" He closed his fingers around her forearm, the rough rasp of his skin in direct opposition to the gentle, careful way he held her.

She blinked down at his hand, surprised that she wasn't more upset. Normally, she wasn't a big fan of strangers touching her. Her gaze moved to Dash, and she wondered why it was different with him.

"Your first impulse is to stand there?" She felt her cheeks warm again, but he sounded surprised, rather than mocking.

Norah tried to think of how to explain that he didn't trigger the usual alarm in her brain, but she couldn't even understand it herself. If anyone except her sisters—well, apparently her sisters or Dash—touched her, she would have yanked away. "No," she answered belatedly. "I'd pull back. If someone else grabbed my arm, I mean."

The revealing heat was returning to her cheeks, annoying her. *Why am I being so extra awkward with him?*

Luckily, he didn't seem to notice anything off about her as he increased the pull on her arm. His fingers stayed gentle, even as he hauled her close to him. She wondered if she was supposed to fight back, but her brain was still preoccupied by her strange behavior, so she couldn't think of the best way to get free from his hold. As careful as his grip was, it was still firm and unyielding. Her forearm looked tiny and frail in contrast to his thick, rough-looking fingers.

He pulled her closer until their fronts were almost touching. She kept her gaze on his face, checking for clues about what he wanted her to be doing in response. All she knew from looking at him was that his eyelashes were as black and thick as a mascara ad, and he appeared to be…baffled.

"Why aren't you pulling back?" he finally asked, pulling her attention away from her study of his eyelashes.

"Am I supposed to?" she asked.

"No."

She frowned slightly, confused.

"Most people do, and we have to train a different reaction. You're the first person I've trained with such a…passive response."

Norah's frown deepened. "Passive?" She didn't like to think of herself as passive. Even in her less physical role in her family's bounty hunting business, her contribution felt active, like she was accomplishing something. Her method of chasing might be computer-based, but it was its own type of hunt. Though…she had to admit that she hadn't done very well in the field. Maybe if she hadn't been so *passive*, she wouldn't have ended up on the wrong end of a gun so often.

Her chin set as determination coursed through her. This was why she was here, after all. She wanted to get better at the physical part so she could do her part to protect her sisters. She was tired of always being the one tied to the railroad tracks. Instead, she wanted to be the hero riding to the rescue, for once. "What should I do instead?"

The corner of his mouth twitched in something so close to a smile that she blinked, startled. "Just what you did," he said.

Shaking off her distraction, she looked up at him, confused. "I thought I was too passive."

"Not in this case." He stepped back without releasing her arm. "Like I said, most people pull back when someone grabs them. That's what the assailant expects you to do. If you step in closer, instead, it throws them off guard."

Norah could understand why the attacker would be thrown initially, but there were still holes in his logic. "I haven't gotten away, though."

"That's the next step." He pulled her in again, and she allowed herself to be tugged toward him, even as the word *passive* rang sourly in her brain. This close, she had to tilt her head back to meet his gaze. "Now, you're in a position to get some hits in. You could knee me in the groin or stomp on my foot or do a palm heel strike to my nose. All my tender bits are at your mercy."

The words *tender bits* coming from cranky Dash made her smile, but his meaning sharpened her grin. "Nothing passive about smashing your...tender bits."

This time he really did smile, and it looked just as fierce as hers felt. "Nope. As tiny and fragile as you seem, they won't see it until it's too late."

Her surge of confidence faltered. "See what?"

He gave a light tap on her sternum. "Your ferocious inner badger."

Her smile returned at full force, and she started asking him to show her how exactly to crush his bits when a thunderous knocking made her jump. His scowl snapped back into place before he released her arm and headed for the entrance.

She watched him flip the deadbolt and yank open the door, as butterflies danced around her insides. When she'd walked in the gym for the first time a few days before, the most she'd been hoping for was to possibly learn to throw a punch. All she wanted was to never again be a liability in a fight, but Dash made it seem like even *more* was possible. With time and training, she might become a true bad-ass. It was a powerful feeling.

"What?" Dash snarled, but even his cranky tone couldn't erase her smile, especially since his ire wasn't directed at her.

"Why's the door locked?" Another voice, almost as deep as Dash's but not half as gravelly, asked. "This place is never closed. I thought you were dead or something."

"Private session. Come back in an hour." Dash swung the door shut, ignoring the other man's protests, and clicked the deadlock back into place.

As he rejoined her where she waited in the center of the gym, she felt a twist of anxiety thinking that all the usual gym clients were locked out, waiting in the alley, getting more and more annoyed because she was having a private session with Dash. "You didn't have to close the gym down just for me."

He gave her a level look. "You don't need a bunch of meatheads staring while you try to learn this stuff. Archer's right—this place is almost always open. He can come back later."

The thought of having an audience as she struggled through the motions made her nauseated, and she gave him a grateful nod. "Thank you."

With a grumbly noise, he waved his hand as if dismissing her thanks. "Let's not waste this time then. Palm heel strikes, when you do them right, can be even more effective than a punch..."

As Dash continued, Norah focused on him, filing every word into the proper place in her brain. At the back of her mind, she was almost giddy with the knowledge that he'd closed down the entire gym for her because he knew she'd be uncomfortable with people watching. The happy butterflies in her belly took flight again, but she batted them down, determined to concentrate.

After all, empty-gym time was precious and not to be wasted.

Norah peeked around the door before stepping into the entry of her house, feeling a bit guilty that she was learning self-defense from someone other than Felicity. Rather than the mostly empty house she'd expected, it sounded as if all of her sisters were home—and all speaking at once. Giving up on her plan of slipping in unnoticed, Norah stepped inside, curious as to what was happening.

"Norah!" her oldest sister, Molly, called from where she was pacing the kitchen, a cellphone pressed to her ear. "You're home. Good. Cara and I need some help in here."

Charlie spun around from where she and Felicity were deep in discussion by the bottom of the stairs, their heads so close they were almost touching. "Wait your turn, Moo. *We* need Norah. We're so close to finding

Mom." Charlie crossed the living room and grabbed a fold of Norah's shirt, as if to hold her in place.

Eyebrows shooting up, Norah looked at her sister's fingers and then met Charlie's amped gaze. "What's happening? You really have a lead on Mom?" Her stomach twisted with a mix of emotions. Although it wasn't a surprise that Jane disappeared after using the necklace as collateral on her daughters' home, Norah still felt sick every time she thought about it. She also hated the thought of her mom going to prison, and she was annoyed that she even cared. After all, Jane didn't seem to mind that her actions were about to make her daughters homeless.

"Yes." Felicity was the one who answered as she bounced across the room to join them. Judging by the excited gleam in her eyes, she wasn't feeling the same messy mix of feelings that Norah was. "It's a good lead, too. Do you remember Evan Sage?"

The name rang a bell, but Norah had to think hard before asking, "He was a deputy who moved away sometime last year?"

"That's the one." Charlie grinned as she cast a sideways glance at Felicity. "He got a job with the police department in a small town in North Dakota—"

"South," Felicity interjected.

"Right." Giving a little shrug, Charlie accepted the correction with good grace. "I always get those two confused. I wish they'd just merge into one big state called Dakota. Anyway, apparently, he's *still* obsessed with our Fifi here, and he texted her when he spotted Jane in some security footage, taking a five-finger discount at their local Wal-Mart just an hour ago. Store security didn't manage to catch her, so they passed the case to the local PD."

"He's not *obsessed* with me," Felicity said mildly.

Without pausing, Charlie continued, "Obsessed Deputy Evan sent over the video files of inside and outside the store. Could you go through them and make sure it's Mom and if you can spot what she's driving nowadays?"

"Of course," Norah said, shoving her conflicted feelings aside as a spark of excitement grew inside her. As much as she knew she needed to learn the skills Dash had started teaching her, her first love was doing research, safe behind her computer screen. "Are the files saved in our shared drive?"

"You know it." Releasing Norah, Charlie grabbed hold of Felicity's arm instead and towed her toward the door where their two backpacks were waiting. "Text us if you find anything. We're going to get on the road and head toward Dakota."

"That's not a thing," Felicity complained as she freed herself from her sister's hold in order to shoulder one of the packs. "You can't just change two states' names on a whim to make up for your geographical shortcomings."

"But it makes so much sense." Grabbing the other backpack, Charlie headed out the door, and her voice grew fainter as she crossed the front porch. "Think of how much embarrassment it would save people. I can't be the only one who gets those two confused."

"Bye Norah," Felicity said, rolling her eyes at her twin. "Bye Molly and Cara!"

The two in the kitchen chorused their goodbyes, and Molly added, "Keep in contact, and don't do anything stupid."

Pausing in the doorway, Felicity called back, "I never do anything stupid."

Molly stuck her head into the living room. "Try to keep Charlie from doing anything stupid, then."

"I heard that!" Charlie yelled from outside.

"Good! Then you'll know not to do anything stupid!" Molly shouted back, although she was smiling.

With a final quick wave at Norah, Felicity left, letting the screen door bang closed behind her. The sound, as familiar as it was, made Norah jump. It seemed to emphasize the finality of her sisters' exit. This might be the last time they have to chase after Jane.

Norah pulled her gaze off the closed door and headed into the kitchen. It seemed a lot quieter without Charlie and Felicity there, even though Molly was still talking to someone on her cell.

"Ready to research?" Cara asked with a smile that turned puzzled as she studied Norah. "What have you been up to? You look like you just ran a marathon or fell into a pond. Possibly both."

Norah hesitated. She was reluctant to answer, but she wasn't sure whether that was because her sisters would feel responsible for dragging her into dangerous situations, or because she wanted to keep Dash her own personal secret for a while. The second option made her uncomfortable, so she quit thinking about it and just blurted, "I was at the gym."

Cara's eyes widened. Even Molly, who was supposed to be paying attention to the person on the other end of the line, looked fascinated. "What gym?" Cara asked, the corners of her mouth lifting as her eyes sparked with titillation.

Before Norah could answer, Molly was saying into the phone, "Gotta go. Interesting things happening here." There was a short pause before she snorted a laugh. "Yes, more interesting than you. It is possible, you know. Love you. Bye." Ending the call, she shoved her cell into her pocket without looking away from Norah. "You went to a gym? Why? Doesn't Fifi torture you enough?"

"Who was that on the phone?" Norah knew her stall tactic wouldn't work—at least not for long—but she needed a few moments to get her thoughts together. Molly and Cara would feel the guiltiest if Norah explained her true reasons for wanting to learn how to fight. After all, she'd been their backup when her failure to defend herself had become glaringly evident.

"John Carmondy, of course." Cara was the one who answered. "Who else does she love except for us, and we're all here—well, we *were* all here, before Fifi and Charlie left."

"It could've been Lono," Norah argued. "She loves her dad."

"Quit stalling." Molly narrowed her eyes into the stern glare that was guaranteed to make Norah fold. Of course her sister saw right through her delaying tactics. "What's going on?"

"I…um… I wanted to take some MMA lessons?" Her voice turned up at the end, and Norah knew she'd failed. Her sisters would see through her lame excuse in a second, and then she'd have to tell them the truth— that she didn't want to be the weak link. She couldn't live with the idea that she might be the reason they were killed or injured, because they trusted her to act as backup and she miserably failed.

Both Cara and Molly were eyeing her suspiciously, and she braced for the coming inquisition. "Why would you suddenly decide that you're interested in fighting of any sort?"

"Uh… It's actually an interesting sport? An art form even." She resisted the urge to close her eyes and sigh at her utter hopelessness.

The silence from her two sisters was charged as they looked at each other and then back at Norah. The sheer glee in both of their expressions made her pretty sure that they hadn't reached the correct conclusion, and she let the air out of her lungs in a quiet breath of relief. "Is all this," Molly sketched a circle in the air, encompassing Norah's entire sweaty and bedraggled form, "because of a *guy*?"

"A really fit MMA guy?" Cara, who was usually her steadiest and most practical sister, sounded positively giddy. "One who insists that the only way to learn is if he puts his strong, sinewy hands on you to guide you through each movement?"

Even Molly's eyebrows flew up at that, and she turned to stare at Cara. "Where'd that come from?"

"That movie Henry and I watched the other night. The one with the hot Samoan boxing coach?"

"Oh, right," Molly said, and then both of her sisters refocused on Norah, making her panic a little.

"It's not… I mean, there *is* a guy, but that's not… He's not…" She trailed off, unable to finish the absolutely ridiculous lie that Dash wasn't hot and that she wasn't attracted to him. Her face burned, and she knew her normally light skin was currently bright red. *Just go with it*, her inner voice urged. It was an easy way out of having to explain her true reasons, which would just make her sisters feel bad. Still, admitting that she found Dash enormously hot felt a little too close to the truth. This was just one more way she could protect her sisters from hurt, though. If that meant a little humiliation on her part, that was a small price to pay. With a sigh, she held her hands up in a shrug. "Fine. He's really, really gorgeous."

A sound that could only be described as a squeal emanated from both of her sisters in stereo, and Norah winced from both the decibel and the attention.

"It *is* a guy! You voluntarily went to a gym because you're interested in a guy!" Cara was positively giddy. "What about the sinewy hands thing, though? Was I right about that part?"

"Our little Norah is all grown up," Molly cooed, making Norah cringe. Molly's delighted laugh was contagious, though, and she found herself giving her sisters a sheepish smile.

"Well? Spill!" Cara prodded, and Norah stared at her blankly. She'd already spilled on the whole Dash thing. What more did her sisters want? Cara rolled her eyes affectionately as she clarified, "What's his name? Description? How'd you meet him? Are you dating or just *working out* together?" Cara's eyebrows bobbed up and down suggestively, making Norah laugh. The truth was, she'd found out about Dash's gym online, and it was rated the best in the area for mixed-martial arts training. She hadn't set eyes on Dash until she'd forced herself to walk into his gym, but that didn't fit with this less-guilt-inducing version of events that she was letting her sisters believe.

Thankfully, her cell phone rang before her silence

went on too long and made the other two suspicious. "Pax Bond Recovery," she answered, dropping her eyes to the floor so her sisters' impatient expressions didn't make her lose her train of thought.

"Which of you Pax girls is this?" Barney Thompson's distinctive voice made her make a face. Spilling all the details about Dash and his sinewy hands would've been better than having to talk to the slimy bail bondsman who held the deed to their family home. *Thanks for that, Mom.*

"This is Norah," she answered. "What can we do for you, Mr. Thompson?"

"Norah…Norah… Oh, you're the mousy blond one! POS's kid. How's he doing?"

"Fine," she lied, not wanting to go into the gory details of the mess her dad, Dwayne "POS" Possin, was currently making of his life—especially not with Barney Thompson, of all people. The only reason they were giving Barney the time of day was that they still hadn't found Jane, and he could make their lives miserable if she missed her first hearing. "What did you need?"

"All business, aren't you?" he asked with a stiff laugh, and she scrunched her nose at her sisters, who were watching her with a mixture of sympathy and apprehension. Norah barely could deal with talking to people outside her family. Making nice with a scumball like Barney was not part of her skill set. "I have another job for you."

Her relieved exhale was silent. Even though he sounded a bit peeved about her not indulging in his desire for small talk, at least he was willing to get down to business. "Who's the skip?" she asked.

"Devon Leifsen."

The name didn't ring any bells, so she repeated it for her sisters to hear. Both of them gave her a blank head shake. "What did he do?"

"You mean, what is he *accused* of doing?" Barney corrected archly.

"Sure." There was a snap in her voice that she couldn't help. Barney was quickly wearing through her thin veneer of patience.

"With your mother's…situation, I would think you'd be more of a stickler about the whole innocent-until-proven-guilty thing." He paused, as if waiting for her to comment, but she held her silence until he finally answered sullenly. "He's *accused* of being a hacker. This time, he was arrested for deactivating home security systems so his buddies could burglarize the places."

Norah drew in a sharp breath as her gaze flew to Cara. Her sister had been kidnapped after their security system had been disabled. Maybe it was just a coincidence, since there were lots of hackers in the world, but Langston, Colorado wasn't a huge place. Cara gave her a questioning look as Norah asked, "Is he local?"

"If you call Denver local, then yeah." Barney sounded bored now that she hadn't gotten defensive about his earlier bait. "Look, it's all in the file I sent over. Find him fast, or you're not going to like the consequences."

Norah was already opening her email app and pulling up the business' account. If there was a chance that this guy helped kidnap Cara, then she was going to relish her part in bringing him in.

"Hello?" Barney's voice echoed faintly from her phone speaker, and Norah twitched her shoulders in irritation. He'd said himself that everything was in the file. Why hadn't he ended the call already? "Hello? Did you hang up on me, you little—"

Returning to the phone app, she pressed the end button. A snort from Molly brought her gaze from her phone screen to her sister's amused expression. "What?" Norah asked.

Cara sighed, but the corners of her mouth twitched in a way that meant she wasn't really that exasperated. "Don't hang up on clients, Norah."

"It was Barney." She turned back to her phone, still wanting to read the file.

"True," Molly agreed, the laughter in her voice slipping away. "But as long as he may have the ability to evict us in the near future, it might be a good idea to say 'bye' at the end of phone conversations."

Distracted by the contents of Devon Leifsen's file, Norah just grunted an acknowledgement. "The skip is a hacker who's been disarming residential security systems so his friends can burglarize homes." She heard Cara's sharp indrawn breath as Norah continued to scroll through the information.

"*Is* he local?" Cara asked, moving to peer over Norah's shoulder.

"Denver," she answered absently, her brain already half in research mode.

"Okay." Molly's hand clap yanked Norah's attention away from her phone. "New plan. I need to act as backup for John when he picks up a skip, so you two are it for research until I get back. Norah, you'll tackle the security footage of Mom, and Cara gets to start investigating the hacker." When Norah drew in a breath of protest, Molly cut her off with a sharp shake of her head. "Cara gets first crack since she was the one kidnapped."

The logic of that couldn't be argued with, so Norah closed the file and stood. "Okay. I'm going to look at the store footage on my laptop."

"I'll start going over Leifsen's file on mine." Cara sounded unusually bloodthirsty. Normally, she was the peacemaker, but Norah could understand. She had huge amounts of rage for everyone involved in Cara's kidnapping, and Norah hadn't even been the one snatched out of their living room. "I could use your help when you're done watching Mom steal stuff."

"Gladly," Norah said before heading upstairs, motivated to get through the store footage as quickly as possible. Helping to bring in a skip was always satisfying, but finding a guy who may have had a hand in stealing Cara away? That would be doubly sweet.

Hours later, Norah decided that one circle of hell was watching store security footage nonstop. She wasn't sure what terrible thing a person would have to do to get sentenced to an eternity of that, though. Her eyes were having trouble focusing, so she blinked rapidly and looked away, taking in the dimly lit details of her tiny room. It was officially a largish closet, but sharing a room made her anxious and unable to sleep, so she'd converted the small room into an improvised bedroom as a teenager.

It wasn't a bad closet bedroom, as closet bedrooms went. Young Harry Potter would've considered Norah's room to be an upgrade. Besides, she'd always been short and slight, so she didn't need much more than her single bed—except when Warrant, their Great Pyrenees mix dog, took most of the space for his hundred-pound self. The closet even had a window set in the wall opposite the door, which showed the fading light of evening. Norah stared outside, still blinking to get her distance vision back after spending half the day staring at her computer screen. It was just light out enough to emphasize the darkness of the shadows. Usually, she appreciated living on the edge of a national forest, but this time of day, when the trees stood stark and spooky against the indigo sky, and her imagination inserted monsters into every creeping shadow, a part of her wished for the ambient light of a big, never-sleeping city.

Her stomach growled, making her jump and then laugh at her momentary startle. It was pretty sad to be scared by her own body's noises, and it definitely meant that she needed a break. Standing, she stretched out the kinks and then headed downstairs to the kitchen. Sitting at the small table that worked as a desk, Cara looked up from her laptop and blinked. Norah had to smile at her sister's cloudy expression, sure that it'd matched hers from just a few minutes ago. The transition from research mode to reality wasn't an easy one.

Cara smiled back before transitioning to a yawn as she glanced at the clock on the microwave. "Whoa, where'd the day go?"

That wasn't really a question that Norah could answer, so she just shrugged and stuck her head into the fridge. Felicity's insistence on all of them eating healthily made it harder to find a quick meal, but there were eggs and cheese and veggies, and Norah could make something sort of speedily with that.

"Molly isn't home yet?" she asked, her brain instantly filled with terrible scenarios of what might've befallen Molly and John.

"She spending the night at John's. The skip pick-up went off as planned, but I'm assuming they have a lot of adrenaline to work out now." Cara smirked.

"Oh." Norah wasn't sure how to respond to that, so she stayed quiet and opened the egg carton.

"What'd you find in the footage?" Cara asked, her tone carefully diffident. When Norah glanced over, her sister was studying a sticky note with more intensity than it deserved.

"Mom stealing things," Norah said baldly, feeling guilty when she saw Cara wince before her sister quickly smoothed it away. "Want an omelet?"

"Sure. It really was her, then?"

"Yeah." Picking up an egg, she held the cool, smooth oval in her hand as she studied Cara. Even as Jane had proved to her daughters over and over that she wasn't a reliable person, it still came as a shock every time she did something like this. Norah wasn't sure if they'd ever get used to their mother's disregard for the law and her own children. "She took a bunch of those travel toiletries and a few smaller electronics and then left in a red Honda Accord with a Colorado license plate. I think the last letter was an L, but I'm not a hundred percent sure about that. She left the parking lot and headed west on the frontage road in front of the store, but she could've gone anywhere from there."

By the time she'd finished summarizing what she'd found after staring at security footage for hours, Cara's expression had returned to her usual calm. "You let Fifi and Charlie know?"

"Yes." Norah cracked the egg she held into a bowl and then added three more. "I wish I could've gotten the entire license plate number."

"You gave them a lot to work with," Cara assured her. "With that and a place to start, they're going to track her down in no time."

I hope so. We don't have much time to spare. Jane's first court appearance was coming up fast. She didn't say that out loud, though. Cara knew as well as she did that they were down to the wire. Instead, she changed the subject. "How's your research going?"

"Eh." Cara wiggled her hand from side to side in a so-so gesture. "Okay. I'm still not sure if he's the one who helped Abbott kidnap me, but even if he isn't, Devon Leifsen is a dirty piece of work."

"Want some help?"

"After omelets? Sure."

The gentle reminder made Norah realize she'd stopped beating the eggs as they'd talked, so she refocused on the meal prep. "After omelets."

With her belly full and her brain already occupied with Devon Leifsen's file, Norah settled back on her bed with her laptop warming her thighs. Probably hoping for leftovers, Warrant had chosen to stay downstairs with Cara as she did meal clean-up. Although Norah appreciated having the space to stretch her legs out, she missed the furry beast's warmth next to her.

She read through Leifsen's entire file, letting the information settle into her brain. He had a few possible connections in Langston, although his home base and main associates were in Denver. He was young—only twenty-three—but he'd managed to rack up a solid list of suspected offenses in the five years since he'd been a legal adult. Norah was pretty sure that his sealed juvie file would be interesting reading, as well.

Like Barney had said, he'd been arrested most recently for his part in three Denver burglaries. One of his accomplices had given him up as part of a plea deal. Before that, he'd been accused of numerous crimes, from bank fraud to planting cameras in the dressing area of a local beauty pageant. Norah's nose wrinkled at that last one.

Not only is he a thief—he's a sexual predator, too. Gross.

Most of the charges against him had been dropped immediately, and he'd never been convicted of anything. He'd never been married, and there were no known girlfriends or boyfriends—past or present— listed. His address matched his parents' house in Golden, and they'd been the ones to bond him out before he skipped bail.

After scanning through the last page of his file, she started searching online for information, starting with his parents, Karen and Bryon Leifsen. They owned several auto body shops along the Front Range, and the couple's names popped up quite a bit in the Golden social scene. Karen had a few speeding tickets, but otherwise the pair seemed to be generally law-abiding—or at least were good at not getting caught.

A light knock on her bedroom door made Norah jump, her laptop bouncing with the sudden movement. "Come in," she called, and Cara stuck her head in.

"I'm heading to bed," Cara said, as Norah's heartrate gradually slowed. "Find anything?"

"Not really." She'd taken in a lot of information, but she wasn't at the point to start processing it yet, so it was just a bunch of facts about Devon Leifsen floating around her brain at this point.

"Goodnight. Don't stay up too late." Cara always told her this, even though she knew Norah probably wouldn't take the advice.

"I won't," she responded as usual, knowing that she'd probably still be digging deeper into the rabbit hole in the wee hours of the night.

Once Cara withdrew and softly closed her bedroom door, Norah moved on to searching for information on Devon's few friends mentioned in the file. One of them, a Chloe Ballister, was in a Denver modern rock band that played at a bar in Langston on a semi-regular basis.

"Of course it was at Dutch's," Norah muttered as she made a note of it. "Everything seems to come back to that place."

A faint beep drew her eyes back to her laptop. A black text box with a flashing cursor opened in the corner of the screen, and she blinked at it as her heart accelerated. As letters appeared—letters that were not typed by her hand—she could only stare in horror.

Hi Norah!

Someone had gained access to her computer. Her

brain couldn't wrap around this fact. Despite her layers and layers of top-notch security, someone had managed to hack into her heavily protected system. Her hand hovered over the touch pad, unsure if she should engage or do her best to kick out this interloper. They didn't seem to be attempting to access her data, however, and the cheery greeting—including an exclamation mark— threw her off guard.

Who is this? she typed, even as a large part of her scolded her for her curiosity.

Devon. Nice to meet you.

Her heart was thundering now. *Devon? Devon Leifsen?* She balled her hands into fists, taking reassurance in the bite of her short nails into her palms. Could it be a prank? Someone pretending to be Devon? The only people who knew she was investigating Devon were Molly and Cara, and neither of them would do something so cruel and pointless. Barney knew, but Norah was willing to bet her laptop that he didn't have the know-how to hack her computer. In fact, she was reasonably sure he had to have help sending an email.

What are you doing? Her shaking fingers made it hard to type accurately.

Chatting with you! She'd never seen such a sinister smiley face.

No, why did you hack my laptop? The voice in her head was now screaming to shut him down, but she had to know why the skip she was researching had hacked her computer and was sending determinedly cheerful messages. All the happy exclamation points made his comments feel creepily wrong. A threat would've felt less menacing.

Because I wanted to introduce myself to the beautiful woman who's investigating me. *waves* Hi pretty bounty hunter!

Norah's gaze flew to the dark window for a terrified second before she looked back at the small, circular lens at the top of her laptop screen. *He's not watching you,* her brain tried to reassure her. *He's just trying to scare you.*

It was working. She was full-on terrified. With trembling fingers, she closed the text box and then shut down her laptop. As soon as the screen went black, she closed the computer and kept her hands pressed against the top, as if to keep Devon from remotely opening it, as impossible as that would be. Her gaze darted around her shadowed room, dark without the light from her laptop screen, and landed on the black window again.

Forcing herself to put the computer aside and slide off the bed, she moved to the window, her heart hitting her ribs so hard it felt as if it'd break out of her chest. The darkness of the room spooked her, but she couldn't turn on a light, not if he was watching her.

He's not out there, she tried to convince herself as she drew closer to the glass pane. He's holed up somewhere miles away, messing with your head from the safety of a friend's couch.

Even despite the logic of that, and the high likelihood that he was nowhere near her house, the shadows took on a menacing quality. Someone could easily be lurking in the darkness, staring up at her, taking delight in her unsettled fear.

Her breaths came quickly, fogging the glass, and she couldn't drag her gaze away from the thousand and one possible hiding places right outside her home.

Wait—was that a flash of light? She blinked rapidly, but that just made it harder to tell if she'd imagined the glow or not. Her stomach twisted as his typed words ran on repeat in her mind. He could be just a few steps away from her house. If he picked the lock, disabled the alarm, and crept up the stairs, he could be outside her tiny bedroom in mere minutes.

At the thought, her gaze flew to her closed door. *Is that creak just the house settling, or did someone take a stealthy step?* She went completely still, listening. It felt like the house held its breath along with her. All she could hear was the rapid pattering of her heartbeat in her ears, telling her to run.

But she was trapped in her closet of a bedroom. There was no escape.

ABOUT THE AUTHOR

A graduate of the police academy, Katie Ruggle is a self-proclaimed forensics nerd. A fan of anything that makes her feel like a badass, she has trained in Krav Maga, boxing, and gymnastics, has lived in an off-grid solar- and wind-powered house in the Rocky Mountains, rides horses, trains her three dogs, and travels to warm places to scuba dive. She has received multiple Amazon Best Books of the Month and an Amazon Best Book of the Year. *Run to Ground*, the first book in her Rocky Mountain K9 Unit series, was a 2017 *RT Book Reviews* Reviewers' Choice Award nominee. Katie now lives in a 150-year-old Minnesota farmhouse near her family.

SEARCH AND RESCUE

In the Rockies, lives depend on the Search
& Rescue brotherhood. But this far off
the map, secrets can be murder.

By Katie Ruggle

Hold Your Breath

Louise "Lou" Sparks is a hurricane. A
walking disaster. And with her, ice diving
captain Callum Cook has never felt more
alive…even if keeping her safe may just
kill him.

Fan the Flames

Firefighter and Motorcycle Club
member Ian Walsh rides the line between
good and bad. But if a killer has his way,
Ian will take the fall for a murder he didn't
commit…and lose the woman he's always
loved.

Gone Too Deep

George Halloway is a mystery. Tall. Dark. Intense. And city girl Ellie Price will need him by her side if she wants to find her father…and live to tell the tale.

In Safe Hands

Sheriff Deputy Chris Jennings was a hero to agoraphobe Daisy Little, but one wrong move ended their future before it could begin. Now he'll do whatever it takes to keep her safe— even if that means turning against one of his own.

"Vivid and charming."

—Charlaine Harris, #1 *New York Times* bestselling author of the Sookie Stackhouse series

ROCKY MOUNTAIN K9 UNIT

These K9 officers and their trusty dogs will do anything to protect the women in their lives

By Katie Ruggle

Run to Ground

K9 officer Theo Bosco lost his mentor, his K9 partner, and almost lost his will to live. But when a ruthless killer targets a woman on the run, Theo and his new K9 companion will do whatever it takes to save the woman neither can live without.

On the Chase

Injured in the line of duty, K9 officer Hugh Murdoch's orders are simple: stay alive. But when a frightened woman bursts into his life, Hugh and his K9 companion have no choice but to risk everything to keep her safe.

Survive the Night

K9 officer Otto Gunnersen has always been a haven: for the lost, the sick, the injured. But when a hunted woman takes shelter in his arms, this gentle giant swears he'll do more than heal her battered spirit—he'll defend her with his life.

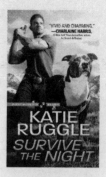

Through the Fire

When a killer strikes, new K9 officer Kit Jernigan knows she can't catch the culprit on her own. She needs a partner: local fire spotter Wesley March. But the more time they spend together, the hotter the fire smolders…and the more danger they're in.

For more Katie Ruggle, visit:

sourcebooks.com

ROCKY MOUNTAIN COWBOY CHRISTMAS

Beloved author Katie Ruggle's new book
brings pulse-pounding romantic suspense
to a gorgeous Colorado Christmas.

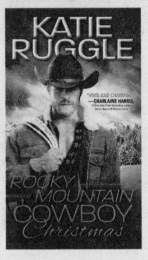

When single dad Steve Springfield moved his family to a
Colorado Christmas tree ranch, he meant it to be a safe haven.
He quickly finds himself fascinated by local folk artist Camille
Brandt—it's too bad trouble is on her trail.

It's not long before Camille is falling for the enigmatic
cowboy and his rambunctious children—he always seems to
be coming to her rescue. But as attraction blooms and danger
intensifies, this Christmas romance may just prove itself to be
worth fighting for.

For more Katie Ruggle, visit:

sourcebooks.com

TURN THE TIDE

There's breathless suspense for everyone in this free e-collection of novellas from some of the brightest new names in the genre: Katie Ruggle, Adriana Anders, Connie Mann, and Juno Rushdan.

Whether you're diving into treacherous waters, racing the clock against global annihilation, or delving deep into an untamed wilderness, these thrilling tales of love and suspense will leave you breathless.

"Vivid and charming."

—Charlaine Harris, #1 *New York Times* bestselling author for the Search & Rescue series

For more from these authors, visit:

sourcebooks.com

FINAL HOUR

Lose yourself in a romantic thriller featuring an elite government unit and the terrifying bioterrorist outbreaks they fight to subdue.

By Juno Rushdan

Every Last Breath

When a lethal bioweapon goes up for auction, Maddox Kinkade's life-or-death mission to neutralize it sends her crashing into the last person she expected—her presumed-dead fiancé, Cole Matthews.

Nothing to Fear

When Gideon Stone investigates suspected mole Willow Harper, an unlikely bond pushes limits—and forges loyalties. Every move they make counts. And the real traitor is always watching…

Until the End

Gray Box operative Castle Kinkade always comes out on top. But when he agrees to protect white-hat hacker, Kit Westcott, surviving might be mission impossible…

COVER TO BE REVEALED!

"Tense and fulfilling. Settle back and savor this one."

—Steve Berry, *New York Times* bestselling author for *Every Last Breath*

For more info about Sourcebooks's books and authors, visit:

sourcebooks.com

WHITEOUT

With a storm coming and a killer on the
loose, every step could be their last...

Angel Smith is finally ready to leave Antarctica for a second
chance at life. But on what was meant to be her final day, the
remote research station she's been calling home is attacked.
Hunted and scared, she and irritatingly gorgeous glaciologist
Ford Cooper barely make it out with their lives...only to realize
that in a place this remote, there's nowhere left to run.

Isolated with no power, no way to contact the outside world,
and a madman on their heels, Angel and Ford must fight to survive in the most inhospitable—and beautiful—place on earth.
But what starts as a partnership born of necessity quickly turns
into an urgent connection that burns bright and hot. They both
know there's little chance of making it out alive, and yet they are
determined to weather the coming storm—no matter the cost.

"Scorching hot and beautifully emotional."

—Lori Foster, *New York Times* bestselling author